IT'S ALL IN THE FAMILY

''Tommy said he asked you out tonight.''

She hadn't expected him to know about that. ''You and I had work to do,'' she reminded him.

''We could have started after dinner.''

She wondered if Tommy had run some kind of guilt trip on Ely. ''Then I'd be going home at one or two in the morning, instead of eleven o'clock,'' she pointed out.

''You should be out dining and dancing, not eating reheated chili with a guy like me. I feel like I've cheated you out of the usual Friday night festivities.''

''Don't worry about it,'' Eliza said. ''Good food, good conversation, and an education on modern-day education were fine.'' She had really enjoyed getting to know Ely and his son better, even if it was for professional rather than for personal reasons.

He walked her to the door.

She turned back to him to say good night, and his eyes caught and held hers, his gaze intense. ''If Tommy were here, he'd kiss you good night, wouldn't he?''

''I suppose he would,'' she answered.

Ely's eyes darkened. ''Here's a kiss from Tommy,'' he said, leaning slowly toward her. Eliza stood frozen in place. She was shocked. He was so nice, respectful. She couldn't believe he was putting a move on her.

''It's all in the family,'' he murmured against her mouth. His lips touched hers.

. . . What strange power did these two brothers have over her?

BOOK YOUR PLACE ON OUR WEBSITE AND MAKE THE ARABESQUE ROMANCE CONNECTION!

We've created a customized website just for our very special Arabesque readers, where you can get the inside scoop on everything that's going on with Arabesque romance novels.

When you come online, you'll have the exciting opportunity to:

- View covers of upcoming books

- Read sample chapters

- Learn about our future publishing schedule (listed by publication month *and author*)

- Find out when your favorite authors will be visiting a city near you

- Search for and order backlist books from our online catalog

- Check out author bios and background information

- Send e-mail to your favorite authors

- Meet the Kensington staff online

- Join us in weekly chats with authors, readers and other guests

- Get writing guidelines

- AND MUCH MORE!

**Visit our website at
http://www.arabesquebooks.com**

WORTH WAITING FOR

Roberta Gayle

Pinnacle Books
Kensington Publishing Corp.

http://www.arabesquebooks.com

PINNACLE BOOKS are published by

Kensington Publishing Corp.
850 Third Avenue
New York, NY 10022

First Printing: June, 1998
10 9 8 7 6 5 4 3 2 1

Printed in the United States of America

Chapter One

The Apollo Grille was the most luxurious hotel bar in Boston. The walls were covered with midnight-blue damask paper and with the high ceilings and recessed lights turned low, Eliza Taylor felt as though she sat in the heart of a deep, plush cavern. Music floated from the baby grand piano half-hidden in a shadowy corner. The tinkling notes mingled with the murmur of low-pitched voices, increasing the feeling of intimacy at the small round tables, which were placed at discreet intervals about the floor.

The only bright spot in the decor was the bar itself. It was easily twenty feet long and was backed by a mirror which reflected its full length, and doubled the light from above. Tier upon tier of liquor bottles with contents of amber, gold, red, and even blue liquid sparkled from behind proud old labels. The elite of Boston's African-American community had made this place their own over the last ten years, and Eliza—through no fault of her own—was a de facto member of that exclusive society, though she hadn't been at the Apolle Grille in ages.

Nearly a year ago, on her last birthday, her friends MJ and Stephanie had coaxed and bullied her into taking the evening off to dine at the four-star restaurant across the hotel lobby from the Grille. The small party had begun here, with a drink among the so-called beautiful people.

That night, Eliza had been at the top of her form. Egged on by her friends, she'd waxed poetic on the subject of plastic surgery, and had found their irreverent comments about the cream of Boston's black society equally hilarious. The name of the bar, Apollo, always filled her classically educated mind with Olympian images, but the men who frequented the Grille were godlike only in the width and breadth of their pretentions. She couldn't believe that tonight she was here with one of *them.*

Eliza couldn't help comparing her date to the other brothers decorating the elegant hotel lounge. He stood out in the surprisingly homogenous crowd of upwardly mobile black men in their expensive suits. He was wearing an equally expensive jacket over well-worn jeans and a plain cotton shirt, but it was his natural grace and easy air, rather than the outfit, that made this man. Tommy Greene was the most beautiful man she'd ever seen. Actually, he was the most beautiful human being she'd ever seen. Period.

His short black hair, worn natural and cut close to his perfectly shaped head, showed off his wide, nut-brown forehead and amazing deep-set eyes. Eliza still couldn't believe she was actually on a date with him. She was the kind of woman who made jokes about men with bedroom eyes. But Tommy's eyes were only the beginning. His high, almost feminine cheekbones were balanced precisely by the hard masculine line of his square jaw. He'd inherited his mother's strong African nose, and it looked even better on him than it did on the famous singer Eugenia Greene. And then, there were his lips. Eliza could barely take her eyes off his mouth. The curve of that generous lower lip was enticing, even to an old battle-ax like herself.

She tore her eyes away, and looked toward the bar again. There, standing with his back to the bar, was *Power*. In an Armani suit, gold Rolex peeking from beneath a starched white cuff, he punctuated important points in his monologue with a wave of a perfectly manicured hand. Eliza liked debonair, self-assured men, but she was far too familiar with the type.

Control was also easy to spot; another suit, less elegant perhaps but just as expensive—probably bought for him by his soon-to-be-ex-wife who, fed up with his obsession with making money, had sent him packing. Eliza would have been willing to bet that if she were on a date with him, she would already have heard "the speech." She'd heard every possible variation, and it boiled down to one oversimplified line: divorce teaches one the most important lesson in life; never let your work make you blind to the ones you loved. The Suit would be lying, of course, but he wouldn't know that.

Success, not to be left out, was also on view. In the darkened, oak-paneled bar, where famous poets had, in the nineteen twenties and thirties, tumbled off their high stools in a haze of expensive whiskey, he was represented by The Artist. His beautiful, chestnut dreads tumbled gracefully over the collar of his black silk suit and halfway down his back. He was entirely focused on his companion, and could barely wait for the end of her sentence before responding. His intent gaze never left her eyes while he spoke. Eliza knew that it didn't matter what they were talking about. He'd be equally absorbed by any discussion. It was a question of style.

She knew all about style. She had a pronounced style of her own, which attracted men just like these. They were amusing enough and, more importantly, since she was a normal, red-blooded, single woman who enjoyed, on occasion, male companionship and even male admiration, they appreciated her. Over the years, she'd found a little adulation in her men quite delightful, though a little went a long way. Success with men had never been as satisfying to her as success in her chosen profession. It was unfortunate that the corollary to this equation was that the more successful she was in her work, the less men seemed to fit into her life.

Eliza knew she was attractive. With enough prep time and good lighting, she could even be called beautiful—for a well-preserved, middle-aged lawyer. Her self-assurance was a match for that of any man. She was a successful, independent woman and proud of it. Like any other animal, in any jungle she could name, she attracted her own kind. She put them at their ease.

Eliza couldn't keep the corner of her mouth from turning upward in a wry smile of recognition.

But this evening, her dinner companion was different. Not that Thomas Greene wasn't successful. Tommy wielded enough power and had made as much money as any man could want. As for status, as the youngest partner ever in the number-one corporate law firm in Boston, he was every bit as golden now as he had been as the top-ranked student at Harvard Law School. He was also perfectly formed in face and body. Eliza had always liked her men to look good, but Tommy Greene was hot. Sizzling hot. Added to that, he was, literally, brilliant. She didn't date idiots, but this man was a genius. It made Eliza feel slightly off balance to be with him. She didn't think she'd ever dated anyone who was both smarter and better looking than she was herself. She'd never made a conscious effort to avoid it, it had just never happened.

Not that she'd been dating much lately. It was too much trouble, and she was much too busy most of the time to even consider dinner and a movie, let alone the complicated dances of the modern relationship. Tommy Greene's invitation to renew their acquaintance over dinner had come out of the blue—and she'd stammeringly accepted without considering the implications.

As a result, she sat silently across the small table from this incredible-looking man, a man moreover who was ten years her junior, and who somehow made her feel like she was on her first date again. She hadn't felt this awkward or excited in years.

"I can't believe it. You look exactly like you did when we graduated from law school," Tommy said.

Eliza knew it wasn't true. There was a patch of gray right at the top of her head which she'd considered dyeing about a thousand times. He couldn't have missed it. She was very familiar, after forty-one years, with the face that stared back at her out of her mirror every morning, and she was well aware of every wrinkle and laugh line. Still, she couldn't help being flattered at the obvious sincerity in his voice. Maybe Tommy

Greene still saw in her the twenty-something-self she'd forgotten over the years.

"Pshaw," she answered, making a joke of it. Eliza was just thankful that they didn't look like too odd a couple, despite the ten-year difference in their ages.

"No. Really," he insisted.

"I can't say the same of you," Eliza teased. "You've certainly . . . changed." She'd started to say "grown," but that sounded too much like something a maiden aunt might say, and while she might feel like she was somehow robbing the cradle tonight, she sure as hell didn't plan to let him know that.

He smiled smugly. "I'll take that as a compliment."

"You were pretty cute back then." Eliza couldn't resist teasing him a little further, testing to see if he'd grown conceited with all his success.

He smiled. "Pretty cute? That's what you thought?"

"Sure did." She nodded.

"I was adorable. Everyone said so."

"You were," Eliza laughingly agreed.

"But you don't think I'm adorable anymore?" Eliza shook her head solemnly. "So, when you say I've changed . . ." he prompted.

She cocked her head, pretending to think about it while she looked him over.

When they had met, he was sixteen, and she, twenty-six. Despite his height and athletic build, no one could have taken them for a couple then. He was the wiz kid—graduated high school with honors at thirteen, Harvard undergrad at sixteen, and then took his law degree with Eliza's class. She was just an ordinary student, working her way toward her degree after a couple of years working in the real world with her M.S.W.

His amazing intellect and her hard work had made them first and second in their class. Being "brains" had brought them together. Her sympathy for the boy had made them friends. And when they graduated, the local papers had made a fuss about this unusual African-American dynamic duo, photographing them together and printing stories about their accomplishments. They'd laughed together at the irony of being lauded just because of the color of their skins, and she'd soothed the pain he'd tried so hard to conceal at being distinguished again as the young black genius. Foolish as it might be, now that she'd seen Tommy again, Eliza didn't want him to see her as his "older sister" or even his mentor anymore.

"Come on," he urged. "Am I more handsome? Sexier? Even more irresistible?" he suggested.

It had been Mary Jane, her secretary, who had brought Eliza to the realization that she was once again on the dating scene. MJ had congratulated her on breaking her long dry spell. As unpleasant a revelation as that had been, the evening was actually progressing quite nicely. Tommy was as intelligent and ambitious, articulate, and imaginative as any of the three specimens of contemporary black manhood at the bar.

Eliza brushed a strand of hair off her cheek, extremely glad she'd taken care with it that morning, blowing it dry and curling the ends. Straightened as it was, her red-brown hair curved gently around her face, the ends just brushing her collar.

She had taken off her suit jacket, and her red silk blouse hinted at a figure that a younger woman wouldn't have been ashamed of. Her measurements hadn't changed too much since her law school days. Maybe her waist and hips were a smidgen wider, but her long legs were the envy of her friends. She didn't have to spend time in the gym, either—though it would probably have been good for her soul. She was tall enough, at five foot six, to control her weight by watching her caloric intake when she felt the need.

She still looked pretty good. Her black linen skirt was just short enough, and her heels just high enough, to show off her long, still supple legs. If she didn't set the room on fire, she didn't think she could be accused of looking like anyone's spinster aunt.

He couldn't wait any longer. "Spit it out, woman. You're making me nervous."

Eliza relented. "Devastatingly attractive?" she offered.

"Hmmm," he murmured. "Devastating. I like that. Thank you."

His intense gaze unnerved her. "You're welcome." Eliza cleared her throat. Then she looked away. Back at the bar.

There was a newcomer at the far end. He looked totally out of place amid all the suave, sophisticated gentlemen of color. His almond-colored skin might have been golden brown in any other shirt, but the lime-green color he wore made him look sallow. His corduroy jacket looked frayed at the edges, even from this distance. Eliza would have been willing to bet his khaki pants had not felt the heat of an iron in a month of Sundays.

As she watched, he knocked over one of the modern, café-style tables. His attempt to right the spindly legged table earned a muffled groan of sympathy from her. Tommy turned to see what she was looking at, but the buffoon was bent double, scrambling for the table setting and not visible to her date. She knew well how impolitic it was to let her attentions stray from the man she was with, even to one so pathetic. Eliza refocused on Tommy—not a difficult task.

"I hear you've accepted an offer at Silliman and Cosell," she said. She'd been disappointed that Tommy had gone into corporate law after a brilliant clerkship with the supreme court. But then, not everyone was interested in juvenile rights law. In fact, not many shared her obsession. Her cases lacked the glamour of criminal cases, and the monetary rewards of civil cases. The clients were, frankly, childish, the hours were ridiculous, and the pay was minimal. Eliza had good reason to choose this specialty, but a man like Tommy probably didn't need his work to compensate for the lack of a real life.

He had distinguished himself in his chosen career, already appearing before the supreme court on behalf of his corporate clients. He had certainly earned his partnership at one of the premier law firms in the country, and the incredible salary that went along with it. It appeared he was as driven as she was to succeed. Unlike other goal-oriented men she'd dated, he seemed to have retained his sense of humor. If only he'd been ten years older, he'd have been the perfect match for her. A disconcerting thought kept recurring, that even with the age difference, he was exactly the kind of man Eliza had hoped to meet at least once before she died.

A tiny inner voice enumerated the reasons Eliza couldn't possibly be serious.

He's a lawyer, her conscience tweaked.

So am I, she argued with herself.

Not a corporate lawyer. Think about it. Their mission in life is to protect a system you hate.

So?

You'd be crawling in bed with the enemy.

Only if I get really lucky, she thought.

Her internal debate ended when Tommy said, "I can't believe I didn't think to call you when I first came back to Boston. In all these years, I've never met another woman like you. How could I have forgotten how beautiful you are?"

Another hour of this kind of treatment, and she'd be in love. It wasn't his flattery that won him another point on the mental score sheet she automatically tallied up on the course of any date, it was the fact that he was more interested in talking about her than in discussing his latest coup. She chalked up a point for modesty.

"I don't exactly travel in the same exalted circles that you do, Mr. Greene." No matter how humble a man appeared to be, a wise woman would always compliment him on his accomplishments.

Eliza was no idiot, and so she followed up on her coy hint that he'd bypassed her own achievements with a sincere compliment. "I'm so proud of you." As flattery, the comment lacked a certain flamboyance. Worse than that, even as the words left her lips, Eliza wished she hadn't said something so ... so motherly.

Tommy didn't seem to notice. He went on with his original train of thought. "No, I meant ... I never forgot you. You were my best friend. I really thought we'd stay close." She couldn't help noting this was another mark of the difference in their age and experience. It hadn't surprised Eliza at all when they'd drifted apart after graduation. That was, after all, what happened when school ended. Of course, she had been celebrating her thirtieth birthday a week after graduation, while Tommy had nearly a year to go to his twentieth. He could be forgiven for maintaining that youthful optimism. But they had gone in very different directions, he to a prestigious clerkship with the state supreme court, and she to the public defender's office.

"I've thought of you often," he said.

"Me, too," Eliza admitted hesitantly. She didn't want to give him the wrong idea. She had thought of him, true, but only as a distant acquaintance, a friend from another life. She'd been reminded of his existence when she'd seen him once in court, but she'd been on her way through to a judge's chambers to consult on a case of her own. He'd been gone by the time she'd emerged from the judge's office, and she had promptly relegated her memories of him to the back of her mind.

She had never had any romantic fantasies about their meeting again or ever being anything more than friends. That had never occurred to her, until a few minutes earlier—when he had said she hadn't changed at all in that deep, throaty voice. As with any new idea, she had to think about this, pull back and analyze the situation. That was the way she was. Cool, unemotional contemplation of every possibility was her forté, in her work and in her life. In court, her dispassionate analysis of each new wrinkle in a case served her well. In relationships, it tended to distance her from other people.

She couldn't help it, though. A rational, cerebral approach to even the most urgent situations kept her firmly in the driver's seat, which was the only comfortable way to maneuver around the potholes and the curves the gods tended to throw in her path. Like this date.

Tommy, on the other hand, seemed to be quite caught up in the moment. "What happened to us?" he asked.

"The usual." Eliza shrugged. "You know how it is. You're busy, and you're far away, and those phone calls to old acquaintances fall into the it-can-wait pile."

"Yes, yes. I guess so. Still, I can't believe I let you drift out of my life so easily."

"We're here now," Eliza offered, averting her eyes and focusing on the drink in her hand. It was pink and fruity.

"You're right, here we are. Together again," Tommy said. "And I don't want to waste this second chance."

She should have ordered something stronger, she thought. Bourbon, straight up, that's what she should have gotten. Then maybe she could have relaxed a little . . . lost herself in the fantasy.

"Now that I've found you again, I don't mean to lose you this time."

Eliza's heart started to pound, hard. *Whoa, girl,* she told herself, *this is getting intense.* Maybe she would order a bourbon next round. Meanwhile, he was waiting for an answer.

"I hope not," she said aloud, her tone much primmer than she wished. She cursed her reserved nature for making it impossible to just let go and enjoy this moment.

"I'm so glad I called you."

"It was nice to hear from you, as I said." She was repeating herself, now. For a woman who prided herself on being articulate, Eliza was at a loss for a better reply. She couldn't understand it; she was usually such a scintillating conversationalist. She tried to redeem herself with a vaguely flattering remark. "I've followed your career in the alumni newspapers. Of course, your return to Boston was reported in the trades." Did that sound as coy to him as it did to herself? she worried. She didn't want to gush all over him, just to sound less polite, less stilted.

"That's the public relations department at S&C for you. A very efficient machine." He shrugged it off. "Remember how we vowed to appear in the newspaper together at least once a year after they printed that article in the *Globe* about out graduation?" He smiled. The memory was clearly a pleasant one.

Eliza smiled faintly. "I was just thinking about that, earlier."

"This kind of publicity seeking wasn't exactly what I had in mind," he said dismissively.

"Why not? S&C is proud to have you as a partner in the firm, and that's nothing to be embarrassed about." Eliza cringed as the words left her mouth. What was the matter with her tonight? She was talking to him as if he were one of "her"

kids. She supposed that this was what came of spending virtually every waking hour with her underaged clients. Now she
was talking to her date as if he were one of her semi-reformed
juveniles.

Eliza loved her work, and she was proud of her success as
a juvenile rights lawyer, but enough was enough. There had to
be some room in her life for other adults. If before Eliza had
been in any doubt that she needed a jolt out of her routine—
maybe even a man like Tommy Greene in her life—she had
just proved it. She had apparently lost the ability to converse
intelligently with other adults.

And what a time for the discovery! Here she sat, in a luxuri-
ant, decadent setting, across the table from a man who personi-
fied the ideal of male beauty, and who had suddenly appeared,
by the grace of the gods, out of the blue. It was a rather
unfortunate coincidence that he was also the closest thing she
had ever had to a little brother, but she just had to put that
aside and concentrate on the present.

This was not the night to examine every word, every action,
for some deeper meaning. It seemed her secretary had been
right. Tommy Greene appeared to have romance in mind. Eliza
told herself sternly to take his compliments at face value and
stop worrying about their earlier relationship.

He presented her with the opportunity to put this plan of
action into effect immediately. "You've done wonderful
work," he said. "Just like we used to talk about in law school.
You really did it. The defender of the innocent. You're almost
a legend. Do you know, you're the only lawyer I know who
actually does defend the innocent."

Eliza ignored that little voice in her head which warned that
his words might be the product of youthful hero worship and
consciously responded to him as if he were any colleague who
embarrassed her with praise. She made a joke. "Counselor,
I'm shocked. You mean to say that you associate with lawyers
who defend the guilty?"

He covered her hand with his own. "You know what I mean.
You're a real hero."

His hand was big and strong and warm. "I just do my job.

Just like you,'' she managed to reply coolly enough, despite the heat coursing up her arm.

''Maybe, when we get to know each other again, you'll believe me when I tell you how big a hero you are. For now, let's just say I've got all the faith in the world in you. That's why I asked you to meet me.''

''Oh?'' She had had the impression, during the phone call he'd made to set up this date, that it had been an impulse that inspired him to ask her out. Had he been planning this meeting for some time? She didn't get any further in her musing. Tommy was standing and turning toward the bar. He waved at someone she couldn't see and stepped aside. The nerd who had knocked the table over was coming toward them, nervously straightening his tie.

''Do you remember my brother, Ely?'' Tommy asked.

Chapter Two

"Yes, of course," Eliza said as she shook Ely's hand. She smiled with a warmth she was far from feeling, automatically attempting to ease the younger man's obvious discomfort at the awkwardness of the situation. Ely Greene had not changed much in the past twelve years. The shy young boy was now a diffident, quiet man, still nervously fidgeting with his hideous tie. "Ely, it's nice to see you again. Tommy didn't mention you'd be joining us this evening."

Tommy didn't seem to notice the slight admonishment underlying her welcoming words, but Ely cleared his throat nervously before saying, with a pointed look at Tommy, "I thought you'd forgotten all about me. You two look so cozy over here."

His elder brother was unabashed. "I was enjoying this reunion so much, I hated to ruin it with your problem. But I didn't forget I'm here for you, too, little brother."

Eliza looked curiously from one man to the other, the pleasant illusions of a moment ago gone as quickly as they had sprung up. She didn't plan to make this any easier for either of them. The wafting strains of soft music and the indistinguishable chatter of the other patrons flowed over her, unintrusive background noise suddenly grown louder with the lack of conversation at her own table. Finally, since they appeared to be at a loss as to how to broach the subject they'd come to discuss, she relented slightly.

"Have a seat, gentlemen." Her dry tone was apparently lost on both of them as they smiled, Ely gratefully and Tommy with a wink. They sat down across from her at the little table. Suddenly, her date had taken on the appearance of a business meeting.

The irony of the situation struck her forcefully. She had thought herself so cool. But it had taken only one look at Tommy's luscious lips, and she had completely abandoned her pattern of carefully choosing suitable candidates for romance based on such factors as compatibility and intelligence. She had thought she was—at her age!—immune to this kind of foolishness, but she had spent the last half hour talking herself into exploring the possibilities of a relationship with Tommy Greene, just because he was so good to look at. Most ironic of all, she had been gearing up to break a lifelong habit of neglecting her personal life for business, and Tommy hadn't been interested in her romantically at all, but had approached her because of her professional abilities.

"We need your advice, as an expert in child custody cases," Tommy said, confirming the conclusion she'd just reached. She would have laughed out loud, if she'd thought her companions would appreciate the humor of the situation. But both men sat side by side, expectantly looking at her, identical expressions on their faces. The family resemblance was quite clear.

Tommy was six-foot-four, giving an impression of masculine beauty on a grand scale. Ely was less imposing at six-foot-one, and he seemed to fade away in the shadow cast by his older brother's massive frame. Seated, however, the difference in their heights was much reduced, and it became noticeable that Ely and Tommy were built along very similar lines.

The breadth of both men's shoulders was impressive. Tommy's handsome face was a gold of a slightly more amber hue, and his haircut was much more flattering to his strong face than Ely's unkempt curls were to his. But beneath Ely's shapeless, five-dollar haircut, were round eyes bigger than Tommy's, his lashes unusually long and curly behind his black-rimmed glasses. Tommy's nose might be straighter, but the bump in the younger man's nose gave his face a strength of character that even Tommy's glowing perfection couldn't overshadow. Tommy's full lips were seductive, but Ely's lopsided grin had a certain charm, too. If only Ely had had a little more of Tommy's easy manner, Eliza imagined he'd have given his brother a run for his money, genius or no.

But Ely could not be called a smooth talker by any stretch of the imagination. "I told Tommy we didn't need a lawyer," Ely said bluntly, as if to confirm her uncomplimentary thought. "But as a member of the profession, he was sure that getting the advice of a notable juvenile rights lawyer like yourself could only help at this juncture. You are something of an expert in custody cases, from what I read in the newspapers, so I figured it was worth a shot."

"Are you involved in a custody case?" Eliza asked, hoping to cut through the formalities and get to the bottom of this mess. She wanted out. The dull throbbing in her temples presaged the coming of a bad headache.

"Not exactly," Ely said.

"Not yet," Tommy corrected.

"I don't think my in-laws would do anything as serious as file for custody. You heard that I got married, I assume." Eliza vaguely remembered hearing about a wedding, and she nodded. Ely continued. "When my wife died, I was in graduate school, getting my master's. Our son was just two years old, and my mother-in-law, Rebecca, offered to take him to live with her. He stayed with his grandparents for two years, and when I got my degree, I took him to live with me. While Jessie lived with them, I visited a lot, and his grandmother was fantastic about everything. She and Hank—Jessie's grandfather—have acted like a second set of parents to Jessie. My mother warned me that it wasn't a good idea to give the maternal grandparents so much of his care, but I couldn't refuse Hank and Rebecca. They love Jessie, and he loves them, and they've always stayed a big part of our lives. Nothing is going to change that."

"Custody battles can get very messy," Tommy interjected quickly when Ely paused to catch his breath.

"But this isn't a custody battle. At least, not yet," he amended when it looked like Tommy would interrupt again. "We're all just talking right now about what would be best for Jessie. I'm sure Rebecca will understand that Jessie needs his father."

"I still don't see where I come into any of this," Eliza prodded gently.

"Hank and Rebecca are planning to move to Arizona—for the climate," Ely explained. "And they want to take my son with them. To live."

"They've tried to convince Ely to let Jessie come live with them before. They don't like the neighborhood he lives in," Tommy clarified.

"Where do you live?" Eliza asked, purely out of curiosity.

"Dorchester."

Eliza pursed her lips in a soundless whistle. That was a very tough neighborhood.

Ely defended his choice. "It's near the school where I teach. I have an open-door policy for my students, so they can reach me outside of school hours. I teach at an old private school, and sometimes the kids need help—more help than I can give them in the classroom, or with something they can't talk about in front of their classmates."

"It doesn't sound like it would be that difficult to make some kind of compromise with your wife's parents—if that's all they're worried about. Couldn't you move to Brookline or someplace and make your office hours longer—so the kids could meet you before or after school?" Eliza suggested, pleased to have made a contribution to the discussion so quickly and eager to get this evening behind her and to go home. But Ely was shaking his head.

"The school won't allow it. Teachers are supposed to teach and have meetings with administration. Meetings with students, outside of class, are not on the curriculum. They'd say that it isn't really my job to counsel the children. If I suspect someone has a problem, a real problem, then I'm supposed to report it to the administration, who will discuss it with the student's parents. You can imagine what good that would do. I mean, half the time the parents are the problem. Dorchester may be a bad neighborhood, but this is a very good school. The neighborhood just hasn't held up the way the school has. But that's not the point here. We're talking about my right to choose where my son and I live,'' Ely said defensively.

Before Ely could digress further, Tommy piped up. "Don't the courts generally choose the parent over the grandparents in cases like this?"

"You should know I can't answer that definitively," Eliza answered. "In our court system, any and every case that goes before a judge is a gamble, and it's worse in family court. Kids and parents don't get a jury of their peers. They get a social worker and a judge. Either or both might feel sympathetic toward the grandparents. They might honestly believe that awarding custody to them, rather than to the father, would be in the best interests of the child. You know how subjective all court decisions are."

"Even family court judges have to follow the law of precedent, though," Tommy retorted a bit sharply.

Eliza bit her tongue, hard. She was getting tired, and she wasn't really in the mood to play nursemaid to these two overgrown schoolboys. Her headache was worsening with each passing moment. She hid her weariness behind one of the stock phrases she used to divert potential clients from unnecessary litigation. "I'm just saying that it's not so cut-and-dried as all that."

Ely looked anxiously from Tommy to herself. "What exactly are you saying?" he asked.

"You might find a case just like your own, or a lot of cases for that matter, that went your way. The court tends to favor a natural parent, male or female, over anyone else, so I suspect that you would. But, once a case goes to the courts, anything can happen. The decision will be made based on the bias of a judge. I suggest you work it out with the grandparents on your own. It's safer. There's no need to involve me in this, or any other lawyer for that matter.'' Eliza used her most authoritative voice to drive her point home.

Slightly miffed, Ely responded, ''I didn't mean to waste your valuable time, Eliza.''

Inwardly, she sighed. ''It's not that.'' She felt herself growing impatient with him, herself, and the whole ridiculous situation. ''You may have been misinformed.'' Eliza looked at Tommy for confirmation. ''A lot of lawyers assume that because men have a proven advantage over a wife in custody cases, fathers are equally privileged in every case.''

Tommy had the good grace to look somewhat abashed. ''Like the case a few years ago in which the father found out his girlfriend had lied about their child being his, and the judge granted him full custody anyway, even though he wasn't the biological father,'' he said.

''Perfect example,'' Eliza said. ''You can't use the statistics, or even the facts in those isolated cases, to make generalizations about your own case. You never know what might happen if you let the state decide your son's future. You're better off keeping whatever semblance of control you have now and trying to use that to persuade his grandparents to let you keep him.''

''And you don't think it would be a more convincing argument that you think Jessie would be better off living with me?'' Ely asked.

''I don't know and, frankly, I don't think my opinion is important in this instance,'' Eliza answered honestly.

Both men sat back, apparently disconcerted by her answer.

''Well,'' Tommy said, recovering, ''thank you for your advice.''

She dipped her head slightly in acknowledgment and finished her drink. The worst was over now. All she had to do was figure out how to make a graceful exit.

''One thing,'' Ely said.

An odd premonition gripped her. She should have ordered that bourbon.

''Yes?'' Eliza asked hesitantly. She braced herself for his question.

"What is your opinion?" She almost groaned with frustration. He was still trying to pump her for information.

Even if Ely didn't realize that she'd had a long, hard day, and even if he couldn't know that—due to her vanity—tonight had not been one of her finest moments, he might at least have had enough feeling for her as a fellow human being not to send his older brother to wine and dine her in order to get her opinion on his legal problems. If all these two had wanted was her professional opinion, she wished that they'd had the courtesy to make an appointment to speak with her at her office, where her personal opinion wouldn't come into a discussion like this one. Why did they have to try and con her with this friendly reunion nonsense? She tried to remember that they didn't know her anymore.

Eliza went with the safest answer she could think of. "I don't have an opinion," she said.

"Please, I'd really like to know what you think," he insisted.

No you don't, she thought. Aloud she said, "I'm afraid I don't have any thoughts on the subject. I just don't know enough about the situation. For all I know, your late wife's parents might be right about being better able to care for Jessie." Ely bristled, visibly, but Tommy laid a calming hand on his arm and he didn't say anything.

Goaded by some inner demon Eliza continued. "I don't know you that well. I did, perhaps, a dozen years ago. I knew your family. But now we're virtual strangers. All I can say is that Jessie is a very lucky little boy to have his whole family looking out for him. Believe me, I'd love it if some of my other clients were shown a tenth of the concern you're all lavishing on this one little boy."

Ely's eyes narrowed. "How can you say that? This kind of discord could destroy my son's world. You of all people should know the damage a fight like this can inflict on a small child."

The anger that had been simmering inside her boiled over. "Damage?" Her voice was hard, cold as ice. It surprised her since the rage she felt was hot, the words burning her throat as they spilled forth like lava erupting from a volcano. "Like the damage caused when a retarded four-year-old is returned to the parents who locked her in a closet for two days because she broke a plate? Or would you say it was closer to the pain felt by a fourteen-year-old whose mother chooses to let her become a ward of the state rather than give up the boyfriend who's been molesting her daughter?'' The rancor that had been building within her since she realized the whole evening had been a ruse was released with each seething word, leaving Eliza feeling drained.

She stooped to retrieve her briefcase from beneath the table and only then looked at the two men, whose horrified faces reflected the impact of her outburst. ''I'm sorry. Those are two of the cases I have been working on lately, and I'm afraid they're . . . hard to leave behind at the office. They didn't really have anything to do with this.'' The clipped words didn't sound apologetic, but both men seemed to accept her excuse for her outrageous behavior.

Ely mumbled, ''That's all right.''

Tommy helped her on with her coat.

''I'm afraid I have a bit of a headache.'' That at least was the truth, even if it was not the reason for her inexcusable tirade.

''Of course. Do you need a ride home?'' Tommy offered gallantly.

''No, thank you. I'll be fine.'' It was a good thing they'd brought separate cars, she thought. She didn't think either of them could have handled the trip home. She caught the eye of each man in turn. Tommy still looked stunned, but Ely's look of shock had been transformed to one of sympathy, making Eliza feel lower yet. That gave her the impetus she needed to reassert the iron control she generally exercised over her emotions.

''I hope everything works out for you,'' she said. Their solemn expressions gave the cliché the weight of a benediction.

Eliza started to raise her hand to wave good-bye, but it was shaking and she quickly lowered it to her side. That slight fluttering motion would have to serve. She couldn't bring herself to shake hands.

''Goodbye,'' she said crisply, with a perfunctory smile. Eliza turned on her heel and walked away. She felt their eyes following her and held her shoulders back, her head up. She was in her car before she started to curse, slowly, and with feeling.

Eliza was mortified. She not only had deluded herself about Tommy's interest in her as a woman, but she'd nearly convinced herself, against all her better instincts, that her attraction to him was perfectly acceptable. To top that off, when she realized how ludicrous the idea was, she hadn't had the guts to admit to him, or even to herself, that her vanity had suffered a blow. Instead, she had resorted to hiding behind her work. Eliza had used the demands of her profession to avoid personal entanglements before, but this evening's display had been downright revolting. Lashing out at her two old friends with all that suppressed emotion, just because their behavior had pricked her ego, was unforgivable. And it was so unlike her. She never blew up. She had been exercising iron control over her emotions since she was a girl.

By the time Eliza reached her home in Brookline she was exhausted, her head ached, and she'd thought of and discarded a dozen possible ways to make her apologies to Tommy and Ely. Perhaps, she thought, as she let herself into her little row house, she deserved to suffer the pangs of unrequited conscience for this one. She couldn't possibly admit to either brother that she'd been stung to the quick by Tommy's disinterest.

She chuckled as she climbed the stairs to her bedroom. An hour ago, she would have predicted a very different ending to this evening. Her current situation was, undoubtedly, her fault. After all her animadversions on the male character, she had allowed her hormones to overrule her judgment. Maybe it would make her more sympathetic to her brethren, she thought, but she doubted it. Edifying as the experience had been, she should have known better. She could chalk it up to a lesson that would remain indelibly etched in her memory.

Jessie almost didn't hear his dad come home, even though you usually couldn't miss the sound of the car pulling up out front.

It was too late to turn out the light. Daddy would have seen it from the street. But there wouldn't be any trouble about that. Dad fell asleep reading all the time. He probably wouldn't even mind that Jessie had been reading one of the books in the Little House series *Little Town on the Prairie* by Laura Ingalls Wilder. It's not like they were sexy or anything. But you just knew Dad was not going to understand why he wanted to read a book that was all about girls. But they weren't bad. This one was so intense, he didn't even hear the Chevy coming. He still couldn't quite believe Mary Ingalls was really going to be blind forever! He jammed the ''chick'' book under his pillow so Dad wouldn't see it and checked to make sure his book of baseball trivia was lying open on the floor next to the bed.

He had timed it, so he knew it took Daddy approximately twelve minutes to lock the car, check all the windows and doors, come up the front walk, wait for the elevator and ride to their unlucky floor. They got their apartment real cheap, Dad said, because some folks wouldn't live on thirteen, and ''Hallelujah! for superstitious people.'' Dad could never remember where he put his keys, so he'd fumble around looking for them for a minute, and then, when he came inside, he'd send Mrs. Gregg home, drop his work off on his desk, grab a soda from the fridge, and finally sneak into Jessie's room to watch him sleep.

There had been plenty of time to figure out the timing. His dad did the same exact thing every single time he came home late. Jessie didn't mind. And he'd gotten really good at faking like he was asleep. He breathed real slow and steady, and kept his head turned sort of into the pillow. With enough practice, you could fool anyone.

His room was in the front of the apartment, and he always left the window open a crack when he waited up for his father. The street in front of their building was pretty quiet late at night, and Dad's old Chevy was so loud you could hear it for blocks. So Jessie usually had plenty of warning.

He'd been hooked on Laura Ingalls Wilder's books since the time he'd gotten stuck having to read one in detention one day. (Wouldn't you know that would be the only book Mrs.

Finley would have in her desk?) And Daddy always had to tell everyone every little thing he did—just to make sure it was okay. Since he didn't know any other boys who read these books, Jessie figured it must be kind of unusual. Anyway, he wasn't taking any chances. He felt sort of silly hiding the books, but, as Grandma always said, "Better safe than sorry." It wasn't like Dad suspected anything.

The whole family called Dad "The Absent-minded Professor," and Jessie knew they weren't really joking, either. He had to admit his father was a little bit weird at times. He figured that was probably where he himself got it from. And as long as Dad was orbiting the sun a little slower than the rest of the planet, Jessie knew he might as well accept it. It wasn't like the guy was a bad parent or anything. Dad was the best. Even if he was a little bit different.

Chapter Three

Eliza arrived at work early the next morning. She met her secretary as she walked into the office building.

"How did it go?" Mary Jane asked without preamble. She was a good friend as well as an employee, and Eliza didn't keep many secrets from her.

"Not good." Eliza smiled ruefully. "You were wrong. It wasn't a date." MJ was one of those women who made men's mouths water. She expected men to notice her and they did— almost without exception. Eliza wondered how she would have fared with Tommy Greene.

"You went out with a man. That's a date."

"It was a business meeting," Eliza said.

"It's your own fault, I'm sure," MJ said. "You probably didn't give the guy a chance."

"Actually, I—" The protest was automatic. Eliza faltered as she realized that she'd been about to admit what a fool she had almost made of herself. She took a deep breath and continued. "I did," she said defiantly. "I gave him a chance."

"How did you?" MJ asked. "What did you say?" She looked doubtful.

"I said I was glad to see him again. What was I supposed

to say?'' MJ groaned and tossed her smooth cap of raven-black hair. Eliza was one of the few privy to the fact that her thick, lustrous hair was natural, as was her baby-soft skin. Her face was too long, her chin too square, and her features were unremarkable, but what MJ had done with her natural gifts was something else again. Her eyebrows were plucked into a delicate crescent, her eyelashes enhanced to make her eyes look huge. Her lips were shaped into a pout to offset her square jaw. In all the years Eliza had known her, she had never seen so much as a smudge of lipstick in the wrong place. Eliza could easily imagine MJ charming Tommy Greene, wrapping him around her little finger.

''You tell him he looks fantastic. And that you're *excited* to see him.'' There was no doubt what she meant. She virtually purred as she demonstrated. Eliza had seen her friend's sex-kitten persona turn men into drooling idiots. She could also become a femme fatale, or even an ice goddess, in the blink of an eye, if she so chose. Mary Jane was a self-proclaimed expert on men. She had ''snagged a good one'' a couple of years before, and had given up playing the field, but she dabbled in her friends' love lives to keep her hand in.

''I couldn't say that, not the way you do,'' Eliza demurred.

''But it was true. When you left here last night, you were as nervous as a cat.''

''Nervous is not the same as excited.''

''Semantics,'' MJ said, dismissing her argument.

''Okay, but what difference does it make? So I didn't say I was excited to see him again. So what? I'm telling you, he wasn't there for that.''

''What did he say?'' MJ probed.

''He said he was glad to see me again, too, after all these years.'' They both winced.

''Don't men know *anything?*'' MJ said plaintively as they entered the office.

''No,'' Rosa answered Mary Jane's rhetorical question. Eliza's other employee was invaluable to the firm of E. Taylor and Associates, not only because she was the best paralegal in Boston, but because her sturdy dependability complimented MJ's color, and her boundless tolerance balanced Eliza's lack of tact. The older woman stood in the doorway of the little room off the conference room where she brewed a fresh pot of coffee every morning. Rosa stepped aside so Eliza and MJ could enter and pour themselves a cup, but they just stood gaping at her.

"Rosie!" MJ exclaimed. "I thought Samuel was the perfect mate."

Rosa was a trim, gray-haired woman in her sixties who reminded Eliza, somehow, of both her mother *and* her father. She was happily married and had more grandchildren than Eliza could count. Rosa bustled about, organizing everything in sight, including her boss's daily life. Eliza wanted to be just like Rosa when she grew up, and she had told her so. She wouldn't have minded her employee's counsel on personal as well as professional matters—however, Rosa had a rule against interfering in her coworkers personal lives. She said a lady lawyer had no need for an old woman's advice.

Which was why Eliza and MJ stared as Rosa answered, "He is. That doesn't make him any kind of genius when it comes to women. No man can ever understand what it is we *really* want to hear."

Eliza was sure Rosa's no-nonsense approach to life's little problems was the reason for the older woman's contentment at work and at home, and she couldn't wait to hear the first, and only, criticism she'd ever heard Rosa utter about her husband.

"You go, girl!" MJ urged. For all her cynical airs, she loved the tidbits of worldly wisdom that Rosa occasionally imparted as much as Eliza did. The two of them clinked their empty coffee cups against each other's and turned to their personal wisewoman.

"I've got him trained pretty good, after forty-some years together, but he still thinks its a compliment when he tells me I look 'great for an old broad.' "

"He's kidding." Eliza had met Sam. He was a courtly old gentleman.

"Half-kidding."

"You do punish him, I hope," MJ said.

"Sometimes. Generally, I take it in the spirit it was intended. He's just like any other man. He doesn't know any better. It doesn't matter how smart they are, or how old they get—they just never learn the true meaning of the word 'diplomacy.' It must be biology. To men, it's us against them—whether it's family or country or their sex. They're all stuck in boxes. I think that missing Y chromosome is what allows a body to make the connection between all the emotions you feel and all the knowledge you have, and all the experience you earn."

"Hey." Eliza felt honor-bound to protest. "Some women aren't all that good at making those connections, either."

"Yeah, but then it's their own fault," Rosa said philosophically. "At least, we have the ability."

"What does that have to do with the dumb things men say they think we like to hear, like "Great Bazongas" or "You look so sweet, I wanna taste that," MJ asked.

"They just can't help it. They think because they love to hear us say, 'That was the best sex I ever had,' that's what we want to hear, too. They don't know we don't want to be reminded we're in competition with every woman they've ever been to bed with," she explained.

"Mmmm." Eliza nodded, thinking she was beginning to get it. "So, you're saying Samuel thinks calling you a great-looking *old* broad is okay because when men grow older they just grow more distinguished and, presumably, more attractive."

"You got it, honey." Rosa smiled approvingly.

"That's why they're always rubbing those potbellies like some kind of security blanket," MJ declared triumphantly, adding, "Well, it's time somebody told them. There ain't nothin' sexy about a beer gut, I don't care how rich or how cool the guy is."

"Well, you can try, dear," Rosa said, shaking her head in her grandmotherly way. They could nearly hear her thinking, "It won't make a bit of difference, but you young girls are surely welcome to waste your time if you want to." They'd heard it before.

Eliza knew their moment was over. "We should get to work," she said.

Rosa nodded. "Your schedule is in your computer. Just hit Control S."

"Wait, I want to know more about the date," MJ protested.

"It wasn't a date. How many times do I have to tell you that. Tommy Greene just wanted some legal advice. That's all."

Eliza went into her office, but MJ wouldn't be put off. She followed her into "the inner sanctum," as her secretary jokingly called Eliza's overflowing office. It had been a beautiful work space at one time, with the huge old antique desk as its center-piece. Now, every surface was covered with paper, journals, and legal tomes. There were even piles of books on the floor by the oak-paneled walls.

MJ pretended to do some filing as she continued the interroga-tion. "Maybe that's all he said he wanted, but he's single, he's straight, he's new in town, and you are definitely available. He might have had an ulterior motive. I saw you when you left here last night. You looked good! I don't guess he'd have been too offended if you asked him back to your place."

"Mary Jane Collins, get your smutty mind off my sex life and get to work," Eliza ordered.

"Somebody's got to remind you that there's more to life than . . . this." Her disgusted glance took in the work piled on the desk, floor, and file cabinets.

"Oh, he reminded me all right," Eliza said ruefully. "Much good that did me."

MJ pounced on that remark. "Why? What else did he say besides, 'It's good to see you again.' "

"Nice voice," Eliza said, complimenting MJ on her mimicry. "But he's got this deep baritone that's like velvet."

"Velvet, hmmm? That sounds promising. So what did he say that reminded you that there are other things in life more pleasant than work."

"We talked about him, mostly."

"Mostly," MJ prompted.

Eliza started to confess but chickened out. "It doesn't matter."

"I'm going to strangle you, paycheck or no paycheck. Tell me!"

"He said I was his hero," she mumbled. Eliza's cheeks grew warm at the memory.

Her secretary grinned. "There, was that so hard?" Only then did MJ realize what Eliza had said. "See, I told you," she said, gloating.

"It didn't mean anything."

"Didn't mean anything?! I'd kill to have a guy say that to me. It's just wasted on you. Didn't your mother ever teach you how to accept a compliment? All you have to do is say thank you. Then you puff up like a blowfish, like me."

"It's embarassing. And, anyway, I'm not the hero type."

"Heroine. And you are, at least to the kids you are. Sometimes even *I* am half-convinced. Not right now, but when you're all jazzed up about getting some sleazebag, you are something else!"

As always, when embarassed, Eliza made a joke. "Oh, sure. Me and Thurgood Marshall. Fighting injustice for love and money."

"That's just what I was talking about. That's your problem exactly." MJ was exasperated but undaunted. Eliza could tell from her mulish expression that her friend and secretary had not finished with her yet.

"I appreciate the vote of confidence. But you might be a tiny bit biased in my favor."

"So, what's wrong with you?" MJ asked. "No beating around the bush now. I'd like to know what's so terrible about you. Then maybe I can stop wasting my time on such a loser."

"I didn't say I was a loser, but I do have a few less than desirable qualities." The conversation was ridiculous, but it was clear to Eliza that MJ had dug in her heels and she wasn't going away.

"Like what?" she asked.

"Oh, you know. The top of this desk hasn't seen the light of day in years, and the way it's going, I'm never going to get it cleared off."

"That wouldn't be heroic, it would be miraculous."

"Okay, but you should see the house. It's a mess. The lawn hasn't been mowed in I don't know how long. The neighbors are going to get a petition going soon."

"My God!" MJ clutched her chest and backed into a chair.

Eliza continued, laughing now. "The dry cleaners have probably sold my clothes. I haven't watched a single game of the Series. Or had dinner with a friend in months. Or a date, as you have so often pointed out."

"It wasn't meant as criticism, just a gentle reminder," MJ interjected.

"There's definitely something wrong with me. You work as hard as I do, but you manage to fit in a movie once in a while, you take classes, you take *vacations.*"

"So should you," was the merciless reply.

"I know. I try," Eliza said. "I can't do it. Rosa is raising something in the neighborhood of a hundred grandchildren and makes all those Halloween costumes, by hand, and she knits and paints, and plays golf, and works and has two gardens, and writes letters, and cooks—"

"There's no great mystery there. She likes to do all those things. We're not workaholics. Does that make us better people?"

"Not in my book," Eliza responded, straight-faced.

"Fine!" MJ stood, signaling the end of the session. "I thought we were getting somewhere here, but if you're just going to make jokes . . ."

"Thanks, Doc, but I've really got to get to work, and so do you." She smothered a smile as MJ threw her hands up in the air with a grunt of frustration. When she reached the door, Eliza said, "I thought the session went pretty well today, didn't you?" But MJ didn't stop, just raised one hand over her shoulder and made an obscene gesture aimed in Eliza's general direction. "Bring me the Lopez file," Eliza shouted at her retreating back.

The tables were turned when Eliza came back from court. Her secretary had completely recovered. She dangled a pink message slip in front of Eliza's face, but pulled it away as Eliza reached for it.

"What is it?" Eliza asked impatiently.

Mary Jane's mischievous smile made her nervous. MJ had the world's softest heart, and was fantastic with young children, which was a great help when it fell to Eliza to cope with preverbal human beings. Unfortunately, as a secretary, her disregard for authority and her irrepressible sense of humor, led her to poke fun at people whose support Eliza sorely needed. MJ's flippant manner could be a hindrance in situations in which arrogant attorneys, straitlaced judges, or harassed parents were justly concerned with some aspect of a case. Eliza generally welcomed her secretary's attempts to bring levity into the workplace, but it had already been a long morning, and she didn't have time to soothe any ruffled feathers this afternoon.

"Guess who called?" MJ trilled, ignoring Rosa's slight frown and the little shake of her head.

Eliza caught the paralegal's motion out of the corner of her eye. "I don't have time for games today. I've got to get all the way across town."

She was due at the hospital to talk to an eleven-year-old whose stepmother's spiked heel had somehow ended up embedded in his ear. Eliza was not looking forward to it.

"Well," MJ huffed, turning and walking to her desk, taking the message with her. "What trauma brought out this charming persona, Sybil, dear?"

Eliza felt the corners of her mouth twitch. MJ might lack some of the social graces, but her outrageous comments could always make her laugh, even at the most unlikely times.

"Oh, drop the attitude, and give me the message, MJ." Eliza tried to look stern.

It didn't work. "I don't know if I should bother. You're probably too busy to call him back anyway. And this is not a voice that should be dealt with in a hurry. Maybe I'll just give him a call myself, to make your apologies," MJ teased.

Eliza recognized the sinking feeling in the pit of her stomach. It was the same feeling she'd had when she'd looked up from her drink to find Ely Greene standing behind his brother. She always got it when she sensed bad news coming.

"Unclench," MJ commanded. Eliza couldn't take offense at

her secretary's impertinence. It was just MJ's way of suggesting
Eliza lighten up a bit. "Tommy Greene wants you to give him
a call. It's not a disaster."

Eliza sat on the message and the two that followed it until
she couldn't stand another minute of Mary Jane's incessant
nagging. A week after their first evening together, she returned
his calls. As before, he suggested that—as it was Friday night—
they should go out and have a drink.

It was simple enough to say no. Eliza's promise to herself
never to repeat their first "date" rang in her mind as she said,
"Maybe if this is business, we can just set up an appointment
for you and Ely to come see me here in the office. Or we could
even arrange a telephone conference."

"Okay." Despite his agreement, Tommy sounded disappointed, or perhaps she imagined it. "If you're too busy, perhaps we could stop by the office on Monday sometime."

He took a lot for granted, Eliza thought, but pleased at having
averted another tragicomedy, she agreed. "Monday afternoon,
around five-thirty. I've got court during the day."

If he recognized her subtle rebuke, he didn't acknowledge
it, but he did sound sincerely grateful as he confirmed the
appointment. "I really appreciate this, Eliza."

"No problem," Eliza lied. She waited for a moment to see
if he had anything to add, then she broke the connection.

She buzzed MJ on the intercom. "Pencil in Thomas and
Elias Greene on Monday at five-thirty." She ignored the grunt
of disapproval from the other end of the line. She didn't bother
to ask whether MJ was displeased because Eliza passed up the
chance of a date—which she was sure her sharp-eared busybody
of a secretary had heard. Mary Jane's censure could also have
stemmed from Eliza's habit of suggesting her staff "pencil in"
items on her calendar. She couldn't quite get over using the
antiquated phrase, despite the fact that her two-woman staff
had insisted on buying the best office management program
computer software had to offer.

Eliza wasn't a high-tech person, as she frequently told her

office mates. She appreciated the ease of access to the on-line law library through Nexus, and she couldn't imagine how she had written a brief or a contract before she bought her word-processing program, but that was where it ended. Even Rosa, though two decades her senior, had managed to completely revamp her skills with the arrival of their first computer. So clearly, age had nothing to do with it. Eliza was just hopelessly old-fashioned when it came to things like this. She could no more imagine using e-mail than she could imagine calmly asking Tommy, "Your place or mine?" after a companionable dinner.

She was not exactly a puritan. She enjoyed men, and everything that came with them. She liked playing computer games, too. But none of it came easily to her. She'd probably been born at the wrong time. MJ certainly seemed to think so. In most ways, Eliza was definitely a woman of the nineties, but she couldn't be as casual about sex as most of the other women whom she knew. The act was too intimate, too revealing.

She was not a prude, nor, despite her computer illiteracy, was she a reactionary. The sexual revolution hadn't exactly passed her by. Eliza had been only eleven in 1968—the summer of love—but as the seventies began, she had begun to explore her own sensuality. The AIDS virus hadn't yet been discovered, and she stood at the brink of adulthood with all the freedom to experiment that the sixties had made possible. But slowly, after her parents died when she was sixteen, her excitement had dimmed. By the time she turned eighteen, looking for love was not part of her personal quest. She half hoped it would take her unawares. And, finally, when she became a social worker, it had. She had fallen in love with "her" kids. There were children who needed all the love and attention she had to give. That had opened her up a little.

She had gone into her adult life feeling less than complete, and her kids had given her back a part of herself that she had thought lost forever. As always, when she thought of those years, Eliza was overwhelmed by an unbearable sense of sorrow. Memories of those days as a social worker brought back memories of her one failure. But she wouldn't let it drag her down. She was no longer that vulnerable, bleeding, young woman. She had recovered from that tragedy and had gotten on with her life.

The sexual relationships she'd had had been satisfactory, but they had never been the stuff of fairy tales. She had never gotten carried away by her physical attraction to any one man— although once or twice she had thought she had found "the one" on an emotional level. But Eliza wasn't a romantic. If she hadn't found a mate by now, she didn't imagine that she ever would.

She had rebuilt her life and herself. If her heart had been lost, forever, she'd replaced it with something just as good. She might not be able to nurture a family of her own, but she was the best friend a helpless child could have in the courts. She might not be in touch with her softer side, but she could tap into the core of white-hot anger that had replaced it when- ever she needed to. Her passion ran as hot and strong as anyone else's. If men found her a little cool, she was still an intelligent, attractive woman who never clung or dragged on them.

In the past few years, she had begun to dread the moment when her dates suggested getting more serious. She had not been able to detect in herself enough enthusiasm for any of them to make that kind of commitment. She missed sex some- times, but it required too much work outside the bedroom. Occasionally, she wished for the distraction of a man's hard arms around her late at night when she couldn't sleep for worrying about one of "her" kids. When she fantasized, it was almost always about kissing. Unfortunately, as far as Eliza was concerned, most men these days didn't spend enough time practicing to become truly expert at it. Kissing was a lost art.

Tommy Greene was probably good at it, Eliza thought. He excelled at everything else he did. But that was no reason to make a fool of herself. She had always remained cool, almost aloof, until she felt a man could be trusted to behave—even in the most intimate situation—like a gentleman.

The pickings grew slimmer as she grew older. Not that she had any lack of escorts when she wanted one, but they all seemed to fit into slots that held little interest for her. She was tired of men who couldn't go anywhere, even on a date, without their cellphones. Of course, she was never out of earshot of her own mobile phone, but she still found it annoying in others. Eliza could peg a guy with little more than a glance; she knew when someone was suffering a midlife crisis, recovering from a divorce, or finally deciding bachelorhood no longer held its appeal. There was no mystery to men anymore. She missed that, too. Although Tommy was certainly different. She'd pegged him wrong, from the start. That was something new.

As uncomplimentary as it had been to find his interest in her was purely professional, she had had a thrilling few minutes that first night. If her ego had been a little deflated after that fiasco, at least she could get a chuckle out of it. Who would have thought that sweet little Eliza Taylor would grow up to be a dirty old lady?

Eliza was pleased with how cool and calm she felt when her secretary showed Tommy and Ely into her office on Monday afternoon. She had let herself get all hot and bothered when she had seen Tommy before, but now, she'd had plenty of time to prepare herself for the impact he made on her senses. She felt a familiar sense of detachment as she surveyed both men from behind her desk. Tommy was certainly breathtaking in a black polo shirt that showed off his muscular physique, tucked into black slacks with gray piping. He looked like a model for an Armani ad, the way he carried the matching jacket over his shoulder. She was completely in control of her breathing.

Ely was, as usual, dressed as if he'd thrown on whatever came first out of his closet. His rayon pants were a washed-out blue and his pale pink shirt had a tiger or some other big cat sewn onto the pocket—like those that were manufactured by Sears or Marshall's and mass marketed in the fall as back-to-school clothes for young men. Even that ensemble couldn't completely hide the masculine beauty that he shared with his more sophisticated older brother. Both men were dressed to type. Her heart rate stayed even.

Tommy had been talking while she'd been assessing them. His deep baritone washed over her like a gentle river, carrying her along on its current without any conscious attention paid on her part. She surfaced as he said something about the situation growing more serious.

"This is the same situation we discussed before?" Eliza asked, pulling her notepad from beneath a small pile of correspondence.

"Yes. Jessie's grandparents are insisting that Jessie should move out west with them. They've mentioned bringing in a lawyer."

"That's why we want to hire you," Ely said, leaning forward eagerly. "Will you take my case?"

"Wait a minute. Let's back up here. Are you absolutely sure you want to do this? It doesn't sound like there is a case here yet."

"Tommy said they may possibly have a better case than we originally thought, if they do choose to go to court," Ely said with a glance at his brother.

"I didn't say that exactly," Tommy corrected him. "But I am worried. Ely forgot to mention something that may give the Tysons' case more weight. He gave Rebecca and Hank temporary custody of Jessie when he was living with them. And he never legally revoked the arrangement. I think Ely will want to stake his claim right away."

Eliza shook her head. "This isn't corporate law, Tommy. This is a child we're talking about here, not a company or a piece of property."

"I know that," he said, aggrieved.

"Let's go over the facts," Eliza suggested.

"The facts are, I want to keep my son. Hank and Rebecca may have more money, and I know they can offer Jessie a lot, but they're wrong to try and take him away from me. Doesn't the fact that they're trying to uproot my eight-year-old son and drag him halfway across the country purely for their own convenience—count against them?" The words were harsh, but Eliza was pleased to note that his voice was even and controlled.

"Not necessarily," Eliza said. "Their situation is changing, why shouldn't Jessie's? Can you sit there and tell me that if you were suddenly offered a dream job teaching at some school

in Idaho you would turn it down rather than uproot Jessie?"
As she'd expected, Ely shook his head slowly. "He's a child,
he'll adjust. The Tysons aren't moving on a whim. They have
to leave for health reasons. You said yourself that they've been
like parents to him. Their attitude is completely understand-
able."

"Wait a minute. Whose side are you on?" Ely asked.

"It's not a question of sides," Tommy interposed. "A good
lawyer can argue both sides of any case."

"But you can't just take a boy away from his father. I may
not know much about the law, but according to psychological
studies, it's very damaging to remove a young child from his
primary caregiver."

"I know," Eliza said soothingly. "But those are very subjective theories. Anyway, we'll assume that Jessie will be sad-
dened, damaged if you prefer, if this rift were to occur. But
some psychologists would probably say Jessie will suffer
whichever way this situation is resolved. In one case, he loses
the influence his grandparents have had on him—a very close
relationship as I understand it. In the other, Jessie has to move
away from his father, a very important figure in any child's
life."

Tommy spoke up. "It still sounds to me like Ely's got the
right here to say where and how his own kid should be raised.
I thought only unfit parents lost custody."

"Sure," Eliza agreed. "And that might well be the outcome
of a court case. But let's look at this another way. So far, we've
been looking at the negative aspects of Jessie's either staying
or moving. Let's look at the positive side. If he stays . . ." She
let her voice trail off and looked inquiringly at Ely.

"If he stays he'll be able to live in his own home, in his
own room, with all his things and a father who loves him and
whom he loves. He'll be among his friends at school in the
community which he grew up in. He'll have the same stable,
comfortable, normal life he's accustomed to."

"If he goes . . ."

"He'll have to adjust to a new home," Ely said slowly.

"Put the most positive spin on it you can," Eliza suggested. "His grandparents and their lawyer certainly will."

"He'll have a bigger room, in a nice house, in a quiet suburban neighborhood, a wonderful new school—Rebecca already checked it out—and two people who will be at home all day, every day, just to take care of him."

"Sounds pretty good, right?" Eliza remarked. "All I'm saying is that there are a lot of aspects to this thing that you have to think about. I'm sure his grandparents think they've got an equally good case." Ely nodded, although the statement hadn't been a question. "All your righteous indignation will not help you in family court."

"I hadn't thought of it that way," Ely said.

"Why should you?" she asked. Normal people didn't look at emotional situations, like custody battles, from an objective viewpoint. Lawyers were expected to. Although they were sometimes despised for it, the job required objectivity.

"That's right. That's what I need you for," he said.

Eliza placed her notepad precisely in the middle of the pile of correspondence she'd withdrawn it from and folded her hands in the center of the desk. "I wouldn't say you needed *me,*" she began. "I think there are other lawyers who could handle this for you."

Both men sat forward, clearly surprised. "But," they said at the same time. Ely continued. "But you're the best."

"Thank you." Eliza acknowledged the compliment with a nod. "But I think you're giving me credit I don't deserve. I'm good, but there are many competent lawyers who could represent you. My caseload is so full right now I don't think, in all honesty, I could give you the attention you deserve."

"There's time yet, nothing's been filed," Tommy said. He added hopefully, "Maybe . . . ?" He let his voice trail off.

Eliza filled in the rest of the question. "I could make room on my schedule?" She shook her head. "Maybe, but I just don't think it would be fair to you, or to any other prospective clients who may have less resources and connections than you do." She spoke with an unmistakable air of finality. Both men were just starting to absorb her unexpected response when Eliza stood and came around the desk. Ingrained politeness forced them to rise as well, and she herded them toward the door.

"I hope it all goes well for you." She held out her hand, and Tommy shook it.

Ely was not quite ready to accept her bombshell yet. "You won't take my case?" he asked in disbelief.

"I'm sure it will be fine." She ushered them out of the door of her office and followed them to the outer door. "Good-bye," Eliza said firmly.

"Good-bye," Tommy echoed.

"Bye," Ely mumbled. His bewildered expression hadn't faded.

Eliza closed the door behind them and then sagged back against it. That was that. She went to her desk and rearranged some of the papers. She made a neat stack of the next day's work, highest priority on top, and then loaded her briefcase with paperwork she hoped to finish that evening. The office walls seemed to close in on her as she surveyed the piles of paper that remained scattered over the desktop, obscuring the highly polished wood from view. She sat down in her chair and closed her eyes. She was glad Rosa and MJ had already left for the day.

The street outside her window was quiet. She'd chosen to locate her office in this building because of its proximity to the courthouse, but as a consequence, when darkness fell, the streets were almost deserted. Once the offices closed up for the day, the people scurried back to residential areas and left the tall buildings empty and dark. Like sentinels, they lined the treeless street, creating an echoing valley through which Eliza tread each night alone: the clicking of her wooden heels or the squeaking of her sneaker soles against cement the only sound to break the silence that had settled over the business district.

As she stood and put on her coat preparing to make the solitary walk to her car, she felt a pang of guilt for having pulled the rug out from under the brothers Greene. But they shouldn't have taken her representation for granted.

She hadn't lied to them. She truly was snowed under with work. If the case had been a more important one, she wouldn't have turned them away—but, as it was, she didn't really feel any compunction about sending them to find another lawyer. She just felt bad because they'd looked so wounded.

But she knew this was the right course of action. For her and for them.

Chapter Four

Tommy told him to let it go, but he couldn't. Every time Jessie looked up at him with those beautiful, trusting eyes, Ely's conscience nagged at him. He had to protect Jessie. Ever since he'd first held his son in his arms, he'd known that that was what he'd been put on this planet to do. Jessie had to have the best, and that meant Eliza Taylor. He had made the right decision, Ely was sure. If he could just talk with Eliza, reason with her, she *would* change her mind. She had to.

Ely inhaled deeply, then let his breath out slowly and reached for the telephone. He lifted the handset. It slipped from his hand, bounced off the cradle, and clattered loudly onto the tabletop.

"Get a grip, man," he said to himself.

Even calling her made him clumsy. His wife used to say he was as graceful as a dancer, in and out of bed, but when Eliza was around, he turned into a klutz. When he saw her, he was a tongue-tied fourteen-year-old, basking in the reflected glory of his godlike older brother, who had always, because of his genius, been surrounded by people like Eliza, women like Eliza. She had been the only one who had ever deigned to notice Ely. During the three years Tommy had been at Harvard, Ely had visited as often as he could. That had been a golden time. By the time Tommy had graduated, Ely was seventeen, and he'd gone from being the annoying tagalong to a friend to his big brother.

Ely taught kids who were the age he had been then. Young girls in his classes were infatuated with him, as he had been with Eliza. He knew these crushes were part of being an adolescent. But Eliza was the only person in Tommy's crowd at law school who had really seemed to see him, and the pleasure of it had reduced him to a stuttering mass of hormones. It had taken just one look from those perceptive brown eyes and he was once again enthralled—twelve years later.

Her face had hardly changed, except perhaps to become more beautiful. The tiny wrinkles at the corners of her eyes made her look even more intelligent. To him, that made her sexier than ever. She was just as he remembered her. Her straight nose widened at the tip just enough to give her face character. Her lips were fine, but not thin, the bottom one a little fuller than the top. He was a man now, not a boy, and he could imagine exactly what her mouth would feel like against his own. At seventeen, his heart swelled at the thought of her. At twenty-nine, his blood sang.

But he had to overcome this thing. For Jessie. Ely just had to get ahold of himself. Eliza had to agree to represent him. Hank and Rebecca had hired a lawyer.

He dialed the phone.

"E. Taylor and Associates." The voice on the phone was that of an older woman. The secretary certainly hadn't been elderly. She had been so young and nubile that his sensuous Eliza had looked like an ice princess next to her.

"Hello?" His voice broke. He cleared his throat. "May I speak to Ms. Taylor, please. Ely Greene calling."

"One moment, please."

Ely crossed his fingers briefly, then skimmed the notes he had made. He was going to apologize for imposing and for his presumption in acting as though it was a foregone conclusion that Eliza would present him and Jessie. When they'd met at the office the previous day, he recognized something in her manner, something he'd seen before. His wife used to get that look whenever she felt taken for granted. It had been years since Ely had consciously noticed it, but he realized now his mother-in-law, Rebecca, usually wore it, and oftentimes, the women he worked with got that same look. It was a woman thing, he supposed. Tommy might tell him to piss off; his father would say, "Go fly a kite," and most of the other men of his acquaintance had similar ways of expressing their aggravation when they felt put upon. But women were subtle creatures. A man had to read their minds. Or take his cues from their body language and facial expressions, as Ely was doing in this case. For his son's sake, he hoped he hadn't lost his touch when it came to soothing ruffled female feathers.

After the apology, if she softened, he planned to wing it. He had an idea or two about why Eliza was opposed to taking his case. Her workload was the most obvious difficulty, but he knew in his heart that if she wanted to, she'd find a way to fit them into her overcrowded schedule.

The woman who had answered the phone came back on the line as he mused about other arguments Eliza might advance. "I'm afraid Ms. Taylor is on a long call right now. May I give her a message?"

"No, I'll wait," Ely said stubbornly. He'd wait all day, if he had to, to speak with her. He'd called into the school to say he was taking a sick day, just in case.

Ten minutes later, he was put through.

"Hello, Ely," Eliza said pleasantly enough.

"Hi. I'm sorry if this isn't a good time to talk. I can call back later, or make an appointment to speak with you another day," he offered, mindful of his resolution not to impose upon her any further than was absolutely necessary.

"I have a couple of minutes now," she replied. He thought she already sounded slightly less chilly than she had when she picked up the phone. Of course, that might have been wishful thinking, but a surge of hope lightened his heart.

"I wanted to apologize for being so thoughtless yesterday afternoon. I didn't mean to add to your difficulties. I should have known better. I know how busy you are."

"Thank you," Eliza responded, after a moment.

Ely clasped the phone more tightly. The tough part was coming up. "I just wanted you to know that I thought about it for a long time before I asked Tommy to call you. It wasn't a hasty decision."

Ely withstood the urge to cross his fingers. Strictly speaking, that was a lie. The moment Tommy mentioned that Ely might need a lawyer, he'd thought of Eliza. But he had also thought long and hard about her before the custody argument had ever come up. He'd followed her rise over the years, from the public defender's staff to her own successful office. He combed the papers for news about her with an interest that bordered on obsession. He hadn't told Tommy, nor anyone else, but he'd been half in love with Eliza Taylor since the first time he met her at Harvard. That feeling had never really diminished. It had been tempered by time and distance, but she was still in his thoughts and in his heart. They said it was impossible to forget your first love.

Over the years, he'd been as proud of her as if she were his own sister. Because of Eliza he'd followed the changes in juvenile rights law, a field that had seen a lot of upheaval in the past ten years or so. Spectacular cases even made the headlines. Eliza had been featured in more than one article. He was probably as much of an expert in the area as any layman could be.

"You are my first and only choice as a lawyer." As soon as the words came out of his mouth, he realized how arrogant he sounded. He'd meant it as a compliment, but it could be interpreted as a demand—one which he was not in any position to make.

Eliza did not sound flattered as she said, "I've already explained that my schedule just won't permit me to take on any new clients right now." Ely waited patiently for further objections. "In any case," she said, "any good lawyer could handle your case. It's relatively straightforward."

She sounded tired. Ely wished he could ease her burden rather than add to it, but he just couldn't.

"Straightforward perhaps, but the outcome, as you pointed

out, is not so clear-cut. I can't take a chance on losing Jessie."
He heard the desperation in his own voice. Well, there was
nothing he could do about that that. He was desperate.

Her voice gentled as she asked, "Have you considered making a move out west? Instead of fighting your in-laws, you
could join them. You can teach anywhere, can't you?"

"I considered it, of course." He wondered if she'd find his
reason for discarding the idea too selfish. It was Jessie's future
he was thinking of, too. Not just his own.

"You did?" She was insultingly surprised.

"I love this area, and I've never lived anywhere else, but
when I realized Rebecca and Hank had to move, I made some
queries about positions that might be available in and around
Phoenix. I'd hate to leave my family behind, but I had to find
out if perhaps the move would be better for my son. If nothing
else, I thought I should know if a move like this would offer
both Jessie and me advantages I didn't know about."

"What happened?" she prompted.

"It just couldn't work," Ely said. "The area is not heavily
populated, and the demand for a secondary school teacher is
not nearly as high as it is here. There are fewer public and
private schools. My qualifications aren't that extraordinary—
for example, my Spanish isn't that strong—and there's a
smaller pool to compete in. Part of the reason I was able to
get a place at a school as prestigious as St. Joe's was because
Tommy and I went to school there. As for teaching in the
public school system, I don't have certification yet. I'd been
planning on getting it in the next few years, thinking that Jessie
and I might both move to public school here. But I wanted to
wait till he was a little older to add the coursework to our
schedule."

He didn't know whether to mention to her that Rebecca was
very opposed to the idea of Jessie's attending public school,
but decided it wasn't relevant. "There's a good chance I
wouldn't be able to get a position at the private school Rebecca
thinks Jessie should attend, and if I didn't teach there, it would
be too expensive for me to pay for. So, either I'd be dependent
on my in-laws for tuition or Jessie would have to attend public

school.'' Rebecca Tyson would never be able to live with that. But Ely didn't think Eliza wanted to hear about the public versus private school debate he and Rebecca had been arguing for years.

"On top of that, there's a good chance I'd have to go back to school myself in order to get any kind of job,'' Ely went on, "and whatever I did get, I'd have no seniority and no guarantee of a permanent position.''

Ely felt the need to justify himself further, but he stopped. He didn't want to overwhelm her, just wanted her to be aware he'd thought this out thoroughly.

"I understand,'' Eliza said. And he believed she really did. She sounded different, more sympathetic.

"I still think you should interview some other lawyers,'' she again suggested, but much less forcefully than she had before.

"Hank and Rebecca have already hired an attorney. Time is of the essence, now. And besides, I couldn't trust anyone else the way I trust you.'' It was true. His faith in this woman had nothing to do with the glowing recommendations Tommy had passed along to him. He had always admired her and her work. Eliza had fought some high-profile cases, both in public and private service, and he had followed it all in the newspapers. Even in that objective media, all reports indicated that she was as caring and sensitive in her work as she had been in person when they had known each other twelve years ago.

"But you haven't spoken to anyone else. How can you be so sure that you won't find someone you like just as much?''

She was weakening. He sensed it. "I just am.''

Ely could picture her so clearly, sitting in that disaster of an office, tapping her fingernail against her teeth the way she used to do in those days at Harvard when she debated some particularly thorny issue with his brother at the Pub.

He had one more piece of ammunition. He had to use it. "If I were a woman in the same situation, you wouldn't send me to another lawyer, would you?'' It was a challenge to her integrity. One he didn't think she could refuse.

"What are you implying?''

"I just happened to read the article you wrote for *Emerge*

a couple of years ago, about this very subject. I remember it well. You said wealthy men continued to maintain control over the disposition of their children even when they died, or divorced, and removed themselves from the child-rearing process. It was primarily through the grandparents that this was perpetuated. Didn't you say . . ." He checked his notes. "Single parents need to stand up for their rights against the grandparents who fight for custody on the grounds that the children would be better off financially in a wealthier household. I believe you argued that money, alone, was not a good basis for determining where a child would be best cared for."

"You're taking all of this out of context. That article has nothing to do with this case." The note of finality in her voice sent a shiver of foreboding down Ely's spine. Perhaps the challenge he'd thrown out hadn't been wise. Just because he thought it irresistible, didn't mean it couldn't kill the whole deal.

"Interview a couple of other lawyers. There are some real sharks in this town. You should be able to find someone who can give you what you're looking for."

Damn, Ely thought. He couldn't believe he'd blown it. And he had been so close. He knew it. He was so busy castigating himself for his blunder, he didn't realize Eliza had broken the connection.

The voice of the woman who had answered the phone finally penetrated his reverie. "Hello? Is anybody there?" she was asking. "Who is it?"

"Nobody," Ely said as he placed the phone gently back in the cradle.

He tried to think about other things. He gave the apartment a thorough deep cleaning, which it needed. He even dusted Jessie's room. He swept, mopped, and scrubbed, James Brown blasting from the old reliable turntable. He sang along. He really got into the chorus of "Please, Please, Please," but it only reminded him of the conversation with Eliza. He made a list of records he wanted. These old LPs were getting harder and harder to find, since the advent of CDs and laserdiscs. He made a mental note to get to work locating the albums he wanted to add to his collection before they stopped producing them altogether.

Finally, the school day was over. He had arranged to meet Jessie after soccer practice in the public library around the corner from the school, since no one from St. Joe's ever visited it. When he got there, he had a bit of a fright. He thought he saw the headmaster, Mr. McGinley—his nemesis. But it turned out to be another old white man sporting the same bald head with white fringe. Ely was engrossed in a book when Jessie found him.

"Hi, Dad," he said. "I wasn't followed," he added, when Ely looked around nervously.

"No, I know," Ely said. "I thought I saw McGinley before, and I guess I'm still a little jumpy." He stacked the books he'd been perusing neatly on the table in front of him. "How about we stop and get a pizza for dinner? I'm not in the mood to cook." He and Jessie both knew there was tons of Grandma Rebecca's homemade cooking in the freezer, all tagged and bagged and ready to pop in the microwave. As Ely had expected, Jessie jumped at the offer of junk food over his grandmother's healthy, hearty dishes.

"Za! Yeah!" His eight-year-old fist punched the air, a perfect imitation of his uncle Tommy's jubilation after a well-executed play on the basketball court. Ely marveled at the intricacies of genetics, while the eighty-something librarian ushered the pair of them out of the library. With a quick glance up at the corner, around which stood the school, Ely turned and started to jog in the opposite direction.

Jessie fell into step beside him. "Uh, Dad?"

Ely couldn't quite find his pace. "Yes, son?" He looked down at his feet. He was wearing an old pair of leather shoes with soles that were as stiff as a board.

"Did you hear me?" Jessie was saying.

"Huh?"

"This isn't the way home." Jessie pointed back the way they had come. "It's back there."

"Let's take the long way, okay?"

"Sure," Jessie agreed. "I only jogged a couple of miles during soccer practice."

Ely barely heard him. Each step he took reverberated through his entire body as his feet slapped the pavement. "At least you're wearing sneakers," Ely said, looking pointedly at his own feet.

"I told you you should get the Air Jordans, Pop," Jessie said cheekily. Then he took off, outdistancing his father in seconds.

"That's not funny," Ely yelled after him. But he couldn't help grinning.

He found it harder and harder to smile as the evening wore on. He didn't mention the conversation with Eliza to Jessie, although Ely had told him that he was staying home in order to make an important call to that lady. Jessie, the soul of indiscretion, didn't bring it up until bedtime.

With youthful directness, he said, "It didn't go too well with the lawyer, huh, Dad."

Ely tried never to lie to him. "Not too well, no. But don't you worry about it. I'll take care of it."

"Uncle Tommy prob'ly knows lots of other lawyers, just as good as her," Jessie said soothingly.

"But I want this one." Ely sighed. "I'll think of something."

"Okay, good night." Jessie went to his room. Ely watched him go. He felt relieved at Jessie's easy acceptance of his promise, but it made him feel anxious, too, because he knew his son was still young enough to believe he could fix anything, and he didn't want that to end, yet.

He wrapped the leftover pizza in tinfoil and washed the soda cans for recycling. Then he turned on the television, only to turn it off two minutes later. His thoughts kept returning to Eliza. He replayed the conversation he'd had with her over and over. He couldn't give up the fight, but he'd left himself with nowhere to go.

Finally, Ely went to the phone. He'd have Tommy set up some interviews with other juvenile rights lawyers. He knew that no one could be as good for them as Eliza, but he couldn't think of anything else to do besides following her suggestion. Maybe after he talked to a couple of other attorneys, he could call her and explain that he just couldn't make the same connection with them that he felt he could with her. That *might* change her mind.

Tommy picked the phone up on the second ring.

"It's me," Ely said.

"Oh." Tommy sounded disappointed.

"Were you expecting a call?"

"Well, I, uh . . ." Tommy stuttered. Ely hadn't heard his big brother sound so flustered in a long time.

"What's up, bro?" he asked.

"I meant to call you," Tommy said.

"Call me about what? Is anything wrong?"

"I called Eliza."

Ely groaned. "You didn't. I talked to her already. Now she's going to think we're double-teaming her. I told you I would handle this on my own." He wasn't angry exactly, because he knew Tommy was just trying to help, but pestering Eliza wasn't going to change her mind.

"I didn't call her about that."

Ely was stunned. He knew instantly what Tommy was saying, but he asked anyway. "What did you call her about, then?"

"I wanted to ask her out. For dinner or something. There's not a law against it, you know," he said defensively. "I know you two have business to discuss, but I'd really like to see her again. Socially."

Ely didn't know how to respond. He'd always thought of Eliza as belonging to him somehow. Tommy never had seemed interested. He hadn't mentioned her since he'd left the university.

"Ely?" When he didn't answer, Tommy asked sarcastically, "Is that okay with you?"

No, he thought, but he couldn't justify saying it. Aloud he said, "I don't think that's such a good idea. I mean, your track record with women isn't that good. I personally know half a dozen who won't even speak to you, or to me because of you."

"Eliza is different." Tommy sounded sincere. But then he always did.

She certainly is, Ely thought. *Not your usual style at all. Why her? Why now?* But he knew he wouldn't want Tommy to date Eliza ten years from now or even twenty. She was his.

"I know you feel that way now," he said slowly, "but what if your feelings change?"

"But—" Tommy started to protest.

"Amanda was different. Pam was different, too. In the beginning. But they ended up the same. What if you decided to, say, dump her, just when my case was coming to court?"

"She hasn't even agreed to take the case."

"Yet," Ely said. "And don't change the subject."

"Look, all I did was call her. She hasn't agreed to go out with me."

"Yet," Ely said again. "But what if she says yes? How can she date you and represent me?"

"I've done it. Remember?" Tommy said smugly.

"Sure I remember. How could I forget?" Ely had thought it very unprofessional. He still did.

"I won that case," Tommy said, stung.

"I remember." Ely gave in on that point. But he wasn't going to surrender altogether. "I also remember telling you that I was going to talk to Eliza again, and I am going to get her to take us on. I know she'll do it."

Tommy knew him too well. He pounced. "She turned you down, didn't she?"

"Yeah, but I still think I can get her to reconsider." He had to.

Meanwhile, he couldn't decide where Tommy's sudden desire to date Eliza fit into the scheme of things. If Eliza were to start dating Tommy—and most women seemed to find him quite irresistible—maybe she'd agree to represent Jessie in the custody case. On the other hand, what if she, like Ely, thought it unprofessional to date the brother of a client. Or, worse yet, what if she and Tommy started something and it lasted only a short time. His brother's love affairs were notoriously short-lived.

"I don't need this right now," Ely concluded, aloud.

"This doesn't have anything to do with you," Tommy said.

"It will. Especially if you break her heart."

"I wouldn't do that. Not to her," Tommy swore.

"I've heard that before, Tommy," Ely said. "I can't afford to take a chance on it. Not this time."

"I don't need your permission, Ely," Tommy said. Ely knew that tone of voice. Tommy was about to dig his heels in. There was no arguing with him once he'd done that.

"No, you don't. You don't need anyone's permission to do anything you want. But, Tommy, if you screw this up for Jessie and me, I swear I'll kick you from here to Baltimore."

"All right, all right," Tommy said. "I'll hold off. At least until we see if she'll take the case. But I'm telling you now, this is just a little rain delay. I'm not forfeiting the game."

"All I ask is a little more time," Ely said. "By the way, Eliza suggested I try some other lawyers, remember?"

"Yeah." His voice was noncommittal.

"Can you get me some names?" Ely hated to have to ask this favor on top of everything else, but it would be faster to go through Thomas than to find the information he needed on his own. "I know I want her, but maybe if I actually talk to a couple of these guys, get specific, I'll be able to tell her I have a basis for comparison when I ask her to reconsider."

"Fine," Tommy agreed grudgingly. "I'll call you tomorrow at school."

"Thanks." He tried to sound more grateful than he felt. "And, Tom, thanks for the other thing, too."

"Okay," Tommy relented, his voice softening. "I'll talk to you tomorrow, bro."

"I'll be waiting."

"Later," Tommy said, as if they'd just been discussing the weather rather than a decision that could affect them both for the rest of their lives.

"Sure," Ely said. "Later."

Chapter Five

Jessie was glad Eliza Taylor was coming to see the apartment, but a little nervous about it, too. What if she met him and changed her mind again about taking their case?

Jessie didn't know very many ladies except teachers, and they didn't count. His grandmas were okay, but regular women, like the ones who dated, were both more and less crabby depending on whether you accidentally spilled something on them (more) or whether you ate ice cream sundaes for breakfast (less). Uncle Tommy said that if he had ever known his mom, he'd know why his dad and his uncle were so picky about choosing a lady to live with. He guessed that meant his mom had been a lot cooler than any date he'd met so far. He wouldn't have minded getting to know one. They smelled pretty good. But women tended to come and go rather quickly, like his mother. She died when he was too little to remember her.

Once, when he was really little—like five years old—Jessie had asked his father why Lizbette couldn't be his new mother. Dad said it wasn't possible, as his baby-sitter was only seventeen years old, and some kind of cousin besides, but he said he knew just how Jessie felt. Jessie said he did not, because when he grew up he had a mother, a cool mom, too. Grandma had been a singer. They had some of her records. Dad said Lizbette was too young. She might want to be a singer or a doctor or something—and if she got married now, she wouldn't have time to watch Jessie and go to medical school, which took eight years, or go to New Orleans, like Grandma, and become a singer. Jessie had not quite liked it, but he agreed Lizbette should have time to decide what she wanted to be.

He did ask Lizbette, when Daddy wasn't around, if she maybe couldn't decide if she wanted to be his mother, and she said she liked the idea of being his mom, but she also liked the idea of being a few others things, like a lawyer. That was when Jessie remembered that it was Uncle Tommy that Lizbette always urged to stay to dinner, and she snuck little peeks at him when he wasn't looking, and also she always tried to hide her wild, kinky hair, when he came over unexpectedly, under a big scarf that made her look like she had a huge lump on her head. He realized that that girly stuff she did probably was what Dad needed some woman to do to him. Jessie kept his eye out, but no lady acted strange around Ely.

The weekend after he had talked to his father about Lizbette being his mom, Dad brought home these videos of an old television show called *The Courtship of Eddie's Father.* It had episodes of an old sitcom about this kid whose mother had died, just like Jessie. The kid, Eddie Corbett, kept trying to find a new wife for his father, Tom Corbett. "Tom Corbett never got married," Daddy said, "and Eddie brought home every single woman in Los Angeles. So just forget it, pal. I don't think we're going to be getting married anytime soon."

Of course, Jessie said just what Eddie would have said— since Daddy seemed to like the show—that Dad and he did just fine together, and they didn't need anyone else. He told Lizbette about it and she laughed. At first he was mad at her, but she said, "I've got to show you the movie version," and she brought him a video also called *The Courtship of Eddie's Father,* an old movie with different actors as Eddie and Tom. In the movie, Tom Corbett did marry Eddie's favorite baby-sitter. So Jessie hadn't lost all hope, though he did think, even then, that he was getting a little old for being baby-sat.

Unfortunately, Grandma and Grandpa Tyson, or old Mrs. Gregg, usually took care of him when his dad couldn't. So Jessie wasn't holding his breath. Still . . . whenever there was a new lady teacher at school, or on the rare occassion when Uncle Tommy talked Daddy into going out on a double date, Jessie always dressed up a little and combed his hair. Just to be on the safe side. He hadn't needed his father to tell him to go change out of his school clothes for Eliza Taylor's visit.

"Jessie, get out here and take your school stuff in your room," Daddy yelled, just as Jessie finished tying the laces on his good, brown leather shoes.

Eliza Taylor was an old friend of Daddy's. Dad showed Jessie a picture of her in the newspaper, and she was very pretty. She was already a lawyer, so that wasn't a problem. And Dad got a sort of funny look on his face whenever he talked about her. Jessie had never seen him act so nervous before. But he knew that Dad had been trying to get this lawyer, Eliza Taylor, to help them for a long time so it might be, as he said, that Ely was nervous about making a good impression tonight. Jessie wore his khaki pants and a nice white oxford shirt—he saved those for special occasions because they had to be ironed, and he and Daddy both hated ironing. Unfortunately, his father had chosen to wear this suit which looked about a hundred years old. It had something wrong with it, although Jessie couldn't figure out what, and it made Dad look like Grandpa.

He tried to get him to change into his khaki pants and oxford shirt, too, but Daddy kept bustling around, rearranging the papers on his desk, and trying to fix the busted leg on the easy chair, and generally getting himself all worked up.

"Chill, Daddy-O," Jessie said, like Uncle Tommy did when he talked Dad into going on a double date. But just then the doorbell rang.

When he answered the door, Ely radiated nervous tension. "Hi, Eliza," he said. The words were casual, but his manner was not. He ushered her into the house, where Jessie stood waiting.

He stepped back and introduced her to his son. "Jessie, this is Ms. Taylor. Eliza, I'd like you to meet Jessie Greene."

Eliza shook Jessie's hand while Ely rocked back and forth, watching them. From his expression, you'd think he'd just brought the two heads of warring states together rather than his small son and an old friend.

"So, you're our lawyer, right?" Jessie asked.

"I'm considering it," Eliza answered as he released her hand.

"Great," Jessie chirped. "Daddy told me all about you."

"What did he say about me?" Eliza asked, unable to keep from smiling at this little old man in miniature.

"You went to law school with Uncle Tommy," Jessie said.

"That's right."

"You must be a brain like he is, then," Jessie concluded.

"Well, I don't know about that," Eliza said. She tried always to be honest with children. They deserved the truth. "My brain is okay."

"Sure." Jessie seemed to accept that. "Are you smart like my dad, too?" He looked over at Ely, who had started toward them at the question.

Eliza waved him away. "What do you mean?" she asked.

"I mean, well, I know Uncle Tommy has a high 'q,' because everyone always says that. But he's not smart like a dad is. He doesn't always get the jokes, for one thing."

"Oh?" Eliza handed him her bag and briefcase, which he gave to his father. "What kind of jokes?" Eliza asked. Jessie didn't answer right away. He watched Ely place her accoutrements carefully on the table by the front door, then he held out his hand to his father. Ely still looked like he was about start bouncing off the walls. Eliza had purposely made no effort to reduce the tension. How these two reacted to the subtle pressure of the interview would tell her a lot about their relationship. As now, when Ely walked over to his son, and took his hand. They both stood, facing her, drawing strength and comfort from the simple physical contact.

"Guess what?" Jessie said. Ely groaned.

"What?" Eliza answered, remembering the old joke.

"That's what," Jessie crowed.

Eliza smiled. "Uncle Tommy didn't get it?" she asked.

"No. Daddy did. You did. But Uncle Tommy isn't that kind of smart."

"Maybe it's just because your dad knows you better than he does."

Jessie thought about that for a moment, then answered, "But you don't know me at all."

Eliza knew better than to try to get around the unbeatable logic of an eight-year-old mind. "True. I see what you're saying. I guess I am sort of smart like your dad."

"Good," Jessie said, satisfied. "You were right, Dad. She's perfect for us." He let go of his father's hand and came toward her. When he reached her side, he motioned for her to come closer. She bent her head toward him.

In a stage whisper, he said, "He said you were the best."

"Okay, Jess, that's enough. I have to speak to Ms. Taylor now. I think maybe you should go do your homework."

"Okay," Jessie said happily. "See you later, Ms. Taylor."

"Eliza," she corrected. He looked briefly to his father, who hesitated, then nodded.

"Bye, Eliza."

"Bye, Jessie." She watched him walk down the hallway. He was a charming boy. He was also clearly at ease with her, now that he'd checked her out. His behavior told her most of what she needed to know. This little boy felt loved and secure. Even in what had to be a confusing situation, with her invading their home and making his father visibly anxious, he trusted his father's judgment. Based on what she'd seen tonight, she would say their relationship was very healthy.

Eliza always visited her clients before agreeing to take a case—and she considered the children, not the parents, her clients. It was a little precaution she'd taken ever since her recommendation had sent a child into a home that wasn't the safe haven she had thought it. She didn't feel any compunction about letting the parents know they were on trial, either. She insisted on intruding into their personal lives, without any guilt about invading their privacy. She had found out the hard way that people did lie to their lawyers. When it came to a child's safety and comfort, she would do anything she felt was necessary to help them.

Eliza didn't think she had to worry about Ely. He seemed to have grown up into exactly the sort of man she would have predicted. He was sweet, appeared to be honest, and still just as idealistic as the young boy she'd known. But it was always better to err on the side of caution in these matters. She had every intention of delving even deeper before she was finished with these two.

Ely watched her as she wandered about the small living room. The front door had opened directly into this room, clearly the heart of the house. A navy-and-cream-striped couch faced the large television and an old fashioned stereo system. The entertainment center took up most of the center wall. The end tables beside the couch were covered with books and photos. A large, built-in bookshelf took up the wall behind her. In front of it was an easy chair, with a floor lamp positioned directly beside it.

Under the room's only window, in the wall facing her, was a cream-colored table which clearly served as a work space for Ely. She took a quick look at it. It was littered with schoolbooks, papers, and a few odds and ends, including an odd-shaped ceramic dish full of paper clips, surely a creation of Jessie Greene's. Her mouth relaxed at the sight of that ill-shapen dish, the ubiquitous sign of parenthood.

She turned and faced Ely again. He stood behind the couch, nervously kneading the overstuffed back with his fingers. It was clear which side of the couch was Jessie's; a hastily folded sweatshirt sat on a large book with Hank Aaron crouched in a battling stance on the cover. In front of his seat on the couch, she glimpsed the tips of a worn pair of sneakers, which appeared to have been quickly kicked underneath the sofa. From this angle, she could see the frayed edges of a large hole in the seam connecting the toes to the instep.

She wandered toward the kitchen. The folding doors had

been pushed open, and from the doorway she could take in the whole small room. Its size required that it be functional, but it was also eat-off-the-floor clean, with shining appliances lining the counter between the sink and the stove. A bushy plant hung in the small window, and the refrigerator was covered with pictures and notes. Against the wall stood a table, with colorful embroidered place mats in front of the two chairs. A matching napkin holder held plain paper napkins, and a large wooden salt and pepper shaker sat next to it. She could easily imagine father and son sitting there, dark curly heads bent over their plates as they prepared to go to school together in the mornings. She blinked the image away. It wasn't the most elegant dining area, but it was too cozy looking to be purely for show, she thought. She resisted the urge to check the refrigerator and freezer. She'd do that at a later date.

The bedrooms were off down the hallway Jessie had taken. She would get a look at them the next time. On the second visit, she didn't give advance notice of her plan to drop by. That was a courtesy reserved for the first time. For now, Eliza was satisfied that Ely had done his best to supply his son with a nice, comfortable home.

"Who will take over his grandparents' baby-sitting duties?" she asked. She might as well take care of a few of the preliminaries while she was here.

"I've got a short list of sitters. I can go over it with you if you like. Rebecca has a pretty busy schedule herself, so other than her normal twice-weekly visits, she and Hank don't generally watch Jessie. If I have a PTA meeting or something, I have to get a regular baby-sitter."

When Eliza nodded, Ely continued. "Rebecca comes over on Tuesday and Thursday afternoons, and Hank joins us for dinner. On Saturday, Jessie and I go to their place, or maybe we'll meet at a museum or the zoo, or go out with them. At least that's what we were doing. Right now, it's a little confusing. Jessie can't have helped but notice that his grandmother doesn't stay for supper when I get home from school anymore. For the past month, I've been dropping him off at their house on Saturday mornings, then I pick him up in the afternoon, or they drop him off here. We've all sort of tacitly agreed to try not to argue in front of him. It doesn't always work, though."

Eliza nodded. "He is a perceptive little boy. I'm sure he has a better idea of what's happening than he lets on."

"I've tried to get him to talk to me about it all, but mainly, he just listens. I'm telling him whatever I think is safe. I never kept secrets from my son."

"You should keep talking to him, and get him to talk to you. Kids are masters at denial. They think they can ignore problems, and they'll go away."

"I told him we all love each other, and especially him, but we have some problems to work out. I'm afraid that it's a lot for him to take in, especially since it all started right after his grandparents told us they had to move away. I feel bad about it, but I don't know what else to do." He looked so sad that Eliza almost wanted to comfort him. But she knew how important it was to remain completely professional at all times.

"As hard as this is on all of you, it's ten times harder on Jessie. Eight is too young to really understand the situation, even if he does hear and see a lot more than you might think. He's totally powerless to do anything about all this strife. So he'll internalize everything, and probably figure out some way to blame himself for the whole mess."

"I know. Unfortunately, there is very little I can do about it." Ely squared his shoulders. "That's where you come in."

"I'll do my best, but you should be aware that I'm no miracle worker. All I can do is use my knowledge of the law to put you in the best possible position."

"That's fine," Ely said gratefully. "So . . . any other questions?"

"I'll make up a list."

"I want to make this as easy on you as possible. I know you don't have the time to take this on, and I want you to use me as much as you can."

"Oh, I will," Eliza assured him. But time or no time, she knew she would give this case the same attention she paid to any other. Ely might think she took it because of their personal history, but Eliza treated every case in exactly the same way.

She provided the best representation for each and every client she took on.

"I mean it. Any legwork you need done ... or typing ... or anything. I can fill out forms, deliver packages, whatever you want. Any background information you have to provide, I'll get for you."

She had warned Ely that they'd be spending nights and weekends together to prepare to go to court. She'd done that before, and she knew exactly what she was letting herself in for. His offer was all well and good, but he wouldn't have any more time than she would.

"I'll have to do most of that myself. I'm sure you understand I have to make sure all the information we present to the judge is completely accurate and unbiased if we end up in court." She watched his face. Her words could be taken as an insult. But he didn't seem to take umbrage at the inference that he might not be the most objective person to do the job.

Instead, he grinned. "That makes sense. I just really want you to feel comfortable about treating me like a friend. I think of you as an old friend of the family, not just a lawyer. I know I've taken advantage of the situation. Now, I want you to take advantage of me."

"I'll remember that," Eliza promised, with no intention of doing so.

"I'm counting on it," Ely said. "After all, I owe you." He continued to grin, unabashed, although Eliza knew he was thinking about the underhanded way he'd manipulated her into taking the case.

"You took a risk, accusing me of being a sexist."

"I knew it would get your attention," he said smugly.

"As a black, female lawyer in this court system, I've encountered sexism and racism in some pretty unexpected places, but I never thought anyone would call *me* on those same things."

"I knew you felt strongly about it. I've read more than one of your articles."

"I think everyone is a little bit sexist, deep down," she admitted. "I've always said I *had* to be one, just to counteract all the chauvinism out there."

He nodded. ''It's ironic, isn't it.''

''I confess I let my prejudices get in the way of my assessment of your case. Now drop it, okay?''

''I did feel guilty using that to change your mind,'' he said.

''I deserved to have my prejudices used against me. It's poetic justice.''

''I've heard of poetic license,'' he said, ''but poetic justice?''

''Same thing, sort of,'' Eliza remarked. ''I made it up.''

He smiled. ''I like it.''

That smile gave Eliza a jolt. The rakish quality of his smile didn't quite fit the hopeless, old-fashioned suit he wore. That smile made her think of Tommy. Despite the similarities in the two men, neither one had ever reminded her of the other before. They were so different. But there was a sparkle she had never seen before in Ely's eyes as he smiled at her dry wit. Those gleaming eyes and quirked lips were more what she expected from his handsome older brother. They were downright sexy— which was not a word she had ever associated with Ely Greene.

The moment passed, and when she looked up again, it was just Ely standing in front of her. She gave herself a mental shake. It was bad enough she'd almost been seduced by Tommy, a man ten years her junior. Tommy's little brother was barely a grown-up. What was he, twenty-nine?

''Did I thank you for agreeing to spend all your free time on us?'' Ely asked, serious again. No trace of Tommy Greene remained. ''I don't know how I can ever repay you.''

''Wait till you get my bill,'' Eliza said, only half-joking.

''It can't possible be high enough to make up for what you're doing for us.''

''It'll be enough,'' she assured him. She hated being thanked so profusely for merely doing what was, after all, her job. And in this case, she hadn't even done anything yet.

They'd agreed he'd pay her a retainer of five hundred dollars a month, which was a hefty amount, given his salary. He'd be repaying her firm for years for the work she was about to do for him, and that was with no guarantee of success. One of the things that made her specialty so unprofitable was that most of the cases didn't earn the participants anything but grief.

When a wife sued her husband for child support, the expense of the court battle was not paid by an insurance company. Unlike a corporate lawyer, Eliza represented people who were not usually arguing over money. No one was going to walk away from this with a profit, not even Eliza. All that was at stake here was a child.

It was enough for her.

"You are worth every penny," he averred. "And much more."

"Let's see how we do, before you pledge your undying gratitude," Eliza suggested.

"It's too late," he said solemnly. "You've already got it." He put a hand on her arm. "Jessie is everything to me. If I lose him, I lose the only thing that really matters." He caught her eye and held it and said, "I owe you my life."

Chapter Six

Tommy Greene was becoming a real pest. He had called Eliza every day for a week, and MJ was becoming insistent that she call him back.

"It's embarassing to have to tell him I've given you his messages over and over again. I feel like a broken tape recorder," her secretary complained. "Just call and find out what the fool wants."

Eliza had already called Ely to ask if he had told Tommy that she had taken on his case.

Ely had answered, "No, I haven't spoken with him." He had sounded distracted, and she had made an excuse to jump off the phone right away. That was five days ago, and she figured Ely must have told him by now. But Tommy just kept calling, and she couldn't imagine why. Or rather, she didn't want to think about what else he might be calling about.

She was already more involved with the Greene family than she cared to be. If he were calling to further renew their acquaintance, Eliza didn't know how she would respond. She'd been pleased to see him again, but their reunions, to date, had been disasters—especially that first night. She still cringed at the memory of it. Eliza didn't think he, or Ely, had any idea that she had misinterpreted his motives for asking her out on that ill-fated "date," but she herself knew how close she'd come to acting like some pathetic old fool of a woman. So Eliza wasn't interested in seeing Tommy Greene socially anymore.

She couldn't deny that she was curious about his persistent phone calls, though.

He finally caught her in. She was, as usual, busy, but MJ refused to take another message.

"You take care of it, girl. Talk to the man, or put him out of his misery. Tell him to stop calling. I'm not handling this one for you," was her secretary's last word on the subject.

Eliza bit her lip, hard, and picked up the phone. "Tommy?"

"Eliza?" He sounded amazed.

"Yeah, hi. It's me," she assured him.

"I thought I'd never get you," he said.

There was no point in dragging this out. "Didn't Ely tell you I took the case?"

"No, I mean, I haven't talked to him," Tommy said apologetically.

"Oh." She'd been right all along. He was still calling her on his brother's behalf. She was surprised at how disappointed she was to have her suspicions confirmed. Anyway, at least the phone calls would stop now. She couldn't help wondering why, if he was so concerned, he hadn't just called Ely.

"That's not what I was calling about," Tommy said.

"What?" The involuntary exclamation escaped before she could stop it.

"I said I was calling because . . ." His voice trailed off. "Because I wanted to talk to you about something else."

"That makes sense," Eliza said sarcastically, barely controlling the urge to make a snide comment like *Looking for more free legal advice?*

"I was hoping we could get together again," Tommy said.

"I don't think so." Her response was automatic.

"We didn't really get a chance to talk the other night," he went on, as if he hadn't heard her.

Eliza was tempted to ask, *Whose fault was that?* Instead she said, "I just don't have any free time right now."

"I know the feeling. But I'm sure we can come up with something." Like a spoiled child, he thought all he had to do was keep asking and he'd get whatever he wanted. She could hear it in his voice. Underneath the sweet, sincere, coaxing tone was a confident note. This was a man used to getting his own way.

He didn't have a clue.

MJ wandered into the room. Eliza rolled her eyes at her friend, who took that as an invitation to sit down.

"How about lunch, then?" Tommy suggested.

"Honestly, Tommy, if I'm not in court, I'm here at my desk trying to dig my way out from under all the paperwork. If you could see my calendar."

"Tell him you're on a special diet," MJ whispered.

Eliza shook her head but couldn't resist asking, sotto voce, "Why?"

Tommy was saying, "You've got to eat sometime. I can come to you. Breakfast, lunch, or dinner. You name it."

"Breakfast, lunch, or dinner," MJ unconsciously echoed. "No jerks."

Eliza hurriedly covered the mouthpiece, but not before a choked laugh escaped her.

"Eliza?" For the first time, Tommy sounded uncertain. Perhaps he was beginning to get the picture. "Are you still there?" he asked.

"Yes, yes. My secretary just came in. I really do have to get back to work."

"How about if we just say I'll call you . . . on . . . Friday afternoon. I'm free that evening, and I'd like nothing better than to whisk you away from all that dreary work. It's better for the digestion."

"This Friday?" Eliza said incredulously.

"Doesn't think much of himself, does he?" MJ commented, not bothering to lower her voice this time.

"You know what they say about all work and no play," Tommy joked lamely.

"I really don't think it's going to work, Tommy."

"We'll leave it open, okay? Take it as it comes." He didn't

give her time to respond. "I'll let you go now. Talk to you Friday." He hung up.

Eliza stared at the telephone, open-mouthed. "He says we'll leave it open and just take it as it comes," she repeated for MJ's benefit.

"He really doesn't know you at all, does he?" MJ said. "Take it as it comes? You?" She grinned. "Maybe you should go out with him, and let him get to know the real you. He'll probably drop you like a ton of bricks."

"Hey!" Eliza protested. "Whose side are you on, anyway?"

"Why yours, of course, bosslady. I'm just trying to be helpful. It sounds like he's looking for someone who's sort of easygoing, mellow. No offense or anything, but that ain't you."

"I can be mellow," Eliza retorted.

MJ snorted. "Yeah, and cows can fly."

"Go away," Eliza ordered.

"That's all I was saying," MJ said. Eliza shot her a dirty look, and she hightailed it out of the room.

Eliza stood, walked deliberately to the door, and closed it quietly. Then she returned to her desk.

She knew she was a little inflexible, maybe even rigid. It was a character trait she'd cultivated after her parents died. The shock of waking up one morning to find herself completely alone in the world had left her feeling like one big, open wound. She'd needed to feel less vulnerable. Her parents had been protective, sheltering her from the world. They'd been a close, complete family with little need for outsiders. When her parents died, Eliza suddenly had had to go from being a shy, retiring young girl to being an adult, trying to keep her life from being ripped apart before she reached legal age.

Her parents had been young and healthy, and they hadn't left a will. Their life insurance had been paid up and had given Eliza a healthy bank balance at the tender age of sixteen. She had had to guard that money, the house, and herself from a system that was as cold and impersonal as her family had been warm and loving.

Eliza had always been something of a loner. With the death of Benjamin and Mary Taylor, she'd retreated even further into self-imposed solitary confinement. Her peers didn't know how to react to such a catastrophe. She had always found it easier to be with her parents' friends than with kids her own age anyway, and after the accident, those of her peers who didn't withdraw from her, she pushed away. Excelling at school became her sole focus, and when she went on to college—as her parents had always planned—it was even easier to eschew the social whirl to concentrate on academic pursuits. She received a full scholarship and graduated at the top of her class. The few personal ties she established were with her professors. So she went on to graduate school and got her M.S.W.

It was when she started to work that she was pulled out of her shell. As a social worker, her clients, especially the children, brought her out of exile, little by little. But the system too often failed its younger constituents. As a part of that system, she had failed, too. After little David Paron died, as a result of her recommendation, she had gone back to school to study juvenile rights law.

Twelve years later, she had achieved all of the goals she had set for herself. Over that time, she'd become comfortable with who she was. That had enabled her to overcome her shyness. She still socialized with two of her college professors, and also enjoyed the company of certain men and women whom she had met through her work, as both a social worker and as a lawyer, including MJ and Rosa.

She still lived in the little house she had grown up in, but that terrified little girl, who had had to force herself to answer each knock at the door with a show of confidence she was far from feeling, had disappeared long ago. Eliza was completely independent. Her work was fulfilling, her law office was successful. Most importantly, she was able to help youngsters who found themselves, for whatever reason, at the mercy of the system that had tormented her. She was proud of that.

MJ could call her uptight all she wanted, but Eliza Taylor felt as mellow and easygoing at this stage of her life as she ever had. One disastrous evening with her old friend Tommy Greene was not about to change that.

When he called on Friday, she had the perfect excuse not to

go out with him. She was going to work on his brother's case that evening and was expected at Ely's house around seven-thirty. She was planning to be there no later than six-fifteen.

Tommy took his dismissal with more grace than she had expected. "Maybe I'll stop by later," he said, without much conviction.

"We'll be working," she warned. "But I'm sure you're always welcome to drop in at your brother's house. Ely and Jessie would probably be happy to see you," she said, purposely implying that she herself would be less than thrilled at the interruption. Eliza didn't care if he showed up or not. Tommy posed no threat to her equilibrium in Ely's homey apartment. The presence of his brother and small nephew would surely prevent him from further pestering her about going out on a date with him. And she herself would be buried in notes and legal forms that would serve as a barrier against his imposing physical presence. It might even be a good thing if he did show up and saw her, as MJ had said, "as she really was." Maybe this attraction he seemed to feel would die a natural death in the unromantic setting of Ely's living room.

Eliza needn't have worried about it. Tommy didn't show up that night. She and Ely and Jessie spent a productive evening. With the boy, Eliza concentrated on school and his view of his home life. She made a general assessment of his physical and psychological development and found him to be a happy and healthy little boy. His grandparents had done their job of parenting very well. They had prepared him (as her own parents had not) to take on life without them by giving him a strong sense of himself, and just enough support to foster his independent and spirited nature.

Eliza said as much to Ely when he came back from tucking Jessie into bed.

"I know," he said. "Much as I'd love to villify Rebecca and Hank, I've got to say their influence on Jessie has always been very positive. Will that hurt us in court?"

"I doubt it. In a way, it would be harder to prove you've been a good parent to Jessie if you'd shared your parenting duties with grandparents who weren't so good with him."

He nodded. "Anyway, I'm glad you think Jessie's okay."

After spending the evening with the two of them, Eliza's last qualms had been laid to rest. This was a family that should be preserved, for Jessie's sake. Jessie and Ely had a near perfect father-son rapport. They were comfortable and affectionate with each other, and it was heartwarming to watch them.

This time the apartment wasn't as scrubbed and spotless as it had been when she'd first visited, but it was clean and the refrigerator was well-stocked—she'd snuck a look while Ely was heating the chili. The hole-y sneakers had disappeared, but Jessie's schoolbag apparently lived in that corner of the couch where she'd first spotted it. Jessie had delved into that scuffed backpack over and over during the course of the evening, and Ely hadn't looked at it once. Eliza had been tempted a couple of times. The respect that Ely showed for the boy's privacy, as well as Jessie's protective air, had demonstrated to her that they were a unit, self-contained and complete, despite their dependence on each other.

Eliza liked being in the cozy apartment even more now that she'd spent an evening in it. The comfortable sofa, the worn rug, even the mismatched furniture created a suitable backdrop for the two males who made her feel so welcome. She was ready to go to battle for them.

"Now, about your situation at work," she started. "You've been at St. Joe's for how long?"

"Since I graduated from college. Seven years now," Ely said. "But in a couple of years, I was planning to start night school. I have my master's degree which will allow me to teach in the public school system, as a substitute, but I need my certificate to obtain a permanent position. It pays better than private school, but it's a lot more challenging."

Eliza made a note to herself to talk more about the challenge later. For now, she would let him ramble on.

"Rebecca doesn't approve of that plan. She feels Jessie and I are better off in the private school setting. It's smaller, more exclusive, and to her mind, safer. She's been on me to move to a better neighborhood since forever. She was very unhappy when Jessie's mom and I moved here, and she and Hank have often offered to help with a down payment on a house in a better area.''

''But it's not just money that keeps you here?'' Eliza questioned.

''No, not at all. I want the kids to feel free to talk to me, even outside of school, maybe especially outside of school. These kids have problems, too. They may be rich and, for the most part, white, but they suffer all the same problems other kids do. Child abuse, substance abuse—theirs and their parents—hunger, neglect, everything. I've had more than one kid tell me things they just couldn't tell anyone else in their lives. They can open up here.'' He waved an arm, indicating the room in which they sat. ''They feel safe.

''School policy, I think I told you, is to inform parents and legal guardians the minute anything irregular comes up. And the kids know it. If somebody's father has a drinking problem, the last person they'd report it to would be the school nurse. Maybe they'd feel a little safer telling a coach, but ... the problems they face usually make them feel even more isolated from the people they like or trust. I want to provide a place to go, someone who seems to be outside the school's control.''

''Then what? I mean, what can you do for them, anyway? Technically speaking, anything they tell you, they're telling the school. Don't you have to report it?'' Eliza was interested, not just professionally, but as a person who dealt with the aftereffects of problems like these in her work.

''I'm supposed to,'' Ely said. ''But what I try to do is talk to them about their options, before their parents get involved. I've sent kids to Al-Anon and A.A., too. I try to respect their right to privacy.''

''You try. But you can't always, can you? Aren't you taking a big chance doing this? If you have to tell on a kid, in the long run, what good does it do to pretend your house is some kind of safe haven?''

He bristled at that. ''I don't *tell* on them. Sometimes we can talk out their problems by ourselves. When it gets beyond that point, I give them the choice of talking to someone themselves, or having me do it for them. I'd never give away their secrets without their permission.''

"Okay." She backed off. "Fine. So while you're busy playing priest, where does that leave your son?''

"I don't neglect him for my students, if that's what you mean. Jessie always comes first, and he knows that. I think I'm setting an example for him to live by and with. He knows he can tell me anything, that he's safe with me. He's too young to really understand what's going on, but I believe he's sensitive to what it all means.''

"That's not what I meant," Eliza said. "I'm talking about your position at St. Joe's. Aren't you taking a pretty big chance with your job, going against school policy like this?''

Ely had to think about that one for a moment. Finally, he said, "I think he knows there is some risk involved. But I think Jessie would rather I lived up to my principles than played it safe. Even if he doesn't, that's what I hope he'll learn.''

"From one or two things he said, I'd say Jessie clearly understands that you are 'up against the school' in some way. He seems to see you and himself as some kind of dynamic duo fighting.'' Eliza looked at her notes. "Is the principal's name McGinley?''

"Yeah," Ely said.

"He sees the two of you taking on this guy together, and he obviously approves. He thinks you're a hero for taking on an authority figure like the principal. But I can understand your mother-in-law's point of view. Where do you draw the line?'' Eliza couldn't keep a hint of cynicism from creeping into her voice.

Ely shifted in his chair. "So far, I haven't had to choose between Jessie and my students. If I did, I know it would be no contest. I just don't have any way to prove it.''

Eliza disagreed. "Aren't you choosing now? By choosing to fight the Tysons rather than giving in by, say, moving out of the neighborhood? As an act of good faith, it might go a long way. But instead, you're taking a chance on losing custody of Jessie.''

"I don't think so," he responded immediately. "There are

a lot of other issues at stake here. Rebecca feels that the school is safe from drugs, from guns, from all the problems she sees in the news. But it's not true. Maybe St. Joe's is a little more insulated than a public school, but alcoholism and addiction are certainly not unknown to the student body. Gangs are even starting to infringe on the edges of the campus. Rebecca and Hank both see these rich, white students and their parents, and she thinks they live in a different world than we do. It's not true. We can't keep Jessie safe by locking him in some ivory tower.

"In fact, I think he might be suffering a little because of this rarified atmosphere. He certainly can't compete with these kids in the money department. There are accusations of tokenism and favoritism I don't think he'd hear if he went to public school. I don't know if they bother him or not. He never says anything to me. But I know it bothered me a little as a black kid in a white school, and even more as a college student. Even if I'm projecting those feelings on to him, I know that he is not getting the benefit of going to school with the other children in this neighborhood, whom he grew up with and whom he still plays with on afternoons and weekends. Maybe he'd feel more a part of this black community if he attended school with his at-home friends, as he calls them.

"Everyone's talking about white flight, but what about African Americans like our parents, who left the ghetto to give their kids a better life and never looked back? I don't want to do that. I don't judge anyone for dusting the street off their shoes the minute they get the chance, but I want to give something back to this community. I want my child to feel that he can, too. I'll go further than that. I'd like Jessie to feel some obligation to other people who haven't had his advantages."

"All right," Eliza conceded. "I agree with you. But I think we've gotten away from the point here. This is all very noble, but what about being practical for a second. What if one of your alcoholic kids falls of the wagon and runs his car into a tree? The parents, and the school, could blame you for not telling them about the problem. Or what if one of the kids decides you betrayed him or her? There's a real chance you could lose your job. Then what would you do?''

"I don't think we need to worry about my being unemployed. Being the only African-American teacher does give me a slight advantage. They don't want to fire me, and they would do anything rather than avoid a scandal or a lawsuit. I've had problems with the administration before, and I probably will again,'' Ely said.

"What kinds of problems?'' Eliza asked.

"Currently, I'm on probation for bringing a student home—to my house—for dinner.''

"Why did you do it?''

"Her father was passed out inside their house, with the doors locked and the alarm on. She didn't want anyone to know about it, and couldn't get into the place without alerting the police. She called me, so I brought her home and Jessie and I had dinner with her. At bedtime, I tucked him in and drove her out to a mall near her place, where she played video games while I called her father every fifteen minutes until he finally came to. Then I took her home. Unfortunately, her father wasn't satisfied with my explanation, and he complained about my behavior to the school. I think he wanted to forestall any report on my part of his alcohol abuse, or neglect, but anyway, McGinley put me on report, and basically kept the father happy. That was pretty much all St. Joe's cared about.''

"How old was this girl?''

"Twelve. And we were with other people the whole time, as well as calling her father constantly. He wasn't worried that I molested his daughter, and the school knew it. They just didn't want him to worry about a scandal. That's why I want to get out of there, when Jessie's a little older. If they did fire me, by some chance, I have good enough qualifications to get a job as a substitute teacher in the public school system until I got my certificate. I've even done a couple of interviews, and made some contacts, not for that eventuality, but to prepare for the future.''

"Okay,'' Eliza said, throwing her notepad into her briefcase. "I guess that's about it for now. I've got your tax records,

Jessie's school and medical records, and a pretty good idea of what the Tysons will try to use against you. I think that will do for now. I will call Rod Daniels and try to set up a meeting.''

''You're going to meet with their lawyer? Should I be there?''

''I know him. We'll just get together informally, and I can get his take on the case.''

The files followed her notepad, and she snapped her briefcase shut. ''You said the Tysons have filed for a custody hearing, so for now we wait for a date to be set. Both sides will be feeling each other out. We'll find out whether they're going to try to prove you unfit for guardianship, or whether they'll just argue that they already have custody.''

''I can't believe they'd do that.'' He looked so deflated.

Eliza felt for him, but she warned, ''They'll probably do whatever their lawyer advises them to do.''

''So what do *you* advise?'' he asked.

''Right now? We wait. The court will give us a date. When we see the judge, he'll either award you or the Tysons custody, or he'll appoint a Guardian Ad Litem to investigate Jessie's situation. The probability is that he'll do the latter, and our next job will be giving the GAL a list of people to interview. I guess you could start thinking who you'd like to have him or her talk to.''

''I'll do that,'' he said.

Eliza wasn't worried about anything yet. She had some research of her own to do, now. She'd put MJ on the project of checking for any criminal charges or complaints lodged against Ely or the Tysons. The preliminary work was pretty routine. She quickly reviewed the evening's conversation against her mental checklist.

''Would you like another cup of tea or anything?'' Ely asked when she looked up. ''Another piece of pie?''

''No, thanks,'' Eliza said. ''I should get home.'' She glanced at her watch.

He mimicked the action. ''It's later than I thought,'' he said. ''I can't thank you enough for giving up your evening.''

''Don't start that again,'' Eliza said firmly, but she smiled.

''I feel guilty for making you work on a Friday night.''

"You didn't *make* me do anything," she assured him.

He changed tactics. "I hope you're not going to spend the entire weekend working," he said, trying to assuage his guilt, she was sure.

"You'd be surprised," Eliza muttered as he went to get her coat.

"I heard that," he said as he helped her on with the wool coat. "Tommy said he asked you out tonight."

She hadn't expected him to know about that. He seemed to expect her to respond, but she didn't know what to say. "You and I had work to do," she reminded him.

"We could have started after dinner."

She wondered if Tommy had run some kind of a guilt trip on Ely. "Then I'd be going home at one or two in the morning, instead of eleven o'clock," she pointed out.

"You should be out dining and dancing, not eating reheated chili with a guy like me. I feel like I've cheated you out of the usual Friday night festivities."

"Don't worry about it," Eliza said. "Good food, good conversation, and an education on modern-day education were fine." She had really enjoyed getting to know Ely and his son better, even if it was for professional rather than personal reasons. It had gone well, she had been able to relax.

He walked her to the door.

She turned back to him to say good night, and his eyes caught and held hers, his gaze intense. "If Tommy were here, he'd kiss you good night, wouldn't he?"

Eliza was thrown off guard by the unexpected question. "I suppose he would," she answered.

Ely's eyes darkened. "Here's a kiss from Tommy," he said, leaning slowly toward her. Eliza stood frozen in place. Time seemed to slow as he lowered his head. Her eyes remained open, wide. She was shocked. He was so nice, respectful. She couldn't believe he was putting a move on her.

"It's all in the family," he murmured against her mouth. His lips touched hers. They were silky and hot. Her eyelids slid closed. Only their lips touched, but she was drowning in the sensation, vivid and intense, yet fluid and muted.

His fingers slid over the fine silk of her blouse, down her arms. He captured her hands in his own and held them, down at her sides. She ached to raise them to his shoulders. Her lips followed his when he pulled away. Her eyelids felt incredibly heavy when she tried to raise them. She was left hoping, praying for more.

He stepped back. "Well, good night."

Her eyes snapped open. Not again.

She nodded, not trusting her voice. Then she turned and walked away, still in a daze. What strange power did these two brothers have over her? First Tommy threatened to turn her life upside down, with a simple dinner invitation. Now Ely— little Ely Greene!—had thrown her into turmoil with one sweet, gentle, searing kiss. It chilled her to her soul to think of the damage these two men could do, without even trying.

Chapter Seven

Eliza spent the weekend catching up on her bookkeeping. Saturday and Sunday zipped by, and she was still deep in the throes of her work-frenzy when Monday morning dawned.

She spent the morning in court, trying to get a continuance which would give her time to find the evidence that would keep the state from returning a retarded four-year-old girl to the house where Eliza suspected she'd been abused by her parents. Unfortunately, the judge was loathe to abuse the parental rights of the girl's legal guardians based on the testimony of only four nurses and doctors at a local hospital and a file folder full of X rays and charts documenting the various breaks, bruises, and other maladies the child had suffered. He wanted a witness. Eliza counted herself lucky to get a month to build her case. At least, little Jenny Raymond would be safe with social services for the next four weeks.

She then closeted herself in her office, ignoring all of MJ's attempts to find out why she wasn't happier about the judge's decision. She was disgusted with herself for being unable to put the surprise ending to Friday night's business out of her mind, and she certainly didn't want to talk about it.

She was at the office until late, and when she finally went

home to Brookline, she was bone tired. Exhausted enough, she hoped, to halt any brain activity not necessary for breathing. She didn't want to think or feel or even move until Tuesday morning. She just wanted to sleep, dreamlessly.

Her white, two-story row house with its sky-blue trim and shutters was a welcome sight, though the unkempt lawn was just another reminder of her folly. The grass in the plot which fronted the eighty-year-old house had grown raggedly since the last snowfall over a month ago. If she hadn't been so distracted this past weekend, she would have called the teenager who mowed the lawn for her and had him come by. As she made her way up the front walk, she made a mental note to arrange for him to come the following Saturday.

The rhododendron her mother had planted by the front steps hadn't shown any sign of flowering in years, but the crocuses Eliza had had planted the preceding September were blooming. The small purple and white flowers were flourishing despite her inattention. Spring had arrived, they proclaimed, without her noticing it. Eliza was too tired for more self-recriminations. She was just glad to be home.

The first jolt of adrenaline slammed through Eliza as she opened her front door. As oblivious as she had been that morning—to the temperature, to the weather, even to the clothes on her back—she was certain she had locked her door. For three days, not a single real emotion had registered in her heart and mind. The first to do so now was pure terror. The door was off the latch.

She nearly closed the door again, ready to run, but out of the corner of her eye, Eliza saw a colorful, woven knapsack lying on the floor in her foyer. Not the kind of accessory she would expect a housebreaker to carry. Eliza eased the door open. The lights were on in the living room, the dining room, and the stairway that dominated the front hall. She was either being robbed by the most inept thief in Boston, or she had a visitor—probably a teenager.

She stepped just inside and leaned over to untie the string holding the cotton knapsack closed. A plastic box full of what appeared to be cheap costume jewelry, and a small transparent

makeup bag containing equally cheap cosmetics, lay atop a
piece of tie-dyed fabric. She lifted out the things at the top of
the bag. Two T-shirts and some wisps of feminine underwear.

Eliza quietly closed the front door behind her. Her fear was
rapidly being replaced by anger. She strode through the house,
looking into the kitchen first, where someone seemed to have
gone through her cabinets. The makings of a jam sandwich had
been left on the island that occupied the center of the room.

She found the culprit in the small study at the back of the
house. Bare feet, sporting toenails painted purple, rested on
the black leather ottoman, just inches from the television set.
Chocolate-brown toes wiggled in time to the music of MTV.
The enormous black armchair with its tall wraparound back
had been dragged from its customary place next to the couch
to its current location in the center of the floor, three feet
from the large-screen television. Eliza stood in the doorway,
undetected by her uninvited guest, trying to keep a rein on her
temper.

The music blaring from the digital sound system was so loud
that an army could have invaded the house without attracting
the attention of Sandi O'Davis, a former client. She curled one
of her dreds around the first two fingers of one hand, while
with the other she tapped a soda can against the arm of the
chair in time with the music.

"Alexandria!" Eliza said sharply.

The girl jumped a foot in the air, nearly dropping the soda
can. "Jeez!" she exclaimed, one hand going to her heart. "You
nearly gave me a heart attack."

"What are you doing here?" Eliza asked, striving to keep
her voice low and even.

"I ran away," Sandy answered glibly. She sank back into
the deep leather armchair as if for protection. Hard eyes, much
too old and wise for such a childish face, dared Eliza to criticize
her action. That defiant tone might have fooled someone who
didn't know the teenager into ignoring her body language. But
Eliza knew it was just a disguise Sandy donned whenever she
felt unsure of herself, or threatened. The wave of fury that had

propelled Eliza into the room ebbed away, leaving behind only bone-deep weariness.

This was the last, unbearable, straw. Eliza's legs threatened to buckle beneath her. The pretense of carrying on as though a soul-shattering kiss from a virtual stranger hadn't thrown her completely off-kilter, added to a staggering amount of mind-numbing work, done at a backbreaking pace, were already more than Eliza could handle. Sleep deprivation didn't help as her poor befuddled brain struggled to assimilate the enormity of this sudden twist of fate. She had had thrust upon her the responsibility for a street urchin with the heart of a hustler and the smile of an angel. She just couldn't contend with this new dilemma.

Eliza backed into the couch and dropped onto it, coat, handbag, briefcase, and all. Her head fell back, eyes closed, as she offered up a quick, fervent prayer. "Lord, have mercy on me." She sensed, rather than saw, Sandy peeking out at her from the oversized chair in which the child had taken refuge.

"Are you okay?" a small, desperate voice asked.

When Eliza opened her eyes, she caught only a glimpse of a smooth chocolatey cheek and the tip of the nose of the girl buried deep in the black leather bastion in which she'd elected to take her stand. *Or seat,* Eliza thought drunkenly. She didn't have the energy to take on this battle tonight. Sandy would make mincemeat of her.

With a good night's rest, her alter ego—E. Taylor, Esquire, attorney at law and protector of the innocent—would reappear. Eliza could only cling to the hope that the helpless, hapless, confused creature she had become would be transformed into her more familiar self, and she would stop feeling as if she were caught up in a nightmare where clients ignored every word of her advice, and followed her home from work. Eliza had to believe that, or she would not have been able to coax Sandy out of the big comfy armchair and up the stairs to the guest room. If her faith had deserted her, she would never have managed to shuck off her shoes, slip out of her power suit and silk undergarments, and into her satin nightshirt, nor could she have paid token service to her usual nightly ritual by washing her face and brushing her teeth before slipping into the cottony comfort of her bed.

Eliza awakened suddenly in the small hours of the night, not—as she had fearfully imagined, just before falling asleep—to the sound of sirens and bullhorns, but to a deceptively peaceful quiet. She padded silently down the hall to check on Sandy and found her asleep with the light on. In repose, that face belonged to a babe of two or three months. Even the traces of hideous lavender eye shadow and deep purple lipstick couldn't detract from that cherubic innocence. Despite her instinctive worry at the thought of yet another unwelcome glitch in her already hectic life, Eliza couldn't help but feel a surge of compassion for the girl.

The first time she had seen Alexandria O'Davis, the girl had been mouthing off to the policewoman who had brought her out of the holding cell in the police station. The case had been referred to Eliza by the public defender's office, which had been so understaffed that day they'd called her to go and interview the girl at the police station—before they'd even seen her themselves. They hadn't even been sure of Sandy's age, but the cops had called to say they didn't believe she was eighteen yet, despite her insistence that she was.

A minor, with no visible means of support, they'd picked her up at a demonstration when she'd attacked a police officer. The man she'd taken on was six-foot-three.

"These kids at these sit-ins or whatever are always hassling us, but this one was unstoppable. I was trying to get between this rookie and some guy who was trying to incite a riot, I swear, and she just launched herself at me. She's tiny. Wait till you see her. Big guys generally don't have those kinds of balls, but this one's a handful. Reminds me a little bit of my own kid. I'm the one who called the public defender. I didn't want her to have to stay here all night."

Eliza had fully expected the rather large cop's description of her potential client's small stature to be an exaggeration, but when she'd seen O'Davis, Alexandria Latiffa, who barely topped the five-foot mark and weighed maybe eighty-five pounds, she realized he had hit the nail on the head. The man really could have crushed her with one hand.

Sandy had proven to be as rebellious and as cynical as anyone Eliza had ever met. She had been nearly impossible to defend, and had her youth to thank, as much as Eliza, for the fact that she didn't end up in juvy instead of in a temporary shelter. She'd been about fourteen then. That was two years ago. Eliza had visited her regularly when she'd been placed in a group home, been called when the girl threatened to run away, and had finally gotten her into the foster care program, with the help of her good friend, Stephanie Mann. She hadn't seen the teenager in the last six months, except when, at Sandy's invitation, she'd gone to her school to speak at career day.

Eliza pulled the spread up over her young charge's fully dressed body and went back to bed.

She woke up again, completely refreshed, at dawn. Eliza spent some time sorting through various scenarios she might be expected to play out with Sandy. As soon as she deemed the hour sufficiently advanced, she placed a call to her old friend at the welfare department. Her mind at rest after a protracted conversation with Stephanie, Eliza outlined her options on a legal pad, and then waited for Alexandria Latiffa O'Davis to awaken.

She didn't have to wait too long. Sandy joined her in the kitchen at seven-thirty. Her face was scrubbed clean, her carrot-red dreds neatly brushing her shoulders. The last time Eliza had seen the girl, the orange cap had been a mess of spiky knots, sticking out from her head every which way. Although the color was natural, passed on by her red Irish father who'd deserted Sandy's mother before his daughter was born, it was such a bright orange it was startling on such a dark face.

Eliza took the neat new coiffure as a good sign. A woman, even a sixteen-year-old womanchild, didn't take the time on her appearance that Sandy had in creating dreds—a laborious process that involved hours of twirling and twisting strands of hair together—without reason. Eliza hoped Sandy's new foster parents had fostered a little self-esteem in the child. And she prayed this new look wasn't because of a boy.

"Morning," Eliza greeted her.

"Yo." Sandy acknowledged her presence without looking at her. She opened the refrigerator and stood looking at its meager contents.

When she didn't make any effort to retrieve anything from within the cool, white interior, Eliza finally said, "Sandy?"

"Yes?"

Eliza was growing annoyed, but she only asked, reasonably enough, "What are you looking for?"

"Dunno," Sandy said.

"Well, there isn't much in there. If you haven't found anything yet, I don't think you're going to."

"Uh-huh." Still she stood, staring into the refrigerator.

Eliza imagined she could feel the room growing colder. "Yo!"

Sandy jumped. "What?" *She* didn't try to disguise her annoyance.

"Close that door, please." Although she hadn't raised her voice, Eliza felt like she'd just failed a test of some kind.

"Okay, okay," Sandy said, unfazed. She came to the counter, where Eliza had left bread, butter, and jam next to the toaster oven. Sandy reached for the coffeepot. Eliza watched her pour the dark steaming liquid into a mug, then top it off with milk and a number of spoons full of sugar.

"Do you want some eggs and/or toast?" she asked.

"Maybe later," Sandy answered, sipping her coffee.

"Okay then." Eliza decided it was time to take the bull by the horns. "We need to talk."

"So, talk." The teenager wasn't giving an inch. Eliza tried, and failed, to look at this scene from the runaway's perspective. Sandy was a true survivor. She abhorred weakness, in herself and others. Despite her nonchalant pose, slouched against the counter, Eliza knew Sandy was preparing to defend herself. Like a dog, backed into a corner, her hackles were raised. But that didn't excuse her rudeness.

"Look, I'm just trying to figure this out. You came to me, remember?" Eliza said. It was the wrong thing to say. If anything, Sandy melted even further into the countertop, the hand holding the steaming mug tilting dangerously, as if the bones in her tiny wrist were too weak to support its weight. Her head lolled to one side, then dropped forward. She stared at the floor.

But the glance she shot at Eliza was as sharp as nails.

"No problem, homegirl. I'm outta this joint." Her street accent was in full force.

"That isn't what I meant," Eliza said gently. "You're welcome to stay here for a few days."

"Whoa, thanks, man," she said, her voice dripping with sarcasm. Nevertheless, she came to the counter and took a seat in one of the tall stools across from Eliza.

"I called social services, and as a court officer, it seems I qualify as an acceptable baby-sitter for a ward of the state."

Even in her desperate straits, Sandy appreciated the humor in that statement. One lip curled upward. "Gotta love that sh— I mean, stuff," she said.

"But only if your foster parents agree." Sandy stiffened. "I can give them a call?" It was the best she could offer. She couldn't see the girl's face, buried in her coffee cup, but she knew the turmoil the teenager was going through.

Eliza waited. Sandy didn't respond.

"Okay?" Eliza finally asked.

Sandy shrugged. Since that seemed to be the only answer she was going to get, Eliza took it as an assent. They didn't have any choice.

The Farbers, Sandy's foster family, were very nice. Eliza had met them briefly at Sandy's new school, when she'd been invited to participate in the career day lecture. They agreed to the arrangement immediately, once she reminded them of that meeting and explained who she was.

"We don't really know what to do about her," Mrs. Farber said.

"Maybe we can talk more, later," Eliza suggested, conscious of Sandy listening intently despite the girl's relaxed stance. "I'm afraid that I'm running a little bit late this morning. I have to get into the office." She gave them the phone number at the office and at her home, "in case of any problems." Eliza wanted to speak with them, but not in front of Sandy. The girl was too fragile.

Mrs. Farber agreed eagerly, and Eliza made a mental note to call them as soon as she arrived at work.

She hung up the phone and checked her watch. "I've got to get dressed."

Surprisingly, Sandy followed her up to her room. Eliza didn't try to get her to talk, although she had a hundred questions buzzing around in her brain, foremost among them: *What had possessed the child to come here?* The tension emanating from her pint-sized houseguest was palpable. She figured it would be better to wait until Sandy unwound a little before asking her anything.

"I want to be emancipated," Sandy blurted while Eliza was applying her mascara.

"Uh-huh." Eliza stalled, thinking rapidly. Emancipation of a minor was never a simple process, and certainly not one she'd have ever thought to apply for for this particular client. Everything about Alexandria O'Davis screamed the need for a home and family of her own.

"I'm sixteen, now," Sandy said belligerently.

"We'll talk about it later," Eliza said, needing time to marshall her arguments against the girl's latest ill-advised scheme. "Meanwhile, why don't you unpack your things and figure out what you want me to make for dinner." Eliza fished a loose business card out of her purse. "Here's my number at the office. Call me with a list of things you like, and I'll do the grocery shopping on the way home." Sandy made no move to take the card she held out to her. Eliza wedged it alongside the makeup mirror. "Nothing fancy. I'm not a great cook."

Eliza took one last quick glance in the mirror. "That's the best I can do with the materials at hand. What do you think?"

"It's okay." Sandy sounded totally miserable.

"I'll let you do me some time," Eliza said. "See if you can make me look a little younger." She grimaced at her reflection, and caught a glimpse of Sandy's relieved expression in the mirror.

When she turned around, the mask was back in place, but

Eliza had seen for herself the hopelessness hidden behind that carefully blank expression. Sandy trailed her out of the room and down the stairs. Eliza felt terrible leaving her there. This was a troubled teenager, she reminded herself. Only two years from legal adulthood. Eliza knew for a fact that this little girl was capable of taking down a full-grown man, or two. A day on her own wouldn't kill her. Eliza was well aware that it would have been more reasonable to fear for the state of the house that she was trusting to this quasi-delinquent, than to worry about the girl. But it didn't help. As she walked resolutely out the door, she still felt like she was abandoning a poor, defenseless kitten.

As soon as she reached the office, she made a beeline for the telephone and called the Farbers.

Mr. and Mrs. Farber each got on an extension. "We don't know what to do with Sandy," Mrs. Farber repeated, as if their previous conversation had never been interrupted. "Lately, things have been going pretty well. She's been trying hard. She's very smart. When she wants to, she does very well in school."

Mr. Farber chimed in with, "Alexandria isn't anywhere nearer to accepting her situation than she was when she came to us. There's a lot of anger in that young woman."

Eliza wondered if his use of the phrase "young woman" was significant. Her cynicism was deeply rooted when it came to foster parents who appeared to be too good to be true. She could easily come up with a number of reasons why Mr. Farber might have decided to categorize Sandy as a woman rather than a child, none of them good. When he began his next sentence, Eliza's suspicions faded. "The other kids are better at controlling their tempers than she is, even Rosie, and she's only nine."

Eliza felt foolish. She had met this man and his family. He'd been thoroughly investigated in order to be accepted in the foster program. And her instincts had told her immediately upon meeting both him and Mrs. Farber that Sandy had been lucky to be placed with them. That he referred to Sandy as a young woman made perfect sense, especially in the context of

this conversation. A man who lumped his sixteen-year-old foster daughter with his "other kids," two foster children, and
two whom the couple had adopted, ranging in age from three
to twelve years, didn't warrant the kind of foul suspicion she
had been harboring. Jackson and Edna Farber were exactly the
kind of gentle, nurturing surrogate parents she would choose
for Sandy.

"If she wants to stay with you for a couple of weeks, then
fine. It might be good for her. But honestly, I can't see her
staying away indefinitely. This isn't a group home. We're a
family. The kids just can't pick up and leave. It's not acceptable." The warning hit home. The Farbers were willing to
include Sandy in their family, but she would have to do her
part.

"I understand," Eliza said. "Do you have any idea why
Sandy chose to leave now? You said she'd been doing well
lately. Has something happened?"

Mrs. Farber sighed audibly. "It was her sixteenth birthday
a couple of weeks ago. She got this idea somewhere about
trying to become an emancipated minor. She talked about it
when she first came to live, but we hadn't heard about it in a
while, until her birthday. She said that was the only present
she wanted. She was very nice about it. She said we shouldn't
spend any money on her, all she wanted was our support. We
didn't really know what to say, and we still gave her a party
and gifts, but we made it clear we wouldn't try to stop her if
that was really what she wanted." Mrs. Farber cleared her
throat. "After that, she calmed down. She stopped acting up
in school and seemed to really settle in here, so we thought
everything was going to be fine."

"Alexandria even painted her room. Purple," Mr. Farber
interjected. "I think it was a relief for her to know that she
had the option. Sixteen was this magic number, and the whole
idea just gave her this feeling of control."

"She explained it all to her brothers and sisters. She said
she could drop out of school, now. It's funny, that's why I
think she started doing so well in school. She felt it was her
choice to be there, and Sandy's such a rebel, she needed to

feel that," Mrs. Farber said. "Same with the situation here at home. Once she felt she had a choice about whether or not she would continue to live here, she was fine with the curfew, and doing her chores, and even doing a little more." She stopped talking, but Eliza didn't think she had finished yet, so she waited.

Mr. Farber was the one who finally continued. "I guess it was Libby, our youngest, who did the damage."

"She just didn't want her new big sister to leave. Those two are so great together, you should see them," Mrs. Farber said, her voice thick with emotion.

Mr. Farber went on. "Libby kept harping on about how Sandy couldn't leave. She kept asking if Sandy loved her. I think it spooked her. More even than I realized. We didn't think she'd run away. We talked to Libby about it, but she only got more upset."

"We hoped it would fade, you know how it is," Mrs. Farber said. "Maybe we should have known better, but ... things were going better than ever. Sandy stopped breaking curfew. Oh, I guess I said that already, didn't I?"

"I think I've got the picture, Mr. and Mrs. Farber," Eliza said.

"Oh, call us Edna and Jackson, please."

"And you can call me Eliza. If you think of anything else, please don't hesitate to pick up the phone," she said.

"Eliza, there's just one thing I do want to make clear. We really like Sandy. She's a rebel, but we figure she'll learn to choose her battles, and she's such a bright girl. Underneath all that anger and frustration, I think there's a real sweet kid trying to come out," Edna said.

"Yeah," Eliza agreed as the other woman paused. She knew exactly how Edna Farber felt.

"But if she's going to come home, it will have to be pretty soon." Jackson murmured his agreement.

"I understand, Edna, Jackson. Maybe I can bring her to visit you while she's staying with me."

"Great," they chorused.

"Next week, perhaps. Let me just get Sandy settled, and we'll see what we can arrange."

"Okay, Eliza. And thank you," Edna said.

"Thank you." Eliza waited for them to hang up before she put down the phone. The couple had given her a lot to think about. Her mind flashed to Ely Greene. He had said he worked out problems with is students. She wondered if he had any experience with a situation like this one.

No! The objection came hard on the heels of the thought. Sandy's dilemma had gotten her mind off Ely Greene and his brother for almost twelve whole hours. She was not going to let thoughts of either of them intrude again. Especially not Ely. And especially not that kiss.

Chapter Eight

"Hey, Mr. Greene, you got a hot date?" Charlie Perkins called as Ely entered his classroom on Wednesday morning. Charlie was a smart kid, and Ely usually enjoyed the energy he brought to class—even though, as the teacher, he had to keep a lid on the boy's enthusiasm. But today, Charlie's joking had hit a little too close to home.

"Simmer down," Ely ordered in his no-nonsense voice.

Charlie smirked at him. The class quieted. Ely thought he'd quelled the snickers and the wisecracks, until several hands shot into the air. His students generally waited until he had raised a subject before volunteering an opinion on it. The hour hadn't even struck yet, so class had not officially begun, and therefore he had yet to introduce the topic of the day's lesson. Only one subject had been raised. His suit.

Ely groaned inwardly as he called on the meekest of the students whose hands had been raised, a girl who'd recently taken to calling herself Baby J. "I suppose it's too much to hope that you have a question concerning the reading assignment."

"Got no questions. I just wanted to say you look *good*, Mr. Greene."

"Thank you, Janet." He derived childish pleasure from using

her given name, knowing it would embarass her. Ely didn't
know why the young white students at this school tried to
mimic the lingo of the streets; they hadn't done that when he'd
been a student at this school. They'd get over it, he supposed.

"So? Who's the chick?" John Baines called out.

"Chick?" Ely directed the question to the whole class.

"Lady," someone shouted.

"Woman," Janet corrected.

"I wore this because I decided to show you people what
real class looks like," Ely said.

"Yeah, right. Who is she, Teach?" Charlie asked.

Ely took a quick look at the clock. "Let's get to work, guys,"
Ely said firmly.

After his first-period class, Ely had an hour free. He planned
to call Eliza at ten o'clock and arrange to see her at some point
during the day, and he didn't think he could concentrate on
anything else until he'd done it. Ostensibly, he was making
this appointment in order to discuss his upcoming court appearance, but Ely was actually hoping he could use the business
meeting as an excuse to get Eliza alone for an hour or two.
Hence, the suit.

Eliza Taylor clearly saw him as nothing but another client,
but that kiss they had shared had given him hope that something
could develop between them. She had not pulled away; in fact,
she had barely been able to walk straight afterward, and it had
been then that he'd decided he couldn't let her go without a
fight. When he kissed her, he had enacted a scene he'd dreamed
about all those years ago—except for the part when he pretended he was just standing in for Tommy.

He hadn't spoken much to his brother lately. When they did
speak, by tacit agreement they didn't mention Eliza. But Ely
knew Tommy was still interested in her. It didn't matter. If he
had to compete with his older brother for this woman, he would.
Tommy was wrong for her. He would let Eliza go on thinking
that being a lawyer was what defined her, because Tommy
thought the same way. His brother and Eliza were alike in too
many ways. Tommy wouldn't make her face herself—because

then he'd have to examine those things in his own life that frightened him so, and that kept him alone.

Tom might be smarter, more savvy, more directed than Ely, but his older brother did not have his staying power. Everything came easy to Thomas Ezekial Greene. Ely knew how to fight for what he wanted. He had more experience. He'd faced his demons when Helen died and he'd been left with a toddler who counted on him for every single thing he needed. As awful as it had been to lose his young wife, and watch the life they'd planned together fall apart, it had made him strong. And stubborn enough to go after what he wanted, without hesitation. He picked up the phone and dialed Eliza's number.

Mary Jane Collins answered on the first ring. "Taylor and Associates."

"Ely Greene calling."

"Eliza is in court, Mr. Greene. May I give her a message?"

"Have her call me later, all right? I'd like to set up a time to see her."

"May I ask what the purpose of the appointment would be?"

"Sure. We need to discuss the next step in this process. She was going to get in touch with me when she spoke to Rod Daniels."

"One moment, please." The secretary put him on hold, but she was back on the line in seconds. "Mr. Greene, Eliza has a meeting scheduled with Mr. Daniels for next Thursday. How about if I have her call you after that?"

Ely was disappointed, but not particularly discouraged. The only problem was, he'd have to wear the suit to school again. His class would have him married off by the end of the week.

"Thank you," he said. "I'll speak with her then."

"Have a good day, Mr. Greene."

"I'll try," Ely answered, but she had already broken the connection.

He started to whistle as he hung up the phone. It wouldn't be long now. Maybe he'd buy a new suit.

*   *   *

Eliza had had a good morning. Judge Dresher finally agreed to garnish Timothy Sanderson's wages since he had neglected to pay a penny of the child support the court had determined that his first wife needed to raise their three children. The case had taken over three years to resolve, and Eliza signed off on it happily. The rest of the day went splendidly, as well. She spoke to Sandy on the telephone, who called to ask when Eliza would be home for supper, which she announced she would be cooking.

Most satisfying was the fact that she had finally successfully shoved the disturbing incident with Ely to the back of her mind, barely thinking of him or that kiss during the course of the day. Eliza was looking forward to celebrating all her various triumphs with Sandy when she arrived at her house that evening. Since her new roommate had moved in, light shone out of every window in the house as soon as the sun went down. It was a waste of electricity, which was politically incorrect, but Eliza sort of liked it. And it seemed the perfect welcome tonight.

But her homecoming was not what she had anticipated. Eliza noticed, as she passed the dining room, that the table had been set—and beautifully—with her best china and silverware. Apparently, her quiet little celebration was going to be more formal than she had anticipated. Unfortunately, when she took in the table, she failed to question one important detail. It was set for three.

When Eliza walked into the kitchen, she found Tommy Greene sitting at the island, drinking a glass of wine, and chatting with Sandy as if they were long-lost friends. Instantly, Eliza's euphoria faded.

"Hello, Eliza. I stopped by hoping to catch you in and Sandy invited me to dinner. I hope that's all right," he said. Eliza could see no graceful way to refuse him.

"Of course," she answered, feeling trapped.

"I understand you're celebrating?" he questioned.

"Not really." When Sandy looked at her surprised, Eliza grudgingly conceded. "I won a case today."

"Tell us about it," Tommy invited.

"What were you two talking about when I came in?" she said, stalling.

"The age-old question, which came first, the chicken or the egg. Sandy is making chicken and spinach quiche. It seemed apropos." He and Sandy shared a conspiratorial smile.

Eliza felt oddly left out. "It smells wonderful in here."

"Dinner won't be ready for about half an hour. You're early," Sandy said. Eliza had rushed home in anticipation of getting out of the power suit and designer hose she'd worn to court that morning, and into something more comfortable before dinner. It was a good thing she hadn't left the office a little earlier, or she would have been home to greet Tommy dressed in her frumpy old bathrobe when he made his surprise visit. She counted her blessings and resigned herself to spending the evening in Tommy's presence. She contented herself with removing her short tailored jacket and kicking off her high heels. The straight black skirt was form-fitting, but not too tight, and her patterned hose were only thigh high. She could remove them later.

Since Tommy seemed to have reverted to the informality of their law school days and made himself at home, Eliza decided to treat him just as casually. After all, nothing had actually changed between them over all these years. She poured herself a glass of wine.

"You brought this?" she asked. He nodded. "Very nice."

"A peace offering," Tommy said.

"I hadn't realized we were at war," she said.

"For dropping in unannounced," he clarified.

"Ahhh." Comprehension dawned. Tommy Greene hadn't been as unconscious of his presumption as she had thought. He just went ahead and did what he wanted anyway.

"Good idea," Eliza retorted, with a lift of an eyebrow to let him know that he'd only narrowly avoided the scolding he deserved.

"I do occassionally have one," he said.

Sandy watched this byplay with a puzzled expression. "One what?" she asked.

"Good idea," Tommy explained.

"It almost makes up for his lack of scruples," Eliza said. "But not quite."

Tommy shook his head. "You've seen through me. I'm still unscrupulous."

"What are you talking about?" Sandy was completely confused.

"It's an old joke from when we were at school together." Tommy and she had always had this way of speaking in shorthand to each other. Twelve years ago, there had been no subtle, hidden meaning behind their words. They'd been close. The best of friends. She'd almost forgotten. "You know Superman?" she said, trying to explain to Sandy. "Well, we used to call Tommy Unscrupulous Man."

"Why?" Sandy asked.

"He gave people the answers to tests."

The girl's expression finally cleared. "Ohhh," she said. "You guys were brains, weren't you?"

"Yup," Tommy said. "Completely uncool. Especially her."

"He was a nebbish."

At Sandy's questioning look, Eliza translated, "Nerd."

"At least I tried. You were a yenta. That's Yiddish for a pushy old broad," he told Sandy. His reference to her advanced age barely registered on her.

Sandy noticed it. "Eliza isn't old."

"Thank you, Sandy," she said. "But I was twenty-nine—"

Tommy interrupted. "And she never let us forget it, either. She was so bossy."

"As I was about to say before I was so rudely interrupted, I was a mature woman. And he was a baby. A little-bitty baby."

Tommy rolled his eyes. "I'll have you know that I was very mature for my age."

"Ha!" Eliza scoffed, but beneath her mock scorn was laughter.

"Everyone said so," he defended himself. But he was smiling, too.

"They just wanted you to keep helping them with their tests," she taunted.

"There wasn't much danger of that, though, once *she* found out about it," he told Sandy.

"How did she stop you?" the girl asked.

"She pounded it out of me."

"Wow!" Sandy looked admiringly at Eliza.

"Nag, nag, nag," Tommy elaborated.

"I don't nag," Eliza protested, looking at Sandy for confirmation of her assertion. Sandy suddenly grew very busy with her dinner preparations. "And if I did," Eliza said, deciding to try another tack, "it was just because you were so unscrupulous. You needed watching."

"We're back to where we started," Tommy pointed out.

And Eliza felt like they were, indeed, back where they had been when they first met fifteen years ago. He was a charmer. Tommy looked so comfortable sitting in her kitchen, it was shamefully easy for Eliza to forget that he'd intruded, uninvited, into this private part of her life. She couldn't seem to keep her distance. But it didn't seem like his presence was a threat. She didn't feel at all intimidated. He had just . . . slipped under her defenses when she wasn't watching.

It wasn't an unpleasant sensation. This was her old friend. One of the few people in Eliza's life whom she had trusted implicitly. That was probably why she had felt so hurt when she realized he was trying to manipulate her. It had only been her vanity that had been wounded, though. And it was ridiculous to hold on to such a petty emotion.

She let it go.

Eliza waited all through dinner for the reappearance of the sullen, defiant child who always lurked right below the surface of Sandy's thin skin. During the few days they'd been together, any conversation with her temporary ward was like a walk through a minefield. Sandy's tough exterior was only a thin veneer, easily pierced by the slightest perceived insult. But Tommy's avuncular manner and gentle chiding were accepted without Sandy's once becoming withdrawn or taciturn. Eliza watched in amazement as the teenager giggled in response to Tommy's playful flattery. Eliza relaxed her vigilance when it became clear that Sandy was in no danger of taking his teasing comments seriously.

Eliza enjoyed flirting with him, too. Once she stopped worrying about where the evening might lead, she found herself pulled into the charmed circle that seemed to encompass the two of them. She had rarely enjoyed herself more. When Sandy excused herself and disappeared upstairs, it seemed the most natural thing in the world for the two of them to start clearing the table together.

They began by carrying the china and silver into the kitchen. It had to be hand washed.

"Just put it here on the sideboard," she said to him. He gently deposited the plates he carried, then followed her back into the dining room to collect the rest.

"That was an amazing dinner. How old is that girl?" Tommy asked.

"Sixteen," Eliza answered. "Going on thirty."

"Wow. She looks about twelve," Tommy said. Sandy's height, slight form, and baby face had fooled a lot of people.

"She's a sweetheart, isn't she?" was his comment.

"Sometimes," Eliza said wryly. She didn't want to talk about Sandy when she might walk in on them at any moment. As she removed the place mats from the table and bundled the cloth napkins for the wash, she changed the subject. "I do think she could have a bright future. But let's talk about your future. You said you didn't know how long you were going to stay at S&C?" She'd been surprised by that statement when he'd made it during dinner, but the conversation had drifted to subjects that might be of more interest to the young, third member of their impromptu dinner party. Now she thought it a good, impersonal topic of conversation. She was honestly interested in what caused him to make that announcement. As she spoke, they had finished clearing the dining room table, and she quickly ran a damp rag over the polished wooden surface. Then, she led him into the kitchen.

"I've been there only a few months, so I've got a lot to learn about the firm, but it seems as though they're moving away from some of their founding principles." Tommy stood next to the kitchen sink, watching her wash the first of the dishes. He picked up a cloth from beside the sink and started to dry.

He kept talking all the while. "The reason I accepted the partnership was because Jerry Banning has always been someone I admired. Some of the practices he set up are really great. For example, he encourages mentoring among the staff. It's pretty democratic for such a big law firm. Staff and associates even get to vote on the partners' bonuses every year."

Eliza nodded. "I've heard some of this. But I've also heard that things are changing over there."

"It felt like I was joining a team when I joined the firm. But since then, I've discovered that there has been a lot of politicking behind the scenes, and three of the most conservative—and senior—partners recently decided to form an executive committee to review all company policies. It doesn't feel good."

"That's a shame," Eliza said. "Still, I envy you the corporate perks."

"You must have gotten those same perks when you worked in the D.A.'s office," Tommy said. "And they weren't enough to keep you there."

"We didn't have things like free tickets to the symphony. Or chauffeured limousines to take us to out-of-town meetings."

"Oh, *those* perks," he said.

"Yeah, them." Eliza felt her lips quirking up at the corners.

"They're nice." His boyish grin was infectious. But he sobered a moment later. "If the company I work for doesn't uphold the principles I believe in, then I'll find one that does," he said with unconscious arrogance.

"Well, S&C still has the best record among top firms in both hiring and promoting minorities and women," Eliza commented. The kitchen was clean and neat again, the pots and pans drying in the rack. She started the dishwasher.

"They do, and that's a policy I can get behind," Tommy said. "It's one of Jerry's main initiatives, so I don't think that's in any danger of changing. Not right away, anyway. But he's getting older, and he might retire. Especially if he's faced with a major power struggle within his firm.'' As he spoke, Eliza took a last quick look at the dining room, Tommy still following her like a puppy. It was pristine. The two of them had even pushed the chairs back under the table when they'd left the room.

She led him into the kitchen again. ''Did you ever consider working for one of the top black firms?'' Eliza asked. She'd always wanted to know, and as long as she was probing into his career choices . . .

''Of course,'' Tommy said. ''Always.'' They sat at the island, facing each other. ''But a lot of them are even more conservative and profit-driven than white firms. At S&C, I'm encouraged to take any pro bono work I feel like doing. Not just so the company can point out, and write off, their 'charity work' but because it's a policy Jerry Banning really believes in. Few, if any, of the African American–owned firms I applied to were as generous.''

''Oh,'' Eliza said, suitably chastened.

''But I'm not putting the companies down. Someone has to prove that a black-owned firm can be as successful and as downright competitive as any white-owned company. It's just that they can get people as good as me, or better, with a snap of their fingers. There still aren't, as you know, that many partnerships available to our people. White firms offer it only in one out of a hundred cases, maybe even one in a thousand. So when I turn down a partnership in a black firm, I'm leaving the position open for another black man or woman to fill. If I turn down a position at Silliman and Cosell, a white man will probably get it.''

Eliza had heard that argument before, and she agreed with it. Unfortunately, there were a lot of people who would call it a giant rationalization. They had a point, too. Tommy's decision was likely to inspire some disapproval within the ranks of their community. Some believed that choosing to work for 'the man' was tantamount to desertion of the African American culture. She wanted him to know that she didn't condone that kind of bigotry.

''I hear you,'' she said. ''I've never approved of segregation, whether it comes from whites or blacks. That kind of separatism can only hurt both sides. In my humble opinion."

"Humble? You? Sure," he said sardonically.

"Really," Eliza insisted.

"But you do approve of all-black firms, I take it, since I didn't see any white faces in your office."

"Yeah, I have to admit it," she said.

"But an all-white firm . . . ?"

"Is all wrong," Eliza said militantly, fully prepared to defend her point of view.

"I agree," Tommy said unexpectedly.

They shared a smile.

"We all know mankind's evolution isn't complete," she said.

"You think when it is, they'll overturn *Brown* vs. *the Board of Education?*"

Eliza shrugged. "Maybe. When everything else is equal, maybe separate but equal under the law will actually work. In this racist society, separate can never be equal."

"I'll drink to that," he said.

"Would you like another glass of wine?" Eliza asked.

"Sure," Tommy accepted without hesitation. They had long since finished the first bottle, and she got another from the refrigerator. He retrieved the corkscrew from a drawer as if he'd lived in her house all his life, and took the bottle from her. She got two clean glasses from the cabinet, and he filled them.

"Here's to evolution," she said, raising her drink. He lightly tapped his glass to hers. They drank.

"So, now what should we talk about?" Eliza asked playfully. "I think we've covered everything."

"Do we need to talk?" Tommy leaned forward and gently kissed her. Eliza felt warm all over, but she pulled back immediately.

"Oh, yes," she said. "For one thing, Sandy could come back any minute, now that the dirty work is done. Kids seem to have a sixth sense when it comes to these things."

''She wouldn't do that to me,'' Tommy said. ''But, okay.''
He retreated to his side of the island. ''What else?''

''What else what?'' Eliza asked.

''You said, 'For one thing, Sandy might return.' What's the
second reason.''

''I don't feel I know you well enough,'' Eliza said weakly.
It was a lie. She felt like she'd known him forever, but suddenly
he'd changed.

''I think you know me better than most people do.''

''I doubt that,'' she said.

''Kissing is a good way to get to know one another better,''
he said. ''You could find out if I'm a good kisser, for one
thing.'' Tommy smiled.

''And is there a second reason?'' Eliza asked, laughing.

''Of course,'' he said. ''I could find out if you were.''

''Hold off, there, man,'' Eliza said. ''We have barely
exchanged a word in twelve years.''

''Not including tonight,'' he interjected.

She continued as if he hadn't spoken. ''And suddenly, I can't
seem to . . .'' She'd been about to say, ''get away from you,''
but stopped because that sounded too frightened. Instead, she
said, ''I don't feel comfortable with you, this, whatever this is
between us. I know I've changed, and I'm sure you have, as
well.''

This time, he waited until she was finished. ''It didn't feel
like it, tonight,'' he said.

''Tonight was . . . nice. Maybe we could do it again . . .
another time. We're both grown-ups. There's no need to rush
into anything.''

''You're right,'' he said. ''No need at all. I've got all the
time in the world.'' There was something calculated in the way
he agreed with her. She had the feeling he was saying it only
so she would let her defenses down again.

She swallowed. ''Great,'' she said.

She watched nervously as he stood and came around the
island toward her.

''I don't need it. Time, I mean,'' he said. He moved like a
panther, graceful, powerful. ''I knew from the moment I saw

you again that I wanted to do this." He nodded at the glass in her hand. "May I?" She'd forgotten about it. He took it from her.

He kissed her again, tentatively. Eliza didn't move. She didn't want to. This was fascinating. Without the element of surprise that had accompanied that first kiss, she was completely calm, almost detached. His lips were hot and fluid against her own. One of his hands rested lightly on her hip.

She listened with one ear for the sound of Sandy's sneakers squeaking on the wooden staircase. Meanwhile, a wave of tenderness for her old friend flooded through her as his arms wrapped gently around her, enclosing her in an embrace that promised to hold fear and loneliness at bay. It was the homecoming she'd anticipated a few hours ago: warm, welcoming, a quiet celebration. The lack of the fireworks that had accompanied his brother's kiss caused her a moment's niggling worry, but she was able to put it out of her mind easily as she let herself sink into the warmth of his body. She floated mindlessly in the pleasant sensation he aroused in her.

Slowly, Tommy lifted his head, a question in his eyes.

"We'll have to do this again," Eliza said. As he lowered his head again, she slipped off her chair and out from under his arm. "Another night."

He took her rejection with good grace. "You never told me about the case you won," Tommy said.

"Deadbeat didn't want to pay child support. The judge finally agreed to garnish his wages," she recapped quickly.

"Good for you," Tommy congratulated.

"Good for the three kids," she corrected.

"Pro bono?" he guessed.

"That was the only way the mother could afford me. After three years of trying to raise her family on a postal worker's salary, she didn't exactly have any savings left."

"Good for *you*, Eliza," he repeated.

"Yeah," she said, with a sheepish grin. "That's one for our side." She had done a good thing. And now, she had been rewarded for it. She walked him to the door.

"Tomorrow's Thursday. Would you like to go out with me on Saturday night?

"You've already got a date for Friday night?" she asked, with a lift of an eyebrow.

He grinned. "No, but I didn't want to push it. I wouldn't want you to think I was trying to rush you or anything."

"You're so thoughtful," she teased, smiling.

He stole one more quick kiss and was gone, whistling, down the front walk.

Sandy was sitting at the top of the stairs when Eliza came up. "So, how did it go?"

"Playing matchmaker?" Eliza inquired.

"Just trying to be helpful," Sandy said. "He's cute."

"Maybe a little too cute," Eliza said.

"There is no such thing as a man who's too cute." Sandy spoke with all of the assurance of her sixteen years. Eliza wasn't about to argue with the girl since basically, she agreed with her. "Besides, I like him," Sandy said.

"Oh well, as long as *you* like him, I guess it's all settled."

"You like him, too," Sandy said defensively. "I can tell." When she caught sight of Eliza's grin, her pout disappeared, but she did warn her, "Don't be laughing at me."

"I'm not," Eliza assured her. "I just feel like smiling." She took on the girl's own defensive tone. "Think you can handle that, huh, tough guy?"

"Why you always have to get up in my face?" Sandy asked, but Eliza caught the glimmer of laughter in her eyes as she shook her head.

" 'Cause I'm bigger 'n you. So. So. What you got to say to dat?" She crossed her arms across her chest, in her best imitation of the homegirl stance.

This time, Sandy couldn't hold the smile in. "You are crazy, lady. Anyone ever tell you that?"

"Sure, but my shrink told me not to listen to the voices any more."

They walked up the stairs together, and Sandy watched her as she took off her makeup and got ready for bed. Eliza felt so close to the teenager, that she was in bed, with the lights off, before she remembered that she still hadn't figured out how to get Sandy out of her house.

Two years before, her friend at children's assistance, Stephanie Mann, had helped Eliza to keep Sandy out of jail. Stephanie worked in the social welfare department, and Eliza and she had started out together as social workers years before. Eliza had encouraged Stephanie—and even sat for her kids—when she went back to night school for her M.S.W. When Eliza decided to return to law school for her second graduate degree a few years later, Stephanie had been all for it. And she was the first person Eliza had called when Sandy showed up on her doorstep.

Eliza had spoken with Stephanie a couple of times since then, and the social worker had emphasized the need to get Alexandria Latiffa O'Davis back into the Farbers' household as soon as possible.

"That girl's a menace, but she was making some headway there. The last month she was there she had an A average in school, and she was getting along nicely both at school and at home, probably for the first time in her life."

When Eliza's complained that Sandy was prickly as a porcupine and absolutely refused to discuss returning to the Farbers' house, Stephanie only sighed and said, "She'll end up in juvenile hall. This is pretty much her only shot. I can't place her again. She'd go straight to a group home, and once there, it's just a matter of time before she's back on the streets."

"I know," Eliza told her friend, frustrated. And she'd been wrestling with the problem ever since. She couldn't force Sandy to go home, and she couldn't bring herself to throw the girl out. She supposed it would all blow up in her face, as usual, but as long as there were moments like the one tonight, Eliza could only hope she could come up with a solution before that happened.

Chapter Nine

Eliza enjoyed her first informal date with Tommy so much that she made another, and then another in rapid succession, with hardly a qualm about the discrepancy in their ages. After all, so far their meetings had been as innocent as they were impromptu, whether Sandy was with them or not. Sandy and Tommy got along like a house afire. Eliza's life was, if not back to normal, at least back on a smoother track. Work provided few surprises, and at least she was making some headway in her most pressing cases.

She met the opposing counsel on the Greene case for coffee and a muffin on Thursday morning. She knew Rod Daniels. He was a good lawyer, and they had no trouble understanding each other as they waltzed around the issues in the case in a dance as familiar as breathing. Of course, they both thought they'd prevail. It was only natural. But when Eliza left him, she was satisfied that she could counter the Tysons' two main objections to Ely's guardianship: his choice of neighborhood, and his ambition to teach in the public school system. It was not unusual for a man to choose to live near his work, regardless of the neighborhood. Their second contention was a bit trickier to combat, but Eliza thought she could put a very altruistic and idealistic spin on his ambitions, which would hopefully impress the judge.

She called Ely at lunchtime to tell him about the meeting, but he insisted on coming to see her, to discuss it in person. The last time they had seen each other had been the night he kissed her. They'd spoken on the telephone since then, of course, and Eliza had convinced herself that her reaction to that kiss was some sort of aberration—the result of too little contact with the opposite sex. With the benefit of hindsight, she realized she'd blown the incident out of all proportion.

Every once in a while, the memory of that moment intruded, usually when she was thinking of the most mundane things, but it was easily forced out of her mind. She had too many other important matters to deal with at work and at home with Sandy to let it upset her. Besides, she was dating Tommy, now. Ely couldn't possibly have any effect on her.

She agreed to see him, at the office, after business hours. He offered to meet her at her house, but Eliza figured they could finish their business more quickly in the quiet, impersonal office space. There would be nothing to distract them from work.

When Ely showed up, at seven on the dot, she was ready and waiting for him.

"It's just as we expected," she said after she greeted him. She ushered him into her office as she continued. "Your in-laws are convinced that they can provide a safer home for Jessie, for now." She waved him into the seat that faced her desk. "As well as financial security for the future."

"So where does that leave us?" Ely asked.

"Well, if the judge sees any merit to their case, he will appoint a Guardian Ad Litem to investigate Jessie's living conditions. The list we've been making, his doctor, his teachers, friends and family, will be given to the investigator, and he will interview everyone." Ely nodded, relaxing back into his seat a little. "The Tysons will provide their own list."

"They'll put McGinley at the head of that one," he said.

"After the GAL has spoken with everyone, he'll report his findings to the judge. As I told you, the judge is required to decide which custody arrangement will best serve the interests of the child. If you hadn't granted custody to your in-laws, their case would be much weaker. It would be up to them to prove you an unfit guardian. But since technically, they are already Jessie's legal guardians, even though he's been living with you, the court will have a little more leeway in this case.'' Ely never took his eyes from her face. His concentration was so intense that Eliza could not look away.

"So, they have to prove that they're better parents than I am?"

Eliza shook her head. "You're his only parent. It gives us a slight advantage. The state does try, most of the time, to put a child with his natural parents. If we have to argue the case in court, we'll have plenty of precedents on our side."

"When do we go to court?"

"We'll just be seeing the judge the first time, and when the GAL reports on what he's found, we'll see the judge again. Then, he'll either hold the case over for a trial, or he'll determine what the custody arrangement will be." She blew a stray wisp of hair out of her face, and wished she'd put it up this morning. It was annoying her.

"So, at the first meeting, nothing will really happen?"

"The judge could agree to revoke the Tysons' guardianship right there and then."

She smiled, but he only leaned forward in his chair.

"Then, it could all be over in a day?"

"Yup. But it all depends on the judge's impression of all of you. Just act natural, and you shouldn't have a problem." He nodded at the compliment. "Try not to be antagonistic toward the Tysons." He blinked and Eliza felt as though she'd just been released from a trance. His gaze was so unwavering, it seemed to have an hypnotic effect of her. She cleared her throat and lifted her shoulder-length hair off her neck to cool it.

"I'm not angry at them," he said accusingly.

"Feelings run high when you're actually sitting across from your opponent in a courtroom. Unjust accusations tend to bring out the trapped animal in most people."

"Okay," he said, digesting the thought. "I'll remember."

"So," Eliza concluded, "I think that's all I have to tell you for now." She was eager to go home, take a shower, relax. She felt tense; every muscle in her body seemed suddenly to have been tied in knots.

It must have been the hectic day she'd had. And perhaps her discomfort had something to do with Ely Greene. After all, she hadn't felt this way before he came in to her office. Eliza figured it had to be his resemblance to his brother that made her so aware of him, so conscious of his physical presence.

"Next comes the court date?" Ely asked, standing.

"That's right. Any time now, I would think." She stood and came around her desk and held out her hand to him. He took it, but instead of shaking hands, he pulled her gently closer and gave her a hug.

The brush of his cheek against her forehead stirred something within her. Eliza pulled away.

"I can't wait for all this to be over," Ely said confidently. "You will join Jess and me for a celebratory dinner, I hope." His eyes shone with excitement.

Eliza hated to put a damper on his happiness, but she was compelled to remind him. "Hey, it's not over yet. Let's not get cocky."

"It's called thinking positive," Ely remonstrated.

"All right, all right," she conceded. "But let's make that date *after* we win." Eliza knew well that once the case had been settled he'd forget all about the idea. Most clients issued invitations like this one, but once their professional relationship was severed, the intense feeling of camaraderie that came of working together was instantly diluted. In a month or less, her relationship with Ely would return to what it had been a few weeks ago. They would be distant acquaintances, nothing more.

"Promise me you'll come to dinner to celebrate with Jessie and me, and I'll consider the subject closed. Until we win, of course."

She couldn't help returning his infectious smile. "Fine. I promise." He moved toward her again, but she backed away, not letting him touch her, and ushered him out of the office.

* * *

The rapport that had been growing, oh so slowly, between Sandy and Eliza ended abruptly when they set out for the promised visit to the Farbers' house the following week. She knew Sandy was punishing her for calling their visit a visit "home," but it all seemed worthwhile to Eliza when six-year-old Libby launched herself into her "big sister's" arms on their arrival at the Farbers. Sandy's face lit up, and for the first time Eliza saw what the young woman Alexandria O'Davis could be—happy, loving, and unafraid. Unfortunately, Sandy withdrew into her shell again the moment they left the Farbers' house. In the car on the way home, she responded to all of Eliza's attempts at conversation with monosyllables. It was enough to make a grown woman cry.

That night, at dinner, Sandy seemed to have reverted to her usual wisecracking self, so Eliza mentioned hopefully that her visit home seemed to have done her good, and perhaps it was time to set a date for her return to her foster family. Sandy became very hostile, so Eliza backed off. She was back to square one. Again.

She thought about calling Ely for his advice, but quickly dismissed the idea when her stomach muscles tensed at the thought of hearing his voice on the phone. There was something about the way he looked at her that worried Eliza. Despite her conviction that once the custody issue had been settled he'd forget all about this newfound friendship of theirs, it was better to avoid him for now. He made her uncomfortable, most probably because he looked so much like his brother.

Waiting for her, when Eliza arrived at the office the next morning, was a copy of a summons for Ely Greene to appear in family court the following Monday morning. She called him to make sure he'd been notified. He had, and she gave him a quick rundown on what to expect in court, and promised to brief him well before they actually went in to see the judge on the details. She also advised him to buy a nice, conservative suit that fit him.

"I have a black suit," he said.

"A nice one . . . that fits?" she asked.

"I'd have to get it out and try it on."

"Ask Tommy to help you," she advised.

MJ buzzed her on the intercom. "Mr. Greene for you," MJ said.

"I'm already talking to . . . Oh," Eliza said.

"Right. The other one," her secretary said.

Great, maybe Tommy can get Sandy back to normal again, was her first thought. She realized the thought had been lurking at the back of her mind ever since their visit to the Farbers'. Sandy and Tommy were great together. Eliza loved to be with the two of them and even found Sandy's constant references to what Tommy said amusing, most of the time. She could barely laugh with the girl without being accused of laughing *at* her, but for Tommy and Sandy, trading insults was their primary mode of conversation. The fact that Sandy seemed to like Tommy so much was made even more incomprehensible by the fact that Sandy had always before held men in aversion. She had tolerated them, even suggested they had their uses but, to the best of her knowledge, Sandy had never trusted one. Until now. But the affectionate bond that had formed between them seemed to strengthen each time they met.

"Which line?" she asked, thinking she would tell him she'd call back when they could talk at greater length.

"None. He's here."

"Here here?" Eliza asked.

"Yup," MJ answered and clicked off.

Eliza looked at the closed office door. She didn't know why it made her so nervous to have Tommy suddenly show up unannounced when she'd been so pleased he'd called, but on top of the scene with Sandy the previous evening, his timing seemed somehow ominous.

Eliza knew that she encouraged the friendship between Tommy and Sandy at least partly out of guilt. She felt terrible about being the cause of a rift between Sandy and her foster family—even if she hadn't had anything at all to do with Sandy running away from home. Perhaps if Eliza had turned her away, Sandy would have worked things out with the Farbers. As it was, Eliza couldn't even bring herself to tell Sandy that she didn't think she could win her case if they tried to petition for emancipation.

Eliza hoped that Sandy's friendship with Tommy might also help soften the blow when it came. Meanwhile, the duo who had invaded her life got along with each other better than she did with either of them. Eliza found it heartwarming to watch the two of them together.

She got back on the line with Ely. "Something just came up, and it's very important. I'm sorry."

"That's fine," Ely said without hesitation. "We were finished anyway, right?"

"Thank you. I'll call you tonight," Eliza said hurriedly, barely waiting for his assent before she severed the connection, but she didn't immediately ask MJ to show Tommy in. She started to stand, to go to the outer office to greet him, but slowly sank into her chair again, to think.

Eliza had planned to talk to Tommy about Sandy, but she had never been able to find a good time to bring it up. Those dates on which Sandy accompanied them were out, of course. Eliza and he had gone alone to the symphony one night, and had met for quick meals a couple of times, but although they seemed to talk about anything and everything, Tommy was a master at keeping the conversation light. There never seemed to be an opening to introduce a subject as serious as Sandy's future. Even though she was sure Tommy cared about Sandy, she wasn't at all confident that his feelings for her ran deep.

Tommy appeared to take the teenager at face value. Sandy made him laugh, and he seemed to genuinely like and respect her. There was admiration in his eyes and voice when he sparred verbally with the little hellion. He alluded to her checkered past occasionally, but he never asked any questions about it, of either her or Eliza.

Of course, he had never seen Alexandria O'Davis's darker side. But Eliza suspected that, even if he had, it wouldn't faze him. He had found a friend, and he treated Sandy with the same brand of tenderness and respect that he did Eliza. And if a delinquent sixteen-year-old munchkin made an odd companion for a charming, sophisticated man like Tommy Greene, Eliza couldn't think of any way in which it could hurt the girl. Why Tommy allowed it was a bit of a mystery.

And she wasn't going to solve it today. Whatever he was here for, it probably wasn't about Sandy. She'd just have to wait until the moment was right to bring that subject up. For now, she could only hope he'd just been in the neighborhood and decided to drop by. She approached the door with all the pleasure with which she might have approached the guillotine. She took a deep breath before walking out of her office.

Tommy was flipping through the pages of a magazine in the small waiting area. He rose immediately when she appeared. She met him in front of MJ's desk.

"Mary Jane, I'd like to introduce you to Tommy Greene. Mary Jane Collins," she said to Tommy, completing the introductions.

Eliza marveled at her friend's ability to keep a straight face. "A pleasure, Mr. Greene," MJ said, with uncharacteristic solemnity.

"Tommy, please," he asked.

"Tommy."

She gave him a cherubic smile. When he turned toward Eliza, showing her his back, MJ gave her a very deliberate wink. Eliza couldn't help smiling.

She motioned for Tommy to precede her into her office. He was two steps ahead of her when she turned to close the door behind them, so Eliza jumped when his arms snaked around her middle and he pulled her back into his body.

"Hi," he whispered in her ear. He nuzzled her neck.

"Hey!" Eliza protested half-heartedly, but she didn't try to stop him as he tilted her head to the left, exposing more of her skin to his mouth. His lips slipped over the sensitive skin just below her right ear.

"I was working," she said as he nibbled on her earlobe.

"I guessed you would be," he said, barely lifting his mouth from her flesh.

"And I can't stop now," Eliza told him as she stepped away from him.

"Me, neither," Tommy said, catching her hips in his big hands and pulling her back to him.

She laughed, but scolded, "This is not the right time or place for this. This is a place of business, Tommy." She slipped out of his grasp and away from the temptation he offered, and quickly crossed the room, putting her desk between them. He followed more slowly, stopping when he reached the far side of the desk.

Tommy crossed his arms, smiling at her knowingly.

Eliza sat down. "What are you doing here anyway?" she asked.

"You don't want me here?" he asked, confident, even cocky.

Eliza pulled her work toward her. "I just want to know why you're here."

"Why not?"

She looked pointedly at the work spread on the hardwood surface in front of her. "As I said, I have got a lot of work to do."

"You can take a few minutes, surely," he said.

"Surely," she echoed. She leaned back in her chair. "What for?" He couldn't be here to make the let's-get-serious speech, Eliza thought. They'd been dating for only a couple of weeks. Nevertheless, she was nervous. Their four or five dates had been squeezed into her schedule, always taking a backseat to her work. She knew she should make more time for him, but she hadn't had any practice at rearranging her life to suit another person in some time, and she was pitifully bad at it.

To give the man his due, the take-it-as-it-comes attitude he'd suggested once seemed to work for him. He never indicated by word or deed, that he resented being at the bottom of her list of priorities.

"It really drives you nuts, doesn't it? That I'm out of my little box?" She hadn't bothered to hide the fact that she considered a date with him a nice interlude in her "real" life. His curious, amused expression baffled her. If he was upset, he had an odd way of showing it.

"What box? What are you talking about?" Eliza asked.

"What heading do I go under? Playtime?"

Uh-oh, Eliza thought. Her intuition and her reasoning had both been right. Tommy wasn't here to give her the let's-get-serious speech, but he was here to ask the big question: Where Do I Fit in Your Life?

She couldn't very well tell him the truth, that he was in her life because he was fun, and she was doing her best to loosen up and enjoy the attention. MJ made fun of her, because she couldn't just sit back and let things unfold, but Eliza really did try. And look where that got her, she thought cynically.

Stall! screamed the little voice in her head. If this interlude had to end, she could at least go out on one last date. She'd been looking forward to their evening at the jazz club. She had nothing to lose. And after over a year of celibacy, she deserved one last night of romance, even if it wasn't real.

She turned to her computer and hit Control S. Her date for the next night came up on her schedule, as well as the name of her favorite jazz performer, Dave Valentin. He was playing at a little club in Harvard Square. "We have a date for dinner tomorrow night. We can talk about this box you feel I put you in then."

Tommy came around the desk and bent over her so he could see the computer screen. Their date for the following evening was highlighted. "Your calendar? Ah, I see you're planning to play with me between filing and visiting dead storage. That's not very flattering, Eliza."

He leaned across her to turn off her monitor, but he didn't straighten up again right away. He turned his head to face her. Bent over her desk, with his hands braced on the arm of her chair, his eyes were on the same level with hers.

"Lady, lady, what am I going to do with you?" he mused.

Eliza felt trapped. Again. He had a tendency to do that to her. "Tommy, I've got to get back to work," she said.

"I know, but answer the question first," he said. "Where do I fit in the scheme of things with you? Am I just a temporary diversion?"

"I don't know," Eliza answered honestly. Oh, well, there went the jazz club. She promised herself she'd go with MJ or Stephanie the next time Dave Valentin was in town.

"Think about it," he advised. He closed the distance between them and kissed her lightly on the cheek. Now she was really confused.

"I will," she promised helplessly.

"Great," he said, his lips trailing from her cheek to the corner of her eye. "And while you're in such a receptive mood, how about a real date?"

"What's that?" she asked suspiciously. But her distrust could not keep her eyelids from drifting downward.

He kissed her closed eyes. "You dress up. I dress up." His lips brushed over the bridge of her nose. "Dinner, dancing, candlelight." He flicked the tip of her nose with the tip of his tongue. "No storage facilities."

Eliza felt a tremendous surge of relief. He wasn't going to press it! Happily, she raised her head, trying to catch his teasing lips with her own. "I store the dead files at my place," she said suggestively. *Why not?* she pleaded with her conscience, which was nagging her unmercifully. *I want him.*

"Sandy's there," he said. Eliza opened her eyes to stare at him, surprised. "You know I like the kid," he excused himself. "But she can do without you for an evening." Eliza clung to the first part of his statement. He liked Sandy.

She tried to joke. "Me, sure. You, I don't know." Maybe this wasn't the right time to ask him for his help with the girl, but she didn't have to completely abandon the idea. His heated gaze focused on her mouth. He flicked his tongue across her bottom lip. Her wayward houseguest was forgotten for a moment.

"She's a big girl. I think she can fend for herself," he said.

Eliza made one last-ditch effort to change the direction of his thoughts about Sandy. "She does that now. In fact, I'd say she takes care of me as much as I take care of her."

"Well, then, let's give her a break. Let me take care of you." His breath whispered across her lips.

She would talk to him about Sandy later. Much later. "Okay," she agreed.

Finally, he pressed his lips to hers, firmly and briefly. "It's a date then," he said. Instead of deepening the kiss, he raised his head and started to straighten up. She caught his tie. He gently disengaged himself. "Tomorrow still good?" he asked.

It must have been the release of all that tension that made her say, teasingly, "I'm not sure about this. You know how nerve-wracking first dates are. A first *real* date would probably be even worse. I'm not sure it's worth it, after all." She was amazed by her own boldness, but he deserved to be punished for that taunting kiss.

"I think they're exciting. Everything's new. There's still so much to learn about each other. And there's that first real kiss," he said.

"I have a strict rule. No kissing on the first date," she said airily. "It's not that I'm a prude or anything, it's just that it's one less thing to be nervous about. All right, so *you* find it exciting, but it makes most people feel awkward. Worrying about spilling food on your clothes, or not being able to think of anything to talk about is bad enough, without that first kiss hanging over your head like the sword of Damocles."

"I always kiss on the first date," he informed her arrogantly. Then, he smiled. "Otherwise, what would be the point?"

She smiled back. "I guess one little kiss wouldn't hurt."

"Little? Oh, no. The first-date kiss has to be long, hot, and wet. It's essential," he stated unequivocally.

"Why?" Eliza asked.

"It breaks the ice for the second date," he answered.

"Aren't you getting ahead of yourself here? How do you know there's going to be a second date?"

"I'm a good kisser," Tommy boasted. "That's why I always kiss on the first date."

"There had to be a reason," Eliza said.

"Oh, sure," Tommy said. "There are lots of reasons."

"Like?"

"Well, once I've got the girl warmed up, I—"

Eliza interrupted. "What the heck do you think you're dating? A car?"

He pondered the question. "Women are a lot like cars," he finally said.

Eliza tried to look offended rather than amused. "Out!" she said, standing and pointing at the door.

"No, really," Tommy insisted, grinning. "They both require great care and attention." She advanced on him, and he backed away. "And they both can cause a lot of damage if they get out of control."

She pushed him toward the door. He caught her arm, pulled her to him, and kissed her. Eliza laughed against his mouth for the first few seconds, but he only deepened the kiss. He took his time and when he lifted his head, it took her a moment to catch her breath.

"I give you a nine for technique, eight for feeling, and ten for breath control," she teased, feeling slightly drunk.

"Okay," he said, letting her go. "That's out of the way." He walked to the door, then turned back to say, "Now we don't have to worry about warming you up." He opened the door.

"You never did," Eliza said, her voice sweet as saccharine. She could hear him laughing all the way to the outer door.

MJ came into the office a moment later.

"So what happened?"

"He said he wanted to go out on a real date."

"What have you been doing up till now?" MJ asked.

"Playing with him," Eliza said. MJ looked as confused as she had. "Like a little kid plays in the park. I've only been diverting myself."

"Well, that's true. But what did he expect?"

"He wants Mommy's undivided attention. I thought he was so cool, with all his take-it-as-it-comes talk. But he's just like all men."

"So what did you say?" MJ asked, nodding sympathetically.

"I said, yes," Eliza admitted.

"When is it going to be?"

"We're supposed to go to a jazz club tomorrow night anyway, so I guess that will be it."

"Good for you," MJ said. "You're always saying jazz is your one weakness."

"Yeah," Eliza said, blushing. Luckily, her skin was dark enough that MJ wouldn't notice.

"Who are you going to see?"

"Dave Valentin." Eliza couldn't help smiling at the thought.

"Uh-oh." MJ said. "Didn't he record the music you gave Robby and me for our anniversary? The one you said was guaranteed to put us in the mood."

"I know. But I'm going to look at it this way. Even if the rest of the evening is a disaster, at least the show will be good."

"If you weren't my friend, I'd hate your guts," MJ said. "Luckily, you are my friend, so I'm happy for you. And I'll tell you, the best thing that could happen to you is if that guy sweeps you off your busy little feet."

"Why, so my work could pile up even higher?" Eliza was genuinely curious about how MJ thought having Tommy in her life would solve her problems. She could barely manage to fit picking up her dry-cleaning into her week. She was so obsessed with work, she had forgotten the outside world existed. She covered her defects recently by hiring a man to take care of her yard, and a maid who came once a week to clean her house, but she was not a normal woman. She could barely find time to call her friends of twenty years, so where in her life could she possibly fit a full-grown man?

"With his money, he could make your life a lot easier."

"His money won't solve my problems."

"Not all of them. But a cook, a maid, and a chauffeur would be a start. I can't believe this. You weren't even looking, and you ended up with a wealthy, handsome, brilliant partner in a major law firm. *And you don't even appreciate it.* He doesn't even want to chuck it all to be a piano player or anything."

"Well, thanks, I guess," Eliza said. "He could have secret desires that I don't know about, like aspirations to become a spot welder or an Olympic equestrian."

"Nah, he's the real thing," her secretary affirmed. "A jackpot, a one-in-a-million shot, and you got him."

MJ was still ragging on Eliza when lunchtime rolled around. "Just don't blow it," she warned. Eliza was standing out by her secretary's desk waiting for Sandy, with whom she was going to lunch.

Her ward chose that moment to walk in the door. "Don't blow what?" she said nervously.

"It was nothing, honey," Eliza said. Sandy didn't look convinced. "Nothing to do with you." She added. "Or my cases," she added quickly. Sandy took most of her clients' cases as personal warnings. No matter how unlikely her chance of ever suffering the same problems as another child, Sandy felt each kid's triumphs and defeats deeply. Eliza thought she filed each case under the heading, "Situations To Be Avoided," as if she would have walked voluntarily into one of them if she hadn't been forewarned.

When Sandy still appeared anxious, Eliza explained. "MJ, Ms. Collins, was just saying I should take good care of my relationship with Tommy."

Sandy smiled, finally satisfied and clearly relieved. "I think Ms. Collins is right. You've got to work it, sistah."

"Listen to her. I seem to remember someone who looked a lot like you telling me that no man was worth the effort."

"He's different," Sandy said seriously. "He's got class."

MJ joined in. "Tommy Greene is definitely worth it, girl." She and Sandy gave each other a high-five.

Sandy's coat fell open, and Eliza caught a glimpse of her clothing.

"What in the world are you wearing?" she asked, horrified. Sandy's smile was replaced with a frown. "Alexandria O'Davis, don't tell me you came all the way down here in the trolley in a slip."

"I've got a shirt on over the top. The bottom part's the same as a skirt."

"If it was the same as a skirt, they'd call it a skirt. That's a slip, not a dress. Are you crazy?!"

Sandy cringed, but she continued to defend herself. "I've worn it before," she said sullenly.

"I've never seen it. If I had, I'd have told you to change into something decent!"

"It is decent. It covers me more than a bathing suit does."

"Do you see a pool around here? Or any other body of water?"

"No." Sandy had withdrawn almost completely into her shell.

Eliza nearly regretted her outburst. Nearly. But someone had to tell the child what was and was not acceptable behavior, and Eliza had been appointed, sort of.

"Come on. We're going to the store to buy you something to wear that can be seen in public. You can't go to lunch in that."

"Why don't I just go home?" Sandy asked. "Then you wouldn't have to be seen with me anywhere."

Eliza knew she should back down. She'd gotten her point across to the girl—if not with words, then with the strength of her reaction. But she couldn't keep the disappointment she felt from her voice as she said, "I didn't say I didn't want to be seen with you, did I?"

Sandy didn't answer. She wouldn't look at Eliza.

"I want to have lunch with you, I just don't think that what you're wearing is appropriate," Eliza said more calmly. Sandy continued to subject her to the silent treatment. Eliza looked at MJ, who shook her head helplessly.

Rosa came to her rescue. "Go on, then. There's a sale at Filene's, and there's a Pizzeria Uno right next door." She gave the frustrated Eliza a nod of approval as they passed by.

"Enjoy lunch," she called to Sandy.

Eliza dragged Sandy along to Filene's and bought her a skirt. It was bright blue linen, cut straight and tailored, and it did not exactly go with the multicolored print top the girl wore. But that didn't matter much as the shirt fell almost past the hem of the short skirt. It was the only item that Sandy had displayed the least bit of interest in, which was why Eliza bought it. She only hoped the teenager would not throw it in the trash the moment they went home.

Eliza wished she hadn't lost her cool over the slip thing. Their lunch date had been the result of a truce, after their latest argument. As soon as they'd made their peace about the visit to the Farbers, they'd gotten into another fight, and it had taken

Sandy almost an entire weekend to forgive her. Much as she
hated the seesaw relationship they had forged, wherein Sandy
was furious with her one day and sullen the next, Eliza couldn't
apologize for her part in the last dispute. When Sandy had
made a date with a boy she met at the local supermarket, she
had been right to give her permission only provisionally, and
to insist on meeting the boy first.

It hadn't taken more than one quick look at his shaved head,
gold front tooth, and blue bandanna for Eliza to decide he was
not to be trusted with her young charge, but she hadn't forbidden
Sandy to go until she saw the motorcycle on which he intended
to take them both to the cinema. Even then, she hadn't actually
nixed the date, but had offered to drive the couple to the mall.
But Lloyd flatly refused, and Sandy became verbally abusive.
Eliza had grown more frigid and unbending as Sandy became
louder and more frenzied. There had been no way for Eliza to
release any of her frustration on the head of the girl who'd
caused it, because Sandy's anger was clearly inspired by feelings of hurt and betrayal more than anything else. Eliza didn't
want to say anything that would add to the teenager's pain and
had tried reasoning with Sandy, but that had been a useless
exercise.

For this latest argument, though, Eliza could apologize. "I'm
sorry I blew my stack," she said.

She felt like she had had to win Sandy over again and
again, and this lunch, which was to signal a new phase in their
relationship, had started badly.

To her surprise, Sandy answered, "It's okay."

"Great, I'm starving," Eliza said, a surge of hope lightening
her heart.

"Me, too."

They ordered two large deep-dish pizzas, and Eliza cast about
in her mind for a topic of discussion that wouldn't offend her
young guest. "I've got a court date for the Greene case." Sandy
had always been interested in her work. It was one of the things
that gave Eliza hope, since Ms. O'Davis had a good mind and
excellent grades, and might just make it through law school

herself, if she decided she wanted to pursue that course of study.

"That's Tommy's nephew. The one whose father and grandparents both want him?" Sandy said, with a bitter twist to her mouth.

"Yes." Perhaps this hadn't been the best conversational gambit. Sandy seemed jealous.

However, the teenager only said, "You're working for his dad, right? So, you think the kid should live with him?"

"Yes, I do. I think Mr. Greene has done a good job raising his son. His grandparents don't want to leave him, but I think they're letting their feelings get in the way of what's best for Jessie."

"So, how come they're trying to take him away, if Mr. Greene did so good and they love the kid?"

"They're moving. And they're worried that Mr. Greene might lose his job."

"Why would he lose his job? He's Tommy's brother, right, so he's got to have a pretty good brain."

"He doesn't really like teaching in the school where he's working. He doesn't like their rules, so he doesn't always follow them. You should know all about that."

"Sure," Sandy said offhandedly. "I wrote the book. Could they fire him? For breaking the rules?"

"They could. But they probably won't."

"What would happen if they did?"

"He'd get another job. He wants to teach in public school anyway. But he's waiting for Jessie to be old enough to stay home alone nights so he can go to night school and get the teaching certificate he needs."

"Sounds like a plan," Sandy said, her disinterest clear. She concentrated on her pizza.

"Have you given any more thought to college?" Eliza couldn't resist asking.

Sandy shot her a look of derision and laughed. "You never give up, do you?"

"Not very often," Eliza agreed, smiling back at her, relieved by her charge's calm, content manner. It seemed she'd been forgiven, and in record time.

"I think I'll order dessert," Eliza announced, feeling the small celebratory gesture was in order. This girl would never cease to amaze her.

Chapter Ten

The Farbers' two-week time limit was almost up. Eliza debated with herself about whether to bring it up with Tommy as she dressed for their first real date. She much preferred discussing Sandy to talking about their relationship, and she was determined to ask his advice at some point.

They met at the restaurant, and as Eliza had joined him at the table and ordered an aperitif, she launched into the subject. "I'm having a bit of trouble with my young houseguest," she stated. Even if Tommy turned out to have nothing to say, she figured that talking about her dilemma might help her come up with a solution.

"She's so defensive when I try to speak with her about going home to her foster parents, and time is running out. If she waits too long, the Farbers won't let her come back. I thought you might have some ideas about how to talk to her. You get along with her better than anyone." She wasn't trying only to flatter him. It was true.

"I have a talent for drawing out recalcitrant females." Tommy smiled.

She gave him a perfunctury smile in return. "I've tried everything I can think of. I invited her to lunch today, hoping that maybe it would be better to talk in neutral territory, but that was a total disaster.''

"She seems pretty sensible to me. I know, she's a little touchy, but can't you just say straight out it's because you like her that you want her to have more than a part-time, overworked lawyer for a mother? You can still be her friend, but she has to go back to her parents. I know she likes her foster home, she mentions it quite often.''

"You make it sound so simple,'' Eliza despaired.

"You make things more complicated than they are,'' Tommy said without censure.

"Maybe I do, but I'm not in this case. Sandy withdraws from me the minute I say anything that even implies she won't be with me forever.''

"I think she knows she's got to go. That's why it's such a sore subject for her. She accepts the reality of the situation. Now, you just need to give her a goal to work for. Set a date, and she'll come around by the time it comes around. She's a strong girl.''

"She seems tough, but she's really fragile,'' Eliza argued.

Tommy surprised her by saying, "I don't think she's tough at all. She's a pussycat. But she tries to hide it. Badly, I might add. I'm not talking about that. I have the feeling she's been through a lot. She doesn't know how often her eyes give her away. But she made it through that pain, she'll handle this. It's not like you're dumping her. You're being her friend and giving her what she really needs.''

"She won't see it that way,'' Eliza said sardonically.

"Then make her see it,'' Tommy said sharply. Eliza looked at him, surprised. "I'm sorry,'' he said. "Obviously, I'm not the best person to give you advice in this situation.''

"No, I really appreciate what you've said. Perhaps I have been pussyfooting around this too much. Sandy isn't stupid. She knows what's coming, and that might well be what's causing the tension between us. I'll try to be more straight with her.''

"Eliza, you do what you think is right. You've known the young lady since she was fourteen: I met her only a few weeks ago. I'm just a playmate. You're more like a parent to her.''

"Whoa, baby. Sandy has parents. Too many parents, what with her mother, two stepdads, and two foster parents. I'm just her lawyer."

"Yeah, right," Tommy said, shaking his head, but he smiled at her. "You know, you are so perfect for me."

"What?" Eliza asked. The conversation had taken an unexpected turn.

Tommy put down his wineglass and took her hand. "You and I are alike in a lot of ways. We both really like this girl, but I'm just in it for the laughs, and you're just in it on behalf of the law. Neither of us is able to admit how we really feel. We are sitting here, having dinner in this romantic setting, complete with candlelight and soft music, and we're still talking about our little . . . friend."

Eliza looked around at her surroundings. She had noticed the elegant decor as she entered the room. She hadn't been to La Signe in years, but it was just as lovely as she remembered. But it was true, when they had started talking about Alexandria O'Davis, everything else had faded away.

She gave Tommy a rueful smile. "I really don't mean to bring my work with me everywhere. I'm sorry."

Tommy shook his head. "You still don't get it. That juvenile delinquent isn't 'work' for you. My brother isn't 'work' for you."

Eliza suffered a panicky moment as Tommy paused before finishing his thought. Had Ely told him about the kiss? Was he about to accuse her of taking more than a professional interest?

"You take their cases on as if they were your own battles. You may not say it. You may not be *able* to say it. But your concern for your clients is personal. You're just too chicken to admit that you care about them."

Eliza opened her mouth to contradict him and closed it again. She knew there was an element of truth to what he said.

"It's not a crime," she said childishly.

"No, it's one of the things I like best about you. I have the same problem. I've never been able to talk about my feelings easily, either."

Luckily, the waiter came with their bill at that moment, so Eliza didn't have to answer him, didn't have to tell him she wasn't hiding her deeper feelings. She just didn't feel things as strongly as other people did.

Once the bill was paid, they left. Eliza didn't want to address his accusation, and Tommy didn't say anything more about it, which didn't surprise her, since it had been a revealing confession as much as anything else.

They barely spoke as they drove to the jazz club. They had already discovered that they both loved jazz. It made sense for Tommy to bring her to the Good Note to see Dave Valentin. Tommy's mother, Eugenia, had been a pretty famous singer in her day, his dad a trumpeter. Eliza had been a fan of both parents before she ever met the Greene boys. She remembered fondly both Tommy and Ely playing and singing in college a couple of times. They were natural musicians. Tommy played piano and jazz guitar, and they both had beautiful voices. Ely was just a kid when she first met him, but he had also been the cutest sax man she had ever seen.

Eliza had been looking forward to the evening with great anticipation since Tommy had ambushed her in her office. Her blood grew heated as the first note sounded. As she had told MJ, jazz had that effect on her. This music was sexy. But the music was not entirely responsible for her excitement. The seduction had begun the morning before, when Tommy had forced her to face him, answer him, feel him. Her senses were heightened by the look in Tommy's eyes as he gazed at her. She was incredibly, unbearably aware of Tommy's knee touching hers under the small table.

"What else do you like about me?" Eliza asked throatily, throwing caution to the winds.

"Everything," he said wisely.

"What'll it be?" the waiter asked. Tommy and Eliza quickly gave him their orders, eager to be alone again in the smoky, crowded room.

"Where were we?" Tommy asked.

"You were saying you like me," Eliza reminded him. "For reasons as yet unspecified."

"Oh, yeah," he said, his deep baritone gliding over her skin like a caress. The opening band was playing an instrumental version of an old Gershwin ballad, "They Can't Take That Away From Me."

He sang softly. His voice was melodious, warm. A gift from his mother. Her voice, a deep, husky contralto, had the same rich quality. " 'The memory of all that. No, no, they can't take that away from me.' " His singing voice left her breathless, her pulse pounding.

"I sang professionally when I was young. I know the lyrics."

"Then I don't need to point out that what you were singing wasn't jazz," Eliza said. "Ira and George Gershwin wrote some pretty songs, but . . ." She shook her head. The band chose that moment to shake up an old favorite of hers, "Ms. Brown to You." "That's jazz," she said.

Tommy leaned close. "But Ira had a way with words," he said. He sang huskily, 'My sweet embraceable you.' The whispered lyrics in her ear made her temperature rise even further.

"Hmmm," she agreed. "Ira has his moments." Eliza fanned her heated face with her napkin, looking sideways at him. She had always liked that song.

"God," he groaned. "You are. Embraceable." He put his arm around her, pulling her toward him. When her head rested against his shoulder, he gave her a little kiss on the forehead. She felt something deep inside open up at that tender kiss. There was some quality to that gentle contact that made her feel more excited than any more intimate touch ever had. It was a little scary, but it felt good. She didn't want to be invulnerable, she just couldn't help it. Perhaps Tommy could crack the stone that had surrounded her heart for so long.

This man definitely had possibilities. He saw through her tough act and, rather than being put off by her lack of feeling, he was even more attracted to her. He seemed to relish the contradictions in her personality that she herself couldn't understand. She hadn't felt this strongly, ever, that she might belong with someone. Tommy had said at dinner that they were alike, so maybe he was just recognizing himself in her, but if so, maybe that was what she needed. He was ten years younger than her, and he was heartbreakingly handsome, and she knew she was asking for trouble thinking about him this way, but maybe he was her perfect mate. Her fairy-tale love. The man she'd given up looking for before she'd even started.

After her parents had died in the accident, she was adrift, lost. After she had made the mistake that cost two-year-old David Paron his life, Eliza felt like she would never be completely human again. Her heart had been broken too badly ever to mend. Tommy Greene gave her hope. Maybe she could recover, after all.

He had started to hum along with the band. She could feel the vibratons in his throat barely two inches from her ear. They traveled from him to her as she nestled against him. Her heightened senses made her aware of his long, hard body, all down her side where their bodies met and merged, his torso next to her breast, his legs against hers, his muscled thigh beneath her palm.

"Dance with me," he said. She didn't want to move away from him, even for a moment. But she nodded, and they stood.

When they reached the tiny dance floor, he drew her close again. She laid her head against his chest and sighed. She had dreamed this once, long ago. Either right before or soon after her parents died. That time was still all confused in her mind. But she had dreamed, like all young girls, of finding someone like Tommy: strong and beautiful, and completely in control of his own destiny. All the things that she wasn't, then. And he would care for her, hold her close as Tommy did now, and fit against her just like this. They would be the perfect couple. Her skin was still smooth and supple. She didn't have too many wrinkles, other than a laugh line or two at the corner of her eyes and her mouth. All in all, she'd aged pretty well. She could pass for thirty. Her high cheekbones and round eyes helped maintain that illusion of youth. If that was enough for him, then she was not going to worry about the age thing anymore.

When Tommy suggested they leave, Eliza was ready. She was eager, in fact, to be alone with him.

Women watched them go, or rather, they watched him. Tommy didn't seem conscious of the attention he attracted. He certainly didn't court it. The reaction women had to him was automatic. He was ridiculously handsome, absolutely delicious. Eliza thought that subconsciously, he must be aware of it. He had that air of absolute confidence.

She liked it. She liked everything about him. His solicitousness as he helped her into her coat. His smile as they joked about skipping Dave Valentin's performance. She teased him about asking her out for an extravagant evening of music and dancing and then leaving before the headliner arrived. He only smiled and shook his head. She couldn't keep her eyes off his long brown hands. She was entranced by his forearms—so much thicker than her slender wrists, and so male, with a fine covering of curly black hair. It was a portion of the male anatomy that she'd always admired.

He brought the car to a stop. He got out and came around to her side of the vehicle, and opened door for her, offering his hand. She stepped out into his arms, appreciating his old-fashioned courtesy. They were both smiling so widely, that when they kissed, his teeth scraped gently against hers. Then she opened her mouth, and their tongues dueled as each of them eagerly explored the warm, dark softness of the other.

She waited for that explosion of feeling that had accompanied Ely's kiss. It didn't come. Tommy tucked her under one arm as they walked up the front stairs to his house. He let her go to unlock the door. She shivered slightly, away from his warmth, and was glad that there was a nip in the air to explain the tremor.

Frankly, she was terrified. What had happened to the passion that she had felt when they danced? It had not been her imagination. She had felt a connection to this man that she had never felt before. He was perfect for her. She had thought it before, and when he took her hand to guide her through the door, she thought it still. The forearms she had memorized during their ride in the car, the broad shoulders and hard chest, the firm butt she had admired, and long muscular legs were hers to touch, to claim. That strong masculine face, those lips and eyes, his close-shaven chin which she'd sheltered under on the dance floor, had tempted her ever since she'd seen him again on that awful first night. He was all hers. But she didn't seem to want him.

The moment the door closed behind them, his muscular arms closed around her. But all Eliza could think of was the slide of his brother's fingers down her silk-clad arms. She remembered clearly the excitement she had felt in the club, the anticipation she had felt when they had left the smoky jazz bar. She tried to recapture it, manufacture it. She closed her eyes and leaned into him, raising her head for his kiss. His lips dropped onto hers, warm, soft, practiced, but she felt nothing. His kiss left her devoid of emotion. She could have cried.

"Eliza?" he said, his voice husky. "Do you want a drink or anything?"

"No, thanks," she said. Her voice to her ears sounded cold.

"Good." Tommy didn't seem to have noticed anything amiss. He nuzzled her neck, started to undo the top button of her coat.

She caught his hands, held them against his chest. "Tommy?"

"Yes?" He lifted his head to look down at her, smiling.

"Tommy, I . . ." Eliza couldn't bring herself to tell him she didn't want him. She didn't want to hurt him.

"What is it? Are you all right?" He touched her cheek, concerned.

"I'm fine. I just think I have to go home now," she said. She couldn't explain. Not even to herself.

"Now? I mean, I'll understand if you don't want to go too far, too fast, but . . ."

She couldn't even look at him. "No, I don't," she said.

"But we can still . . . neck," he suggested, his voice playful. His eyes still burned when he looked at her, but he was in control. She knew he was trying to make it clear that he would abide by her decision. If she knew anything about men, that grudging note of respect in his voice was probably for her, for hesitating. It was some strange obsession they all seemed to share. They wanted the women that were most unattainable.

"I'm sorry, but . . . I'd better go."

He nodded regretfully. He had misinterpreted her motives. She could tell by the slow but resolute way he rebuttoned her coat. He thought she wanted him too much to stay. She was sorry to have to leave it at that, but explanations would have to come later. She needed time to think.

He walked with her out of the house, to where her car was parked in his driveway. She had met him here before dinner, so that she could drive herself home. Only four or five hours ago, it had seemed so delicious, so illicit, to leave her car parked in the man's driveway, just in case. She had thought then that the date might not end until the following morning.

He tucked her into the front seat and gave her a kiss good-bye. It was a great kiss. But it left Eliza cold. She pulled out of the driveway. Tommy waved from the front porch. The glow of the porch light behind him created a halo effect around his head and shoulders, and tears came to her eyes. He looked like a dark angel.

The next day at work, MJ confirmed Eliza's suspicion that she had a serious psychological problem.

"You are ill, girl," were her secretary's exact words.

Eliza dropped her head into her hands. "I know," she said. "What's wrong with me?"

"We've covered all that," MJ snapped. "What's wrong with him? He is sex. He's as good looking as Denzel Washington, and *he's* not married."

"Denzel is married?" Rosa yelled from the other room. There was no mistaking the disappointment in her voice.

"Yes, darling, sorry," MJ called out to her. To Eliza, she said, "I thought everyone knew that."

Eliza couldn't summon even a hint of a smile. "I thought he was sexy." She pictured Tommy Greene, smiling, in the sexy black suit he'd worn last night. "I still think so."

"So, what are you talking about here?" MJ asked. "He has bad breath, sweaty palms, what?"

"When he kissed me, it was like . . . You know when you were ten and you got to kiss the cutest boy in school in a game of spin-the-bottle? Every girl's fantasy. A fairy tale. But here you were, trying not to look stupid in front of everyone—and you couldn't forget for a second that his girlfriend, who was the prettiest girl in the class, was sitting there next to you, watching.''

MJ was nodding, "I hated that. And when you stopped kissing, she smiled at you like she didn't have a care in the world.''

"That's not what I was talking about. It's the way you feel, like you know you should be really enjoying the kiss, but really it's just sort of painful.''

MJ grimaced sympathetically, but she joked, "We're ten now?''

"It was just the best example I could think of,'' Eliza said, shortly.

"You don't date enough, girl. That happened to me last week.''

"It did not, you've been with Robert for two years.''

"The week before that, then,'' MJ insisted.

"Something like this doesn't happen that often. You said yourself, men like Tommy don't grow on trees.''

"It happens often enough. When you're looking for a good man, beauty becomes more and more subjective. In the end, even the good part becomes a little iffy. You know what they say, you've got to kiss a lot of frogs to find a prince.''

"So, what did you do?'' Eliza asked. "When it happened.''

"Lost his phone number,'' her friend promptly responded.

"That's cruel. Tommy didn't do anything to me. He's the same sweet, gorgeous guy he's always been. I'm the one who's got the problem.''

"You could tell him. Maybe the two of you could work on it,'' MJ suggested. "It might even be fun.''

Even MJ didn't know how deep the problem ran. She could confide in her friend and colleague about most everything, but Eliza couldn't imagine baring that part of her soul, even to her closest friend. How could she tell anybody that she had a deep freeze where her heart should be?

Eliza shook her head. "I don't think so,'' she said. She lowered her head into her hands. MJ shrugged, at least momentarily out of advice for her. Eliza let her head fall forward even further, until it hit the desktop.

Hopelessly, she banged her head lightly against the wood. "Stupid, stupid, stupid," she chanted as her forehead connected again and again with the smooth, hard surface of the desk.

Chapter Eleven

Eliza spent the rest of the day thinking about Tommy, expecting him to call at any moment. To her relief, he never did, and so Eliza ended that Friday, as she had the night before, tossing and turning in her bed, going over the events of the previous evening again and again in her mind. She kept coming back to two impossible problems. The first and most perplexing dilemma was how to tell Thomas Greene he didn't turn her on. The second problem was his response to the situation with Sandy. She had hoped Tommy would help her. She hadn't realized how much she'd counted on that. But he'd made it clear that he thought Eliza should just present the girl with the facts.

She wouldn't have minded discussing it further, but she couldn't exactly dump him one minute, and then ask him to help her with her resident juvenile delinquent the next.

Saturday morning, she awoke resolved to put off the one problem in favor of the other, more pressing matter. She called Tommy's service and left a message explaining that she'd be preparing for Ely's court appearance all weekend and, as they were due in court Monday morning, she wouldn't have time to see him. At the earliest, out of familial loyalty if nothing else, Tommy probably wouldn't contact her until after court adjourned some time Monday. She'd bought herself a few days.

As for Sandy, Eliza decided to tackle the problem head on. She did it that Saturday morning, counting on the weekend which stretched out ahead of them to iron out any problems this discussion might raise between them. She made their meal—western omelettes, her grandmother's home fried potatoes, freshly squeezed orange juice, and coffee. She called Sandy, fixed two trays and brought them into the den, where she had already turned the radio to some nice bluesy music so Sandy wouldn't be tempted to turn on MTV.

"You know I like having you here, don't you?" she asked when they had both settled with their meals in front of them.

"Mmmm," Sandy grunted. Eliza attributed her young friend's noncommittal response to the huge mouthful of potatoes she'd just shoveled into her mouth and didn't take offense. Before continuing, she decided to wait for Sandy to take a breather. It was a bit of a wait. For such a little girl, she could really pack it in. She had inhaled half of the food on her tray before she stopped to take a sip of her coffee.

Eliza seized her opportunity. "But you do know that living here is not a permanent solution?"

"Yeah," Sandy said, contemplating the remainder of her omelette with a jaundiced eye. She picked up the salt shaker and liberally doused the contents of her plate, including not only the omelette and potatoes but also the toast and the orange slice which Eliza had used as a colorful garnish.

Eliza couldn't figure out if the action was a subtle protest. All she could do was ignore it. "We've got to figure out what to do next," she said. "I know you want to petition the court for emancipation, but in my professional opinion, they won't consider you as a prime applicant."

Sandy had resumed eating, but the hand holding her fork came to a halt midway between her chin and her mouth as she absorbed Eliza's statement.

She asked indignantly, "Why not? They know I can take care of myself. I did it before."

"The fact that you ran away and were not apprehended for

over a year is not a point in your favor. You were a truant, homeless panhandler and by the court's standards, that made you a criminal, not a responsible adult. I know how amazing it is that you were able to survive on the streets, but emancipation is a privilege which the court grants to kids who are top students, maybe working already, with a support system of friends or relatives who will be willing to help them adjust to living independently.''

Sandy ignored the last part of her sentence. She seized on the one part of the argument she could answer knowledgeably. ''It's legal to drop out of school, now I'm sixteen. I know lots of kids who did it.''

''You were only fourteen. It was not legal. Anyway, there are practical considerations to the policies. What kind of work can you get without a diploma?''

Sandy grimaced. ''What do they think? If I make it through high school, I'm gonna be a doctor? I'll be up for some minimum wage job at a fast-food joint, even if I do graduate high school.''

''Don't you see,'' Eliza said. ''That's exactly what they will be thinking. You are a ward of the state, and they want you to grow up to be a productive member of society. That's their responsibility.''

''They ain't doin' too good,'' Sandy said. ''They ain't prepared me for nothin' but whorin'. It's amazing I ain't already makin' my living on my back. I coulda done that easy, but I come here instead.''

''I'm glad,'' Eliza said sincerely.

''They got nothin' to offer me, so why won't they let me take care of myself? Lincoln freed the slaves, but just 'cause I'm a kid, I ain't got no rights. I know I ain't got no future, not even if my fosters wanted to adopt me or something, which they are not gonna do, even if they could get permission from Mom, who they ain't gonna find.''

''I know, I know,'' Eliza soothed. She was familiar with Sandy's frustration. She had often felt it herself. ''But at the risk of sounding like I'm on their side, which I swear I'm not, I have to say that I don't think you should be going it on your own right now. The Farbers really care about you, and I think they can help you." The girl bent her head over her plate. "No, Sandy, don't look away." Eliza waited until Sandy raised her eyes again before continuing. "I honestly think you belong with them."

To her surprise, Sandy didn't take offense at the remark. "The Farbers are okay. They're nice to me an' all. But they don't have a clue who I really am," Sandy said simply.

"Give them a chance to get to know you. And give yourself a chance, too," Eliza begged. "They have helped a lot of kids."

"No one as old as me, though."

"No. They usually take younger children. But they saw something in you that made them choose you. They did. And maybe they can make you see it, too."

"They just took me 'cause I'm a runt. I look a lot younger than I am. I even act a lot younger than I am sometimes. But," she said, tossing her head defiantly, "I'm no kid. I've done too many things even you don't know about." It was obviously a painful confession for Sandy, but Eliza thought it was a good first step. It was probably the closest the girl could come to saying that she was ashamed of what she had had to do to survive. If Sandy could only admit that she was frightened by the emotions evoked by the Farbers' caring attention, perhaps she would stop running. "Sometimes I feel older than you, or the Farbers, or anyone," Sandy said sadly.

Eliza well knew that it would take years of therapy, or at least a decent shot at life, to give this child back the ability to feel loved, and to feel worthy of it, but at least she could say, "I'm sorry, Sandy. I know you've seen a lot, and you've had to do things that you don't want to talk about, but we're not talking about the past now. We're talking about the future. And whether you believe it or not, you have as much of a right to a happy, normal life as anyone. You can make one for yourself. You could even go to college. And the Farbers can help."

Sandy sipped her coffee. "It's cold. I'm gonna warm this up in the microwave. Can I do you?"

Eliza hesitated a moment, not wanting Sandy to leave when they had come so far. By the time the girl came back from the kitchen, they could be right back where they started. The little progress they had made could be lost. But Sandy stood waiting. Eliza held out her coffee cup, wordlessly. At least that way she knew Sandy would be back.

Eliza had calculated wrong. When Sandy didn't return after a few minutes, she went into the kitchen and found nothing but the coffee cups, emptied, washed, and drying on the countertop. She took the steps upstairs, two at a time. Sandy's stuff was undisturbed, as far as she could tell, but the girl had disappeared.

Sandy returned that evening, late. She refused to say where she had been. Eliza tried probing her gently for answers, then demanding them, and finally, gave her uninvited houseguest an ultimatum: either she could talk to Eliza, or she could pack up and go back to the Farbers. She had twenty-four hours to make her decision. When even that didn't get a rise out of Sandy, Eliza ordered them a pizza and went to her room to sit on her bed and stare at herself in the mirror until the food arrived, trying to take comfort from the image of herself reflected there. She looked at herself objectively. Sure, the face that stared back at her was mature, but it was also quite attractive. And behind that high forehead was the brain of a very capable lawyer. That woman would not be bowed by the system or by her own frustration.

Sandy was no more communicative over dinner than she had been a half hour before. At least her appetite did not seem to have suffered as a result of their confrontation. She ate half of the large pizza and drank a glass each of milk and leftover orange juice. Eliza didn't subscribe to the theory that foods like liver and brussels sprouts tasted so foul that they had to be good for you. Pizza was a satisfying meal in and of itself, and according to an article she read once, it had all the nutrition of a complete meal. Her "parental" duties discharged, all Eliza had to do was find a way to get through to her before Sandy either ran away again or slipped through the cracks of the social welfare system permanently.

The next morning, she was still being subjected to the silent treatment. Eliza reminded her of the evening's deadline and left her alone.

At ten o'clock, Ely called. "Jessie and I are going on a picnic. Would you like to join us?" he asked.

"I don't know if I can get away," Eliza answered, tempted.

"Not to discuss the case, or tomorrow, or anything, unless you want to. I just thought maybe you'd like to recharge your batteries with us before you fight for us in court."

"I don't know if this is such a good idea," Eliza said, but there wasn't a lot of conviction to the protest.

"If you've got something else you need to do, like vacuum the house or clean the bathroom, Jessie and I will do it for you. We'd love to."

"Oh, right," Eliza said, but she was weakening.

"Or if you still have something to do for tomorrow, maybe I can help, type something or whatever. Iron your clothes? It's Sunday, and we'll have you home by two, three at the latest. Even God took one day off."

"I don't know." Eliza debated internally. What if Sandy disappeared again?

"It's the perfect opportunity to see the two of us in our natural setting. Maybe it will inspire you, give you more ammunition to use in court." When Eliza didn't answer, he added, "Look, Jessie really wants you to come with us, to say nothing of me. Please don't say no," he cajoled.

That decided it. Eliza wasn't anyone's warden, and she deserved this. She hadn't been on a picnic in years. *Besides,* her conscience nagged, *you can't disappoint that sweet little boy.* She knew Ely was manipulating her, but it was with the best of intentions.

"Okay," she agreed. "When and where?"

Before she left, she went to the guest room and told Sandy. "Ely Greene and his son, Jessie, have invited me to a picnic in Grant Park. I'm sure you are welcome to join us."

"No, thanks," Sandy said. Eliza thought she saw a flash of an emotion, pain perhaps, in the girl's eyes, but it was gone before she could categorize it.

"I can stay if you think you might want to talk," Eliza offered.

"I have till tonight," Sandy answered gruffly. Eliza didn't know if she was being strung along or not, but didn't see that she had any choice. She refused to stand guard over the girl, even if that was what she should do. The next move had to be Sandy's.

"I'll be back by four at the latest."

She turned to leave, but didn't quite make it to the door before she turned back to look at her housemate. "Sandy?"

"Ummm?" Sandy didn't look up.

"Please don't leave." Sandy's angry eyes met hers. That other emotion she'd glimpsed was there somewhere, too. Could it be jealousy? Eliza dismissed the idea. The teenager couldn't begrudge her a picnic in the park. Besides, Sandy had turned down the invitation to join them. "Okay?" Eliza pressed for an answer.

"All right, all right," Sandy said.

It would have to do.

Eliza met the Greenes, father and son, exactly at noon, at the entrance to the park. They walked past the jogging path, on their way to the picnic area. They watched as the young men and women traveled around and around the track, and Eliza felt a twinge of guilt about her sedentary lifestyle, as she often did when she was reminded of the current exercise craze. There were others watching the joggers, as well. They passed a group of young men loitering at one end of the field, rating the women. Eliza grimaced as their comments became louder as one particularly well-built young woman passed by.

She shot a surreptitious look at Ely and Jessie. The boy seemed oblivious to the fracas. Ely looked from the young men, to the young woman—who had to be about the same age he was—and then looked at Eliza consideringly.

"You've got better legs," he said finally.

The boost to her ego was just what she needed, Eliza decided, and so she didn't take him to task for the sexist comment.

"So, aren't you going to say something about me?" he asked.

"Fishing for compliments?" She laughed.

"I hope so. I mean, it would be nice." He pointed at a very muscular guy, whose breasts, Eliza would have been willing to swear, were bigger than her own. "How do I compare to him?"

"Favorably," she said.

He nodded. "Do you really mean it? I could work on beefing up a little, if you prefer that type."

"No, no. He looks like an ape. You look . . . good," Eliza said, suddenly embarassed.

"Thank goodness," Ely said, letting out his breath with an exaggerated whooshing sound. "I would have done it, but I would have hated it."

"You don't like lifting weights?"

"Not all day and night. And you should see what those guys *eat!*"

"Speaking of food, what have you got in there?" she asked as he spread a large red and white tablecloth on the ground.

"You'll see," he said, opening the food containers and presenting them for her inspection. The boys had brought a bucket of fried chicken, biscuits, and potato salad from a take-out joint, but Ely had also filled two large Tupperware bins with fresh vegetables and fruit.

"Okay?" Ely asked. When she gave an approving nod, he started serving the food. "Pure cholesterol for the young at heart, and cholesterol demolishers for the old folk," Ely said. She suspected he'd included himself in the second category, even though he was twelve years her junior, just barely closer to her age than to his son's. But Eliza refused to think about being old today. She felt rather carefree, for a change. She wasn't going to let one chance remark ruin it. It wasn't like she and Ely were on a date. She spent enough time worrying about her age when she was with Tommy. She refused to let such morbid considerations ruin this innocent family outing.

They all sat down and proceeded to eat. *Norman Rockwell would have loved this scene,* Eliza thought as the tension ebbed from its favorite lodging places in her neck and shoulders.

Jessie had kept up a steady stream of conversation since he'd eaten his first bite of potato salad. "I hate the Power Rangers," he said as he started on his chicken. "Have you ever seen them?"

"I think so," Eliza said. "But I don't watch a lot of television. All of my friends' kids wanted to be Power Rangers for Halloween, so that's when I found out about them."

She smiled as she thought of it. Her old friend Stephanie hated the program, but her kids loved it. She had forced Eliza to watch part of an episode and wouldn't turn off the television until Eliza had agreed the show was banal and annoying. Eliza had understood. Stephanie just wanted someone to be on her side.

"The whole show looks phony, like those old Japanese monster movies."

"Oh, yeah." Eliza hadn't made that connection, but she laughed. "These big Godzilla feet smash those fake little towns, and you can't possibly be scared."

"There's computer animation now, and everything. But the Mighty Morphins are so lame! Everything about them is sad. Especially the fight scenes."

"I know." Eliza shook her head.

"I take karate, and you can tell those guys do, too, but the scenes where they're doing karate are so stupid. I used to like the Teenage Mutant Ninja Turtles, but I'm older now, and that stuff isn't real at all."

"Do you like karate movies?" she asked Jessie.

"Some of them. *Kickboxer* was a classic. At least, the first one was. Van Damme can fight. And Seagal does some good movies."

Eliza grimaced. "Too violent for me. The karate's okay, I guess, but all the guns and bombs are annoying."

"But they're about real stuff anyway, like the environment and stuff."

"Do you think so?" Eliza shook her head. "I haven't seen that many, but I don't like what they say, even about karate. They act like we invented it, and they're always saying Americans are the best. Do you believe that?"

"*Best of the Best* was based on a true story. That was about when the American team beat the Koreans for the world championship.''

"I saw that one. They made all the Koreans, except one Korean American, into these brain-dead, psycho killers. I don't think that was the true story. Even if it was, which I really think is impossible, they didn't show any good Koreans in that movie, and I know that there are lots of good people in Korea.''

"Of course.'' Jessie looked shocked. "It's a whole country. And they're great at karate. It's not just about fighting. Karate is a way of life, like . . . I don't know, like church or something,'' he said.

"So, doesn't that bother you, when you see those movies?''

"No. Because I know it's just a story.''

"But you just said *Best of the Best* was true.''

"Just the fighting parts. Those are cool, and I bet they did them just the same as in the real fights.''

"I guess I know what you mean,'' Eliza agreed. "I used to like this show called *Kung Fu* when I was a kid.''

"I've seen it,'' Jessie said. "You really liked it?'' he asked in disbelief.

"I thought it was great. I can't believe it's back on.''

"It is,'' Ely joined in. "I've watched it with Jessie a couple of times. He thinks it's boring.''

"It's okay. But it's so slow.''

"I admit it's silly,'' Eliza said. "But at least he had a positive message about Eastern culture. Those other guys, Norris, Seagal, and Van Damme are always great 'white' fighters, defending America from the yellow hordes.'' Jessie looked perplexed. "I mean, it's just that I think the movies are prejudiced.''

"Oh,'' he said, nodding. "But what isn't?'' he asked, matter-of-fact.

"Don't say that,'' Eliza said. "You're only eight. You can't be a cynic.''

"What's a cynic?'' Jessie asked, looking from her to Ely.

"Someone who thinks everything is screwed up,'' his father answered briefly. "They think there's no point to anything because nothing will ever change.''

Jessie thought about that for a moment. "I'm not one of those, then. I think it's all gonna change."

"That's a relief," Eliza said.

"Sure. Things that are stupid have to change," Jessie said with conviction. "Lots of things are changing all the time. Even karate movies have different kinds of phases. Like *The Karate Kid.* They're still making rip-offs of that."

"I loved that movie," Eliza said.

"It was pretty good," Jessie said guardedly.

Ely rolled his eyes. "Everyone's a critic."

"If they're going to do karate competitions, then why don't they just do the real thing. Those are the best!"

"Have you ever gone to one?" Eliza asked.

"Not yet," Jessie said. "But I've seen them on TV lots of times. Why? Have you?"

"Yeah," Eliza said. When Jessie looked at her with new-found admiration, she explained. "I have some friends who used to compete."

"Wow! You're lucky."

"Luckier than them. They've had broken wrists, arms, twisted knees, lots of injuries." Jessie's expression made it clear he did not share Eliza's feeling that this was a downside to the sport. "I agree with you, though," she admitted, "the live fights are better than any movie version."

"I bet!" he said enthusiastically.

Eliza felt like the office, Sandy, even Tommy, were a million miles away. This was just what she had needed. She had been transported from the world she inhabited to this magical place where the sun shone on a population almost completely composed of children who ran and played without a care in the world. She could almost imagine herself one of them.

Jessie ate even more than Sandy, but he talked nonstop. "My favorite subject is science, and I'm going to be an astronaut when I grow up," he stated.

"That's good," Eliza said.

"I thought you probably wanted to know that, being a grown-up and all. Even if you didn't ask me last time."

"Thanks," she said sincerely. "It's good to know these things."

"Why do grown-ups always ask that?" Jessie asked, seriously. The question, and the tone in which it had been asked, made Eliza feel as if she had been accepted by this child as someone he could confide in, a trusted advisor, rather than just another one of the grown-ups he referred to.

She considered carefully before answering. "I guess because it's something other adults asked them when they were kids."

"Oh." Jessie seemed content with her answer.

"So, how long have you known you wanted to be an astronaut?" Eliza asked.

"Since I was a little kid," Jessie said.

Ely smiled. "He has the Milky Way and the constellations painted on the ceiling of his room," he said.

"They painted it when I was a baby," his son reported. "It's still in good shape, too. Only there's one sort of big crack in it, but that's right where Orion's sword would be, if he really had one, so it's no problem."

"I didn't notice." Eliza had taken a quick look at Jessie's room on her second visit to their apartment, but she must have neglected to look up. She remembered a collection of dinosaurs, a shelf full of board games, a childish suite of furniture built into and around a bunk bed, and a lot of books. She'd noticed, also, baseball paraphernalia and a soccer ball.

"What sports do you play?" she asked, since Jessie seemed athletically inclined.

"All of them," Ely answered for him. "He's a natural athlete."

"Good." She addressed the comment to Jessie. "Astronauts have to be in great physical shape."

"They also have to be good at math," Ely said, looking pointedly at Jessie.

"I said I'd work on it," Jessie said indignantly. Clearly, this was the subject of an ongoing debate.

Ely raised his arms in surrender. "Okay, okay. I'm sorry. I couldn't resist."

"You should have," Eliza chastized. "It's nice and peaceful here. No nagging allowed."

Jessie shot his father a triumphant look. "Do you want some more lemonade?" he asked Eliza solicitously.

"No, thank you, I'm stuffed. You boys sure know how to host a picnic."

"I told you she'd like fried chicken from KFC better than sandwiches."

"No nagging includes I-told-you-so's," Ely said.

"Okay," Jessie said, flopping down onto his stomach and regarding Eliza curiously. "Do you like sports?" he asked.

"Sure, but I'm out of practice." Eliza calculated quickly, and realized she hadn't played a team sport since she left high school over twenty-some years ago. That was not a fact that she was going to pass on to Jessie. It would be inconceivable to an eight-year-old. It was difficult enough for her to believe it.

"How about Frisbee? I brought one with us."

"Huh? Oh, sure, but not right now. Maybe later." Eliza couldn't even remember the last time she'd tossed a Frisbee around. At least it was during her adult life, though.

"Before you do anything else, please take this trash to the can over there," Ely said. "And let us digest our meal."

"Okay, I'll do my kata," Jessie said, jumping to his feet.

"Good idea," his father approved, but the kid was already walking away.

After he threw out the used paper plates, utensils and wrappings from their meal, he chose a level spot about halfway between their picnic blanket and the garbage can. Eliza watched as he started a complicated series of karate exercises.

"He's really advanced for his age, isn't he?" she asked.

"His teacher says he's a natural," Ely said proudly.

"I wasn't. I felt like an idiot. I really liked it, though."

"You study karate?" he asked, unsurprised.

"Not anymore. You?"

"I did take a few lessons when Jessie started, so I'd have some idea of what he was talking about. I didn't have the time to keep going to classes. He's a yellow belt already. I'll never catch up with him now.''

"But you can help him with his math," Eliza consoled him.

"Yeah." Ely smiled ruefully. "Unfortunately, that's not the kind of thing a second grader really appreciates."

"Don't you believe it," Eliza said. "He thinks you hung the moon."

Ely chuckled. "For now," he said gruffly.

"Don't knock it," Eliza advised.

"I know how lucky I am," he said seriously. "Every time I look at him, I'm reminded of it." He stretched out on his side, beside her, one hand under his head, watching his son. "It's hard to believe he's mine. He's so much his own person," he said, looking up at her.

Eliza looked from Ely, who lay on her right, to the boy shadowboxing on her left. *This was how it might feel to have a normal home and family, instead of a way station for runaways,* she thought. She looked down affectionately at the man who lay beside her. Of course, she'd dress Ely differently.

He was wearing jeans that were much too big for him. They sagged in all the wrong places, rather than showing off his natural attributes. His puce shirt was shiny from many washings, and over it he wore a ratty old cardigan of a nauseating yellow shade that did nothing for him. Eliza hadn't exactly dressed up in her finest clothes for a day in the park, but her sky-blue slacks were tailored cotton, and her white shirt and warm pink sweater were both practical and attractive. Even Jessie's navy sweats with red piping and his matching windbreaker were more flattering to the boy's dark complexion and muscular little body than his father's clothing was to him.

Jessie finished his routine and strode back to their picnic blanket, panting. Eliza applauded until he gave a quick, embarassed bow. He dropped to the ground and sprawled out at her feet.

"You're looking good, Jess," his father praised him.

"I've got to stretch more, get my kicks up higher," the boy said.

"Do you have girls in your class?" Eliza asked.

"Sure," Jessie said, somewhat surprised by the question.

"When I took karate lessons, it wasn't as popular as it is now. I was the only girl in my class. Hardly any guys took it, either."

"Here in the states," Jessie corrected.

"You're right. It has taken a while for karate to become so well-known here in the states," Eliza said wryly. "In the Far East, kids have been taking lessons for generations. Touché." She laughed. He was such a bright kid. "What I was going to say was, when I started studying karate, my kicks were my best thing. Because of ballet and all that, I could get up high."

"So, you want to take ballet, Jess?" Ely teased his son.

"No, I'll just keep stretching," he said with a grin. "Do you still study?" he asked Eliza.

"No. I lasted only about a year. It taught me some stuff I still use today, though. Like when I walk down a street, I'm very aware of where I am in relation to everything around me. Our teacher was really good, and that was like our homework. One time we had to concentrate on walking in the exact middle of the sidewalk for a month."

"I'll try that," Jessie said.

"I sort of got into the habit. And another funny thing. If I walk down the street by a wall or a hedge, I always have to land on my outside foot at the end of the thing obstructing my vision, so if someone jumped out at me, I could kick out at them instantly. I don't even know if I could actually kick anybody, but it's weird how I still think about it years later."

Jessie was nodding. "Our sensei makes us do things like that, too." He opened the container of chicken and fished around until he found a leg. When he looked up and found Ely and Eliza staring at him, he offered them the bucket.

"No, thanks," Eliza said.

"You're going to eat again?" his father asked him.

"Just this piece," Jessie said, recovering the box and taking a napkin. "I guess that means you guys are still digesting?"

"Yeah," Ely answered. "I guess it does."

"I'm gonna go take a look around, okay?"

"Sure, knock yourself out," was Ely's dispassionate response.

They watched him walk away.

"I can't believe he can eat after that workout," Eliza said, amazed.

Jessie came bounding back before Ely could answer her. "Dad, they're getting up a soccer game in the field. Can I play?"

"How old are these kids?" Ely asked.

"Some are bigger than me, but Shawn Wilson and his mom and dad are there, and he's playing."

"Okay." Ely checked his watch. "Forty-five minutes, that's all. We've got to get Ms. Taylor home." Jessie took off like he'd been shot out of a cannon. "I'm coming to get you at one forty-five," Ely shouted after him.

Ely dropped his elbow to lie flat on the blanket beside her. Eliza spread her legs out straight in front of her and leaned back on her elbows. She let her head drop back, enjoying the sun on her face. The silence between them was a companionable one. She closed her eyes, completely relaxed. She couldn't remember feeling this comfortable with anyone in a long time. Casting her mind back, she realized she could never remember feeling *this* serene with anyone at all.

"Eliza?" Ely murmured.

"Yes?" She opened her eyes and looked down at him. He was lying full length on his side, his head, pillowed on his arm, a few inches from her hip.

"Just checking," he said. "I can't believe you're here."

"Me, either," she said, leaning her head back and closing her eyes again.

Chapter Twelve

Ely didn't speak again for a long time. Eliza thought he might have fallen asleep.

When suddenly he did speak, she had relaxed so completely she was surprised by his voice.

"You're obviously very good at what you do," he said. Eliza sensed a "but" was coming. She waited for it. "But you're so busy. When do you find the time to enjoy it?" he asked.

She didn't open her eyes. "Enjoy what? My work? All the time. That's *why* I'm so busy."

"That's not what I meant. What about when you're not working?"

"I'm always working." Eliza laughed. "But I do it because I like it. Even when I'm up to my neck in paperwork, I wouldn't choose to do anything else."

"That's what you do, but that's not life," Ely said.

Inwardly, Eliza groaned. Just what she needed. A lecture on stopping and smelling the roses. And she wasn't even dating this guy.

"It's just as important to enjoy the things that are real. Jessie is a constant reminder for me."

Bully for you, Eliza thought, but she didn't say it aloud. Below her annoyance, she felt a pang of sorrow. She had known for a long time that she would probably never have a normal life with a hubby and kids to come home to. She was too closed off, like a prisoner in isolation. She hadn't chosen it. She didn't want to feel shut off from the rest of the world. But with Thursday night's encounter with Tommy still fresh in her mind, she had no choice but to accept the way she was.

Long ago, her soft heart had been buried deep inside her somewhere, and it would take a miracle, an earthquake on a phenomenal scale, to raise it up again. Occasionally, some stray emotion impacted on the tomb that housed the organ, as on the day she'd attended David Paron's funeral. The tiny angel on the coffin had done it then, sent a stake straight through her flesh and deep into the pit of her stomach, pinging against the stone that entombed her heart.

Ely's casual comment should have been deflected by the same impenetrable wall that had stopped her from falling for Tommy. It must have been this false sense of peace, after the havoc of the last couple of weeks, and especially the last few days, that allowed his arrow to find the mark.

"Ease off, Professor," she warned, keeping her tone light and playful. "We're not in the schoolroom. No lectures, please."

"Sorry," he said immediately.

A tear found its way from behind her closed eyelid and slid down the side of her face. First Sandy and now this. But she refused to give in to self-pity. Her life was full and complete. More importantly, if she had a so-called normal life, where would kids like Sandy go when the system failed them.

"We've got to talk about *something,*" Ely said. "I'm going to fall asleep."

"So, sleep." Eliza didn't want to talk. She just wanted to listen to the leaves rustling in the trees and the distant shouts of children. Why shouldn't the afternoon continue as it had begun? She was enjoying the peaceful, calm quiet.

"You smell good," he said. The simple comment disturbed her. She wanted to absorb the sunlight into her skin, lose herself in the sweet smell of freshly grown grass, watch the leaves flicker playfully in the light spring breeze. She raised an eyelid. Ely's eyes were still closed. Perhaps he'd give up if she didn't say anything.

"What's that perfume you're wearing?" he asked. Eliza sighed. He wasn't going to quit. So much for relaxation.

If he wanted to wake up, she'd wake him up. Carefully, she reached over his legs and dipped her fingers into his glass of lemonade.

"You really want to wake up?" Something in her voice must have alerted him. His eyes flashed open. Too late.

He looked up in alarm at her sitting over him, but before he could move, she dropped the sliver of ice she'd taken from his drink down the back of his shirt.

"What the—?!" he spluttered, rolling up into a sitting position and pulling his shirt from the waistband of his jeans. He tried, unsuccessfully, to shake the ice out. Eliza laughed as he twisted and turned and tried to get his hand up the back of his shirt.

It melted before he could get it.

"It was just a tiny sliver," she said, her voice still quivering with laughter.

"Thought that was funny, did you?" he asked.

"It woke you up," she stated.

"I was hoping for stimulating *conversation,*" he said. "But if you want to play games . . ."

"No, no," Eliza said. "I'd love to talk."

"It's a little late for that," he said. "Let's see if you're ticklish." He grasped her ankle in his hand and started to untie her tennis shoe.

"Stop that," Eliza said, trying to pull her foot out of his grasp. He was too strong for her. He pulled off her shoe and sock and took his time deliberately plucking a thick stalk of grass from the ground.

Eliza was very ticklish. "Truce!" she cried.

"Truce?" He held the blade of grass an inch from her toes.

"Truce." She offered her hand.

He released her leg and took the proffered hand. "Chicken," he taunted. "You can dish it out, but you can't take it."

"Why should I?" Eliza asked, tossing her head. "I have nothing to prove."

"Ha!"

He still held her hand in his. "Your fingers are so slim." He traced an invisible line from the ball of her thumb to the tip of her middle finger, then back again.

"My hands are pretty big. Almost like a man's hands," she said. A shiver ran up her arm.

He held her hand up and put his up against it. "Mine is a man's hand. Yours is just a little thing." He curled her fingers into her palm, making a fist.

"What are you doing?" Eliza asked.

"Nothing," Ely said. But when she thought he would let her go, he picked up her other hand from her lap and held her two hands between his much larger ones. His fingertips brushed the backs of her wrists. "My hands are bigger than Tommy's," he said.

"Oh?" Eliza suddenly realized she hadn't thought of Tommy much that afternoon. Not much at all. It was sort of odd, given that Ely and Jessie both looked a lot like him. She would have expected to have thought of him sooner than this.

"He has small hands for a man his size. They're . . . delicate, almost." Ely held her hand up to his again. "They're bigger than yours, though."

"I never noticed," Eliza lied. She had definitely taken an interest in Tommy's hands. She had thought they looked like the hands of an artist. You could never tell from Ely's hands that he was a scholar. His palms were calloused and a little rough, like a laborer's.

"We're not much alike," Ely said. He interlaced his fingers with hers.

Eliza looked from their hands to his face. "What?"

"Tommy and I are very different, don't you think?" he asked.

"What are you trying to do?" she asked.

"Confuse you," he answered promptly.

"What?" Eliza squawked.

"I'm trying to confuse you," he said slowly and deliberately.

"Because I can't seem to say two sentences around you without sticking my foot in my mouth. I act like an idiot whenever you're around. I thought I'd try mixing it up a little. Take a less direct approach."

"Approach to what?" Eliza asked, uncomprehending.

"I really want to kiss you again," he said. "And I didn't think you'd approve."

"You're right," she said, but even to her own ears, the words lacked conviction.

"You're dating my brother, you're working with me. It would be totally out of character for you to say anything else. That's why I had to distract you." He raised their hands up between them. Their fingers were still intertwined, his palms flat against hers.

He had tricked her. She felt the first stirring of fear as he said, "What else could I do? You're my hero. And I was desperate."

"Maybe we should talk about tomorrow," Eliza suggested.

"What about it?" Ely asked. He was starting again. That intent gaze mesmerized her.

"Court?" She waited for him to say the words that would send her flying away from him.

Instead he echoed her. "Court?"

His thumb moved back and forth over her wrist. She was afraid he'd feel her pulse racing, and she tried to tug her hand out of his grasp, but that just brought him closer.

"We'll be appearing," she said, in a breathless little voice that didn't sound at all like her.

"I know. I bought a new suit. Just for you."

"Not for me, for the judge," she managed to say.

"For you, and for the judge." Her eyes were drawn to his mouth, and she couldn't tear them away.

"We have to be clearheaded in court," she said, talking to herself as much as to him.

"I know. You told me. I'll be cool."

"Not you, me. This is important. We shouldn't—" She stopped rambling, tried to gather her thoughts. "I have to focus

WE INVITE YOU TO JOIN THE ONLY BOOK CLUB THAT DELIVERS HEARTFELT ROMANCE FEATURING AFRICAN AMERICAN HEROES AND HEROINES IN STORIES THAT ARE RICH IN PASSION AND CULTURAL SPICE...

And Your First 4 Books Are FREE!

Arabesque is the newest contemporary romance line offered by Pinnacle Books. Arabesque has been so successful that our readers have asked us about direct home delivery. We responded to your requests. You can start receiving four bestselling Arabesque novels a month delivered right to your door. Subscribe now and you'll get:

◇ 4 FREE Arabesque romances as our introductory gift—a value of almost $20! (pay only $1 to help cover postage & handling)
◇ 4 BRAND-NEW Arabesque romances delivered to your doorstep each month thereafter (usually arriving before they're available in bookstores!)
◇ 20% off each title—a savings of almost $4.00 each month
◇ FREE home delivery
◇ A FREE monthly newsletter. *Zebra/Pinnacle Romance News* that features author profiles, book previews and more
◇ No risks or obligations...in other words, you can cancel whenever you wish with no questions asked

So subscribe to Arabesque today and see why these books are winning awards and readers' hearts.

After you've enjoyed our FREE gift of 4 Arabesques, you'll begin to receive monthly shipments of the newest Arabesque titles. Each shipment will be yours to examine for 10 days. If you decide to keep the books, you'll pay the preferred subscriber's price of just $4.00 per title. That's $16 for all 4 books with FREE home delivery! And if you want us to stop sending books, just say the word...it's that simple.

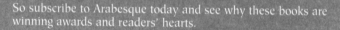

See why reviewers are raving about ARABESQUE and order your FREE books today!

WE HAVE 4 FREE BOOKS FOR YOU!

FREE BOOK CERTIFICATE

Yes! Please send me 4 *Arabesque* Contemporary Romances without cost or obligation, billing me just $1 to help cover postage and handling. I understand that each month, I will be able to preview 4 brand-new *Arabesque* Contemporary Romances FREE for 10 days. Then, if I decide to keep them, I will pay the money-saving preferred subscriber's price of just $16.00 for all 4...that's a savings of almost $4 off the publisher's price with no additional charge for shipping and handling. I may return any shipment within 10 days and owe nothing, and I may cancel this subscription at any time. My 4 FREE books will be mine to keep in any case.

Name _____

Address _____ Apt. _____

City _____ State _____ Zip _____

Telephone ( ) _____

Signature _____ AR0698

(If under 18, parent or guardian must sign.)

Terms and prices subject to change. Orders subject to acceptance by Zebra Home Subscription Service, Inc. .
Zebra Home Subscription Service, Inc. reserves the right to reject or cancel any subscription.

on what's directly ahead. And so do you. Otherwise, all our work will be for nothing.''

"This is the most important thing I've ever done. Jessie's happiness means everything to me. But that's tomorrow.''

A gentle tug of her hand was all it took for him to bridge the little distance that separated them. When his lips touched hers, Eliza's fear vanished beneath a wave of passion. She had relived that first kiss so many times, but she hadn't remembered this velvety texture, this sensual rush. It was just as shocking as the first time.

This fumbling, bumbling, ridiculous man could really kiss.

It was sheer joy, just like the first time. Desire coursed through her. Eliza fell into the tide of pleasure mindlessly. She was pure sensation; every pore in her body screamed for more. This was what she had missed when Tommy kissed her, this overpowering sense of need, this compulsion to be even closer, to feel the heat and scent of him on her skin. She was barely aware of their surroundings. Eliza struggled to remember that they lay on a blanket, under the open sky, where anyone could see them. It didn't matter.

His kisses enthralled her. Her hands were drawn to his face. She touched his jaw, stroked his cheek. One hand stole behind his head, and she tangled her fingers in his soft, kinky curls. His lips left her mouth, and his head dropped down as he tried to catch his breath. She pulled his head back up, her hands at the nape of his neck, and sought blindly for his lips.

She couldn't get enough of the feel of him, the taste of him. He pulled away, and she stared at him in amazement. Sanity slowly returned. She'd gone from complete disinterest to sensual oblivion in ten seconds flat. How had he done that to her?

His face swam before her eyes. Eliza blinked. Her vision cleared. "Oh, my," she said.

Ely looked as astonished as she felt. "Wow," he breathed, his eyes searching her face, his expression bewildered. Slowly, those luscious lips curved into a smile. "You are good at *everything* you do."

Eliza broke away from his intense gaze. She had completely lost control of herself. "What time is it?" she asked.

"Half past one," Ely answered. "Why?"

"I just thought it might be time to collect your son," she said. "And it is."

"Not quite yet. We need to talk about what just happened."

"There is nothing to say," Eliza said. "It was a mistake." She started to pack up the last few things in the picnic basket. When Ely didn't move, she reminded him. "You told him one forty-five."

"We've got a few minutes," Ely said. "What do you mean, there's nothing to say?" He took the picnic basket from her nerveless fingers.

"Which word didn't you understand?" Eliza said testily. She picked up the checkered cloth and shook it out.

"You have nothing to say?" He shook his head in disbelief. "Well, I do. That was fantastic. It was incredible."

"Great," Eliza muttered. "It was the perfect kiss. Now forget it," she said more forcefully.

"How can I just forget it?" he asked. "I want to do it again."

"Well, we can't. It should never have happened." Eliza finished folding the blanket and stood looking at the ground, over his shoulder in the direction Jessie had gone, up at the sky, anywhere but at Ely. He closed the distance between them, took the blanket from her, and set it on top of the basket beside them.

"What are you afraid of?" he asked.

Eliza clamped her mouth shut. She refused to have this conversation. There was no point to it. Nothing could come of that kiss. And he knew that.

He reached out as though to put his hands on her shoulders, and Eliza stepped back. She hated to act so cold, but she couldn't help herself.

"Don't," she ordered. "Ely, you said it yourself. I'm your lawyer. I can't get personally involved. This was not a good idea."

"It might not have been smart. But it turned out to be a great idea." He stepped toward her again.

She said hastily, "I'm seeing your brother." He looked as

if she had struck him. Ironically, Tommy's kisses didn't move her at all, while Ely's had awakened her sleeping heart. But he didn't know that. He didn't know that that long-dead organ was aching at the thought of never touching him again. And he couldn't know. It was too frightening. If a simple kiss could cause this kind of turmoil, Eliza shuddered to imagine the damage that might be the result of a deeper relationship with Ely Greene.

Jessie couldn't help noticing Dad and Eliza were very quiet as they walked her to her car. Something must have happened, because when he had left them to go play soccer, they had been smiling and laughing, and now they looked real serious. When they ate lunch, he was sure they had both been in a good mood—he'd noticed because neither of them had looked that happy before. Now, they didn't even say good-bye.

He and Dad watched her drive away, and Daddy sighed as they turned to go back to the Chevy. Jessie didn't ask any questions. He could always tell when Dad was depressed, and he tried not to pester him then. When they got home, he turned on the TV while Dad put away the picnic stuff. He did some channel surfing, but there was nothing good on.

"Stop that, please." His father's voice sounded sad, so Jessie put the remote down right away. A minute later, he wished he hadn't. The Power Rangers were on. They were the worst. He would have turned the TV off, but he left it on because if he did turn the television off, his house would be too quiet. That was how it always was when Daddy was thinking sad thoughts.

It didn't happen too often, maybe around Christmas when he was little, but lately, since the fight with Grandma Rebecca started, his father sometimes couldn't keep his spirits up. Usually, after Daddy talked to Eliza, he felt better. So it had to be really bad news this time, because they had just spent most of the day with their lawyer, and Dad was sadder than ever.

Jessie wished there was something he could do to help. He knew from past experience, though, that he just had to wait it out. When it was over, his father would be extra happy and in the mood to celebrate. Meanwhile, at least the Mighty Morphin Power Rangers were loud and colorful. He watched, disgusted, as they shouted the words that turned them into ninja characters. Jessie was pretty sure they wore the ninja suits to hide their faces, so people wouldn't know it wasn't the actors doing the karate, but stunt men.

His mind drifted back to the conversation with Eliza. She was too cool. She had taken karate herself, when she was in college, before she knew Dad. Better yet, she had some friends who competed. She could take him to an exhibition. He would ask her later, and maybe talk to her about his father. She must know what it was that was upsetting him. But he didn't know whether he should ask her about that. He'd have to play it by ear. Jessie hoped this didn't mean that something had gone wrong with their case.

Eliza didn't have time to think about Ely once she arrived at home. Sandy was waiting for her.

"I coulda gone if I wanted to," were the first words out of her mouth when Eliza walked into the kitchen. The teenager was obviously spoiling for a fight.

"I'm glad you didn't," Eliza said calmly. "Do you want to talk?"

"No," Sandy said. "I'm just sayin' I can go and come when I want, and I'd like to go back to the Farbers in two more weeks." She hesitated before adding, in a slightly less defiant tone, "If they'll let me."

"I know for a fact that they're looking forward to it. They wanted you to come home sooner. But I'm glad you've stayed, and I'm looking forward to having you here a little longer." Surprisingly enough, it was perfectly true. Eliza thought she might even miss the brat if she weren't around.

Sandy, true to form, flounced off without another word to the living room, where seconds later, the sounds of MTV reverberated through the walls. Eliza went up to her room and sank onto her bed. She toed off her tennis shoes, and lay back, her forearms over her eyes. She was completely exhausted.

She woke up at 2 A.M. lying just as she'd fallen—fully dressed, legs still dangling over the edge of the bed, feet on the floor. She was tempted to get up and get some work done. Her mind was going at a million miles a minute.

She could go over the notes on Ely's case. But there was nothing more to be done, really. She had gone over all of the information and organized her arguments as much as possible. There was no point in writing out any kind of statement because she'd have to respond directly to the Tysons' accusations. It was better not to be married to any one line of reasoning until Rod Daniels presented his case, and she could see how the judge responded, and which issues seemed to concern him most. It would be better to be alert, on her toes, ready for any surprises Mr. Daniels might have up his sleeve.

Sleep was the best preparation for the next morning's activities, but Eliza did not think she could manage it. The deep, dreamless state of unconsciousness from which she'd just been roused was unusual, and the direct result of the shocks she'd suffered in the past few days. Her body and brain had shut down. This hyperactive state of mind was her natural response to the stress she'd been under. She'd been here before. But never had she felt so completely adrift, as if a windstorm had swept through a lifetime of paperwork and sent thousands of pages up to the sky to come tumbling down in disarray.

Sandy. Tommy. Ely! Her relationships with all of them left her feeling confused, out of her depth. One she might have managed, but three at once was beyond her.

She tried to figure out when everything had spun so far out her control. That first night at the Apollo Grille with the Greene brothers had certainly had an impact on her, but she thought she had learned her lesson. She had resolved not to let herself be drawn into the deceptively attractive sphere of these two handsome, vibrant men. She had decided not to let her guard down again. Why hadn't it worked?

And she'd known Sandy for two years, had fought with her and for her as passionately before as she had at any time this past month. When she had met the girl and taken her on as a client, Sandy had been in much more dire straits. Eliza had, then as always, rushed into the fray, and emerged again unaffected. Why, now, did the girl's pain threaten to overwhelm her?

She had to stop thinking this way, she told herself. She was not completely powerless in this situation. She knew what she had to do. She would have Sandy settled in with the Farbers in two weeks. She only had to hold on until then and maybe try to mend a few fences. And she'd tell Tommy, when he called, that it was over between them. It was the only solution. She'd come up with an excuse that wouldn't hurt his feelings or his pride. It was unlikely he'd even question her decision. What could she mean to him, after all? They had had a couple of weeks together, after twelve years of no contact. He'd fade away again into her past, to be remembered fondly when she saw his name in the newspapers. And she would fight for Ely in court, and ignore the incomprehensible attraction he held for her.

Chapter Thirteen

Ely had been inside the courthouse only once before, when he'd been selected for jury service. He hadn't been chosen as a juror, so he'd never been in any of the courtrooms, let alone family court. He walked past the white marble columns flanking the entrance and felt like he'd stepped into a movie, or perhaps into someone else's life. It couldn't be him walking into this place to challenge the two people who had helped him raise his son. It had to be a nightmare. After Helen died, he dreamed often enough of losing Jess—in a forest, in his own house, and in endless dark caves—but never had he dreamed anything as frightening as this.

The echoing vault of a ceiling was real, though. There was an immediacy to the colorful scene that was not a part of the dream world. Ely listened to the low, unintelligible whispers of the people around him, the scuffle of well-shod feet hitting the marble floor, heels clicking. The dark, sombre clothes of the lawyers and their clients depressed him, and he longed for Eliza.

She met him at the entrance to the courtroom, as promised. When he saw her, his knees went weak with relief. She was his lifeline, his anchor.

"Hi, Eliza." Without her, he'd been floating somewhere between that high ceiling and the cold stone floor. He needed her to be pulled back into himself. Once she was with him, he could breathe normally again, and he could face the fear.

"Hi, Ely."

He wanted to touch her, but he held back. "I don't know if you'll remember my mother and father?"

Eugenia and Geoffrey Greene wore smiles which didn't quite hide the concern in their eyes, but they greeted Eliza with apparent pleasure.

"Both of our sons have been talking about you a lot lately," his mother commented.

"I can see why," Dad said gallantly. "It is a real pleasure to see you again."

She was her lawyer-self, today. Her red-brown hair was pulled tightly into a bun, pinned back away from her face. Her tailored suit—slim black slacks, vest, and jacket—made her look more feminine than ever, though Ely didn't think it was supposed to have that effect. He liked it. But he had to forget about all that and concentrate on the business at hand. Rebecca and Hank had appeared behind Eliza, as if from nowhere. They didn't look at him as they walked through the door.

"Any last-minute instructions, coach?" he asked as they prepared to follow his in-laws into the courtroom.

"Just remember to speak clearly, and don't ramble," Eliza said. She turned to his parents. "I'm sorry, this courtroom is quite small. You might be more comfortable waiting out here." They nodded and wandered away, while Eliza turned back to Ely and eyed him critically.

She straightened his tie. "All right." She looked up at him and froze. Ely knew what she had seen on his face. Passion, lust, or naked desire, whichever name one chose, it was something animal, something he hadn't been expecting. Eliza had made that simple wifely gesture so naturally, he'd had no time to prepare himself, to school his expression. In all his years, even during his marriage, he'd never felt such an ache for a touch.

She gaped at him. He braced himself for her revulsion. What kind of an animal would be thinking about her that way at a time like this? But he didn't find disgust or scorn in her eyes. Her gaze flew from his eyes to his mouth to his necktie, and she cleared her throat. At that moment, that second, he knew. Whatever might happen between them, he knew now that the heat that had flared between them when they kissed had not been a fluke.

He could see that that moment between them had shaken her, but Eliza said nothing. She turned on her heel and walked into the courtroom, and he followed a couple of feet behind.

She had him sit next to her, and the judge entered, almost immediately. Ely felt nervous, and Eliza seemed to know it. She covered his hand with hers for a moment, then arranged her notes on the table in front of them. He had known there would be no jury, but he was surprised that there was no box for them. He'd pictured courtrooms as always having that gallery. The lack of one made him feel less like he was on trial, which was good.

"This court will be called to order, the Honorable Judge William Garson presiding." The judge seated himself at his bench, and he nodded at the occupants of the room in general as the clerk finished his announcement.

"Tyson vs. Greene?" he asked, pointing in the direction of first Hank and Rebecca and their lawyer, and then Ely and Eliza.

"I've read the petition," the judge said. He looked up from the papers in his hand, and looked over his glasses at them. "You are the Tysons?" he asked, looking toward Hank and Rebecca.

Their lawyer said, "Yes."

"Mr. Greene?" Ely nodded.

Mr. Daniels stood. "We have petitioned for the custody of Jessie Greene on the basis of a temporary grant of custody awarded in 1992, by the father."

The judge nodded. "I see. Mr. Greene is clearly fighting this."

Eliza stood. "Yes, Your Honor. Jessie has been living with his father for the last four years and, of course, he lived with him for the two years before Mr. Greene was widowed. It was purely a temporary arrangement, and both parties understood that at the time. We hope you will revoke that temporary agreement here today.''

''On what basis?'' the judge asked.

''Jessie Greene is and has been in the custody of his father for most of his life. His grandparents, the Tysons, have been a large part of his life, but his primary caregiver is his parent, and we feel it is in his best interest not to disrupt the normal, stable home life which his father has created.''

She sat down. The judge looked again at the folder in front of him. He cleared his throat. ''I'd like to hear more about these allegations that Mr. Greene has placed his child in danger on a number of occasions.'' Ely felt bile rise up in his throat at the thought that his mother-in-law and father-in-law were really going to go through with this.

Her lawyer indicated Rebecca should stand. ''Mr. Greene is a teacher at St. Joseph's Academy,'' she said. ''That's the school Jessie attends. But he's always getting in trouble because he encourages the rougher element of the student body to rebel—''

The judge interrupted. ''To rebel against what?''

''The school, Your Honor. He won't follow the rules, and he's been put on probation because of it. He's even been suspended, and he's under probation again now.''

''In what way does that endanger his son?'' the judge asked.

''Well, a couple of years ago I was baby-sitting one day, and some of the boys from St. Joe's came to the apartment with their gang.''

Ely leaned over to whisper in Eliza's ear. ''That was four years ago. I'd forgotten about it.''

Eliza stood. ''Your Honor, this is ancient history.''

''This isn't a hearing, Ms. Taylor. Your client will have his chance to tell his side of the story. Sit down, please.''

Eliza sat and wrote him a note. ''What's she talking about?'' Ely listened to Rebecca finish the story with one ear while he wrote out what had happened for Eliza on her legal pad.

''These five big boys, who looked too big to be in Ely's class—he teaches eighth grade—they barged in the door when

I told them he wasn't at home and said they'd wait till he came home. I asked them to leave, and they had the nerve to threaten me. So, I took Jessie and left. I think one of them might have had a gun. Now, what's he doing inviting those kinds of boys into a house with a child in it?''

"Mr. Greene?" the judge asked, looking at Eliza.

Ely stood without being prompted. "I didn't invite those boys to my house, but I am known around school as a teacher who will talk to students outside of class. They came to talk to me because one of the boys had been in my class at St. Joe's a couple of years before, and he wanted me to talk to his friends about his little brother, who was, at that time, a student of mine whom they were thinking of jumping into the gang. I talked them out of it, which is exactly what his older brother had been hoping. Then, I talked to the boy they'd been trying to get to join the gang so he wouldn't make the same mistake his brother had.''

"How did these boys get your address?" the judge asked.

Ely's eyes dropped before that sharp-eyed gaze. "I do give it out to my students." Ely had never felt guilty about it before. "When I think they need help," he hastened to add. "Or, if they come to me." The judge was scribbling a note of his own. "I feel that I should be able to help the kids, outside of school. That gang incident was a perfect example. Because they felt free to come to me, I kept a boy from joining their ranks.''

"But you are exposing your son to these troubled kids. In your home.''

"Most of the kids aren't involved in anything nearly that serious. It helps them to see me outside of class to discuss their personal problems.''

"And you are currently under suspension for this?"

"I'm on probation, but not because of that incident. It was four years ago, Your Honor. The school did not even know about it.''

Hank spoke up. "You should have informed the school. And the police.''

"Mr. Tyson, please," the judge said calmly.

"Nothing but good came of it. Jessie was never in any danger."

"Nothing but good?" Rebecca gasped. "Those hoodlums were in your house."

"I'm sorry they scared you, Rebecca, but they're not bad boys. Not really. They were just trying to look tough."

"Let's continue," the judge interposed. "What are you currently on probation for?"

"One of my students called me. She's twelve years old, Your Honor, and her father locked her out of her house one evening, by accident. By the time she got home from volleyball practice, all of her friends were at dinner, and she didn't want to embarrass her father by telling any of their parents about his mistake. So she called me. Jessie and I went and picked her up and she had dinner with us. I called her house until her father answered the phone. Then I took her home."

"You had dinner with a twelve-year-old student?" The judge was incredulous.

"The school has not accused me, in any way, of corrupting the girl. There is no question of that. They put me on report solely because students and teachers are not supposed to spend time together outside of the school without the written permission of a legal guardian."

Although the judge appeared to be slightly mollified by his explanation, Ely didn't like the way he paused to scribble, again, on his notepad.

Eliza stood and motioned for Ely to sit. "Your Honor, these anecdotes are perfect examples of the kind of caring, sensitive teacher and parent my client is, and I'd like to ask that we address the issue at hand. Elias Greene is, and has consistently proven himself to be, an excellent parent. The Tysons have been very close to the Greene family, and I don't think they would contradict that statement." She looked challengingly at Rod Daniels, and beyond him, Hank and Rebecca.

Daniels rose to answer her. "I beg to differ. My clients are very concerned that Mr. Greene has and will continue to jeopardize the safety of his home and his son. Because of his blatant refusal to follow his employer's stated policies, he's

constantly in danger of losing his job, which is his sole source
of income.''

"Mr. Daniels, this court is not interested in what might
happen, but only in the situation as it now stands. Mr. Greene
is currently gainfully employed, I take it?''

"Yes, Your Honor, he is,'' Eliza answered.

"But he's planning to quit his job,'' Rebecca cried out.

"Is that true, Ms. Taylor?''

"Mr. Greene might seek employment in the public school
system, after he obtains his teaching certificate, Judge Garson,
but at the moment, he has made no such move.''

"Mr. Greene, do you believe you will be able to retain your
position at St. Joseph's Academy?''

"I do, Your Honor,'' Ely responded.

Hank spoke up again. "For how long?'' he asked.

"Once again, I would like to remind you, sir, that we are
dealing with the facts here, not speculation,'' the judge said
reprovingly. "But I admit these incidents have me worried,
especially in that last case, which shows some questionable
judgment on Mr. Greene's part. I think I'll appoint a Guardian
Ad Litem to look into the situation more closely. When his
report is in, I will notify both Mr. Greene and Mr. and Mrs.
Tyson, and we'll decide at that time who shall have custody
of the minor child, Jessie Greene.''

Rod Daniels was leaning toward Rebecca and Hank when
the judge stood up to leave. The three scrambled hastily to
their feet and Ely rose, too, with Eliza beside him.

"So,'' she said, when the judge had left the courtroom.

"You said he'd probably appoint that investigator,'' Ely
said, watching her impassive face as she gathered up her notes,
including his account of Darren Johnson's unexpected visit to
his apartment.

"You didn't tell me about this, Ely,'' she said.

"I forgot about it, to tell the truth. Besides, who would have
thought they would bring that up?''

"Exposing your son to gang members in your own home
through your carelessness?'' Eliza said disbelievingly. "Rod
Daniels would be a fool not to use that.''

Ely braced himself. "So, how bad is it?" he asked.

"It's pretty much what I expected. We've got some back-tracking to do on that boy in the gang, but otherwise, we're exactly where I thought we'd be."

"Are you sure?" Ely asked. She looked completely in control, as professional as he'd ever seen her, but he sensed she was disappointed.

"Absolutely. Let's go find Mr. and Mrs. Greene. I'm sure they're waiting to find out what happened. You can tell them, in all honesty, things look good. We may have lost a little ground with the rehashing of that incident, but it's nothing to what Hank and Rebecca lost when the judge refused to listen to their concerns about your job." She smiled, and Ely followed her out of the courtroom. They met his parents out in the hallway.

Despite what Eliza had told Ely about the outcome of the hearing, she was surprisingly disappointed at the judge's decision to appoint a GAL to investigate. She had hoped, against hope, that perhaps the judge would just grant Ely custody. She called the office from the car to tell MJ she was going straight home instead of returning to the office. Rosa could e-mail her if she needed to review the documents on the Raymond case.

When she arrived at home, Eliza didn't even look for Sandy. She went directly to her bathroom and started the water running for a nice hot bath. Unfortunately, her soak in the tub did not improve her state of mind as she had hoped it would.

Her disappointment was way out of proportion to the events that had occurred in family court. She should be content with the current status. But she had never wanted to be finished with a case as much as she did this one. If the judge had ruled today in her client's favor, she could have left the courtroom a free woman. Eliza could have, and would have, walked away from Ely, from Jessie, and even from Tommy, without a moment's hesitation, just calling to bid them a polite farewell. The Greene family would get along just fine without her.

Eliza had been more than a little surprised to see Ely's parents in the courtroom that morning. She had gotten into the habit of thinking Tommy and Ely were different from other men, produced by some strange force of nature. Nothing so mundane as ordinary parents could have created the two men who had so thoroughly made their presence felt in her life, her city, even her courthouse.

Geoffrey Greene was a small, thin man. His skin was that shining blue-black that seemed to defy age, and he had an intensity about him that was almost palpable. He was wiry, and a little edgy, the perfect contrast to his wife, whose calm manner was reflected in her serene beauty. A light-skinned woman, slightly taller than average, she was barely an inch shorter than her husband. Her voluptuous figure, which had made her a poster girl for the black soldiers during World War Two and the Korean War, had not suffered from the birth of her two children. The hourglass shape was still intact, if slightly wider.

Seeing them next to their younger son, it was hard to believe that this elderly couple had produced such extraordinary offspring. Eliza remembered their faces at her law school graduation ceremony. They'd been awestruck by Tommy's accomplishments, overwhelmed and overjoyed. They had also been fiercely proud.

She wandered down to the kitchen to make herself a cup of tea. Sandy was rolling chicken in batter. She had ordered a deep-frying pan from some outfit on television, and she fried some vegetable, dairy, or meat product nearly every day. Today, Eliza couldn't help turning away from the pot of bubbling oil. She did not fault Sandy's cooking, despite the teenager's preference for foods that were high in fat, cholesterol, and refined sugar. It was just that the smell of frying chicken reminded her of the picnic lunch she had shared with Ely the day before.

Her young houseguest ignored her presence. Her terse responses and sullen silence all day Sunday had worried Eliza, and she eyed Sandy balefully while she waited for the water in her teakettle to boil. The girl bopped around the kitchen, humming as she cooked, and pretending that she was alone.

Eliza couldn't resist mentioning, "You're going to have to talk to me sometime." Sandy didn't answer her. That was fine with her temporary guardian. Eliza was going to have to issue an ultimatum soon, but right now, all she wanted was a little peace and quiet.

Her nice orderly life had been turned totally upside down, and Eliza felt as though she'd been turned inside out.

Work was her only refuge. The office was as busy as always, but at least her workday was comprised of the usual series of triumphs interspersed with compromises and setbacks. It was familiar territory, she could handle it with ease.

She looked at Sandy's sullen face and decided she needed some time alone, to think. She took her cup of tea into the living room and sat drinking it and brooding. She had dealt with some hard truths about herself over the years. Eliza knew she was responsible for her solitary existence. She had thought herself closed off forever—isolated and alone—but she had been content with what she could achieve.

Eliza had satisfied her parents' ambitions for her, as well as she could remember them. She could count, always, on the work she found so fulfilling. The interest from her inheritance provided a small but livable income which made it possible for her law firm to run on the slightest of profit margins. As long as she wasn't actually losing money in her business, she would be fine. And, in fact, her little firm was doing well. Her clients were a mixture of well-to-do individuals who came to her because of the publicity from the high-profile cases she had won over the years. Referrals from clients well satisfied by her representation also brought in new clients. Then, to keep her from getting soft, there were her welfare families, often referred by the public defender's office where she had gotten her start.

The shy little girl, who had been brought up to believe in fairy tales, and happily ever after, had managed to succeed in the real world without any help from anyone. When her close-knit family had been ripped apart that rainy night so long ago, she hadn't thought she could survive without them. But she had. And now she'd grown used to being completely alone.

Her parents had been devoted to each other, and to her. She didn't know what they would think of the mess she had made of her personal life. Her strongest memories from childhood were of the three of them doing things together: the zoo, the symphony, and dinner with their close circle of friends. Eliza couldn't remember ever having birthday parties with kids her own age. She didn't know if she had just been too shy to enjoy them and had therefore blanked them out, or if her introverted nature had prevented her from having them the parties in the first place.

She had buried her parents, buried David, and grieved for them, but that had been a long time ago. She had thought about it often as, year after year, she had closed the door on any relationship that threatened the life she had chosen. At first, she had wondered why she was so different from everyone else—why she didn't feel the need to pair off, start a family. But Eliza had become comfortable with her choice. Around the same time some of her friends started to consider divorce, it ceased to bother her that she had never married. She had watched families break apart—helped friends pick up the pieces—with the same lack of empathy she felt as she watched good relationships grow stronger over the years. None of it affected her.

But something was happening to her, changing her. Tommy, Ely, Jessie, and Sandy had all converged upon her, and they were making her react in ways that were totally foreign to her nature. She hadn't been this unsure of herself since that awful night when her childhood had ended so abruptly.

Except once.

When David had died, she had felt the world disappear from beneath her feet. But she'd been over it and over it in her mind, and she couldn't have done anything differently. She had forgiven herself. She hadn't put that little boy in the way of the car that killed him. True, Eliza had recommended that his father be granted custody, but it had been proven beyond a doubt that his mother was unfit. And Bruce Paron loved his little boy. His grief at the funeral of his small son had brought tears to everyone's eyes. His sobbing had finally made her own tears flow.

She was not inhuman. Eliza knew she was not actually made

of stone, no matter how icy she sometimes felt herself become. As Tommy had deduced, she did care for her kids. She took her cases very personally. That was not all just ambition. It was true feeling. But for the first time in her adult life, her feelings threatened to grow out of control and that frightened her.

Her tea had grown cold. Eliza went to the kitchen to empty and wash the mug and found Sandy weeping. The teenager held her hand under a stream of cold water flowing from the sink faucet.

"What did you do?" Eliza grabbed the child's hand and examined the burn on her palm. "Why didn't you call me?"

"Don't yell at me," Sandy said, sniffling.

"I'm sorry. I'm sorry," Eliza said. She winced in sympathy as Sandy hissed in pain.

"It hurts," Sandy said, gulping hard to stop the tears.

"Of course, it does," Eliza said soothingly. "We'll take care of that. Come with me."

She shepherded Sandy out of the kitchen and up the stairs to her bedroom. "Sit on the bed, sweetie," she urged. As soon as Sandy sat down, she ran into her bathroom to get some ointment to deaden the pain in the injured area. Eliza dabbed the healing balm gently on the burn and blew on it. "Are you hurt anywhere else?" she asked, turning Sandy's hand over and reaching for the other one.

The girl tried to pull away. "I'm fine."

"No, you're not," Eliza said, holding her two little wrists gently but firmly. Eliza felt the small scars on the back of each of Sandy's hands before she saw them. The small tattoos were crude, the black ink barely visible against the dark skin. Carved into the skin, just above the wrist on the back of Sandy's right hand, was her office number; on the left, Eliza's home telephone number.

"Oh, Sandy," she breathed. "What did you do?"

"I prayed you didn't move," Sandy joked, tough as nails, despite the fact the tears on her face were not yet dry.

Eliza smiled at the joke, but her throat had closed up in reaction to the emotion she felt. Her heart was breaking again.

That organ was suffering a lot of wear and tear lately. She would have thought three strong blows in such a short time would have been too much for it. She supposed she was glad it kept weathering these sudden jolts. She was certainly thankful that it was working again. Hard as it was to admit, she had missed it.

Chapter Fourteen

When Eliza arrived at work the next morning, Ely had left a message on her voice mail. "Hi, Eliza. It's Ely calling, Tuesday at six forty-five. I know you're not in the office yet. I didn't want to wake you up, but I wanted you to get this message first thing. It was so strange to sit next to you yesterday and try to think of you as my lawyer and nothing more. I couldn't quite do it." His voice sounded so natural, not strained or false, just the man, stating his case, his way. "We do need to talk, whatever you may think. I do, anyway. And this way, I can get it all out without any interruptions." He cleared his throat, the only sign that he'd been as nervous making this recording as she was feeling listening to it. She could picture him, nervously fiddling with the phone cord, or a rubber band, while his vision focused on some point deep inside. She'd grown used to this odd combination of traits, hands that stayed busy, while his face was still, contemplative, and intent.

"I don't think Tommy has anything to do with this. I don't know how things are between you. I haven't felt comfortable talking with him about you, and so I haven't." His voice gained strength as he went on. "I love my brother. I don't want to hurt him, but I think what's between us, you and me, is very special. However, you made your feelings clear. You want to ignore it.

"If I could think of the perfect, witty, irresistible line to make you forget everything that stands between us, I would. But I can't. All I can say is, it has to be better for both of us, and Tommy, too, to be honest about this.

"You couldn't love him and respond to me that way. At least, I don't think so. Damn, I've never been good at this. I'm a disaster with women I really care about. Did Tommy ever tell you how I ended up proposing to my wife? Oh, God, I'm an idiot." There was a pause. Eliza was hooked on the rambling monologue. She hoped he didn't hang up.

He hadn't. "So, I proved my point. I know I shouldn't be talking about Helen with you now. But Eliza, if you're still listening, please believe me, I only want . . . I want you to talk to me. Call me."

Eliza sighed. This wasn't going to go away. She picked up the phone to call him back, then dropped it back in the cradle. She couldn't remove herself from the case. It wasn't her style. And she couldn't ignore him. He deserved better than that. She would have to deal with this, openly and honestly, the way Ely was doing.

For the life of her, she didn't know what to say to him. Every instinct screamed, *Duck and cover!* She wanted to believe this would just blow over, but Eliza knew herself better than that. Ely's kisses had opened some floodgates within, and Eliza was afraid of the emotions he had released.

He touched her. She cared about him and his son. She felt closer to him, even now, scared stiff and completely witless, than to any other human being she knew. It was a physical thing. It had to be. But why him? If it had been Tommy, she might have been able to understand. Except for the difference in their ages, he was the perfect match for her. He was suave, sophisticated, successful. He was, as MJ had said, all that and a side of fries. Ely was a babe in the woods in comparison to his brother, and to herself.

Stop that, she told herself. *You've got to get a handle on this.* The only solution she could think of was to keep her distance, physically and emotionally. "You can do this," she said aloud, reaching again for the phone.

It rang just as she was about to pick it up.

"Tommy Greene on line one," MJ announced over the intercom a moment later.

Eliza dropped her head in her hand. "Problem number two."

She hadn't realized she'd said it aloud until MJ spoke over the intercom. "What's problem number one?"

"It's a long, complicated story," Eliza said, wishing MJ could straighten out the sticky situation she had gotten herself into with the two Greene brothers the same way her she managed so efficiently to get her out of the conflicting appointments she sometimes made without thinking.

"Tell me later," MJ said. Eliza didn't answer. She didn't know if she could even confide in her good friend about this mess. "Meanwhile, Tommy's waiting."

"I know," Eliza said.

"Are you going to give him another chance?" MJ asked.

"I don't think there'd be any point." Eliza broke the connection before her friend could start enumerating the various reasons for her to reconsider. She was just as convinced as MJ that Tommy was as skilled a lover as he was a lawyer, but not even if she were guaranteed the best lovemaking any woman had ever experienced, in life or in dreams, was she about to tell him that his kisses left her cold. Especially not as long as there was the smallest likelihood that he might pass that information along to his younger brother.

How had she gotten herself into this?

The phone was blinking at her insistently. She picked it up. "Tommy?"

"Hi, hon," he said easily. "Didn't you get my message?"

"What message?" Eliza asked.

"I called last night. Sandy didn't tell you?"

"We had a difficult weekend."

"Could you possibly make some time for me in the near future, Ms. Taylor?" he asked confidently.

"Sure," Eliza said. She had to see him, had to tell him face to face that she didn't think things were going to work out between them. It was the right thing to do. She couldn't put it off any longer. The weekend's respite hadn't helped anyway. She wished she had a good reason to give him, but after all this time she still hadn't thought of a plausible reason for ending their fledgling romance, other than the truth. She'd just have to play it by ear. If there was a god of irony, he was laughing his head off at her right now. "How about lunch tomorrow?" she asked.

"Can't," he said. Eliza's relief was short-lived.

"Wednesday? Lunch or dinner?" he asked. She scrolled down her calendar.

"Dinner," Eliza said. "I've got a luncheon meeting." She'd have loved to insist on a meeting during daylight hours, but didn't think it would be fair to him to put this off any longer than necessary.

"Dinner, Wednesday it is," he said, his good humor unabated. "I'm looking forward to it."

"Mmmm," Eliza mumbled again. She couldn't manage to voice the standard reply, *Me, too.*

After that, she couldn't seem to bring herself to call Ely from the office. MJ had been in and out all day, plying her for information. Mainly, her friend had been pressuring her to share her game plan for the date with Tommy, but that was not to say she had forgotten Eliza's slip of the tongue about her other, more pressing dilemma. MJ had even sat down across from Eliza's laden desk on the slightest pretext, and fished for details about problem number one.

When Eliza wouldn't tell her, she got miffed and started snapping at her.

When she stomped into Eliza's office to bring some letters she'd typed, MJ whined, "I thought we were friends. I thought I knew you."

"We are, and you do, but that doesn't mean I have to tell you every single thought in my head, does it? I don't bug you for details about your personal life."

"That's because I tell you everything. Stop that."

"What? I didn't say anything."

"No, I mean that thing you're doing with your teeth. Stop tapping on them. You know it gives me the creeps."

"I didn't realize I was doing it," Eliza apologized. But MJ would not be mollified. When she left the office at six that evening, she was still in a huff. Eliza knew from experience that it would all blow over by morning, but MJ's irritating behavior had only made her feel more tense.

Finally, at eight o'clock that evening, she dialed Ely's number, while standing in the kitchen, drinking a fortifying glass of red wine.

Jessie answered. "Hello?"

"Hello, Jessie. It's Eliza"

"Hi, Eliza," he said, his voice became guarded. "What's up?"

"Nothing much." Eliza tried to sound unconcerned for his sake. "How are you doing?"

"Fine." Jessie still wasn't completely reassured.

"I'm just calling to talk to your father about getting together again soon," Eliza said as Sandy came into the kitchen.

"Sunday was uh . . ." She hesitated. It was a little more difficult to get the words out than she expected. She averted her face so Sandy, who was prowling through the kitchen cabinets, couldn't see her expression as she lied. "It was fun, wasn't it?" Her voice sounded false to her own ears; the bright cheery tone didn't ring true.

"Sure," he said.

She didn't think he was buying it. "Seen any good karate movies lately?" Eliza asked.

"There's a new Jackie Chan movie, but it's PG-thirteen, so Dad hasn't decided if I can go yet," Jessie said, loosening up a little.

"I'll try and use my influence on him." Since Ely had apparently allowed Jessie to see other action movies, Eliza wouldn't feel any pangs of conscience in making good on her promise to the little boy.

"Thanks," he said, all reserve gone and heartfelt excitement in its place.

"No problem, kiddo," Eliza said, pleased to hear Jessie

sounding like himself again. Sandy put a bag of popcorn in the microwave.

"I'll get Dad," he said eagerly. She could hear the pounding of his feet as he ran to find his father. It made her smile. Sandy did not smile back, but instead turned to watch the digital display on the microwave count down to zero. The muffled sound of popping corn was all that broke the silence. Eliza felt her smile fade.

"Hello, Eliza." The dry timbre of his voice made her shiver.

"Ely."

"What did you say to Jessie? He's been moping around all day. Two minutes on the phone with you and he's flying."

"I said I'd try to convince you to let him see Jackie Chan." Sandy grimaced as she opened the microwavable bag and a cloud of steam puffed out.

"You've seen it?"

"Ha!" A bark of laughter escaped unexpectedly. Right, she had plenty of time to go to the movies. "Ah, no. But I've heard it's okay. A friend of mine has a girl about Jessie's age who's also into the martial arts. They saw it." Sandy left the kitchen without saying good-bye. Eliza hoped she wasn't angry again. She thought they'd established a tentative truce the night before.

"I was going to let him go, anyway." She heard Jessie whooping excitedly in the background. "Go celebrate in your room, Jess. I can't hear Eliza with you making all that noise."

"Call me when you get off the phone, Dad. I want to tell Fred we can go."

Jessie's voice faded as he spoke. She could picture him walking down the hall to his room.

"Daddy!?" She heard the boy call a second later.

"Yes," Ely said, barely restrained impatience in his terse reply.

"Can you ask Eliza to come to dinner real soon?"

"I'll ask her, Jessie. If you give me a chance."

"Got it," Jessie said. "I'm outta this two-bit popcorn joint."

"Did you get my message?" Ely asked.

"Of course. I couldn't call before."

"So can we talk?"

"All right," Eliza said.

"When?"

"This would seem to be a good time," she said, her voice bright and airy, though her heart was pounding.

"I don't think this is something that should be discussed on the telephone," he said.

"I do." Eliza was sure of it. She didn't owe him a personal interview. She hadn't led him to believe she was interested in a relationship, as she had his brother. Eliza felt a twinge of pain in her neck. This wasn't the way her life went.

"I don't have a choice, do I?" Ely said without resentment.

"No. That's one of the things I wanted to say. I want to set up some ground rules here," Eliza said decisively. She thought she sounded a lot more sure of herself than she was, which was good.

"Like what?" he asked.

"Let me finish," Eliza said sharply.

He subsided. "Okay."

"I can't believe I'm having this conversation, but, since we are doing this postmortem, I have to say that I don't think you should have kissed me. Not the first time and not in the park."

"I shouldn't have, but I did. I don't think it makes any sense to ignore it," he said reasonably.

"I'm not ignoring it. I'm saying what I should have said the first time you touched me. I can't work this way."

"Eliza, I'm sorry," he said. She believed him. She was sorry, too. "Let's not do this over the phone. Let me come and see you."

"I don't want to see you. What I want is your promise that it will not happen again."

He didn't answer right away. Eliza grew nervous as the silence stretched out between them. Finally, he said, "I can only promise to try. I can't give you a guarantee."

"How old are you? Sixteen?" The sarcasm might have been unwarranted, but she wasn't in the mood to play nice. "This isn't negotiable," she said firmly. "If you can't agree, I'll have to withdraw as your lawyer."

"I'm just trying to be honest. I don't know if I can make it to the court date without touching you. I'm not sixteen anymore. You aren't either, but when I'm with you, I don't know.''

"I keep forgetting how young you are," she said, hoping to embarrass him.

"This has nothing to do with our ages." He was not at all embarrassed. For the first time, he sounded angry. "And you know it," he said. "Tell me you kiss every man like you kissed me."

"That's irrelevant." Suddenly, she was on the defensive.

"Like hell it is," he said. "As long as we're being honest, you're the one acting like a child. This is not a silly adolescent infatuation. If it were, you wouldn't be saying any of this. You wouldn't be afraid to talk to me, face to face. And you would certainly be willing to explore this thing between us, this attraction or whatever you want to call it."

"I . . . It's not that I . . ." Flustered by his attack, she tried to go back on the offensive. "You are the one who stepped out of line." Her voice lacked a certain forcefulness. She sounded defensive.

"And you went right along with me. I know you feel something for me. Look, Eliza I'm not trying to put this off on you. It's precisely because I'm not a child that I won't pretend nothing's going on—in spite of the fact that you're running scared, lady, and we both know it." He paused for a moment. Eliza assumed he was trying to get himself back under control.

But when he spoke again, his temper did not seem to have cooled at all. "I'll live with your ground rules, as you knew I would." That promise shook her even more than his anger had.

Eliza was shocked by the depth of her disappointment. For all that she wanted to take back control of her body, her mind, and her life, Eliza had not realized how much she loved it when Ely touched her. Until he agreed not to. Then, her mind and body both betrayed her. She wanted him beyond reason. She ached at the thought of never having him.

"But I'm not doing this because Jessie and I need you. I'm going along with this power trip of yours because I think you believe that what's between us isn't really serious." She should have been relieved, but instead, she was terrified. He still wanted her, despite everything. He might have agreed to her arbitrary terms, but he wasn't giving in.

"Maybe you really can't see what an incredible stroke of luck this is." She flinched. She couldn't help it. Luck was not a word she would have applied in this situation.

"I don't want to shake you up, Eliza, any more than I have to. But when this case is over, you won't be able to put me off so easily. So you have a while to figure out what you want to do, sweetheart. Approximately three months, in fact."

She wouldn't give in, either. Not to him or to herself.

His voice softened. "I'm not going to let you go back into that shell you've built around yourself. I can't." Ely had barely raised his voice, but she felt like she'd been beaten, pummeled with a blunt object.

The no-touching rule had made so much sense when she thought of it. But he had turned it against her. He'd agreed to abide by her terms, but he didn't agree with them. And he was right. It wasn't really a solution. She still had exactly the same problem she'd had before. She had always been the cool one: calm, self-possessed, and in control. She had never responded to a man the way she did to Ely.

She would kill herself before she would act like the rich old men of the Apollo Grille who fawned over their young girlfriends, but she was still as attracted to him now, at this moment in time, as she had been when he kissed her. They weren't touching. She wasn't looking into those eyes of his, but she felt him, his frustration, his desire, as if he were only inches away, rather than miles. It was not Ely she would need to worry about, but herself. In her mind's eye, a picture formed of herself as a frowzy, middle-aged woman, staring hungrily at his lean young body.

She opened her mouth to speak, to say, *Ely, I admit this attraction between us frightens me.* She wanted to say it. But she couldn't get the words out with that horrible picture in her head. She had always imagined she would grow old gracefully, with the kind of dignity Rosa had in such abundance.

"Eliza? I wish I could say I was sorry," Ely said. "But I'm not. I'm glad I found you again," he said gently.

She sat, frozen, powerless to do more than grip the phone. Eliza was suddenly deeply thankful that she hadn't gone to speak with him in person. She would hate for him to see her like this. She didn't like herself much at this moment. She felt like one of those weak, foolish women in the self-help books: women who love men who trample all over them. In her case though, the book would have to be titled, *Women Who Can't Love Men Whom They Should and Instead Want Men Who Are Wrong For Them.* If it weren't so pathetic, it would be funny.

"Good-bye, Ely," she finally managed to say.

"I'll see you soon," he said. The familiar parting line echoed on and on in her mind, long after she returned the phone to its cradle. It sounded like a promise—or a threat.

The next day was Wednesday. Eliza had scheduled the date with Tommy for that night. Eliza had hoped her dinner with Tommy would be in as unromantic a setting as possible. She tried to reach him at his office several times that day to suggest various restaurants, but he was never available. At four o'clock, he left a message with Rosa. He would meet Eliza at her place after work.

"Rats!" she said, when Rosa delivered the pink slip. Her paralegal didn't bat an eyelash. MJ would have been all over that exclamation, but her dignified colleague acted like she hadn't heard a thing. "Rosa, can I ask you something?" she ventured.

"All right," she said cautiously.

"You must have heard MJ and I talking about Tommy Greene?" Rosa nodded. "Do you have any, um, words of wisdom for me?"

"Sorry, honey, it's not my area," the older woman said, shaking her head.

"Well, what would you do if someone was interested in you, and you were attracted to his personality, but his kisses did nothing for you?"

"Nothing?" Rosa asked for clarification.

"You know." Eliza blushed. But as embarrassing as this conversation was, it would all be worthwhile if Rosa responded with her usual efficiency. She'd have suffered a lot more than this for a diplomatic solution to her current problem.

"I'd just tell him straight out he left me cold. No point in beating around the bush. He's a nice young man, but full of himself. I don't think it will hurt him to learn that not every woman is a pushover for looks, charm and money."

"Thanks a lot," Eliza said, dryly. At least he would have to behave himself at her place. With Sandy there, he wouldn't have the opportunity to try to seduce her. Of course, her opportunities to give Tommy her farewell speech would be limited, as well. But if all else failed, she could always walk him out to his car. She tried to visualize the scene and failed miserably. She didn't want to be making this speech to him. It was Ely she wanted to tell, *Your kisses mean nothing to me.*

Dreaming wasn't going to help. As usual, she was late leaving work, and arrived home a scant fifteen minutes before Tommy was due to show up. She'd have to rush to change. The moment she entered the house, Eliza was struck with the feeling that the evening was not going to be as casual as she'd planned. Wonderful smells emanated from the kitchen, and soft music played in the dining room as she walked by.

She had nearly passed the entryway to the room when she literally did a double-take. The table was set with flowers, candles, china, and gleaming silver, as it had been the first time Tommy had "dropped by." But tonight, it was only set for two. She stopped and steadied herself.

She struck her palm to her forehead as she suddenly realized Sandy was setting them up.

"Sandy!" she called.

"Yo," came a voice from the kitchen.

"What the heck do you think you're doing?" Eliza stopped in midstride as Tommy met her in the kitchen doorway with a glass of wine in hand, and a kiss on the cheek.

"You're early," she said stupidly.

"You're late," he admonished. Eliza could see Sandy beaming at them from behind his shoulder. She snapped her mouth shut. She was clearly not going to have a chance to vent her spleen on the girl for her unwanted interference.

Sandy jumped off her high stool. "I'd better get going. I'm taking a bus to the movies. A double feature." She winked and was gone before Eliza could utter a word.

"Seems like things are going better between you two now," Tommy commented.

"Yes, I think so," Eliza said, still trying to take in the sumptuous feast spread on the counter.

"The first course is already on the table, madame," Tommy said with an elaborate bow. "I will be serving dinner tonight, for my lady's pleasure. After the bruschetta, we shall dine on a delicious penne with spring vegetables in a light cream sauce, which I made for you with these two dainty hands, and fresh Italian bread, which I purchased for you at your local patisserie. The pasta course will be be followed by free-range chicken marinated in a dry white wine." He described the meal as he escorted Eliza into the dining room and seated her.

"I would have waited and given you a moment to slip into something a little more comfortable, but timing in cooking, as in any worthy endeavour, is everything. Sit, eat," he commanded.

"I'm just . . . I don't know what to say. It's lovely," Eliza said. Why, oh, why couldn't she love this adorable, pushy rogue, she thought as he teased her for keeping him waiting for five long days before the famed "second date."

He wiggled his eyebrows at her, and Eliza couldn't help laughing. But she sobered as she realized he didn't have a clue about why she'd invited him out this evening.

"Wait, Tommy, I have to tell you something," she said as he jumped up and came around the table to her.

"It will have to wait, my dear," he said, leaning over to brush her forehead with a light kiss. "I must attend to my pasta sauce."

Her left her alone. Eliza despised herself for giving him no hint of her true feelings. This couldn't go on.

When he came back, she told him, "Tommy, I really need to talk to you," but he silenced her by placing a finger over her lips.

"Let's not be serious tonight, darling." He did a pretty decent impression of Cary Grant's suave British accent. "I'm trying to create a mood,'' he said, dropping the actor's manner-isms and giving her a sweet, teasing smile. "Don't ruin it."

Eliza debated internally throughout the meal whether to bring this farce to an end, but Tommy was irrepressible. He was witty and charming, and he barely gave her a chance to talk at all as he joked about the dinner preparations, his conspiracy with Sandy, and his undying sorrow that five whole days had gone by without seeing her. When he brought up that last item, Eliza tried to begin her explanations, but each time he cut her off with a warning shake of the head or a humorous anecdote about the craziness at work, which he offered apologetically as an explanation for his seeming lack of devotion.

"Shall we take our wine in the living room?" he asked, when she had eaten enough to satisfy him.

"Sure," Eliza agreed, resigned. She gave in to the inevitable. He seated her on the couch and then took his place beside her with a sigh of satisfaction.

He raised his glass. "To us," he said and took a sip.

Eliza didn't drink to his toast. "That's what I've been trying to tell you," she said.

"What?" he asked, taking her drink from her hand and putting it and his own on the coffee table. Eliza watched him nervously as he turned to her, a smile playing over his lips.

"This is difficult, and you're not making it any easier," she started.

"I'm not?" he said innocently, then took her chin in his hand and kissed her.

"No," she said aginst his mouth. "I'm trying to talk to you."

"Can't we talk later?" he asked, covering her mouth with his own again before she had a chance to answer.

Eliza closed her eyes, willing herself to feel something, any-thing, searching within for the slightest spark, the tiniest frisson of desire. Nothing. She felt only the same warm glow that had permeated her body every time he kissed her.

"This just isn't working," she said in disgust when he raised his lips from hers.

"What?" Tommy asked, his eyes narrowing.

"I wish it were," Eliza said honestly. "But I don't feel for you the way you feel for me. I've tried. I just can't."

Tommy examined her face closely. She watched comprehension dawn. Then, surprisingly, he laughed.

"What's so funny?" Eliza asked, annoyed.

"I thought it was just me," he said, sitting back, grinning.

"What?" she said, her voice rising in disbelief.

"I thought I was the one who was . . . Well, going through the motions." She hit him with one of the pillows that lay under her hand. "It was the nicest way I could think of to say it," he said apologetically. But his eyes were still twinkling at her.

"Tommy, are you saying you don't feel . . ." She, too, searched for a delicate way to phrase the question, but gave up. "I don't turn you on, either?" she asked finally.

He shook his head. "No," he said, chuckling.

She searched his eyes for a sign that he was making this up to save face and could find none.

Eliza started to laugh. "I can't believe this."

"I'm so glad you said something," he said.

"So am I." When she finally took her last gasp of laughter, he sat regarding her with a wide smile on his face.

"It's a shame," Tommy said. "We're so perfect for each other. My mother is already planning the wedding."

Eliza's smile faded. "How far were you planning to go?" she asked, wondering if perhaps they would have ended up married if she had continued to pretend.

"As far as I could," he said, obviously taking the question quite differently from the way she had meant it.

"Thanks a lot," she said, her vanity slightly piqued. She flung the pillow at him. He caught it.

"Hey!" Tommy protested. "I did it because I love you, Eliza."

He was suddenly serious. "I really love you." He gave her a one-armed hug, holding the pillow in his other hand. She relented.

"Me, too," she said, settling back against him on the sofa.

"So, what do we do now?" her friend asked.

"Do you want to watch TV?" she asked him back.

"Sure," Tommy said. He gave her shoulder a squeeze before he let her get up from the couch to turn the television on.

Chapter Fifteen

Daddy was acting like he was back to normal, singing while he dusted the bookshelves and all, but Jessie knew something was wrong. He suspected it had to do with their case. Daddy said court went okay, but there was something he was keeping to himself. Eliza had called, and she hadn't sounded worried, but he didn't know her as well as he knew his father. She could have been acting like nothing was wrong just to make him feel better. Grown-ups did that all the time.

But Jessie knew his father wasn't really happy. He caught him staring straight at the TV a couple of times when there was, like, a dumb commercial on. And once, when he was supposed to be reading a book, he didn't turn the page for twenty minutes. Jessie watched him.

There was definitely something going on. Something shady.

He tried to ask him about it after a couple of days. "Are we going to win the case, Dad?"

His father was tucking him in, which he was too old for, but couldn't refuse because he didn't want to hurt Dad's feelings.

He sat on the side of Jessie's bed. "I told you before, Jessie, I'm not *absolutely* sure of what's going to happen. I have a good feeling about it, but I don't want to make any promises I can't keep.''

"What does Eliza think?'' Jessie had probed.

"She thinks we've got an excellent case. She's going to do her best. But Grandma and Grandpa love you and so they're going to be trying their hardest, too.'' Jessie didn't know how he felt about Grandma Rebecca these days. He loved her and he knew she loved him, but this all seemed to be started by her. Grandpa, he was sure, was just going along with her. And Daddy wouldn't say anything bad about her, either. But sometimes Jessie felt very angry at her for making everything so hard.

"It wouldn't be so bad to live with them, would it?'' his father asked.

"No, I guess not. But I'd rather be with you,'' Jessie answered, trying hard not to sound like a whiney brat. He was proud his dad talked to him like an adult, and he tried to behave like one.

"Me, too,'' Ely said. "Whatever happens, you know we all love you and only want what's best for you. You understand that, right?''

"Do I get a chance to tell the judge how I feel?'' he asked.

"I'm working on it,'' Daddy said. "You're my ace in the hole. Who could say no to this face.'' He squeezed Jessie's cheeks in his hands and made kissy noises at him, trying to make him laugh. Jessie tried but he couldn't summon up a real smile.

Grandma wouldn't change her mind no matter how much he begged. He knew her. Once she had decided, that was it. He might be able to con his dad with a cute smile, but Grandma didn't give in on anything, not his after-school snack or his bedtime or this. Grandma always did what she thought was right, whether Jessie liked it or not.

It wasn't because she was stricter than Dad that he didn't want to live with her. Mainly, he wanted to stay with his father because Daddy didn't have anyone else but him. Grandma had Grandpa. If they took Jessie away with them, Daddy would be all alone. Plus, Dad was one of the coolest people Jessie ever met. The kids at school, all the way up to the seniors, said Ely Greene was the best. He might get goofy sometimes and, of course, some of his habits were very embarrassing, but mostly Jessie thought they were just alike. He and Daddy were a perfect match.

When Daddy kept right on pretending everything was all right, even though Jessie knew it wasn't, he decided to pay a visit to Eliza. He thought she would tell him the truth, especially if he asked her straight out. He knew Daddy wouldn't let him go, so he skipped soccer practice after school on Friday and took the bus to her house without telling his father.

He wished he understood better what exactly had happened in court. All he knew was the judge had asked them to come back again. Dad had been nervous about that, but he just said the judge wanted to make sure Jessie lived in the best possible home, and he needed more information to decide where that was, so the judge gave him a sort of guardian investigator, and they had to wait for three months until he collected all the information, and then they would make a presentation in court—like Jessie did at school. Jessie thought that whoever got a better report card won.

But he didn't think that was what had gone wrong, exactly. He only knew his dad was not really happy about something, and he not only wouldn't tell Jessie what it was, but he also acted like he had to keep it a secret.

Eliza would know if his father had anything to worry about or not. Jessie hoped she would tell him. He knew he was just a kid, but this was his life they were talking about, for Pete's sake. He had a right to know if he should be worried.

When he reached Eliza's house, a girl answered the door.

"May I help you?" she said.

"Is Eliza here?" Jessie asked her.

"Not right now, no. Was she expecting you?"

"No, I just wanted to talk to her," Jessie said.

"Who are you?"

"Jessie Greene. What's your name?" he asked politely.

"I'm Sandy. I'm living here for a while. Do you want to come in and wait?"

Jessie glanced around. He wasn't supposed to talk to strangers, but this girl didn't look like a flake or anything. He figured if she lived in Eliza's house, she couldn't be dangerous or bad. So, he went inside.

Sandy was nice. She gave him soda and chips and then brought him into Eliza's living room.

"This is my favorite room," Sandy said, when she saw him looking around. "It's cool to hang out in." She patted the couch and Jessie sat on it beside her.

"So, you're Jessie," she said.

"Yeah. Did Eliza tell you about me and my dad?"

"A little." She got a sour look on her face, like Grandma sometimes did when she didn't like his questions.

"What did she say?"

"She said your dad and your grandparents are fighting for custody," Sandy said.

"Is that all?"

She shrugged. "That's about it, kid. What more do you want?"

"I hoped she said she was going to win."

"She always thinks she's going to win. She has to, otherwise she couldn't do her job," Sandy said. "Anyways, far as I can tell, you're in a win-win situation."

"What do you mean?" Jessie asked.

"Well, it's like this. If Eliza wins, then you get to stay with your dad. From the sound of it, he'd never dump you, right?"

"Of course not," Jessie said, starting to get mad.

"Hey, chill, it has been known to happen."

Of course, Jessie knew of kids whose fathers left them, because of divorce and stuff. But his dad wasn't like that. And anyway, his daddy was fighting for him and all.

"I know," he said, trying to stay cool.

"Anyways, even if Eliza loses, then your dad gets to have his own life and you've still got a great crib. Your grandparents are moving to some big, fancy house out west, right?"

"Yes," Jessie said slowly. He was thinking about what she'd said about his father.

"It sounds good to me. I know a lot of other kids who would

be happy to have a couple of houses like that. Your folks want to give you everything, and they got the money to do it, too.''

"What did you mean when you said my dad gets to have his own life?'' Jessie asked.

"You know,'' Sandy said. "More soda?''

"No, thanks.'' He was trying to think. "You think he'd be happy without me?''

"Hey, I don't even know the man,'' Sandy said, shrugging.

"Did Eliza say that? I thought she wanted me to stay with him.''

"Maybe she does. That's her job, right?''

"But she wouldn't be our lawyer if she thought I should live with my grandparents, would she? That wouldn't be right.''

Suddenly, Sandy looked at Jessie like she hated him. "Who are you to judge Eliza?''

"I didn't mean to say anything bad about Eliza. She's great. That's why I came to see her.'' He had thought Sandy was cool, but she didn't seem very nice now. Jessie tried to explain. "I need to know what Eliza thinks.''

"You've got it good. So go home and quit crying about it. You're selfish and spoiled. Why don't you just go live with your grandparents and save Eliza all this trouble? Your daddy will be better off without you anyway,'' Sandy said, like she was tired of him.

"I don't want to move away.'' Jessie couldn't help whining.

"I'm sorry I yelled at you,'' Sandy said. She didn't sound like she was though. She sounded annoyed.

Jessie didn't like her anymore, but he said, "That's okay,'' because he knew she wanted him to.

"You're old enough to make your own decisions, right? When I was your age, I was living with my third or fourth family, and didn't have nowhere to go or you can bet I wouldn't have been there. You can do whatever you want. If you want my advice, I'd say you tell your dad you don't want to live with him no more so he can stop worrying about his job and all.''

Jessie didn't think it would make his father feel better if he told him he wanted to leave, but he knew his dad's job was important to him. Eliza would know.

"Don't you think Eliza will be mad? Daddy said she'd been working nights and weekends on this case."

"She just wants you to be happy," Sandy said. He knew that was true, anyway, but Jessie didn't know what to think anymore. Sandy was watching him. "If you tell her you want to live with the gramps, she'll go for it," she said. Maybe his dad was worried about work. It had definitely been one of the things he had talked about a lot with Eliza. And it made sense he wouldn't want to tell Jessie about it if that was what was bothering him.

"Come on, kid. I'll take you home," Sandy said.

The bus ride was long, and he managed not to cry or anything in front of her. They talked only a little bit. Jessie had plenty of time to think. He tried to break it down, like Daddy told him to do when they talked about his problems.

Grandma Rebecca and Grandpa Hank were sure they were right. Even though Sandy didn't believe it, Jessie was sure Daddy and Eliza were also sure. Everyone said they just wanted him to be happy. But he wasn't. No one was.

Daddy had a secret. That was for sure. Jessie had tried to figure it out. He thought the secret was something about him— like Dad thought Mommy had wanted him to live with her mother. Daddy told him plenty of times that Mommy would be glad if she could see how happy Jessie made her parents. Or maybe the problem was Jessie shouldn't love Grandma and Grandpa so much. Daddy kept saying he shouldn't blame them for loving him. If it wasn't their fault, then maybe it was because Jessie loved them. Daddy would never tell him that.

He almost started to cry again when he was thinking about this, so he made himself think about what he could do instead. He could be bad to Grandma and Grandpa so they wouldn't want him anymore. That was what he had planned to ask Eliza. He'd gone to Eliza's house to ask what he could do to help them win. But Sandy was right that he could also help by just stopping the fighting. If he said he wanted to live with his grandma it would be over. So, maybe that was the best way to help. But he didn't think he could lie so great. His father would know right away that he didn't mean it.

Jessie guessed Daddy wouldn't be too happy, either, in the beginning. But maybe, once the fighting was finished, his father could go on with his plan to teach in public school. Grandma Rebecca wouldn't like it, but if she had Jessie with her, he didn't think she'd make a big stink about it like she did now. She'd probably leave Daddy alone.

As far as he could figure, the big question was, if he stayed, could Daddy still get what he wanted like Sandy said he could if Jessie left?

He didn't want to make her mad again, but he tried asking her, "You really think Dad would be okay if I moved?"

She shrugged again. "I guess he would. He's a grown-up, right?"

Daddy might be a grown-up, but Jessie knew his father would be very sad and lonely if he left. The question was, would he get over it? They had talked about it once. Daddy said they would still see each other, visit and talk on the phone. It wouldn't be the same, he said, but no matter what happened, they would be okay. They were a family, a unit, he said. Together or apart.

Sandy dropped him at the bus stop. "It's probably better if I don't go to your house," she said.

"Right," he agreed. "I can get home from here fine. I do it all the time." He marched away, trying to look cool. He didn't cry till he got back to his room.

Jessie was more confused than ever. He still didn't know why his father was sad underneath, but now he did know he had the power to stop this thing. He kept turning the thought over in his mind. Could he convince everybody he really *wanted* to live with his grandparents? What would happen if he did? When would they be moving? And how often would he see his dad?

He thought maybe he should try and talk to Eliza again, but he was afraid that Sandy girl would be there if he called or tried to visit her house. If he called her at her office, then maybe she'd have to tell his father. They were working together. He couldn't think of anyone else he could ask, though. When he found Daddy asleep on the couch the next morning, he knew he had to do something.

Ely dropped his list at Eliza's office on Wednesday. After their telephone conversation the night before, he had to be very careful not to scare her away. She was waiting for him to say something that would scare her away but he refused to give her any excuse. He was polite and friendly and that was all. Not by look or deed did he give any indication that anything untoward had happened between them.

Amazingly enough, the ungrateful wretch still wasn't happy. She was sulking. His eight-year-old son had done it often enough for him to recognize her expression.

"I'm still trying to make an appointment to speak with Mr. McGinley," she told him.

"He doesn't have to talk to you, if he doesn't want to, right?" Ely asked.

"No, it's completely up to him," Eliza explained. "On the plus side, pretty much everyone else we want to speak with has agreed to a preinterview with me."

"So, we are making some progress?" he asked for confirmation.

"Of course," Eliza answered.

"Is there anything else I can do?"

"Just be patient," she advised.

"I've always been patient," he said.

He woke up the next morning, for the second day in a row, on the couch. Jessie had a steaming hot cup of coffee ready for him.

"Thanks," he said.

"Dad, what's the matter?" Jessie asked seriously.

"It's nothing," Ely assured him, but when he looked at himself in the bathroom mirror, he understood why his eight-year-old son had not believed him. His clothes were rumpled, his hair was completely flattened on one side, and his eyes were bloodshot because of the last two almost sleepless nights.

Ely was much more down to earth than Tommy, even if he did, as his family asserted, walk around with his head in the clouds. He would have been happy to change his image, but he had always enjoyed his life the way it was, crazy ideas and all. He only *seemed* to be so thickheaded in comparison to Tommy, who acted on every thought and to whom thoughts came faster and better than to ordinary people. But it made sense that it was his older brother to whom he was compared.

For example, it never would have occurred to him to ask Eliza out on a date, if it hadn't been for Tommy.

Ely's chest constricted as he imagined Tommy dining with her, in the candlelight, a tableau he'd seen that first night in the hotel bar. He tried to picture Tommy kissing her, but he couldn't. He couldn't find it in him to believe his fast-thinking, smooth-talking older brother could break through to that other Eliza.

If she wasn't his type, she was even less like the women his brother usually dated. They tended to be warm, intelligent, ambitious women who wanted to have a good time with no strings attached. Tommy was out of his depth with a woman like Eliza. She was fire and ice, passion backed by cold logic. She had always been that way, even as a law student. Even after all they'd been through, he didn't know what demons lay beneath that calm, professional surface, and he wasn't absolutely sure that he wanted to know. But he did want to find that woman he'd glimpsed in the park.

She was dating his brother. She had said as much. He thought that she'd thrown that at him to keep him at bay, but Ely was sinking fast. What if, in three months, she just walked out of his life again? He couldn't let that happen. She was a tough nut to crack, but he had to keep trying.

For the moment, there was nothing he could do. She would withdraw from the case if he didn't cool it. But when the custody battle was over, he wanted to have a plan. Something devious—since she'd see through anything obvious. She was brilliant. Smarter, as his son had pointed out, than his brother, who was the most intelligent person he knew. He loved her mind.

If he couldn't outsmart her, and he doubted he could, he'd have to come up with something else. At least he knew she wasn't immune to him. That gave him some hope. Maybe he'd kidnap her. He shook his head, smiling sardonically at his reflection in the mirror.

"I don't suppose she'd fall victim to the Stockholm Syndrome, do you?"

"What did you say, Dad?" Jessie called from his room next door to the bathroom.

"Just thinking out loud." He could picture his son shaking his head in disgust. Jessie was embarassed by his father's habit of talking to himself. "Want to go out for breakfast?" he shouted.

"I'm right here," Jessie said from the doorway, a wide smile nearly splitting his face in half.

"Guess that's a yes, then," Ely said. "Let's go."

"Uhhh, Dad. Don't you want to change first?"

"Oh. Sure. That might be wise."

Jessie came with him to his room and sat on the bed watching him as he changed. "Are you going to do something about that?" He was looking at Ely's hair.

"Yeah. I'm gonna wear a hat." Jessie's grin was infectious and Ely laughed. It was good to see his son smile like an eight-year-old again. He wondered how long it had been. He couldn't get Jessie to talk to him lately—not like they were accustomed to doing. But at least that scared, concerned look that had been in his son's eyes when he'd awakened Ely was gone. If it was in his power, Ely planned to make sure it didn't come back.

Chapter Sixteen

Alexandria had undergone a complete and total transformation overnight. Eliza couldn't get over the change. The former thorn in her side had become an angel. She stocked the refrigerator with all of Eliza's favorite foods, cooked them, cleaned up after herself, and generally tried to be helpful. It was bizarre.

The most unnerving aspect of the metamorphosis was in her appearance and manner. Gone were the short, short skirts, transparent blouses, and ripped, baggy jeans. Sandy found a belt somewhere and cinched her pants at the waist, mended the holes in her pants and tops, and never appeared, either inside the house or out, in any attire that would make her temporary guardian blush. She started wearing less makeup. Along with the change in her adornment, came a change to the face and body she'd been adorning. She was cheerful and pleasant, morning, noon, and night. Eliza smelled something fishy in the abrupt about-face, but she could detect no hidden agenda in Sandy's conversation or actions.

She decided to sit back and enjoy it. This Sandy was a joy to come home to. She asked Eliza for a list of her favorite books and began to read them. Then, they discussed them. Over breakfast and dinner, she was a lively, funny conversationalist, with a unique point of view. Ms. O'Davis had also gone through Eliza's videotape collection, and they talked about movies, as well as literature, and, of course, the law, which she drank in whenever she could get Eliza talking about her work. Even when the two of them didn't agree, they had fun. Eliza decided she would definitely miss the girl when she left.

Since her company was so much more amusing, Eliza found herself doing more with Sandy, who fit her very flexible schedule around Eliza's already tight one. They ate, shopped, listened to music, and even sat together in the living room, reading. When Eliza couldn't get home for a couple of nights, Sandy came down to the office one evening to help with the filing. MJ, Eliza, and Sandy laughed and fooled around while they worked, Eliza sorting and categorizing, MJ and Sandy making folders and filing, respectively.

"What is this, like a year's worth of paperwork or what?" Sandy asked as Mary Jane presented her with yet another full box of file folders.

"No, this is all new," MJ assured her.

"What do you usually do with this stuff? When you can't kidnap some unsuspecting dope and get her to do it?" she asked.

"I do it," MJ said. "With Rosa."

"I help," Eliza piped in.

"Sure you do, Miz 'Liza," MJ agreed, shaking her head at Sandy. In a stage whisper, she added, "You've got to humor the bosslady. Let her think whatever she wants."

"Fine," Eliza said in mock indignation. "I won't bother you anymore after tonight." She bent over her paperwork.

"Oooo, I'm scared now," MJ said, rolling her eyes. "What are we going to do next time?"

Sandy giggled. "How did you end up working together?"

"I answered an ad," MJ said sorrowfully. "Worst mistake I ever made. It sounded like a dream job—good pay, decent chance of advancement, heavy phones but light typing and, get this, *light* filing."

"Hey," Eliza protested, laughing. "The firm was brand new. I had, like, one and a half clients, and at most there were only two hours of work a day—although you managed to stretch it out."

"That's how she hooked me." MJ winked at Sandy. "I took the bait, she reeled me in. Once she got me, of course, she became an instant success and the rest is history."

It was Eliza's turn to roll her eyes. "Yeah, MJ, I owe it all to you."

"I think it's cool," Sandy said. "Before I met Eliza, I didn't think there were hardly any women lawyers. Then I came here, and all there were were girls."

"Thas right," MJ drawled. "They should have us on *Oprah.*" She chanted, "Ohhh, this is Liza and I'm MJ. We're the homegirls of family court today ba duh duh duh ba duh duh duh."

Sandy joined in, parodying the theme song from a popular television show. "Ohhh, this is the story about how my life got turned upside down on the streets of Boston, I was running around till the cops ran me into the ground I was hurtin', I was buggin', I thought I was caught till I turned on to the homegirls of family court ba duh duh duh, ba duh duh."

She and MJ looked at Eliza expectantly.

"Oh, no," she said.

"Come on," they said.

Hopelessly out of rhythm and with no clue as to how they were doing this, Eliza sang out the first thing she could think of that rhymed. Her friends made the strange noises which she recognized as the usual accompaniment to rap songs.

"I am Eliza and I don't know how to make up a rhyme in the here and now. But it seems I must, and seems I ought because I'm a homegirl of family court."

Sandy and MJ made the sputtering noises of a dying car engine, ending the song. They applauded, while Eliza felt heat rise up in her cheeks.

"What are you trying to do to me?" she asked.

"We're gonna drag you into the twenty-first century, Ms. Taylor, no matter what it takes," MJ threatened. "You may find our methods unorthodox," she warned with an evil grin. "But I guarantee we will succeed."

"Don't threaten me," Eliza said in the same playful tone.

Sandy rubbed her hands together briskly. "A quick test. The subject is . . . African-American icons of the nineties. What famous female singing team suggested, 'Let's Talk About Sex.'"

Eliza played along. "I know this one. That's the short fat girl and the tall thin girl that wear the matching, albeit somewhat unsuitable, spandex outfits, right?"

"Nnnnn," Sandy buzzed. "Wrong answer. The correct response would have been Salt-N-Pepa."

"Give her an easy one," MJ suggested. "Try someone closer to her own age." They conferred in whispers.

"That's too easy," Sandy complained.

"Try it," MJ urged. She whispered something further in Sandy's ear that made the girl smile and nod.

"Okay. Are you ready?" Sandy asked.

"As I'll ever be," Eliza said.

"Question. He was the first African American to costar in a prime-time dramatic series—for which he won three Emmys, by the way—made a dozen record albums, and has had four top-rated television series in the last ten years."

"I know this one," Eliza said smugly.

"Listen carefully," Sandy said. "For dinner and a movie, can you, Eliza Taylor, name his most recent sitcom?"

"The Cosby Show!" Eliza declared triumphantly.

"Nnnnnn," MJ buzzed. "I told you she wouldn't know."

"Cosby is the name of the show," Sandy said reproachfully. *"The Cosby Show* was, like, ten years ago."

"You watch it," Eliza said. "I've seen you."

"Sure, but those are reruns. I said his most recent sitcom."

"All right, so I don't know my TV trivia. Do I have to watch MTV and prime-time television drek in order to be a citizen of the twenty-first century?"

"Yup," MJ said, nodding.

Sandy answered more slowly. "I think you do, Eliza. Otherwise, you won't know what's goin' on."

"I read the newspaper to find out what's going on," Eliza defended herself. "This stuff is not exactly earth shattering."

"No, but it's what America's youth is interested in, and as you, yourself, have said, our youth is our future. Therefore, I submit that the future of this country is in the hands of our youth, and since this country is the only major superpower left, the future of the entire world is in the hands of our youth." MJ bowed.

"I apologize," Eliza said. "I'll bone up, and you can test me again next week. Now, can we get this work done and get to dinner? I'm starving."

"Sure," MJ said. "But I have one more little question for you. And you don't even need to study to answer it."

"Okay," Eliza said. "That sounds good."

"What's the deal with you and Mr. Thomas Greene?" MJ asked.

Sandy looked at her expectantly. Eliza shot her secretary a dirty look. "We're friends," she said. "I told him I wasn't interested in anything more, and he was fine with that."

MJ looked disappointed. Sandy appeared more curious than upset. "*Why* aren't you interested?" she asked.

"Good question," MJ seconded.

Eliza narrowed her eyes at her old friend, who quickly became busy with the labeling machine. Eliza didn't want to talk about her sex life, or lack thereof, with her impressionable young ward of the state. "We're just not right for each other. Sometimes things click between two people, and sometimes they don't." That was as graphic as she planned to get. Sandy didn't look satisfied, so she added a reassuring footnote. "Believe me, honey, I didn't hurt his feelings or anything. If you want to know the truth, I think he was relieved."

"Hmmph," MJ said, then looked up. "Ooops, sorry."

Sandy argued. "I'm sure you just misunderstood. He really likes you."

"I really like him, too," said Eliza, standing and picking up a pile of folders the contents of which she'd just finished sorting. "That is why we're going to be good friends." She gave the stack of files to MJ. "That's the end of it," Eliza said firmly. She was sure that MJ picked up on the double entendre.

"Sure, bosswoman, I got it. Come on, kid. If she doesn't

know to hold on to a man like that, there's nothing we can do for her. That kind of native intelligence is not something you can teach.''

That line of questioning abandoned, the three women finished their work and went to dinner.

It wasn't until a couple of nights later that Sandy brought it up again. "When is Tommy coming by? I'd love to cook him dinner again before I go," she said.

"I'm sure that can be arranged," Eliza said, pleased to have the opportunity to give the girl a glimpse of the developing friendship between herself and her recent former beau.

"Great. Do you want to call him? Or should I?" Sandy asked.

"I'll call him right now," Eliza said.

Two minutes later, it was settled. Tommy would have dinner with them the next night.

"Great," Sandy declared, with enthusiasm. From the speculative look in her eye, Eliza would have been willing to bet that she was planning on doing some more matchmaking. Hopefully, when the teenager saw how she and Tommy were together, she would give up on this fantasy. In the hopes of forestalling an embarrassing incident, Eliza tried to broach the subject then and there.

"Why is this so important to you, Sandy?" she asked.

"I just like him. That's all. He's not like other guys. And you're great. You deserve someone like that."

"What is wrong with our just being friends?"

"Men and women can't be friends," Sandy decreed in tones of absolute certainty.

"Sure they can," Eliza said, appalled.

"No, they can't. When they are just friends, then it's too easy to be tempted by someone else."

"Tempted? By another woman, you mean? So what?"

"Men leave," Sandy said.

"Not always. I have men friends whom I've known for years, whose weddings I've attended. A good friendship lasts, and I think Tommy and I will have that. I hope he does find someone to love, because that will make him happy and I want him to be happy. Just like he wants me to be happy. That won't end just because, or if, one of us falls in love with someone else.''

''Yeah, so where are all your other 'friends'?'' There was a trace of bitterness in Sandy's voice. She was not the surly, uncooperative street urchin of before, but a hint of that girl's overriding distrust colored the new Sandy's words.

''I have lots of friends, of both sexes, that you haven't met in the weeks you've been here. That doesn't mean we're not friends.''

''If you never see them, what makes these people friends?'' Sandy asked, less sullenly.

''When I see them, or talk to them, we catch up on each other's news. I know they care about me, and my life, and I care about them. If I ever needed help from them, just like if I ever needed your help, I know I could call and they'd be there,'' Eliza explained patiently.

Interpersonal relationships were not exactly her forté, and she thought it a shame Sandy should be learning about this kind of thing from her, but she was sure of one thing, Sandy's questions had an urgency to them. They had to be answered right away. However poor her social skills, Sandy trusted Eliza to some extent—enough to give her this rare glimpse at the scared little girl inside the street-smart young woman. If she had only a superficial knowledge of this area of human relations, gleaned more from observation than from personal experience, it was still worth sharing with Sandy, who hadn't had the opportunity to either observe or experience good, caring relationships. Eliza was guessing that, flawed as she was, her answers were better than none.

''But if you never see them, then you don't know. You can't really be sure they're still your friends.''

''It's true. I just have to trust them. But that's part of my being their friend. Trust is a gift.''

''What happens if they lie to you, then? You'd never know it. They could be saying and doing all the right things to your

face, but they could be doing . . . anything behind your back.''
Sandy painted the nasty scenario in an emotionless voice. She
had been lied to, neglected, and betrayed more in the course
of her short life than most. As a result, she was very self-
protective. Eliza hoped that her answers to Sandy's questions
would enable her to look at strangers less as potential dangers
and more as potential friends.

"If I trust someone, they can lie to me, I suppose. But the
reason I trust them is because I don't think they'll do that."

"But once you give them your trust, it's too late. What if
you're wrong?"

"Too late for what?" Eliza asked.

"Too late to figure out what they're really after. What if
you're wrong?"

"Wrong to trust them? I guess that's how you get hurt. But
it's also how you make life more pleasant."

"If Tommy says he'll be your friend, but really he's just
saying that because he doesn't want you to know you've upset
him, then he could get mad at you, right? And then you'd trust
him, and he could be planning . . . anything."

"It's possible, but that's why Tommy and I talk, to build
the friendship. We're learning about each other."

"Do you trust him?" Sandy asked.

"Sure, as far as I know him. The better I get to know him,
the more I'll trust him."

"What would make you stop?" Sandy asked.

"Why? Do you think I shouldn't trust him? I thought you
liked him."

"I do. But what if he decided to get even with you for
dumping him?"

"How?" Eliza asked, wishing she knew what it was that
Sandy was so afraid of.

"I don't know. He could sleep with somebody else."

"That's fine with me. That wouldn't hurt me. I don't own
him. Nor do I want to." Suddenly Sandy looked as if she
wanted to cry.

"Why are you asking me all these questions about Tommy
and I? What do you really want to know?"

"Nothing," Sandy said. "I'm just talking." She kept her eyes averted.

"Has Tommy done something to hurt you?" Eliza said, fishing for a clue to explain this line of questioning.

Sandy looked up, surprised. "Tommy? No."

"Me, then. Have I done something?"

"Not really," Sandy said.

Eliza replayed the conversation in her mind. There had to be something significant in one of Sandy's questions. But Eliza could think of nothing. The girl had gotten particularly upset when Eliza had said she wouldn't be hurt if Tommy slept with someone else.

"Was it because I said I didn't own him, or want to own him? It's not that I don't think we belong together. I do. It's just that I don't own my friends. They're not possessions. Tommy is a person, not an object."

"But you just said he belongs with you," Sandy insisted, in control once more and apparently more convinced than ever that this romance was a match made in heaven.

"He belongs *with* me, as my friend. He doesn't belong *to* me. No one belongs to anyone."

"That's the truth," Sandy said, her voice bitter.

"But that doesn't make him, or you, less precious to me."

"What difference does that make? If you don't want him." Her rough outer shell was back in place, hard as a diamond. Sandy smiled and tossed her head, but Eliza knew she was hurting. And she thought she knew why.

"Sandy, do you think I'm sending you home because I don't want you?"

"You're throwing me out, so obviously," the girl said, biting her lip.

"You're not getting rid of me, you know. I'll still be checking up on you and bugging you, just like always." Sandy didn't respond. "I mean it. Your friendship is very important to me." Eliza despaired. There was no way she could convince the teenager with words. She would just have to prove it.

"Everyone disappears, eventually," Sandy said. The statement was made in a matter-of-fact tone that Eliza couldn't combat.

"Some people are not reliable. I know your mother and that stepfather you liked, what was his name—Sid?—they couldn't handle the responsibility. But that's not why I can't keep you. I can't give you the home you need because I work all the time. You need someone to be there all the time, to help with school and boys and friends. You need a full-time mother like Mrs. Farber. And you need a house like theirs, full of kids and pets and everything, not a house like this one where all there is to do is watch television all day and cook my dates lavish dinners." She got a smile, finally, with that last line.

Sandy softened. "Do you think Mom and Sid might still be together?"

"They could be. Someday, you'll find out. When you're ready, I'll help. Meantime, don't spend all your time waiting for the people you care about to betray you. Life is too short."

"I bet if you cut back on work a little, you could find time for someone like Tommy." This girl never gave up.

"Probably," Eliza said wryly. "But it's not in the game plan right now."

"Why not?"

"You're too young to understand," Eliza said gently. She seemed to be saying that a lot lately. "Come on, it's time to watch *Cosby.*" When Sandy looked at her in surprise, she said, "I'm studying for the final exam, remember?"

"Then you should watch *Brotherly Love,*" Sandy suggested.

"Brothers?" Eliza said. "I've had enough of brothers for a while. Maybe some other time."

But between dinner with Tommy the next night, during which Sandy watched them both like a hawk, making it impossible to relax, and reporting to Ely concerning the interviews with his son's doctor, teachers, and friends, Eliza could not escape the Greenes. She had made all the necessary arrangements for Sandy's return to the Farbers, so her house would soon be her own again, but she still felt unsettled.

She didn't know what she was going to do about Ely. He'd

done nothing more to make her uncomfortable, but she was still uneasy. He'd been completely circumspect in his business dealings with her, but she felt the tension between them building. The promise he'd made haunted her. She had to settle things with him somehow, before his case came to court.

Chapter Seventeen

Principal McGinley's secretary finally agreed to speak with Eliza, even though her boss wouldn't. Eliza was thrilled to have this chance to speak with someone who was close to the enemy camp, so to speak, but in order to get the interview she had to go to her, at St. Joe's. Ely had told her that the administrator was hard but fair with the children, and he had no reason to believe she would behave otherwise with him, but warned that Mrs. Hadley was very loyal to her immediate superior.

Ely had wanted to join them, but, as it turned out, the only time Mrs. Hadley had available to talk was during one of his classes, so Eliza spoke to her alone. Mrs. Hadley was a small, frail-looking woman. Her pale, wrinkled skin and tiny, clawlike hands gave an impression of immense age, but her pale blue eyes were outlined in darker blue and shadowed in a pastel purple, and she fussed with her fluffy, blue-white hair like a young girl. Her speech was concise and clear. Her mind was still sharp as a tack.

Eliza felt her out carefully, and found her to be just as Ely had described her. Her loyalty to the current principal took second place only to her loyalty to the school itself. She made no apologies for the policies Ely found so untenable, although under Eliza's adept questioning, she acknowledged the arbitrary and sometimes counterproductive nature of some of the rules.

Eliza went to find Ely after she had gotten her questions answered. She was going to conduct a second interview with his friend, Marissa, after school was over in a couple of hours. Marissa was a paraplegic. The one good thing about conducting the interview with Mrs. Hadley at her desk a few feet from Principal McGinley's office was that Ely and Eliza could arrange to talk together with Marissa in a location that was most convenient for her, the teachers' lounge.

Eliza was looking forward to speaking to Ely's friend and colleague, as Marissa's account of Ely's "indiscretion" with young Miss Gina Cerrone was definitely going to be the most sympathetic. If she wasn't able to completely exonerate him, she would certainly be their best witness, on paper, and in court if necessary. Eliza had talked on the telephone with Marissa and had found her quick summary of the story to be sensitive and believable. She provided, if nothing else, justification for Ely's actions with her articulate, logical arguments, which Eliza thought would counterbalance the school's irrational hard-line stance on the matter.

Ely's class hadn't ended yet. She stood outside the door, watching him interact with the class full of young teenagers, until he turned and saw her. He beckoned. Eliza hesitated for a moment and then went into the room. One of the little wise-acres in the back of the room let out a low, long whistle. Ely ushered her into a chair without missing a beat in his lecture.

A proper-looking young lady at the front of the room raised her hand as soon as he paused. "Mr. Greene," she said when he nodded at her. "Is that your girlfriend?"

Her teacher gave her a long-suffering look. "No, this is my lawyer, Ms. Taylor."

Immediately, several hands shot up into the air. Ely waved them all down again. "Before you work yourselves up into a frenzy, I'd like to explain a couple of things to you. This woman is an attorney. She graduated at the top of her class from Harvard Law School. For that reason alone, she deserves your respect. Some lawyers work for the district attorney and prosecute criminals, some work for big corporations, and I think you've all heard of divorce lawyers. Ms. Taylor is a juvenile rights lawyer. She specializes in cases involving children, anyone who is not yet eighteen. I'm sure you all have questions for her, but we have only a few minutes left of class, so I'm afraid you're out of luck." He paused to direct a stern glance to the back of the room. "Let's not hear any rude comments or noises, please."

Arms waved wildly in the air. Eliza had "done" parents' day before, most recently at the public school Sandy O'Davis had been placed in. These students were younger and better behaved. Looking out at the sea of glowing, innocent faces, Eliza felt like standing and saying, *Ask anything you want.*

"Can a kid hire you by himself, without his parents?" asked the first child Ely called on. Ely shook his head and looked at Eliza questioningly.

"It's okay," she said. Without rising from her chair, she turned to the girl who had asked the question. "Sometimes, a child can hire me, but usually it's the parents who pay me. Sometimes, the court appoints me to a case."

"Why did the lawyer in *The Client* ask for one dollar from that kid?"

"It's sort of complicated, but suffice it to say no legal contract is binding without the exchange of legal tender." The boy who had asked the question looked totally baffled by her answer. "Okay," Eliza revised, "you know how you shake on a deal?" A couple of heads bobbed up and down. "Why do you do that?"

"It's like, you made a promise with your mouth, then you make it with your body," one girl said.

"It's the same thing. It's like shaking hands. It's firm. You can't see words, and even if they are written down, they're just words. But you see the money. It goes from one person to the other. You've got something real in your hand, just like when you shake hands." A couple of heads nodded, and Eliza smiled.

"Have you ever lost?" a kid shouted out from the back of the class where no hands were raised.

Eliza was quick to answer. "Yes." She should probably not

reward such rudeness, but the kids in the back were the kind whom it was most difficult to engage and whose interest she would go a little further to encourage. "Yes, I have. And sometimes, I don't lose or win, but rather I come to an agreement with the other side. We all decide to compromise, so nobody loses."

"Time's up," Ely said. "Class, you're dismissed. You already have your reading assignment. It's to be done by tomorrow."

The children closed notebooks and binders and stood collecting their books and bags. The hall outside was suddenly thronging with students, and the class filed out to join them.

Ely came to her side. "Lunchtime," he said. "The hall will be empty in a few minutes."

"I'll wait," Eliza said.

Ely fidgeted with his tie, which was narrow and black and looked like something one would wear to a funeral. It did not match his suit. While the suit he had worn to court had been a little outdated, this outfit was clearly gleaned from the back of his closet. The jacket and slacks were of two different materials, wool below and polyester on top. They were both gray, but completely different hues, one a yellow and the other with a bluish tinge. He had already told her he owned only that one suit, since he usually didn't wear one to work. She surmised he had dressed for her visit.

"Do you . . . uh . . . want to have lunch?" he asked diffidently.

"I swore when I left graduate school that I would never eat in a cafeteria again," she said.

"There's a little café around the corner," he said.

"Okay," she agreed. There couldn't be any harm in having a business lunch in a public place. And he was probably eager to hear about her meeting with Mrs. Hadley.

She told him about it as they walked to the restaurant. "She was pretty much as you described her. She's honest. Her loyalties are clear. The school first, McGinley second. But she agreed that your only crime was breaking the rules. She didn't think you had seduced the girl or anything like that, and was shocked when I asked if she did.''

"So she didn't think I should have been suspended?''

"Yes, she did. But she said, and I quote, 'We wouldn't employ a teacher whom we couldn't trust with the students. We investigated the incident, and there was no suggestion that Mr. Greene's infraction went any further than coming to the girl's home outside of school hours and spending a few hours with her off of the school grounds. There was no evidence that anything indecent occurred or he would have been dismissed.' Hopefully, she'll tell the GAL the same thing.''

Ely was quiet for a moment, pondering this. "Could I lose Jessie just because I didn't leave a twelve-year-old girl sitting out in front of her house alone until all hours of the night?''

"I've told you before, it's going to be up to the judge. It's certainly not evidence that you're unfit to be a parent. But it doesn't help your case. The Tysons' accusation that you are endangering Jessie in behaving irresponsibly is pretty hard to prove. But this kind of behavior does make you look a little flaky. Why did the girl call you?'' As Ely opened his mouth to answer, Eliza continued. "That was a rhetorical question. I know why. I'm just pointing out that it's a little unusual. Taking her to your apartment for dinner and then out to a mall to play arcade games doesn't sound like the normal reaction of a grown man. If they try to paint it blacker than it was, though, I think they'll end up with mud on their faces. It was rash, and ill-advised on your part, and your judgment could certainly be called into question. The proper people should have been notified.''

"She didn't want anyone to know her dad was passed out on the floor inside the house. It could hurt his career. She trusted me.''

"Her father, however, didn't trust in your discretion, which is probably, as you yourself have said, the reason he reported the incident to the school. He wanted to forestall any report you might have made.''

"Here we are,'' Ely said, standing aside to let her enter first.

As the door closed behind them, he exclaimed, "There he is again."

"Who?" Eliza asked, looking around the room.

"Out there." He directed her attention out the window to street. There was no one there. "I keep seeing this guy everywhere I go." He followed her to an empty table.

"Someone you know?"

"No. It's strange. I've seen him near my house, near the school, and even once at the market."

There were a few people walking down the street, but no one stood out. "What does he look like?"

"He's gone now. He's middle-aged, medium height, slim build. Nothing special. I can't get over the feeling he's watching me."

"He could just live in the neighborhood," Eliza suggested.

"I know. I'm probably imagining things. He keeps appearing and disappearing."

"Next time you see him, talk to him."

"I will." He gave a little laugh of embarassment. "I sound paranoid, don't I?"

"Not really. I'm sure you're wrong. You're just a little edgy. These things usually end up being nothing. But you never know. Just keep an eye out." Eliza hoped he was imagining things. Ely might not be the most ordinary parent she had ever met— he had his quirks—but she could work with that. What they didn't need right now was a mad stalker on their plate. The description was reassuring. Stalkers were nearly always, like rapists, people who were known to the victim. Ely clearly didn't recognize the man at all.

"The soup is always good here," Ely mentioned.

"I think I'll have half a sandwich and a cup of soup."

"Sounds good," he said. "Me, too." She felt almost as comfortable with him as she had before their picnic. Eliza hoped that this signified a turning point in their relationship.

When the waiter came to the table, they placed their order quickly and then got back to the discussion they'd been having when they reached the café.

"So, do you think Rebecca is right? I should have been

home taking care of Jessie instead of out baby-sitting Gina Cerrone.''

"I think you did what came naturally. Most people would have left her to fend for herself. You're not the type to turn your back on a child in need. Any child. Unfortunately, you've got a young son who needs you, too.''

"But I was with Jessie until bedtime. She had dinner with us.''

"I know. That's just it," Eliza said. "You brought this girl home. I'm sure I would be grateful, if I were the girl's father. But this is exactly the kind of thing Rebecca's talking about. You brought this person, who was not any relation to you, into your house. I know she was in trouble, but Jessie has to come first.''

"We all had dinner together," Ely repeated. " Jessie, too.''

"I know, but, like I said, that's the problem. Look, one of the reasons I've remained single is because I put too much of my time and energy into work. There's nothing left over for anything or anyone else. I've got this young woman living with me now, a girl who I represented on charges two years ago.''

"She answered the phone once, I think.''

"Probably. Luckily, she's sixteen years old, and she can pretty much take care of herself, because with my schedule, I barely see her. Having her visit for the past few weeks has made one thing very clear to me. I work too hard to take care of a child.''

"You sound like every single parent I ever met," Ely said. "We all feel guilty about not spending more time with our kids.''

"Ely, she's not mine. None of 'my' kids are mine. I spend all of my time with them, but I don't have time for doing things with them like going to the park or the zoo. I handle their cases, try to give them moral support. But I'm not like any of the parents you know because I'm not a parent.'' Eliza felt safe talking about this with him. "I shudder to think what kind of mother I'd be when I can barely fit in dinner at home two nights a week with my temporary guest. My point is, I found out early that I was this workaholic, and I accepted it and didn't have a family. You made a different choice. You have a son. You've raised him, and from what I can see, you've given him all the love and attention he's needed to grow up well. But you've drawn the line between work and family a little thin.''

"Are you giving me advice on parenting?'' he asked, not offended but surprised.

"No. Well, yes, I guess I am,'' Eliza said. "As your lawyer, but yes. You jeopardized your relationship with your son by choosing to bring Gina into your house. That little girl was not your responsibility, and yet you took her on. No one could have guessed her father would be such a jerk, but—''

Ely interrupted. "I had to do something. I couldn't just leave her out there with nowhere to go.''

"I sympathize, but you've got to understand that Mr. and Mrs. Tyson have a point, too. You do sometimes choose your work over your son. You left him with a baby-sitter to baby-sit someone else's child, without even being asked to do so. Jessie isn't going to complain. Kids don't. But his grandparents want to protect him, just like you do.''

"I know. I know,'' Ely conceded. "Something's bugging Jess, but he won't tell me what it is. Communication has fallen way off in our house. I haven't told him about our . . . us . . .'' He sent a speaking glance at Eliza. "And now I think he's got a secret or two of his own.''

"Like what?'' she asked.

"I don't know. I think it may be the case.''

Eliza was finished with her lunch. She folded her napkin and placed it neatly on the table. "I'm sure he'll open up to you sooner or later. You two have a nice relationship.''

"Thank you. But I'm a little worried. If he doesn't tell me what's bothering him soon, I'm going to have to force it out of him.''

"Don't do that,'' Eliza said immediately. "If it is about the case, he'll talk to you soon enough. If he's not ready to tell you, then he's not. I think with children that age it's better to let them come to you. We've explained the whole custody issue to him. When he needs to know more, he'll ask.''

"Mmmm,'' Ely murmured his assent.

When he didn't say anything more, Eliza asked, "Shouldn't you be getting back?"

"Oh, yeah, sure," he said, as if awakening from a trance. He waved the waiter over and asked for the check. He paid and they left.

When they had started walking back to the school, Ely brought up a comment she had made earlier. "You gave me advice about parenting, as a lawyer, so I'm going to give you my advice about parenting as a parent. I'm sure you'd be a very good mother." Eliza didn't respond. He had his illusions about her, and there was no arguing him out of them. After a moment, he continued. "You may not be a parent, but what you do for *your* kids demonstrates exactly what kind of parent you'd be. You can call it giving them moral support, but what you do is a lot like loving them. I've seen how you are with Jessie. You may not have time to take your clients to the zoo, but you are nurturing, accepting of them as people."

"I think you're biased," Eliza said.

"I'm sure. But I've had a lot of practice at sizing up parents over the years, and I'm not bad at it. In fact, I'm usually right."

"Me, too," Eliza said. "But usually isn't good enough when it comes to something like this. I've been right in every case but one. At least, I was never proven wrong. But that one exception . . ." She let her voice trail off.

"Yes?" Ely prompted.

"A child died because of my judgment." Eliza couldn't believe she had just said that. She never talked about David Peron's death. It was hers. Her personal tragedy.

"How's that?" Ely asked. Eliza shook her head. "I mean, I can't see you standing around letting a child get beaten to death."

Eliza winced, but she did admit, "I wasn't there." She was sorry it had slipped out.

"He *was* beaten?" Ely asked, horrified.

"Hit by a car," Eliza muttered. Little as she wanted to discuss this, she couldn't let Ely think the terrible assumption he had made was the truth.

"And that was your fault?" Ely asked.

"He was two years old. I was the one who recommended he be placed in his father's care." Eliza was surprised at how calm she sounded. She felt very shaky, confessing aloud her part in the toddler's death.

"So, you're responsible?" Ely wouldn't leave it alone.

"I was the one who left him with the man who . . . let him get away."

"A two-year-old? Got away from his father and wandered into traffic?" Eliza nodded, unable to trust her voice. "That's tragic, but not exactly unheard of, Eliza. No one's infallible. How were you supposed to predict that?"

She recoiled. "I didn't say I—"

"You're trying to affix blame for a situation that could have happened to anyone. Anywhere. It's terrible, but it's true. It happens without your help."

They had arrived back at the school, and Eliza had had enough. More than enough. The meeting with Marissa was supposed to take place after Ely's last class.

"I've got some phone calls to make. I'll meet you in the teachers' lounge at three o'clock," Eliza said.

"Wait." Ely stopped her as she turned away. "I didn't mean to upset you."

"You didn't." Eliza tried to lie, but her voice broke, giving her away. Usually, she was such a good liar. Unfortunately, her talent had deserted her at the wrong time. "I'll get over it," she amended.

"Forgive me?" Ely searched her face. His hangdog expression made her feel guilty.

"Nothing to forgive," she assured him. "I'll be fine. It was a long time ago. And . . . it was probably good for me to talk about it like this." He still looked sad, and sorry.

Eliza waved a hand in the air, erasing his transgression, absolving him. "Don't worry, Ely. It's all right."

He held her gaze for a moment. She nodded.

"Okay, I'll see you later," he said. "Teachers' lounge."

Eliza walked away. She felt surprisingly good, after all—lighter—as if a burden had been lifted from her shoulders. They were right when they said confession was good for the soul, she decided, virtually floating down the hallway. She tested herself, picturing David's face, an image that she recalled at odd moments, which had the power to depress her for weeks. Today, it was like remembering a snapshot that she hadn't seen in a while. Eliza sighed, relieved. It couldn't hurt her anymore. She was free.

Chapter Eighteen

The interview with Marissa went beautifully. The woman was model lovely, with long, chestnut hair that fell in waves down her back. Her ivory skin and serene brown eyes belied her toughness and resilience. When she caught Eliza in her gaze, Eliza forgot that she was in a wheelchair. Those big round eyes were as clear-sighted as a child's, but the intelligence and honesty in them required anyone talking with her to respond with the same.

"It was lucky the girl called Ely," she said of the incident with Gina Cerrone. "And Ely behaved very responsibly in my opinion. Instead of leaving her to get into trouble on her own, he came to get her, brought her home and kept her safe until he could reach her father and turn her over to her parent with a clear conscience. He kept Gina's confidence, so that she wouldn't be worried about calling an adult if she got into trouble again. He should never have been put on probation for that. The school should have thanked him, or at least defended him in the face of Mr. Cerrone's ridiculous accusations. I would have done exactly the same thing."

As for the gang members invading his home, all Marissa had to say was, "I like to think that's exactly what teachers are trained to deal with. That's the kind of opportunity we hope for—those of us in the community who see these kids getting caught up in the violence and danger on the streets. The chance to talk to them before things escalate out of control.

"I knew those boys. The one who thought to come to Ely in the first place was a sweet kid before he joined that gang. If they had visited me, I like to think I could have opened my door to them, talked to them. I don't believe Ely or Jessie were ever in any danger—although I can understand why Jessie's grandmother was frightened, since she didn't know the kids. But none of them was over fourteen."

"Thank you," Eliza said, with heartfelt sincerity, when Marissa had done with her explanation of Ely's problems with the school. "You understand the Guardian Ad Litem appointed to the court will be asking you some of these questions."

"Yes, Ely told me." Marissa was an amazing woman. Confined to a wheelchair after an accident in her college days, she'd continued her schooling and gotten her teacher's certificate and had been teaching at St. Joe's ever since. "I just hope it helps," she said. Marissa was one of the most popular teachers in the school, not only because of her sweet personality, but because she was a hard taskmaster who didn't allow the kids to make any excuses. She got them to work harder and to succeed more than they would have thought possible.

"The Greenes should not be split up, certainly not because of Ely's devotion to his work."

"You tell the GAL what you've told us, and I believe we've got a decent chance."

Ely had been sitting quietly through the interview. He spoke for the first time as Marissa prepared to leave them. "I am glad you're on my side."

"Of course, Ely. We're all on the same side and don't you forget it. They may be giving you grief now, but you'll get yours back."

He leaned down to give her a kiss on the cheek, and she patted him on the back. "You'll do fine. And I've got to get going. My husband is waiting for me at home."

"We won't keep you any longer," Eliza said, walking toward

the door. Ely beat her to it and held the door open for Marissa. They both stepped out in the hall to watch her roll silently away down the corridor lined with brightly painted lockers and colorful posters.

Eliza turned to Ely. "You were right." The wide grin which she could feel stretching from cheek to cheek was not at all her usual style, but she couldn't help it. She felt fantastic. Ely's friend and coworker could not help but make a favorable impression on the GAL.

Ely smiled back at her. "She's amazing, isn't she. That woman is the best thing about this place." Eliza wasn't in the mood to lecture him about the irreverent tone he used when referring to the venerable old institution for which he worked. She preferred to savor, for a moment at least, the thought of this articulate new ally on the witness stand.

Unthinkingly, Eliza reached out to flick a piece of lint from the dark wool of Ely's jacket sleeve. If she had thought about it, she might have remembered how the simple act of straightening his tie in the courtroom had caused her entire body to catch fire. And that had been in the middle of the morning, in front of his in-laws, his family, and the judge! She should have known better than to touch him again when such a casual gesture affected her so strongly.

Somewhere, up or down a staircase perhaps, she could hear young voices echoing, but there was not a soul in sight. They were completely alone. Ely had reserved the teachers' lounge for their interview, so the room stood empty behind him. Presumably, as they hadn't been interrupted once in the past hour, his colleagues had taken any work they had to do home with them.

It had been an innocent mistake. She had only brushed her hand across his upper arm, but the simple act of touching him sent a spark of electricity through her. Ely's jaw snapped shut with an audible click. Eliza looked up into his dark eyes. They were molten chocolate.

She swayed toward him. He stepped back and she followed, her eyes never leaving his face. He reached out a hand to cup her elbow and drew her with him into the lounge. He stopped and waited. Eliza didn't hesitate. She moved forward, until she stood toe to toe with him, with barely two inches between them.

"Eliza?" he croaked.

Eliza had the same frog in her throat. She cleared it. "Ely," she said. He reached around her and gave the door a gentle push, and it swung closed behind her. She raised her hand to his cheek. His skin was hot and silky beneath her fingertips. They skimmed over his jaw, toward his full mouth. His upper lip was shadowed, a bit rough with a day's growth of beard.

Ely dropped his head back and stared up at the ceiling. "Oh, God," he groaned. Eliza stretched up on her toes and kissed his chin. His head came up and he gulped rapidly, his Adam's apple bobbing up and down. She put her hands on his shoulders to balance herself and nuzzled his smooth, warm neck.

His arms closed around her in a big, teddy bear hug. Eliza sighed and rested her cheek against his chest. He smelled of chalk dust and shaving cream and beneath that, of himself.

"I hope you know what you're doing," he said into her hair as she undid one of his shirt buttons and slipped her hand inside the warm cotton to the even warmer flesh beneath.

"Am I going to get into trouble for this?" he asked, stroking her back to the rhythm Eliza set as she painted circles on his rib cage with her palm.

"We both are," she said.

She was seducing a client. It was forbidden. It was stupid. It was beyond her control. She needed his caress, even if it broke her into a million pieces.

She slipped the hand that still rested on his shoulder around his neck and pulled his head down to hers. He caught her top lip between his and sucked it into his mouth. She clung to him. He lowered his head slightly and she tried to follow, but he ducked to plant a swift kiss on her chin, open-mouthed, leaving an imprint that cooled as his breath whispered over the wet spot. His hand went to the back of her neck, and he held her still as he teased her with featherlight kisses at the corners of her mouth. Finally, his tongue flicked over her teeth and invaded the soft, warm depths of her mouth.

She was wide open to him, her tongue dueling with his for her chance to explore his hot, velvety mouth. The startling fact was that he was in control, deepening the kiss and then threatening to withdraw before plundering her mouth again. She had thought his previous kisses remarkable, but this one was a kiss to last a lifetime, tantalizing and yet deeply satisfying.

He was as shy as his brother was self-assured. He was as unkempt as Tommy was well-groomed. But it was Ely, not Tom, who made her feel like liquid fire ran through her veins. She had tried with Tommy. She had wanted him to be the one to bring her to life again after her long abstinence. It could have worked between them. Tommy was just like her, driven by ambition and, despite his charming manner, guarded in his emotions. If they had gotten together, for a week or for a year, no one would have been hurt.

Ely was all wrong for her. He was the kind of man she had always avoided—the type who fell in love forever. She never fell in love at all. They had no future. They even looked ridiculous together. Worst of all, when things didn't work out, he'd be hurt. Eventually, he would realize she was only using him to hold loneliness at bay and was incapable of loving him as he had been loved by his young wife, as he deserved to be loved again by some extraordinary woman like Marissa, like himself. The thought teased her, niggled at the back of her mind: *This is all wrong.* But she had never felt so right. She couldn't get enough of him, the smell of him, the taste of his skin, the feel of his body against hers. When the kiss ended, her lips fell to his collarbone.

''Don't stop,'' she said.

He lifted her off her feet and carried her to the couch. She couldn't open her eyes, didn't open them even as he left her there. Instead, she willed away the doubts, the fears that nagged at her. *Just this once,* she thought. *I'll get my fill of him, whatever it takes. Then, I can walk away.* She took a deep breath and readied herself to open her eyes and start the seduction all over again. Then, she heard a clicking sound and realized he had just left her to lock the door.

She was relieved and frightened at the same time. There was

no turning back now. He came back to the couch and stood over her. She felt fragile, as if the slightest touch would cause her to shatter. She hadn't felt this vulnerable since she'd been a child. But there was a strong thrumming within her, a beat that could not be ignored. She opened her eyes. His shirt buttons were all undone. Funny, Eliza couldn't remember doing that. She drank in the sight of his smooth muscular chest, sculpted in bronze.

His hand touched her cheek, then traced the swirls of her ear. He sat down beside her, his hip against hers. She lay quietly, looking up at him. She put her hand on his thigh and left it lying there, absorbing the feel of him through her palm. With his free hand, he covered hers. His other hand left her face and spanned the delicate skin of her neck. He skimmed down her chest, fingers splayed, and the movement pushed her jacket aside. He looked into her eyes as his hand covered her breast. Her stomach muscles tightened. Her nipple hardened into a tight little kernel beneath his palm. He must have felt it, because he looked down and smiled, like a little boy making a wonderful new discovery.

He started to unbutton her blouse, slowly. Eliza felt a delicious languor spread through her as he pushed the material aside and lowered his head. He kissed the curve of her breast, then drew her nipple deeply inside his mouth. She gasped at the exquisite sensation and squeezed his thigh. Her free hand went to the back of his head, but he caught it and held it against his chest as he drove her crazy with his tongue and teeth. Eliza wanted to wrap him in her arms, bring him closer. Beneath one hand she felt his thigh, beneath the other, his breast, but she wanted more. She wanted to feel him against the length of her.

"Ely," she gasped. "Please!"

He raised his head and smiled at her. Leaning over, he kissed her lightly. "Don't rush me," he said against her mouth.

A breathless laugh escaped her. "Rush you? I wouldn't, uh, dream of it," Eliza said with some difficulty as he nipped her chin with his teeth. "I'm trying to be encourag . . . couraging," she explained. He moved to her other breast, making Eliza tremble in anticipation of more of this excruciating torture.

"At least let go of my hands," she pleaded. "I want to touch you."

"Be my guest," Ely said, placing both of her hands against his chest. His expression was open, joyful, almost childlike. It did not go with his expert lovemaking. He framed her rib cage with his big calloused hands, gently pressing his thumbs into her abdomen. She slid her hand down over his stomach and just under the waistband of his jeans. She pulled him to her with a slow, steady tugging.

"Eliza," he said, pleased, and perhaps a little shocked. He stretched out beside her, almost on top of her.

"Kiss me again, Ely."

He leaned over her and slanted his mouth over hers. She slipped her arms around him and pulled him closer, then ran her hands down his back, as far down as she could reach. His body was taut and insistent. She squeezed the backs of his thighs. His breathing grew harsh.

There was a knock at the door. They both ignored it, until a deep male voice cried, "Who's in there?"

"Oh, no," Ely groaned. He jumped up and started to button his shirt.

"You're going to let him in?"

"No, he's got a key. It's the janitor." Eliza sat up and quickly started to straighten her clothing. They heard the key turn in the lock.

"Fred?" Ely called out.

"Oh, hi." The door opened slowly. "What up, Teach?" The custodian was a dark-skinned man of about fifty. He looked at them questioningly.

"My lawyer and I were just finishing up here."

Fred looked Eliza up and down, then raised an eyebrow at Ely. "Your lawyer, huh? Nice going. She's the prettiest mouthpiece I ever saw. Now I understand that suit." He winked at Eliza. "Hope he made a good impression, miss."

Eliza nodded, uncertain about whether that was supposed to be a joke. She took a quick look at Ely in the awful suit. A good impression? In that ridiculous outfit? If she had a thing for clowns, maybe.

"You finished in here? I gotta clean the room." Fred directed the question at Ely, but Eliza answered.

She had herself under control again. "Yes, we're going." She went to the table where they had interviewed Marissa and gathered up her notes. It seemed hours since she had conducted the question-and-answer session, scribbling on her yellow legal pad as always. She felt like the notations had been made by a different woman.

She reined in her flight of fancy. She had acted, for a short time, in a totally uncharacteristic manner, but it was over and done with. Sanity had returned, and with it, a wave of shame at her behavior. Here was another unfamiliar sensation to add to the new experiences she'd been having lately.

Eliza was no prude. She'd had her share of men in her forty-one years. But she had never shameless seduced anyone before, let alone someone as unsuitable as Ely Greene. He was too sweet and devoted and passionate for a woman like herself. As young as he was, he'd already been married and widowed and made a great start in raising his son. She had never been anybody to anyone.

That was why, when they reached her car, she said, "Ely, I'm sorry. That was my fault, and I shouldn't have done it."

"Let's not start this again," he said.

"No, really. I, you, were right," she said, looking anywhere but at him. "It's not just you who needs to keep your hands to yourself. I shouldn't have touched you."

"Eliza," he said, grabbing her by the shoulders and turning her to face him. "The sweetest words I have ever heard in my life were your saying, 'I want to touch you.' Don't run away now."

"Please don't," she begged.

"I admit, the timing couldn't be worse. I'm being investigated for child molestation, or abuse, or neglect, which is not something I ever thought to hear myself say. But however we got here, let's not go backward."

"I'm going home. You can go wherever you want." She

spun away from him and pulled her car door open. He caught her before she could slide into the driver's seat.

"Eliza!" She tried to push him away, but he was too big and too strong to be moved.

"Damn you!" she cursed. He let her go, but he didn't move away. He had her trapped between the car and his body. Her elbow caught him in the stomach as she tried to squeeze past him. He grunted, but still didn't move. He just waited until she realized she wasn't going to be able to get away from him.

"What do you want from me?" she cried.

"For now, I'll settle for a kiss good-bye."

"Let me go, Ely."

"Come on," he taunted her. "What are you so afraid of?"

"That's not going to work this time."

"What does work with you? Tell me. How do I get through to you Eliza?"

"It's not that simple," she said, full of self-loathing. She had already violated every principle she believed in. She couldn't touch him again. Her heart pounded so hard in her chest, she thought he could see it if he looked, but he was looking into her eyes instead, looking for an answer she wasn't sure she was ready to give.

"Nothing about this is simple," Ely said sardonically. "You think I'm impressed by this tough act of yours? I'm not. How can you act like this after what just happened between us? Eliza, I know you're not this cold."

"I am. I have to be," she insisted.

"Why?" he asked, exasperated.

"Let me go, Ely." She pushed at him again, but he grabbed her arm and pulled her to him and kissed her hard, putting all of himself into that kiss. She pulled back against the hand that held the back of her head, but he didn't let her go. She mumbled a protest against his lips, but he just deepened the kiss, plundering her mouth until she went limp against him. Still he didn't release her, but his lips softened. His relentless attack on her mouth changed to a more subtle assault of her senses as he drew her unresisting body into his and bent into her, fitting himself against her, nearly lifting her off the ground.

She felt herself capitulate. She was overwhelmingly aware of the textures of his body—his warm, wet mouth against her own, his rough-skinned hands stroking her throat, and his fingertips on her cheek. His hard chest pressed into hers. His strong legs were like tempered steel against her thighs. Under her hands, his wool slacks were soft and rough at the same time.

When he lifted his head, her rage had drained away, leaving her pliable, weak-kneed and weak-willed.

"Come on, Eliza. We can do this. It's not exactly what I had planned, but I can't wait three months for you. I can't even wait another day."

"All right," she agreed, surrendering. She needed this human contact. Her body was starved for it. Her soul, too, longed to make the connection again. She needed him. She couldn't deny it, or herself, any longer.

"Tonight," she said. "Can you get a sitter?

"No problem," he answered in a flippant tone, but heat still flared in his eyes.

"Your place?" he asked with barely concealed impatience.

"I think so. I'll call you to confirm."

Eliza wanted Sandy out of the house. She was about to commit an unpardonable crime and didn't want any witnesses. She couldn't justify her actions to herself, let alone anyone else.

Eliza didn't know if it was worth it. She did know that now that the decision had been made to break her own absolutely immutable rule, she could hardly wait.

Chapter Nineteen

It had been planned that Sandy would go to the movies with MJ that night. It took less than a minute to arrange for Sandy to go home, after the movie, with her new best friend. The only explanation Eliza gave was that she wanted to be alone. MJ might speculate about whether she needed the time alone to work or to deal with her romance with Tommy, but Eliza was certain her friend would not guess at the real reason she'd asked for her help in obtaining an evening of solitude. MJ would never, in her wildest dreams, suspect Eliza of doing anything so wrong as sleeping with a client.

She couldn't imagine herself confessing the truth, even though she didn't think MJ would condemn her for what she was about to do. She'd made a mess of it even with Ely, who thought her objections were just an excuse for keeping him at arm's length. She knew he didn't truly believe an affair between them would hurt his case.

She should have been able to convince him. She risked losing all objectivity in his case, which made her feel that she was cheating him, as his lawyer. As ineffective as she'd been at explaining the legal ramifications of corrupting the attorney/client relationship, she felt even guiltier at the prospect of getting involved with such a gentle man. She knew Ely was investing more in this affair than she was, and that made her a cheat on a personal level, as well.

It hadn't been so bad with Tommy. He knew the rules. But Ely was a true romantic. Unfortunately, this was not the stuff of fairy tales. He didn't know her. In fact they were virtual strangers. Until a month ago, they had not had any contact in a dozen years. He had this image of her as some kind of heroine, but she was far from the courageous woman he thought her.

She had warned him. Again and again. And she planned to issue one final warning tonight. Before he touched her, or she him, she was going to have a little talk with Ely about their situation.

She was barely able to maintain her lawn, let alone a love affair. She had clients all over the state depending on her to be there for them. She rushed to bail her juvenile delinquents out of jail at all hours of the day and night. She even had them stay with her. Sandy was not the first child to use her home as a temporary shelter, although she was the first to do so without an invitation. She didn't have time for Ely, or Jessie. Her kids' lives were chockful of crises and real emergencies and, by extension, her life, too, was in constant turmoil. It wouldn't be fair to subject anyone who hadn't chosen it to that lifestyle. And especially not a small boy.

She couldn't get seriously involved with anyone, and she had more than a sneaking suspicion that Ely was going to get pretty serious after tonight. Knowing this did not stop her from pulling her favorite cocktail dress out of the closet after she'd showered. Whichever way the evening went, Eliza felt sure that she could handle it in this dress. The dress made her feel feminine, even sexy, and gave her confidence, she rationalized. There was nothing more to her choice of attire than that, although MJ called it her lucky dress, because she'd worn it to an awards dinner and won the honor she'd been nominated for. Eliza refused to consider the implications.

When Ely rang the doorbell, she was ready and waiting. Her nerves had made it impossible for her to settle down, and by the time she swung the door open to greet him, she was so tense she felt as though she could have burst from the pressure.

Ely didn't say hello. He just stood and gaped at her.

"Come on in," Eliza urged, and he followed her into the small foyer, where he turned to watch her close the door.

"Wow," he said.

She knew what he saw. Her mind flashed to the image she'd seen in the mirror before she left her room. She wore black high heels and sheer black stockings which showed off her muscular calves. Her royal-blue dress was short enough to display the length of her legs. It fit smoothly over her torso. The bodice was tapered at the waist and rose upward in a vee, the cool blue satin fitting snugly over her chest. It stopped just at the upper curve of her breasts, and left her neck and shoulders bare. The color complimented her café-au-lait skin. She wore a velvet ribbon of the same blue around her neck, with a small diamond broach pinned in the center, which matched the diamonds sparkling on her wrists.

With the dress and stockings, it seemed only fitting that she wear dramatic makeup. Bright red lipstick matched the polish on her nails, and a hint of the same red on her cheeks. Mauve eye shadow with purple highlights made her eyes look huge. Her hair she had swept up off her neck and twisted into a smooth wave right over the nape of her neck. She had curled a few strands of hair to fall in wispy tendrils that drifted over her ears, down her neck, almost to her shoulders. When she had examined herself in the mirror, she had liked the effect she'd created. With Ely looking at her, Eliza felt beautiful.

"Thank you," she said. She took his jacket but was careful not to touch him. He didn't take his eyes from her for a moment, but followed her into the living room.

"We need to have a little discussion," Eliza said. "Would you like a glass of wine?" She had already brought an ice bucket with a bottle of Chardonnay into the room, as well as some glasses, and when he nodded, she poured a glass for each of them. Then she sat down. He joined her on the couch, but seemed to sense her need for a little space between them. He didn't touch her, though he was only a foot or so away.

"What do we need to discuss?" he asked gamely.

"You are much younger than I am."

"I knew this was bound to come up again sooner or later," he said, with a slight shake of his head. He settled back into his corner of the couch. "What difference does it make. So you're forty and I'm thirty. They're just numbers."

"I'm forty-one, and you're twenty-nine, but the real problem with the age difference is that I think we're at different stages in our lives. You want to fall in love and settle down. If I were going to fall in love and live happily ever after with some man, I think I would have done it by now."

Methuselah speaks," he joked. She ignored him, crossed "age difference" off her list, and proceeded to the next item.

"Which leads to the next thing on my list. You were married once. I never have been. I want you to think about that for a minute."

"Eliza, this is ridiculous."

"Okay, you're not in the mood for deep contemplation. All I'm trying to say is, we're very different. You listen to your heart. I tend to analyze everything. Everything. That's why you were married at twenty-one."

"Because I follow my heart."

"And I've never been married at all because I never listen to my heart. I prefer reason, which tells me I'm not good at relationships. I can't sustain them. You understand?"

"You're terrible at relationships," he parroted. "Because you're overly analytical?" He looked very pleased with himself when she nodded. He still looked pretty smug when he pointed out, "It doesn't make us incompatible, obviously."

"I wasn't saying it did. I thought I should point out though that I'm not here with you because I've been carried away by emotion. We're both adults. We have physical needs. I certainly do."

"I noticed," he said, his devilish smile back in full force.

"Well, so. I just think we're both very compatible sexually. We, or I, got somewhat carried away this afternoon."

"Me, too," he chimed in.

"But I want to reiterate that—physical attraction aside—it is not a good idea for us to become personally involved."

"I understand that," he said. "I just can't seem to remember it when I'm near you."

"I need to be clear-sighted, unemotional, to argue your case to the best of my ability." That was the last of her arguments.

He reached out to touch her cheek. She cupped his hand between her cheek and her shoulder before Eliza remembered the plan she had made. She wasn't going to touch him until he understood what he was letting himself in for. She leaned forward to get her notes from the coffee table. He let his hand fall, resting his own on the sofa back.

"Ahem," She cleared her throat nervously. "I know we've talked about this already."

"Yes, we have."

"But I can't help feeling I'm not making myself clear."

"You are. You have. I got it." He smiled. "We're breaking the cardinal rule. You know me. I'm not big on rules," he said, his voice smoky.

"But there is a good reason for this rule," she persisted.

"Which you've explained," he said. "I'll take full responsibility. You want me to sign a release?"

"We both have full lives and all of the attendant responsibilities—me to my work and you to your son."

"Okay, I'll accept that. Anything else?" He was nodding, as if he agreed, but there was a glint of laughter in his eyes that made her think he was just humoring her. Eliza wanted to shake him, tell him this was serious. She, at least, was not interested in a long-term commitment to him, and she honestly couldn't make one. It wasn't in her nature, and it certainly didn't fit into her plans.

"I'm afraid my priorities don't include taking on your problems outside of the courtroom. That may sound selfish, but I felt I had to be honest with you before things went further between us."

"Are you sure you're being honest? Or are you just scared?"

"You're not listening to me. If you were, you'd know that you should be scared, too. Whether you agree with me or not, you can't afford to get in over your head with me, any more than I can with you.''

"Eliza?"

"What?"

"You think too much, did you know that?'' He leaned toward her. "Of course you do, you just said it. Is that everything on your list?''

"Ummmm.'' She flipped through her index cards, but she was just stalling. She had no more to say. His big hand reached out and covered hers, and he took the three-by-five slips away and dropped them on the coffee table. His eyes stayed on her face, drifted briefly down to her bare shoulders and back again.

"I feel like I should be wearing a tuxedo or something.'' He was only inches away now.

"Do you own a tux?'' She was momentarily distracted from his lips, so close to hers.

"No,'' he admitted sheepishly, touching her forehead with his own. "I never needed one before.'' He smiled.

"We'll talk about your wardrobe later,'' Eliza said, willing him closer.

"My what?'' he murmured against her lips. "My clothes?'' His mouth was a hairsbreadth from hers. "What's wrong with my clothes?''

Eliza smiled. "You can't be serious,'' she whispered. "They're awful.'' She raised her head up, but he moved just out of reach.

"Everything?'' he whispered across her lips.

"Everything.'' She took his chin between her hands and brought his mouth down toward hers.

He touched his mouth to hers lightly for a moment.

"Hmmm,'' he murmured happily. "You noticed,'' he said smugly.

"It's hard to miss.'' The double entendre was intentional.

"You want to dress me?'' he asked, self-satisfied.

"Not right now,'' Eliza answered impatiently.

"Later, then,'' he insisted.

"Much later, fool.''

He kissed her then, finally. His hand slid from her shoulder to her elbow and around her back, and he pulled her body across his. Her arms went around him, and her hands explored his broad, hard back.

"Let's go upstairs," Eliza suggested, when she could draw a breath to speak.

"Mm-hmm," he assented. He slipped one arm around her shoulders and the other under her knees and lifted her as if she weighed no more than a child. She might have enjoyed the ride, but she wasn't sure she trusted him.

She wrapped her arms around his neck. "Put me down before you drop me."

"I won't drop you." He kissed the tip of her nose. "I promise."

She pushed her hand beneath his shirt.

"What are you trying to do? Make me break my word?"

She started to withdraw her hand, but he said, "No, it's okay. I was just teasing you." She stroked his chest under his shirt, greedy to see him, touch him.

"Lawyers don't have a sense of humor," she said.

She pointed to her bedroom door, and he brought her inside. He laid her gently on the bed and then ran his hand down her legs to her feet. He took off her shoes. He picked up one foot and started to massage it.

"Stop that," she said. "It tickles."

He brushed a fingernail up the length of her sole, making her squirm. "Hey," she protested. "Don't."

"Tickling isn't what I had in mind, but I'm easy. I'll start any way you want." His tone was bright, but his eyes had darkened.

"Come here," Eliza said, crooking her finger and beckoning him. He leaned over her, and she unbuttoned his shirt. "Take it off."

He stood up again and stepped back. He took his time unfastening the buttons at his wrists, then shrugged his shoulders out of the garment. It hung precariously for a moment while Eliza took in the broad expanse of his shoulders, then the blue denim top slid down to the floor. She followed the motion, taking in his chocolate-brown chest and the narrow waist that disappeared into his jeans, his slim hips and long legs. His powerful thighs were shown off to advantage by his pants, which were, for once, the right size for him. She watched the play of muscles in his upper arms as he pulled open the snaps on his jeans and pulled down the zipper. Her lips parted slightly to allow more air into her suddenly constricted throat. He stopped, his eyes on her mouth.

"If you keep looking at me like that, I'm going to have to rip that dress off."

"We can't have that," she said and sat up, turning her back to him. "Unzip me, please."

His fingers were warm and sure as they slid down her spine. She leaned back into him and turned her head, and he kissed her over her shoulder, one of his hands splayed across the small of her back, the other gently holding her chin. Curling her fingers into the sheet and holding on tight, she managed to turn her head away. When he would have turned her fully into him, she restrained herself and held back.

"All right, now we'll get undressed, together," she offered.

His hands dropped from her chin and he closed his eyes, taking a deep, shuddering breath. "Need any help?" he asked huskily.

She felt her lips curve into a smile. "I think I can manage." She turned around, so she was once again facing him and skimmed the low-cut dress down over her breasts and waist, to her hips. She shivered as he drank in the sight of her black bustier with widened eyes. His pupils were completely dilated, his eyes, black pools.

"You first," she said.

He bent down, never taking his eyes from her, and took off his shoes and socks, then stood slowly. His jeans unsnapped, his open zipper offered a tantalizing view of his flat abdomen. He looked so handsome, Eliza felt her breath catch in the back of her throat.

"Your turn," he said, once again turning the tables on her.

She was up to the challenge. She brought one foot up on the bed and slowly skimmed the thigh-high black stocking down to her toes and off, then casually dropped the little ball of sheer black silk to the floor. She repeated the action, baring her other leg. She hesitated for a moment, then pulled the hem of her dress down again to just above her knees and smoothed it over her thighs, and stared at him challengingly.

He pulled down his jeans and kicked them off. Dressed only in his white shorts, he straightened. The pale cotton brought out the color of his dark skin, and Eliza felt her breath quicken in anticipation of touching all that lovely cocoa-colored flesh.

She hooked her thumbs beneath the material of her dress, which had bunched around her waist, and pushed it down. She wriggled, working the sleek satin past her hips, over her thighs and down her legs, and left it lying at the end of the bed. Her black silk panties matched her satin bustier, covering her hip bones with a demure fall of black lace.

Ely slid off his shorts and stood naked before her. He was sleek and surprisingly muscular—and beautiful. She swallowed at the size of him, already aroused, waiting for her. She reached behind her back to open the clasps of her bustier, but Ely didn't wait. He advanced, slowly but surely, as she fumbled with the hooks. He leaned over her, and deftly unhooked the last two clasps which held the undergarment in place.

There was nothing of the awkward, stumbling professor left in the man who eased her back against the pillows and lay down next to her. He looked his fill at her before dipping his mouth to her breast. When she couldn't stand the gentle assault for a second longer, she threaded her fingers in his soft, kinky hair and tugged his head up. As their lips pressed together and their tongues touched, all the sweetness of the verbal foreplay ended, and they explored each other thoroughly, almost roughly. Four hands impatiently roamed and explored the unfamiliar terrain they had exposed to each other.

His hands gentled, and he whispered in her ear, "I guess this answers my question. You are great at everything you do."

She pushed his head up and glared at him. "I didn't realize I was being graded."

"I didn't mean . . ." He stiffened and then grinned as she smiled at him.

"Gotcha," she crowed.

"I thought you said lawyers didn't have a sense of humor," he said, kissing her hard full on the mouth.

"I lied," she said simply. "I have one. It's just slightly perverse—according to the people who know me best."

He stroked the inside of her thighs and the triangle of black silk between them.

"I hadn't noticed your having a sick sense of humour," he muttered as his full lips danced over her cheek and down her jaw. He cupped her sex in his hand, gently, experimentally.

"I'm here with you, aren't I?" Eliza managed to say, before he removed the last flimsy barrier between them. Then she had to stop talking to concentrate on his expert caresses.

He tormented her until she pleaded with him to stop and then, finally, covered her mouth with his as he covered her body, positioning himself atop her. When he finally entered her, she bit her lip so hard it bled. He withdrew and drove himself deeper, and she raised her hips to meet his, a rising tide within carrying her to him again and again.

He moaned, and urged her on with his voice. "Eliza, my love, my sweet. Yes . . . oh, yes."

She matched him stroke for stroke and cried out with her climax, "Ely!"

She had always been a cool lover, giving as much as she took, but always in control of herself. Before tonight. She and Ely were both panting, bathed in sweat, as they lay side by side on the white damask bedspread which they hadn't even bothered to push aside. She had never been so unrestrained, but when he turned his head and smiled at her, she felt vulnerable in her nudity.

She slipped out of bed and grabbed her lightweight cotton robe, quickly wrapping it around her before she asked him, "Would you like a glass of water or something?"

"Sure," he said.

As she walked toward the bedroom door, he asked, "Are you okay?"

"Yes," Eliza answered, "I'm fine." She paused in the doorway. "Are you all right?"

"Better than all right," he said. "You were amazing." As

she turned again to go, he said, "I said that already, didn't I? It's just, I don't think I'll ever get over you. You're so full of surprises."

Look who's talking, Eliza thought. Aloud she said, "I didn't expect . . . this, either." She waved her arm. The gesture took in Ely, the bed, and their clothes scattered on the floor.

He pushed himself up into a sitting position, swung his legs over the side of the bed and reached down for his shorts, which he drew on gracefully, no sign of the fumbling schoolteacher about him now.

"I feel like I just went to heaven, but I also feel like I just came home. You know what I mean?"

Eliza didn't know what to say to that.

"Take this room, for example. It's nothing like you, but it's just what I would have pictured." Eliza looked around her bedroom. It was comfortable. The curtains and the bedclothes were white, the headboard was shiny brass. The dressing table was pine, stained white, as was the bureau and the nightstand. The room was lost somewhere betwen the French provincial and early American styles. Her carpet was turquoise. Southwestern paintings dominated the room and offset the blandness of the furniture. It all fit together somehow, the one exception being the African wood sculpture of a mother and child she'd bought and had a stand built for, so it would be the first thing she saw in the morning and the last thing she saw at night.

She supposed the room revealed something about her personality but looking around now, trying to see it through Ely's eyes, she couldn't think what it might tell him about her.

"I'll be right back," she said, slipping out of the door and padding down to the kitchen. She enjoyed the cool air that wafted from the refrigerator and stood in front of it for a moment or two before she fetched glasses and poured them each an Evian. She dawdled over the simple tasks, feeling shy about Ely after what had passed between them. When she went back upstairs, he was asleep, naked except for his boxers, in her bed. As she sipped her water, her eyes poured over him, taking in all the details she hadn't noticed. Those black eyelashes might have touched his high cheekbones, if they hadn't been so curly.

He was her old friend's little brother, Ely, but he was also, unbelievably, her new lover. Relaxed, in sleep, he could have been the fourteen-year-old boy she'd befriended for a short time in law school. But there, at the corner of his eyes, a wrinkle, and in his curly black hair, a strand or two of gray. He was all man. She climbed into her bed, careful not to disturb him, but then lay on her side, her head propped on her elbow, examining him with such intensity she was surprised he didn't wake up under her scrutiny.

She traced his mouth, his wide brown nose, enjoying having him semiconscious and in her power. She stroked his thick eyebrows, getting used to the feel of them, bristled under her fingertips. He stirred, settling himself more comfortably into the thick comforter beneath him, and his lips parted. She couldn't resist, she leaned over to kiss him gently.

"Helen," he murmured.

She reared back in shock, and his eyes flew open.

"Oh, hello," he said sleepily.

"Time to go," Eliza said.

"What?"

"Wake up, sleepyhead. I brought your water. You've got to go home, now."

"Now?" he asked, finally beginning to wake up.

"No big rush, but I do have to get some sleep tonight." She pretended to yawn. He rolled over, sat up, reached for his jeans. When he had worked them on, he stood.

At the sight of his sculpted back, she felt a moment's regret at ejecting him from her bed. His broad shoulders and slim hips were no surprise, even his awful wardrobe couldn't hide those. It was his washboard stomach that drew her gaze as he turned to look quizzically at her.

"You're an odd woman, Eliza Taylor. If I were a little less secure, I'd think you were trying to push me away again."

"I just prefer sleeping alone," she said, straightening her robe around her legs to avoid looking at him.

"Don't want me to see you drool, eh?" He chuckled, stretching. Eliza's eyes were drawn to his magnificent abdomen. She was a little disappointed when he slung his shirt on. Thankfully, it was wrinkled blue denim. Though it had obviously seen better days, at least it didn't detract from that magnificent physique. He tucked in his shirt and zipped up his pants. She felt a pang of almost physical pain as he closed the snap on his jeans.

It was followed by a strong feeling of relief that getting rid of him was proving to be so easy.

"I'll walk you to the door," she offered, as he sat on the side of the bed to put his shoes and socks on.

He didn't immediately don his footwear, but turned around to catch her chin in his hand and kiss her. She had thought the wildfire that had burned so hot earlier had been doused when he'd uttered his late wife's name. But the embers still smouldered deep in the pit of her stomach, and his kiss quickly fanned them to flame again. Eliza pulled his hand from her chin and gave it a kiss.

"I'm sorry, but I've got to get some rest," she excused herself.

He bent to put on his shoes and then stood and helped her up. She led him out of her room and down the stairs where she unbolted the door.

"Good night, Eliza." He started to lean down toward her, but she side-stepped him and opened the door.

"Good night, Ely."

"I'll call you tomorrow," he said.

Eliza woke up with no memory of having fallen asleep. After Ely left, she had taken a shower, and had covered every available, tingling inch of her body with moisturizer in a vain attempt to erase the indelible impression his body had left on her skin. Finally, she had crawled between her white sheets, exhausted. The next thing she knew, it was morning. And nothing had changed.

She had nurtured the hope that just because they had been intimate, didn't meant they had to give anything of themselves to each other. But it hadn't worked that way. She could still see his face, that full mouth, those hooded eyes that looked at her with such emotion. She could still hear that sleepy voice murmuring his wife's name, and remember the hurt she had felt. It wasn't supposed to be that way. The sex was supposed to have lessened her feelings for him. That was the most mystifying, and terrifying, thing of all. It wasn't just her body that responded so strongly to him. He could make her emotions skyrocket or plummet, with a look or a word or a touch.

She padded down to the kitchen to pour herself some coffee. Just then, the doorbell rang. Eliza walked to the door and opened it. Her jaw fell open.

"Good morning," Ely said. He was still dressed in the same clothes he'd been wearing the night before.

"What are you doing here?" she asked.

"I couldn't wait to see you again. Aren't you going to invite me in?" He shouldered past her into the house and walked straight to the kitchen.

Gathering up her courage, Eliza followed him. "Didn't you go home?" she asked, as he wandered around the kitchen.

"No," he said. "I smell coffee. Oh, there it is. Is there a coffee grinder on this thing?"

"Yeah," Eliza said. "The coffeemaker's on a timer. First it grinds the beans, then it pours them into the filter."

"Fresh-ground, fresh-brewed coffee ready and waiting when you get up in the morning. Nice."

His air of wonder annoyed her for some unknown reason. He took a sip of coffee and looked at her as if to share his joy. Those appreciative looks made her feel like shaking him until he understood this was no game. He had to be more wary, or he'd be destroyed. Maybe even by her. She wished he were more grounded, more like herself, so she wouldn't have to worry about him.

She settled for saying dryly, "What will they think of next?"

Ely gave her a baffled look and set his cup down on the counter. "I should have known you weren't a morning person. He moved toward her, saying reflectively, "I did sense it."

He took her mug from her unresisting fingers, keeping hold of her hand as he set the coffee cup on the island. "But I couldn't wait." With a gentle pull on the hand he still held, he drew her closer. He raised her hand to his lips and kissed her fingertips, then left them resting against his mouth as he circled her waist with his arms. His shoulders pushed her arms up, and Eliza found herself raising them and wrapping them around his neck.

"Mmmm." He gave a contented murmur, as he hugged her to him. "This feels good."

His cheek rubbed against hers for a moment, and Eliza found herself enjoying the feel of his rough jaw against her smooth skin. She rested against him, breathing in the faint smell of his minty breath, and the stronger musty odor emanating from his body.

As though he read her thoughts, he said, "You smell good. I need a shower. Do you mind if I use yours?"

"Uh, no," Eliza said, but she was reluctant to let go of him.

She was relieved when he didn't step back right away, but instead hugged her even closer, whispering, "Thanks," in her ear. He kissed her closed eyelids, sending a now familiar shiver down her spine. He must have felt it run through her, because he said, "You're trembling. Are you okay?"

"I'm fine." Eliza felt a little sore from the unaccustomed exercise of the previous night, but she'd have died before she admitted that to him.

"Good," he said, kissing the tip of her nose. "I was a little worried when I left here last night that I wouldn't be welcomed back."

"Uh-huh," Eliza responded, distracted. This gentle hug was nice and comforting, but it also brought her lower body in contact with his, and something stirred in the pit of her stomach. She slipped her thigh between his legs and rubbed it against him without conscious thought. When she realized what she was doing, it was too late.

"I'm glad I was wrong," he said, before his mouth claimed hers for another of those heart-stopping kisses Eliza was growing to like so much. When he finally raised his head, she was as aroused as he was. The hurt and anger she had felt at his slip of the tongue the night before was all but forgotten.

"Go ahead," Eliza said, as airily as she could, and turned away quickly so that he would not see how deeply his kiss had affected her.

"When I get back, I can cook us some breakfast, if you want," he offered.

She picked up her coffee cup before she turned back to him, gripping the handle hard, so he wouldn't see her hands shake. "I'll do it," she said. "How do you like your eggs?"

"Scrambled, soft." He hesitated for a minute, then started to walk away. As he reached the kitchen door, he turned back to her. Hastily, she looked down into her coffee cup, hoping he hadn't seen the naked lust that had to have been shining from her eyes. "In bed." He grinned, like a child again, this time one who was after a forbidden treat. Then, he went out of the room, and she listened to him climbing the stairs, two at a time.

Eliza, much to her own amazement, made breakfast, put it on a tray, and carried it up to her bedroom. There, she rolled the spread down to the foot of the bed, and sat on top of the white sheets, eating a croissant while she waited for Ely. He came out of the bathroom with a towel wrapped around his waist and another draped across his shoulders.

"That's a pretty picture," he said, while she thought he looked sexier than anyone she'd ever seen, with glistening droplets of water on his calves, chest, and in his hair.

He climbed on the bed beside her, took a strip of bacon from the one plate on the tray, and crunched on it happily.

Chapter Twenty

Ely knew that Eliza was totally discombobulated by his appearance on her doorstep and expected her to question him about it sooner or later. But he was content. She had let him back into her house, even into her bed, without an argument, and after her abrupt dismissal the night before, he'd been worried. But her response to his kisses reassured him. She was hooked.

"Where did you sleep last night?" Eliza asked casually.

"Didn't I tell you? I don't sleep much. Most of the time, I'm good on a few hours." He was lying through his teeth, of course. He needed his REM time as much as the next guy, but in the early hours of the morning he'd decided that was going to be his excuse. She seemed to be buying it. So, he put an innocent look on his face and planned to bluff his way through.

"I understand about your needing your sleep, so I thought I'd get out of your way—let you get some rest. I found a diner and had a cup of coffee and read." She was staring at him in disbelief, so he changed the subject. "How are you feeling? Did you sleep well?"

"Uh, yeah," Eliza muttered.

"Great." He dug into the eggs. He was starving, but for the

main part, he wanted her again. Badly. It would take a little time, as she had retreated behind the protective walls she had built around herself, but he had felt all those layers crumbling away, last night, leaving her vulnerable and soft and lovable. He wanted to reduce her to that boneless, sensual creature once again. Ely finished the eggs and bacon quickly and ate a flaky croissant in three bites while she daintily finished her golden, buttery crescent. She was as stiff with him as she had been before they made love. As stiff as a board, in fact.

He watched her closely, noting the way she moved so carefully and deliberately. It dawned on him slowly that she was holding herself so stiffly not just because of her natural reserve, but because of the physical after-effects of their lovemaking. She was probably sore as hell. As she finished the last of her coffee, he took the tray and placed it on the floor beside the bed. She brushed imaginary crumbs from her robe, seemingly at a loss as to what else she might do with her hands. He watched them flutter for a moment, like two little brown birds, before settling on her lap.

"Did I do that?" he asked, gently touching a small black-and-blue mark on her throat.

"What?" she asked, moving restlessly under his hand.

"A bruise." He leaned over and kissed it, sliding his hands around her neck and starting to massage it.

"I bruise easily," Eliza said. "Don't worry, I can't even feel it."

"Can you feel that?" he asked, gently rubbing the stiff muscles in her shoulders.

"Mmmm-hmmm," she murmured, her eyelids sliding down. Despite her relaxed pose, he could feel the taut muscles that lined her back and neck. He slid her down, so she lay flat on the bed. Her eyes opened and she looked up at him. He caught a glimpse of something that looked suspiciously like disappointment in those glistening orbs.

"Turn over," he commanded.

She rolled over onto her stomach, but not before he saw relief replace the disapproving expression that had crossed her face when he'd pulled her down onto her back. She was still angry at him. And herself as well, he guessed, for giving in to her passion. That was just too bad. He was calling the shots this time.

He reached around her and took hold of both edges of her robe where it parted just above her breasts. He pulled the two sides back and down to her elbows, exposing her shoulders and her back to his eyes and hands. Slowly he stroked away her tension, rubbing and kneading the flesh from her hairline to the base of her spine.

To distract himself from the ache in his groin, he started talking. "I remember the first time I wanted to touch you. There was this one night. I don't know if I should tell you this. It's going to sound like some adolescent fantasy. But anyway, I was seventeen and you were what, thirty—"

"Twenty-nine," Eliza said promptly. He smiled.

He ran his thumbs down her spine, applying just the slightest pressure to the bones that protruded through her firm golden skin. "Twenty-nine. I thought you were the most beautiful, smartest, sweetest woman I had ever met. And you were being nice to me. I remember it so clearly. It's one of those moments in life, one of the good scenes that you remember forever."

"I don't know if I want to hear this," Eliza said. "I don't think I can handle being the star of your prepubescent wet dreams."

"Pubescent," Ely corrected. "And it wasn't a wet dream, it was a party. New Year's Eve. You don't remember."

She turned her head toward him, but her eyes were still closed.

"No, you wouldn't," he answered his own rhetorical question stalling for time. He wasn't sure he should continue. He didn't want to scare her, and he knew that she was just waiting for an excuse to send him away. He had to take this slowly.

"What happened?" She might not have remembered, but her curiosity was piqued.

He went on. "You danced with me. A slow dance. I was so nervous, my palms were sweating. But you didn't notice, or at least you didn't say anything. We danced and we talked, a little. I had just broken up with my girlfriend—her idea, not mine—and Tom was teasing me all night about not having a date on New Year's. But you said she was obviously an idiot, and I was better off without her.'' He had fallen in love with her right then, deeply in love.

"Glad to be of help," Eliza said. Clearly, none of this rang a bell with her. Well, he hadn't expected her to remember.

"At midnight, you kissed me. First, you told Tommy to wait in line and then you kissed me instead of him.

"I did?" She had finally relaxed under his ministrations.

"Like this." He kissed her shoulder, tenderly, mouth closed. She started to move her arms, but they were trapped in the folds of her robe. He smoothed his hand over her back. "Wait. I'm not done yet."

He shifted his position, next to her, until he was kneeling beside her, looking down the length of her legs. He pulled her robe up and up, until her long brown legs were uncovered, and the excess material of her silky red wrap-around was pooled at the top of her thighs, covering her buttocks. She lay completely still, waiting. He took one of her feet in his hand and stroked the sides, applying pressure with his thumbs. Then he did the same with her other foot.

"Relax," he said, when he felt her tense up. "I know you're ticklish." His hands moved up over her ankles to her calves, manipulating them as he had the muscles in her back.

He dipped his thumbs in the hollows behind her knees and then ran his hands all the way up the back of her legs to the crease at the top and started to work his way down, pressing his palms and fingertips into the taut flesh of her thighs. When he reached her knees again, he stopped for a moment. Then he worked his way up again, slowly and steadily. He concentrated on each inch of flesh, not allowing himself to be distracted by the contours almost hidden by the swathe of red silk above.

When he reached the material of her robe, he slipped his hands beneath it and cupped her bottom, feeling the weight and the perfect roundness in his palms for a moment before he continued upward. He gently kneaded the perfect globes with his fingertips. His thumb slipped into the cleft, and Eliza gasped and turned her face into her pillow.

He felt a sudden surge of anger at her resistance. He was not a nameless, faceless automaton, and he wouldn't allow her to turn him into one. He slipped one hand around her, between her body and the bed, and palmed the wet, hot core of her as he urged her to turn over and face him. Her eyes were closed tight against him.

"Eliza, look at me," he ordered gruffly, his anger fading as quickly as it had come. His hands moved over her body without conscious thought. Already he knew, instinctively, where and how she craved his touch. After the exhaustive exploration of the night before, he knew all of her secrets. He felt more in tune with this woman than he had with any other. "Open your eyes and look at me," he said again.

When those big brown eyes looked up into his own so warily, his heart ached to ease her fears, as intensely as he ached to bury his body in hers.

"Say my name," he ordered. Her eyes filled with tears. "Say it," he insisted mercilessly.

"Ely," she whispered. Then louder, "Ely."

Their joining was slow and deep, and as they rocked into each other in a slow, steady rhythm, she begged, "Don't stop. Please, don't stop," over and over again while silent tears wet both their cheeks.

Soft words of comfort came from his lips in a stream of reassurance. "It's all right, it's all right. Don't cry, Eliza." Even as he climaxed, he was saying, "Everything will be all right."

It was a sadder, sweeter sexual release than he could ever have imagined. When she came, she was still silently weeping. There were women for whom crying was a relief, and a blessing, and Tommy and others had told him about lovers who cried during sex. But he didn't believe their tears were this painful.

When he withdrew himself from her, and lay down beside her, she turned her head into his shoulder and kissed him, but Ely knew they had a long way to go before he could convince this woman that there was more than sex between them. Even during the act itself, she resisted with everything she had.

He had known she was afraid. She had made it very clear.

The fear hadn't stopped her—she had too much courage—but her silent tears had told him how much it cost her to let go. Eliza could no more scale the walls she had built around herself than she could cut off her own hands. The fortress she had erected was a part of her, as integral to the woman as her strength, her integrity, her honor.

It was that sense of self-imposed isolation, an awareness of the other self that she kept locked away, that had been challenging him to draw her out, to jump the chasm between them. But it wasn't a mad rush or a strong push that would get through to her. He would have to be patient and cunning.

He didn't know what pain had caused her to lock her emotions away, but ever since he had gotten a glimpse of the beautiful, passionate creature who lived inside those walls of stone, he wanted to free her. That other Eliza had discovered some secret passageway and occasionally ventured out: she had visited him one New Year's Eve twelve years ago and he'd seen her with Jessie in the park. He had a feeling that Eliza's other "children" were able to call her forth as well. It made sense. She could trust them. They couldn't, and wouldn't, intentionally hurt her. She was safer loving them than loving him. His wife's death had taught him well how love could hurt.

In that moment, he knew he faced the most dangerous battle of his life. If he lost it, he lost love again, and this time, he didn't think he would recover.

The kids in school were saying Dad was in love with his lady lawyer. There were a lot of kids saying things about Dad. They liked his father, so the whispers and snickers were mostly not too bad. But still, it bugged Jessie that they were talking about him that way. They were joking about him and Eliza. Some kids said that Ms. Taylor was out of Daddy's league. Some girls thought he wanted to kiss her. A couple of the older kids said Eliza and Daddy were probably "doing it."

Jessie knew his father did "it," because they had talked about sex—but he didn't think Daddy would do such a thing with Eliza. She was their friend, not one of those girls Uncle

Tommy sometimes fixed Dad up with. Jessie had been in Eliza's pretty house, all white and clean, with everything matching in each room, and he couldn't picture her doing "it" with his father. The whole idea was just plain dumb.

Eliza was his friend, too, not just Dad's. And she was their lawyer. And he was pretty sure that lawyers couldn't date regular people. Uncle Tommy was a lawyer, and Jessie knew he dated only women who looked like models and TV stars. His uncle said once, to Daddy, that he didn't believe in dating women he worked with because it was too messy. Jessie was pretty sure Eliza wouldn't date his dad because they were working together on his case—and she didn't like anything messy at all.

Even if Eliza and Dad did have a date, Jessie didn't think they would kiss or anything like that. His dad was a space cadet, who forgot just about everything, and Eliza Taylor was the opposite of him. She was beautiful, and really smart, and very together. She and Dad just didn't match up.

He had to admit that they were hanging out with Eliza a lot, though. They even went to her house when she wasn't there. Daddy straightened out the tool box in her basement, then repaired little things in her house. Jessie swept the walk. They never told Eliza what they did. Even Sandy wouldn't tell her. He didn't have to lie about it either because Eliza never mentioned it, at least not in front of him. Dad said she suspected they had done it, and it was driving her nuts.

"Why?" Jessie asked.

"It's hard to explain, Jess," his father said. "She doesn't want us to do things for her—she wants to do everything herself. But since she's helping us out, I want to help her out."

"So, why don't you just tell her we did it?"

"It's more fun this way," Daddy said and winked.

Jessie didn't understand, but he went along with it anyway. Then came Eliza's birthday. He and Daddy went to her house again, but this time they didn't keep it a secret. While Eliza was at work, Dad had him make a big banner that said "Happy Birthday" and they hung it in the living room. Sandy helped. He still didn't like her much, but she was a friend of Eliza's, so Jessie tried to be polite. She left anyway, after a little while, when Dad explained what they were doing.

After Sandy left, they made dinner. Well, they made most of it. They made a quiche, and then wrapped it up in cellophane for her to reheat when she came home. Daddy told him to write notes like, "Look in the fridge" and, "Put quiche in stove for fifteen minutes." They left notes all over the house with instructions. "Take a nice, long bubble bath," and "Go to the living room." Dad left a tape in the stereo with another note which said, "Happy Birthday from Eugenia Greene. Turn me on." Dad had Grandma Greene record a song just for Eliza.

Daddy called the weird setup a no-hassle-no-pressure birthday-party-for-one.

Mary Jane called them from the office to say Eliza had just left. Then, they did the last-minute things on Dad's list, like preheat the stove and open the wine. At the very last minute, right before Eliza drove up to the house, they started the bath. Then they ran to the car and drove down the street, parked, and watched her come home. They even ducked down below the dashboard so she wouldn't spot them—just like the cops did on TV. That part was fun. But otherwise, Jessie didn't think it was much of a birthday party since Eliza would be spending it alone, and they hadn't wrapped any of the gifts.

"Believe me, Jessie," his father said, "she doesn't want us there. Eliza likes us, but I don't think she likes birthdays like we do."

Jessie liked it better when they went to her office on Saturday afternoon, and Dad and MJ worked while Jessie kidnapped Eliza and took her to the aquarium on the trolley. Before they got to the office, Jessie worried about Eliza getting mad at them for showing up at work, but Dad explained that she really needed a day off, and probably the only way she'd take it was with Jessie. When they got to her building, MJ was there, waiting for them. She was very happy they were going to get Eliza out of her "inner sanctum." Daddy told her about Jessie's nervousness, and she hugged him and said she thought he was doing Eliza a big favor, tearing her away from work. Eliza deserved a break, MJ said.

They ganged up on her. They said, "You cannot say no to that cute little face." And Jessie gave her his best "please" smile.

Daddy had been right about this being a nice present he could give Eliza all by himself. They had an excellent time. It was really starting to get warm, and they ate ice cream and peanuts and just fooled around, like two little kids instead of a kid and a grown-up. Eliza said she felt like a kid playing hooky.

"What's hooky?"

"Cutting school. In my case, cutting work." She looked a little sad when she said that, so Jessie tried to cheer her up.

"Don't feel bad. Dad promised you he'd make everything much easier in your office, so you wouldn't miss the time."

"I know," Eliza said, but she didn't look like she really believed him. Jessie knew she'd see he was right. His father would never break a promise.

They had a good time anyway, and when Jessie took her back to her company, she seemed very happy with the new fax/copier Dad had ordered for her.

"Not a present," he said, before she could say the no that he could see forming on her lips. "I charged it to your account. But you needed this machine. It will save you and your staff a lot of time and effort." While Eliza was deciding whether to agree to that or not, he hurried to say, "And here is your brand-new modem." Eliza looked like she'd rather play with the copy machine, but Daddy showed her how to do a flash session and other useful stuff, and soon they couldn't tear Eliza away from the computer, just like Daddy promised.

They left her alone to work for a couple of hours, but came back at dinnertime and pulled her out of the office to take her for a meal and a movie. She said she couldn't go with them, and they were not going to change her mind, but Dad just picked her up and carried her to the door until she said, "All right, all right. I'll go. Just put me down." Even though she tried to look mad, Jessie could tell she wasn't really.

She was even there when Dad and he had their serious talk about the future. "Sandy said you might not be able to teach at public school if I stay with you. Maybe it would be better if I went to live with Grandma and Grandpa, after all,'' Jessie told them that night at dinner when his dad kept bugging him to talk about it.

''Sandy did?'' Eliza asked. ''When was that?''

''One time,'' Jessie told her. He wasn't about to admit in front of his dad that he took the bus all the way to Eliza's by himself without permission. ''Is it true?''

''Not exactly, Jess,'' Daddy said.

Eliza nodded. ''I'll tell you what. You don't worry about what Sandy says. She doesn't always know what she's talking about. I know she thinks she does, but she doesn't.''

''But why shouldn't Daddy teach somewhere else? St. Joe's isn't that great. Does the judge have something against public school, like Grandma?''

''We don't know yet. Some people think private school is better. Your dad or I will tell you if you need to worry, though.''

''I will, sport,'' Daddy promised.

''So, Dad and me can probably go to public school?'' Jessie pressed.

''Maybe. We'll do our best,'' Eliza said, and with that he had to be satisfied.

Chapter Twenty-One

Eliza thought she had put some of Jessie's fears to rest with their little talk. It was more than she'd managed to do for herself lately. Sometimes, she felt like her life had resumed the pattern it had had before Ely turned it upside down. At other times, she felt like she'd been hit by a runaway train. The tension between herself and Tommy had completely disappeared, and Sandy was behaving like an angel. But Ely . . .

Whenever they were alone, which was admittedly a rare occurrence, he would caress her or tease her into touching him. Ely had always been quiet and clumsy around her, so she was surprised at his deft playfulness when they made love. One day, he even pulled her into the coat closet in her own foyer and kissed her until her senses reeled while Jessie and Sandy watched a television program in the living room. He left her there, panting and disheveled, with a muttered, "Popcorn's probably ready."

When she'd smoothed her hair and tucked in her blouse, she followed and found him ensconced in the big armchair, eating popcorn with the children. It was as if it had been a different man who had made love to her amid the heavy wool coats and rubbery rainwear. The hands throwing kernels of buttery

Roberta Gayle

popcorn into Jessie's mouth could not have been the same long-fingered hands that had slipped beneath her silk blouse to stroke her bare skin as his lips plundered hers.

She could not escape him. MJ must have given Ely a printout of the to-do list in her computer. From her long-term projects list, he had taken on the task of ordering her a new printer, with fax and photocopy capabilities, and had installed her newer, faster modem one afternoon while his son took her on a surprise visit to the aquarium. As much as she appreciated his efforts, she was still convinced that a relationship between them was impossible. If he was trying to prove otherwise, he was wasting his time.

But there was no arguing with him about it. He nodded and agreed with her, and then went right on doing whatever he pleased. MJ had commented on his attentiveness, but she didn't seem to suspect any ulterior motive to his actions. She knew about the birthday party that he had arranged in her house, and came to the conclusion that he seemed to understand Eliza in a way no one else did.

"I never would have thought of it, but once he explained the idea to me, I knew you'd love it. You did, didn't you?" Eliza had to admit that she did. It had been the perfect gift. No pressure, no obligations, no jokes, just pure sybaritic pleasure. His insight had even extended to knowing she'd enjoy Jessie's little touches, which added warmth to an evening that had been so thoughtfully planned and attuned to her desires that she hadn't been able to get it out of her mind since.

"Eliza, you can't be expected to notice this, because you are completely blind, virtually dead, when it comes to men, but Ely Greene is fantastic. I wish all our clients were like him."

"I thought his brother was more your type," Eliza said to her secretary.

"Hey, suave, rich, and handsome is hard to beat, but sweet, sensitive, and huggable is the way to beat it," MJ shot back.

"You can't be serious. Ely?" She pictured him with her fashion-conscious secretary and smiled widely. "You and Ely?

Don't make me laugh. Even I don't generally date guys who shop at Kmart. And you're much worse than I am.''

"Who died and made you Julie Brown?" MJ said, annoyed. "He reminds me of my little brother."

"Roger?" Eliza's jaw dropped open in amazement.

MJ bristled. "What's wrong with him?"

"Don't get me wrong, Roger's all right," Eliza answered. "But even you have to admit he's not exactly Boston's answer to Denzel Washington."

"It's hard to tell with your own brother, but Ely Greene is definitely more than all right. He's so adorable, it's sexy. I know you wouldn't think of him in that way, since he's a client, but try to be objective about this. He's all that and a side of fries, too."

Eliza felt relieved and slightly offended at the same time. MJ's faith in her ethics didn't allow for a hint of doubt about her professionalism when it came to this man. She didn't entertain a moment's thought as to whether Eliza might have, or might even still be, encouraging Ely's behavior. She assumed Ely was merely demonstrating to his lawyer the same gratitude her other clients felt. The insulting part of the equation was that, apparently, a man MJ thought of as the sexiest thing in pants couldn't possibly see Eliza in a different light than she did. His assiduous attention, in her view, could only be motivated by gratitude, and was his attempt to repay Eliza for her legal representation.

Ely turned up everywhere which was, she guessed, why Sandy had been so cruel to Jessie. She confronted her resident juvenile delinquent the same night Jessie opened up to Ely and herself. Sandy was waiting up for her, a mug of herbal tea steeping on the kitchen counter. The girl was so helpful and considerate these days that it was hard to believe she was the same truculent youngster who had shown up on Eliza's doorstep without warning, and with a giant chip on her shoulder. Now, Eliza knew why. Unless she missed her guess, this was the work of a guilty conscience.

Eliza refused to let herself be distracted by the aromatic tea or anything else. "We need to have a little talk, Sandy."

"Okay," Sandy said affably.

"About Jessie Greene," Eliza added.

"Oh." The teenager knew she'd been caught. It was clear in her expression. Still, Sandy was nothing if not a fighter, and she wasn't going to go down without a struggle.

"The kid's cute. A little bit of a crybaby, though."

"He's eight years old."

"So? Libby's six, and she's tougher than he is," Sandy said. "Jessie's nice and all, and it was cute those signs he made for your birthday, but if he had a mama, they'd be callin' him a mama's boy."

"Any chance you might have something to do with his recent behavior?"

"Me?" Sandy pretended astonishment.

"Yes, you, Miss Thang. Why in the world did you tell him he should live with his grandparents? Even if you don't care if you scare him to death, why would you do such a thing to me?" Eliza knew that appealing to Sandy's better nature would not yield any explanations, so she tried heaping on more guilt. "You know how hard I've been working on this case."

"You work hard on every case. I thought this would be easier on you. I heard you on the phone saying the Tysons loved the kid. When Jessie asked me, I told him the truth."

"But you don't know the truth," Eliza protested, baffled. As thoughtless as the girl could sometimes be, she didn't believe Sandy would do something so hurtful as pass on a casual comment from a one-sided conversation unless she did it on purpose. The only explanation that made any sense was that Sandy was jealous of Jessie. Perhaps she saw him as a threat to her relationship with Eliza, but how, or what kind of threat, Eliza couldn't understand.

"You said to Ely you would be sorry if he had to give up his chance to work in public school, but that might be the only way to go. And when we talked at lunch, you said that was what Jessie's grandparents were bugging about."

Suddenly, it dawned on Eliza that Sandy wasn't jealous of Eliza's relationship with Jessie, but of the little boy's relationship with his father.

"Yes, but that wasn't a public broadcast. Especially not for Jessie. He's nervous enough as it is. His whole life is hanging in the balance."

"All right," Sandy conceded. "I'm sorry. But in my own defense, I do want to point out that it was him who asked me."

"You? Why?"

"You weren't around."

Eliza was sure she was right. Sandy was jealous. But she'd never get the teenager to admit it.

She let it go. "Point taken. Meanwhile, I thought I'd invite Jessie and Ely to your farewell dinner Saturday, so you could straighten the kid out yourself. We already told Jess you didn't have a clue as to what you were talking about. All that's needed is for you to confirm it."

"My dinner?" Sandy said, pouting. "But that was supposed to be just you and me."

"But it's the only time I can think of," Eliza said apologetically.

"Right," Sandy said sarcastically.

"When else? You're leaving the next day. I can't think of any other time. Can you?" Eliza had tried desperately to think of another time or place for the two youngsters to meet. She hadn't wanted to mar Sandy's last evening in the house with the unpleasant chore, but she hadn't been able to think of a more suitable time for an informal meeting.

"How about if we invite Tommy, too?" she offered.

"Really?" The change in Sandy was instantaneous. Her scowl was replaced by a smile.

"Sure, why not? It's all in the family," Eliza said wryly. "You and Tommy have become good friends, haven't you?"

"Sure, but . . ." Sandy's enthusiasm had waned very quickly.

"If you don't want to invite any of them, I won't."

"I already did," Sandy said sheepishly.

Suspicion dawned. "You invited Tommy to our dinner?" Eliza asked, knowing the answer to her question was yes.

"Oh, Sandy, are you still trying to get us together? I thought I explained this pretty thoroughly. Tommy and I are friends, nothing more."

"Okay," Sandy said. "I get it."

"What do you get?"

"You're not interested in Tommy since—" She stopped abruptly, apparently deciding she'd said enough. Her disapproval was evident.

"Since what?" Eliza pressed.

"I'm not blind," the girl replied. "I've seen how you and Ely look at each other."

"Ely? He has nothing to do with Tommy and me. Sandy couldn't possibly know what she and Ely had been doing. Even MJ hadn't guessed.

Sandy rolled her eyes. "If you say so. Anyway, if they're coming over to dinner, I guess my inviting Tommy was okay." Eliza struggled for a moment with the desire to pursue the argument. She didn't like the implication that her professional relationship with Ely Greene had anything to do with her relationship with Tommy, or the lack thereof.

But she couldn't make a point of it, not without raising questions she couldn't answer, so she dropped it and said only, "Of course, it was okay. It's your night."

She thought Sandy's smile was a little grim, but she let it go. Eliza felt odd, after that, inviting Ely to dinner, but she explained to him that it was for Jessie's sake. Sandy had an apology to make.

Ely accepted her explanation without a word and said that he and Jessie would be there.

When the night of Sandy's farewell dinner rolled around, Sandy had added MJ, and her significant other, Robby, to the guest list, as well as Tommy. With Ely and Jessie attending, it was beginning to look like quite a party.

Eliza was in her bedroom, putting on her makeup, when she noticed Sandy standing in the doorway, watching her.

"How long have you been standing there? Come in." They had had fun, preparing for this evening, and Eliza was feeling surprisingly good. A month ago, she would have been dreading the evening before her. Sandy, Tommy, and Ely had shaken her up, made her reevaluate virtually everything she believed about herself. And despite that upheaval, Eliza was actually looking forward to having them all at her table that evening.

"You look great," Sandy said enviously.

"You're biased." Eliza surveyed the results of her handiwork in the mirror. Not too bad. She had nice eyebrows. She didn't even need to pluck them. They were not exactly delicate arches, but they came to a peak, a little off center. She'd inherited them from her father.

"I wish I had hair like yours," Sandy said. Her wistful expression reminded Eliza of herself when she'd admired her mother as she prepared for an evening out with her father. Like her own mother, Eliza saw the young girl beside her as the true beauty.

"Your hair is beautiful, it sets you apart," Eliza said of the carroty dreds.

"Hey, it's a look. But I could never be as elegant as you."

"I could never be as hip as you."

"Ummm, Eliza, nobody says hip anymore."

Eliza smiled at Sandy's reflection. "See what I mean."

"I can't believe you don't know how beautiful you are," Sandy said.

"I'm fine with the way I look. But I was a beanpole when I was a kid, and you never forget how that feels. I was always the tallest in the class, and so skinny I didn't even feel like a girl. I always wanted to be petite, like you."

"You look like a model. Your legs come up to my throat."

"We're a pair of fantastic-looking women," Eliza said, pulling Sandy down on the stool next to her so they were both reflected in the mirror. Sandy shook her head, but Eliza continued. "Look at your skin. It's so lovely, golden and smooth." She touched Sandy's cheek. "Soft, just like a baby. Which you are. You have beautiful eyes. Great bone structure. I wish I had your chin, mine is too pointy." While Sandy took stock of herself in the mirror, Eliza quelled the impulse to ask whether she was planning to change for the party.

Her willpower was severely tested, but she managed to control the urge. Instead, she said, "I do have nice eyebrows, though. Don't you think?"

Luckily, perhaps as a reward for her self-restraint, as they walked together out of Eliza's room, Sandy asked, "Could I borrow your velvet shirt?" and Eliza's mind was put at ease.

Tommy was the first to arrive. Eliza was putting the final touches on the hors d'oeuvres.

"Talk to him while I finish up in here," she told Sandy.

The dinner was just about done, so Eliza didn't feel too guilty about letting Sandy check on the meal while she got Tommy a drink.

"Vodka and tonic?" she asked.

"Thanks." He nodded.

He had brought Sandy a gift. "It's a velvet shirt," he said with a self-deprecating smile. "Just like the one she's wearing."

"That one's mine. She borrowed it." Eliza handed him his drink. "She'll love having one of her own," she assured him.

"Great," he said, obviously relieved.

"You're a good guy, Tommy."

"Just what a man likes to hear," he said with a wry smile.

"You are," she insisted. "You've really helped Sandy, and she's not an easy person to know." She nodded toward the brightly wrapped box on the coffee table. "You know her well."

"So, are you saying now that *I'm* too good for *you?*"

"Heck, no." She laughed. "I'm way too good for you."

"Now the truth comes out," he said. "So, all that stuff about your not being interested in the kind of long-term relationship I was looking for . . . ?" She was amazed that he could talk about this, joke about it.

"An excuse, so as not to hurt your feelings," she teased him back.

"How do you know what I'm looking for?"

"I know the signs. Enough men have left me for The One." Eliza was only half-joking.

"I didn't."

"You would have. Eventually," Eliza said. "You thought you wanted me, but you're really looking for a younger, prettier, more flexible . . . me."

"Why do you put yourself down like that?" he asked.

"I thought I was paying myself a compliment."

"Sure you were," Tommy said, his lips twisting into a wry smile.

"Thanks, friend, but I'm not putting myself down. I just happen to be a good judge of character. You are a very nice guy. I am also a very nice guy. It's sort of my mission in life . . . preparing men to make a commitment. To other women."

"Why not to you?" Tommy asked.

"What would I do with them? I've spent more of my life taking care of myself than not. I wouldn't know what to do with a guy who wanted to take care of me." Ely's face flashed before her, but Eliza suppressed it.

"That's an interesting take on male/female relations. Do you boil all of life's more perplexing mysteries into paradigms of two sentences or less?"

"What mystery are we talking about here?"

"Love, sex, etcetera. Sometimes called the battle of the sexes. As old as Adam and Eve."

"I don't think there anything mysterious about it," Eliza said.

"You don't? Everyone else seems to. From Plato to Shakespeare to Terry McMillan. It's the subject of never-ending debate."

"It's just reproduction. Human beings have just managed to complicate the process with the trappings of civilization, like marriage."

"*Trappings* of civilization?" he mused aloud, sitting on the couch and looking at her with a smile playing across his lips. "Interesting choice of words."

Sandy came into the room and sat on the couch next to Tommy. When Eliza would have changed the subject, Tommy said, "Don't stop. I'm sure Sandy will be as interested as I am in your theory."

"What theory is this?" Sandy asked.

"It's not a theory. It's a known fact that the human animal is biologically predisposed to pair off—maybe for life, maybe not. It's a clever arrangement that allows for the feeding and rearing of our young."

"Got it," Tommy said.

"Unfortunately, most people refuse to submit to the inevitable biological and physiological demands of their 'animal' natures. They fight it every step of the way in the name of religion, and progress, and civilization. They think it makes us less animalistic, but I think we're just afraid of what we don't control. They make rules to govern our sexual behavior, not to elevate it. Mankind attempting to subdue Mother Nature. It's absurd."

"I always knew you were a rebel at heart," Tommy said.

"Why, because I didn't fall for your charms?" she retorted.

"There had to be a reason," he said arrogantly.

Sandy laughed. "Maybe you were too smooth for her."

"I cannot have been the only woman to prove immune," Eliza said.

"There must be dozens of women who don't think you're all that," Sandy added.

"Remarkably few, actually," Tommy replied, straight-faced, but with a gleam of laughter in his eyes. Sandy giggled.

"Don't laugh at his delusions, girl. I think it may be dangerous. Like waking up a sleepwalker," Eliza said.

But Sandy couldn't resist. "I know it's hard to believe, but some women do prefer their men sort of . . . frumply. Bad hair, cheap clothes, no money."

"Bite your tongue!" Tommy exclaimed in mock horror.

"I like 'em big and stupid, but I think Eliza's into the intellectual, nerdy type."

"She told you this?" Tommy was amused.

Eliza was not. "I did not."

"She doesn't need to. Just look at her and—" Thankfully the doorbell rang. Eliza jumped up and started out of the room.

Behind her, Tommy asked, "Who?"

"That's probably him now," Sandy said. Eliza stopped short and turned slowly to face them. She glanced at Sandy sharply, but there was no guile in those big brown eyes. The doorbell pealed again.

Just when she was about to turn back around and go to the

door, Tommy suddenly put it together. "Ely?" He looked at her speculatively. "You could do worse," he opined.

The doorbell chimed again.

Sandy jumped up. "I'll get it."

"No, you stay here. Open your gift. I'll get it," Eliza said, feeling as though she'd just made a narrow escape, though she couldn't have said she was out of the woods, yet. Anything could happen.

Mary Jane and Rob were at the door, and she breathed a sigh of relief and brought them into the living room. Sandy and Tommy had their heads together on the couch; the box that contained his gift was unwrapped. From Sandy's forlorn expression, Eliza supposed they had used the few minutes during which they'd been left alone to say their good-byes.

Sandy's face lit up again when she saw MJ. She greeted her friend and renewed her acquaintance with Robby. While Eliza prepared drinks for the newcomers, Tommy brought his glass over for a refill. For her ears only, he said softly, "I think your whole theory is just a smoke screen you've constructed to avoid facing the truth."

"Oh, Mr. Man, what is the truth?"

"You don't know what you want," he said. "You and my brother are alike in that way."

"I seem to remember your saying it was you and I who were alike?"

"I thought so then, but now I'm not so sure. I thought we had the same problem—an obsession with our work. But that's not what you're after. You and Ely run around ignoring reality, both of you. He floats about in a cloud of principles and ideas, and you're lost in a morass of ethics and theories."

"Ely and I have nothing in common," she protested automatically.

"I'd say you have at least one thing in common. You're both alone."

"I know. He's still in love with his dead wife."

"What makes you think so?" Tommy asked.

"Don't you?" she asked, rather than answering his question. She couldn't very well tell him about Ely's slip of the tongue.

''No, I just think he's hopeless when he comes to romance. I've double dated with him and, believe me, he needs all the help he can get.

''You and Ely could be good together, if you didn't automatically rule it out. You both live for kids. Anyway, there's no point even thinking about it. Even if you two tried to get together, it probably wouldn't work out.''

''That was a joke, Eliza,'' Tommy elaborated, when she didn't respond.

''Sure,'' she said. She wanted to tell him, *Less of a joke than you might think, my friend!* She was so relieved he hadn't taken Sandy's suspicions seriously that she felt a little giddy.

He trailed her as she left the bar to give MJ and Robby their drinks. She watched him out of the corner of her eye as he and the others laughed and talked as if they'd known each other for years. For a moment, he seemed too perfect, almost unreal. Then another face blotted out Tommy's—a younger, softer, less sophisticated version of the perfect man. In her mind's eye, she saw his features realigned into less godlike form. She felt a surge of warmth toward her companion, her good friend. The brother she was not in love with. Eliza shook herself. The thought had come from nowhere.

Chapter Twenty-Two

Ely sat next to Jessie at the dinner table, teasing him about eating his salad with his dinner fork and his dinner with his salad fork, and she felt her heart swell with the feelings she had for the two of them. She wasn't embarassed anymore— by the difference in their ages or the picture he presented. He had taken pains to dress for dinner, and his designer shirt with maroon piping actually matched his gray slacks, but even the new clothes had not made any difference to his perpetually wrinkled appearance, and the bad haircut could not be counteracted. But it wasn't the clothes that were different. It was the new Eliza.

The thought she'd had before the dinner party came to mind. She had changed a lot in the last month. She knew now that she would never be the same.

As she looked around her dining room table, she realized that she was surrounded by a loving circle of friends. She was no longer the isolated ice princess she had thought herself. Perhaps she had never been that person.

She had been a shy girl. Then, in reaction to her parents' death, she'd become a solitary, reserved young woman. She had thought of herself as suddenly losing touch, her emotions

shutting off in reaction to her failure to protect a little boy
named David Paron. She remembered the look on Bruce Paron's
face at the funeral as the small casket had been lowered into
the ground. He'd been cleared of any wrongdoing. Eliza knew
as well as anyone that no one could watch a toddler one hundred
percent of the time. But still Eliza had turned away from him
at the funeral. She had tried to blame him, to relieve some of
her own guilt, and had ended up punishing herself instead.

In shutting off the pain of that day, she had lost a part of
herself, and then she had buried the memory of who she had
been. The transformation, which had seemed instantaneous and
complete, had been a gradual change that had permeated her
consciousness, until one day it felt like she had always been
that way. But she had met MJ since then, and Rosa, and all of
her young clients. She had maintained old friendships with her
favorite college professor, her mentor in law school, and with
Stephanie, who had worked with her at social services. These
people were not only loving and supportive of her, but also
loved and nurtured by her.

And then, Tommy and Ely had reentered her life. And Sandy.
That little chat with Tommy before dinner had confused her,
but as her guests' conversation and laughter filled her dining
room, Eliza understood. He didn't see a match between herself
and his brother as impossible, because when Tommy looked
at her he saw through the facade she'd so carefully constructed,
to the real flesh-and-bone person underneath—the Eliza Taylor
she had hidden from herself.

Tommy was chatting with Robby, MJ's significant other,
and the two men, both incredibly handsome specimens, laughed
together, liking each other already on only a few hours acquaintance. Eliza had liked Robert right away, as well, and thinking
back, she realized she had welcomed him into the warm circle
of her intimates. It all came together for her, at that moment.
As she looked around at her friends, her family, she understood
herself, finally. Ely had made her feel vulnerable, and that
frightened her, but those feelings had triggered the release of
other emotions she had thought long dead. Suddenly, she saw

herself differently. Perhaps, she had finally figured out who she really was.

It was not these revelations that made Eliza lay her fork down, afraid to try to force food past the lump in her throat. It was the presence of Sandy, dressed in her borrowed velvet blouse, her dreds glinting golden in the candlelight, her face made up with understated elegance, that threatened Eliza's self control. It wasn't the transformation itself—from gamine street kid to self-possessed young lady—that caused tears to well up in her eyes, but rather, it was how the transformation had been achieved. Eliza had opened her home and, she admitted ruefully, her heart to the juvenile delinquent. Despite all the wrangling and turmoil, the frustration and even rejection, a bond had been forged between them. Eliza was filled to bursting with a new empathy for the girl. Or perhaps she had always felt it, but could only now acknowledge that she knew how it felt to have been cut off, lost and alone, and to have found her way home.

When dinner was over and everyone had finally left Sandy and herself alone, Eliza was struck by the urge to tell the girl how much she cared about her, but she didn't have the faintest idea how to go about it.

"I'll take care of the dishes," Eliza offered, instead.

Sandy had already begun to clear the dinner table, so she went on with her task as she answered, "Sure, I'll just help get these things into the kitchen."

"Are you all packed?" Eliza asked, aware she was trying to convey all of the emotions inspired by Sandy's imminent departure with this display of concern for the mundane details of the separation.

"Except for the shirt Tommy gave me," Sandy answered. She, too, was unable to open up and say any of the things she felt. So, they tidied up together. As they worked in silence, side by side, Eliza felt the unspoken words as a physical presence hovering in the air around them.

"Go on then. Put that in your bag," Eliza urged.

"Let's finish this up first," Sandy suggested. "I'd like to help." Eliza knew that that was the closest she would come to sharing her feelings.

When they were about half done with the table, the doorbell rang again.

"Someone must have forgotten something," Eliza said. "I'll be right back." She opened the door to find Tommy, his back turned to her. He was staring up at the night sky.

"What's up?" Eliza asked. He turned around and came toward her without saying a word. She said, "Come right in," and was about to step out of his way when his hand snaked out and caught her arm. He hauled her to him and kissed her, hard.

"Tommy," Eliza spluttered as she emerged from the assault. "What the heck do you think you're doing?"

"You said I was ready for a commitment, but not with you, and that's why there was no spark between us. I did some thinking about that, and decided maybe you had something there. You're beautiful, sexy, almost irresistible. So, I thought I'd give it one more try. If I'm going to become seriously involved with anyone, you are the ideal woman. We've got a lot in common. We like each other a lot. And I enjoy being with you."

"Tommy, I don't think you understood me—" she started to explain.

"I don't think I did," he interrupted. Tommy looked at her, his eyes glowing. "So, you want to give it another try?"

"No," she said quickly. He hadn't moved. He was laughing at her.

"So." She stood stiffly, not sure she appreciated his strong-arm tactics. "What did that prove?"

"I'm not the one who can't commit, Eliza. I'm ready to do it. It's you who has the problem. You are looking for something I can't give. *That's* why there's no chemistry between us."

She smiled wryly. Thomas Greene might have had some insight into her character but, with this latest off-the-wall idea, he had lost her.

"Come on in, you fool," she suggested. Though she knew she was right, Eliza wouldn't object to debating his harebrained conclusion. She was definitely not looking for a relationship.

He had it all backward. If it made him feel better to project his fantasies onto her, that was fine with Eliza.

"All right," Tommy agreed. "Just for a minute."

Sandy was leaving the next day for the Farbers, and Eliza had been invited to come to dinner in a couple of weeks—but for Tommy, this was presumably his last good-bye.

He entered the kitchen a few feet ahead of her and said, "Hi again, Sand."

Sandy had been bent over the dishwasher and she jumped, rattling the dish trays.

"It was just Tommy," Eliza said as Sandy turned around. "He had forgotten something . . . sort of." She smiled at him.

Sandy said, "I've finished the clearing up. Everything's in here, now."

"How about if we save the washing up for the morning," Eliza suggested.

"Let me help," Tommy asked. She looked at him in surprise, but then thought back to the first night he'd helped her in the kitchen. He'd proven himself quite adept.

"Is this a regular hobby of yours?" she joked.

He nodded. "I have a thing about dishpan hands." He leered at her. "They excite me."

Sandy laughed. "Well, then you do the washing, and I'll dry, and Eliza can put things away."

"I didn't plan for you to spend your last night here doing dishes," Eliza protested.

"It'll be fun," Sandy said. "Besides, I'd feel guilty leaving you with all of this to do by yourself. The party was for me."

"It was thrown for you, not by you," Eliza argued.

"Let us do the dishes with you, Eliza," Tommy said. "I'm not in the mood to go home, yet."

"And I don't want the evening to be over," Sandy added.

Eliza threw up her hands in defeat. "Okay. I tried." Tommy filled the sink with hot, soapy water. "Don't blame me when you get all pruney."

As Tommy and Sandy chatted companionably by the sink, Eliza moved around the kitchen, straightening up and putting away the odds and ends that Sandy handed to her. Her thoughts went back to that kiss at the front door. She had felt shocked, and a little bit angry, especially when he wouldn't let her go, but that was all. She didn't feel any sorrow or regret. Tommy just wasn't the right man for her.

The change had come about almost without her realizing it. She was in love with Ely. Not in like, not even in lust, but actually in love. It was not her mind and body that were at odds after all, but her brain and her heart. Eliza was not the victim of some premenopausal attack of hormones, nor was she some dirty old woman.

It was actually sort of funny. She had been hoping to meet someone different from the cool, collected, successful men she'd been involved with throughout her adult life, but the pendulum had swung too far in the other direction. Ely's life was in shambles. He was hanging on to his job by a thread and his family was falling apart. A man with Tommy's sophistication and ambition and Ely's courage and strong principles would have been perfect. Instead, she found herself involved with the prototypical absentminded professor. Her heart had finally awakened, and it had settled on someone twelve years younger than herself, who just happened to be in love with his late wife.

Eliza was awakened from her reverie by a water fight. "Hey, you two!"

They turned to her with identical expressions on their faces, a combination of guilt and rebelliousness that made them each look about five years old. At least Ely, for all his foibles, didn't make her feel a hundred years old.

"She started it," Tommy defended himself.

"Don't be such a baby," Sandy said, unrepentant. Sandy flicked Tommy with the dish towel, and he retaliated by splashing her with soapy water.

"Hey!" Eliza said sharply. "Are you finished with the pots and pans?"

"Yes, ma'am," Tommy answered. "Everything's shipshape and Bristol fashion." He saluted.

"Would you like a nightcap?" Sandy asked.

"I don't think so," Tommy answered reluctantly. "I should

be going.'' They both walked him out to the door. He gave
Eliza a chaste kiss on the cheek. ''I saw the way you looked
at Ely during dinner,'' he whispered. ''You two would make
a great couple.''

''You're impossible,'' Eliza said but couldn't help smiing.

He turned to Sandy. ''Do I get a kiss good-bye?'' he asked
with a wicked smile.

She returned his smile with a demure one of her own. ''Only
if you promise to leave for real this time. Everytime you say
good-bye, I suffer.''

''Sassy,'' he scolded, but he kissed her tenderly on each
cheek.

''Be—'' he started.

''Good,'' she said with him and rolled her eyes.

''Try,'' he urged.

''I'll take it under advisement,'' she said.

''She's been living here too long,'' he said to Eliza.

''Not for me,'' Eliza said softly, slipping her arm around
the girl's small waist. Tommy winked and then walked out the
door, pulling it closed behind him.

Sandy leaned against her for a moment, but straightened up
almost immediately. ''I guess it's time for bed,'' she said.

''Yeah,'' Eliza agreed. They walked together and parted at
Sandy's door. As Eliza reached her own bedroom, Sandy called
after her,

''Eliza?''

''Yes?''

''Thanks for the party . . . and everything.''

''It was fun,'' Eliza said, and right then, she even meant it.

''Yeah.'' Sandy turned back to her room. ''Night.''

''Good night, sweet dreams,'' Eliza called after her softly.
When she went into her bedroom, Eliza found she wasn't sleepy.
She wished Ely was there.

It was difficult to reconcile her feelings for the sweet, helpful,
diffident client with her passion for the skillful, innovative lover
she had found him to be. Ely, on the other hand, didn't seem
to find any of it particularly disconcerting. In fact he was a
rock. Her rock. And she would not have minded borrowing a

cup or two of his self-assurance tonight. Especially in light of what both Sandy and Tommy had had to say.

Eliza went back over the evening in her thoughts—Sandy's accusation, and Tommy's insight, and her own, dancing first one way and then the other. She finally had to conclude that she would never understand either of the Greene brothers. It was impossible to second-guess Tommy's motives in promoting a match between her and Ely—if, indeed, that was what he had meant to do. Ely, too, remained a mystery to her. That she loved him was something she could no longer deny. But that fact changed nothing. They were clearly wrong for each other.

So, there was no reason for her to go to his house the next day, after she dropped Sandy at the Farbers'. Nevertheless, she found herself that evening knocking at his door.

"Eliza, this is a nice surprise," he said, as he ushered her into the apartment. "Has something happened?"

"No, I just wanted to talk," she hastened to reassure him.

Ely's smile encouraged her. He was so patently pleased to see her. "That's great," he said.

"Isn't Jessie here?" she asked as he leaned down to kiss her.

"He's at his grandparents' house for the night," he murmured against her lips. She gently disentangled herself.

Eliza had not been able to resist the urge to see him, but she did not want to tempt fate. She had only wanted to talk to him, to be near him. But she had counted on Jessie's presence to stop her from giving in to temptation and making love with him again. That was not in her plans.

She backed away until she felt the door behind her. "Lets go out then," she suggested.

He agreed at once, his good humor unabated. "Okay."

They each drove their own car to the restaurant Eliza had chosen. It was cozy, but not too dark or intimate. The place had a family feel to it, although on a Wednesday night, there were more young couples and businessmen dining in the establishment than families. Despite the less than fashionable time and day, the eatery still had the atmosphere Eliza had hoped for.

"Ely, I don't know how we got into this situation, but I feel it's time to end this charade."

He looked at her, puzzled. "What are you talking about?"

"We've been acting like a couple of teenagers . . . groping around in the coat closet for goodness sake! These stolen moments and forbidden kisses might be fine for a fourteen-year-old, but I'm forty-two."

She had almost said it had been fun, but checked herself at the last minute. "I haven't done anything like this in years, and I can't deny the fact that I've enjoyed certain aspects of this relationship. But you've got to concentrate on what's important here."

Ely understood immediately. "The case," he said simply.

"*Your* case. It's in jeopardy."

"What's changed?" he asked.

She thought of Sandy's comments, and his brother's, but their suspicions had not really been the impetus that sent her to him. It wasn't the fear of detection that had caused her to visit Ely. It was her awakening heart, her own feelings, that frightened her. Her objectivity was gone, already. That was a given. But perhaps if she could create some distance between them, she could at least maintain the appearance of arguing dispassionately and unemotionally for her client. She didn't think, at this point, that she could continue to be Ely's lover and keep her feelings for him hidden. Sandy had seen through her already. Perhaps Tommy suspected, too. They couldn't take any more chances. Too much hung in the balance.

"I just don't believe we can go on like this," she said. "Not if we mean to win. And I do."

He nodded. They sat in silence for a moment, then he chuckled.

"What is it?" she asked.

"When you came by tonight—when I opened the door and saw you standing there—I didn't think this was how the evening would end."

That was what she loved about him. The way he thought and the way he didn't hold back. She wished she could be as free, as honest, as Ely was.

Eliza gave him a wry smile in response. "So, we're agreed. This . . . interlude, pleasant as it was, is over."

"I don't suppose we could just pretend we didn't have this little talk till after dinner?"

"After dinner there would be dessert," she said dryly.

"And coffee?" he suggested.

Eliza grimaced and changed the subject. They discussed the case through dinner. The weakest point was his tenuous position at school. The GAL could probably make something of that, if he or she chose.

"I don't know why the administration is going along with Mr. Cerrone. It just doesn't make sense to me," Ely said, shaking his head. "I brought the girl home. The GAL can't think that I robbed Jessie of anything by doing that. I couldn't break her confidence. And in the end, it all worked out. If it happened again tomorrow, I'd suggest, strongly, that the boy or girl call a friend, go to the house of a peer, but I still don't think I'd report what happened to the school. And I sure as hell wouldn't call the cops."

"I know, I know," Eliza sympathized. "It was a mistake, and St. Joe's attitude seems all out of proportion to the events. All in all, I don't think it's going to kill us. It doesn't prove you're unfit. I'm a little more worried about the incident with the gang members. Have you been able to reach any of those boys?"

"Jake—the older brother—is hard to find these days. He doesn't live with his parents anymore. I think he'd explain very well why he came to see me. And if the judge or the GAL saw him, he'd know Rebecca over-reacted. He's not a big kid. And there's nothing the least bit scary about him."

"I imagine that out on the streets, he looks tough enough."

"Maybe," Ely admitted reluctantly. "But he could tell the investigator the truth. Jessie was never in any danger.

"How old is he now?"

"Sixteen, I guess."

"And a runaway. Not a great witness. We're just going to have to put the best spin on the story we can. If we can find him, we can talk to him before we decide to let anyone else interview him. But I suspect that either they'll go with Rebecca's assessment or Marissa's. Meeting or talking to the boy would probably not serve much purpose.''

"I wish you could meet him."

"I wouldn't mind talking with him. It would be great to find out I'm wrong about his usefulness to us."

On their way out of the restaurant, Eliza spotted an old friend. She introduced Ely to him without hesitation.

"George Baker, meet Ely Greene, a client. Ely, this is George, one of the best private investigators I've worked with." For the first time since the brothers Greene had reentered her life, Eliza didn't feel she had to explain her relationship with this man. She wasn't embarassed, nor did she feel the need to justify their dinner date. It was a business meeting, and that was all.

There was no change in George's curious, watchful expression. His stock in trade was reading people, and Eliza was very pleased at his apparent acceptance of her statement. They talked for a few minutes, and then she and Ely left the restaurant and George behind. But when the door closed behind them, Ely said, "That was the guy!"

"What guy?"

"The one I keep seeing everywhere I go."

"He's been . . ." Eliza swallowed hard. "He's the man that you thought might be following you?" There was only one explanation for it. He must have been hired by the Tysons. When Eliza had spotted him, he'd been half-turned away from her, looking at the telephone. She'd recognized him only because of his hat. She'd always teased him about that fedora. It put her in mind of fictional private detectives of the forties and fifties.

If Ely had mentioned the hat when he described his 'shadow,' she wondered if she would have recognized the P.I. from his description. Eliza doubted it. She hadn't expected Rebecca Tyson to have her son-in-law watched. It was not an uncommon practice in custody cases, but in Tyson vs. Greene, Eliza had thought both parties trusted each other more than that. The surveillance had probably been suggested, or maybe even arranged, by Rod Daniels.

She felt her cheeks grow warm as she realized what Baker might have seen her doing. That day, when they had kissed in the parking lot at St. Joe's, for example, had been the same day that Ely had first mentioned the man who was following him. George Baker must have been there, somewhere, taking pictures.

"We may have given the Tysons exactly what they needed."

"What?"

"Pictures of us. At St. Joe's. In the parking lot."

"I remember. There's nothing wrong with our being together."

"That depends on who you talk to. Your brother wouldn't have a problem with it, but the judge might."

"Falling in love with you would make him think me an unfit parent?"

"Having an affair with your lawyer could make him believe that you're irresponsible or worse, especially if the GAL's report has already caused him to doubt your judgment."

"What can we do?"

"You might want to get a new lawyer."

"We've been through that before," he said.

"But now there's even more reason to take my advice. This could be prejudicial to your case."

"If that's my only choice, I'll take my chances with you," Ely said firmly.

Eliza wasn't eager to get herself taken off the case, though she would not have blamed Ely if he decided to make that move. Before she could give him any more legal advice, she needed time to think.

They said good night and separated. As she drove home, Eliza's mind worked furiously as she tried to think of ways to get around this unexpected setback. She still thought she could do a good job for Jessie, but she didn't know if the judge would believe a word she said. The question was, had she destroyed her credibility by having an affair with her client? Eliza felt certain the testimonials she had gotten from his friends, family, and colleagues would be effective in countering the opposition's assertion that Ely had neglected and endangered his son's life. But she wasn't sure her arguments would carry the weight they should.

If the Tysons presented evidence of an affair, Judge Garson could form a bias against *her*. That would color his assessment of her presentation of the facts. Of course, every judge had a bias in every case, but once doubt was raised concerning her professional conduct, the judge had ample cause to discount her arguments.

There was no way to tell, until it was too late, how much damage had been done. And she wasn't willing to risk it. But, for the life of her, Eliza didn't know how to fix it. She'd been willing to give up Ely, the lover, for Ely, the client. She didn't think she was ready to to walk away from him altogether. Not yet. Not until she knew he and and Jessie were together and safe.

Chapter Twenty-Three

Jessie had thought about it a lot, and he'd finally decided he had to stop the fighting in his family. By the time his grandparents moved, with or without him, there wouldn't be a family left. But when it came time to tell his grandparents about it, he choked. He had locked himself inside the bathroom so many times, Granny Reb was starting to get worried that there was something seriously wrong with him. Jessie thought he might be getting an ulcer. There was a kid in his class who had one, so he knew it was possible. Of course, Weenie Reinfelder was nothing like him, but if Weenie could get an ulcer from stressing about getting A's and stuff like that, Jessie figured he could get one from lying to everyone he loved.

Every time he started to tell Gramps and Granny Reb that he wanted to live with them instead of Daddy, his stomachache grew worse. But there was no way out. There'd been a big fight at school, and he heard his father had a meeting with Principal McGinley. He didn't know exactly what happened, but Jessie knew that if his father was fighting with a parent, in public, then that guy must have done something terrible to his kid. St. Joe's wouldn't care. McGinley cared only what the parents said, not the kids. If Jessie agreed to live with his grandparents, then maybe Dad could just tell McGinley where to shove it and start teaching at public school right away.

Eliza had been in court all morning and found the stack of urgent messages from Ely Greene waiting for her on her return. The number he left was at home.

"I've been fired," he said without preamble when he heard her voice on the phone.

"Oh, no." That was just what they needed on top of everything else.

"I had a fight with Gina Cerrone's father."

Eliza couldn't believe her ears. "You *what?*"

"He was there, at the school, drunk. He was looking for me."

"And he got you." She couldn't keep the note of censure from her voice.

"I know, I know," Ely said. "I've called myself every kind of a fool, but . . ."

"That won't help anything," Eliza said wearily. "This couldn't come at a worse time."

"Jessie knows. Did he call you?"

"I don't know." She flipped through her messages. "He didn't leave a message if he did."

"I was sure he called you. He asked me if I talked to you yet."

"Is he there with you?"

"I haven't seen him all day. He left a message on the answering machine. I hoped he was with you."

"How did he sound?"

"He tried to act like everything was cool, but I know he's upset. He asked for permission to sleep over at a friend's house, but he didn't mention which one. Just said he'd call back later."

"He was afraid of something like this, remember? He was worried about your job."

"I know. The problem is, I don't know what he's thinking. He didn't mention school at all. Damn! I was sure he had spoken to you."

Eliza heard the fear in his voice. "Don't panic. That would be the worst thing you could do. We'll talk to him," she soothed. "But first, we have to figure out what we're going to tell him. Can you come to the office?"

"I'll be there in half an hour," Ely said.

By the time he arrived, Eliza had dealt with or rescheduled the most urgent items on her agenda for the day and had started to reassess his case. It didn't look too good. The GAL would report why Ely had been fired. The school was sure to paint Ely in the worst light possible. On top of that, the Tysons had the ammunition provided by the private investigator.

"The most important thing is to get you another job," Eliza told Ely first. She had decided to deal with their other difficulties after they had Jessie home again. "Didn't you say you could start subbing right away, even without your teaching certificate."

"Yes," Ely responded.

"That should make Jessie happy."

"I didn't realize that he knew so much about my plans. But he really does approve, I think. I've got to talk to him."

"The first thing we do is make some calls. We've got some research to do. We have to present the judge with the strongest evidence possible that Jessie won't suffer from the loss of your position."

"He won't be able to attend St. Joe's for free anymore, now that I'm not on the staff there. And I don't know if I'll be able to come up with the tuition."

"You've got savings, right? That's how you paid me my retainer."

"That's for his college education."

"First things first," Eliza advised. "The Tysons' lawyer will argue that you won't have job security. Our argument has always been that Jessie should continue in the same stable environment he'd accustomed to. We don't want to suddenly pull him out of the school he's always attended. Not right away, anyway. We want to prove you've got the wherewithal to keep him in St. Joe's, even though the tuition is no longer waived. I think that will be more likely to impress the judge. And we don't want to make Rebecca Tyson any more determined to remove Jessie from your care. If she thought Jessie might leave St. Joe's, she'd be livid.''

"You're right. And he can always change schools later.''

"Maybe. I think you'd better plan to keep Jessie enrolled at St. Joe's indefinitely. Sometimes the judge will award temporary custody, pending further review.''

"But I don't know if Jessie will want to do that. Without me there, I'm not sure he'll want to stay.''

"I think he'd prefer it to living with his grandparents,'' Eliza argued.

Ely nodded slowly. "All right, so now we find Jessie and tell him, right?''

"Right, and I know where he is.''

"He called you,'' Ely exclaimed. "I knew it!''

"There was a message on my answering machine at home. After I spoke with you, and checked with MJ to make sure he hadn't called here and just neglected to leave a message, I thought of calling in to my answering machine. He's at the Tysons'. He went there to tell them that he wanted to live with them. He wanted me to tell you. That's why he called my machine.''

Ely shot out of his chair. "Why didn't you tell me! I've got to talk to him.''

"Wait. You and I should talk about a few things first,'' Eliza suggested.

"We can talk on the way.'' He was out the door before he finished the sentence. Eliza had no choice but to follow.

"That crazy kid,'' Ely muttered as they walked to her car at a fast clip. "What does he think he's doing?'' Eliza slipped behind the wheel of her car. He gave her the general direction, and sat back, pensive.

"He told me that he heard about your fight at school, and he wanted you to be able to leave and go back to school yourself for your degree without worrying about him.'' That little boy's gruff voice on her answering machine had been the most pitiful sound Eliza had ever heard. "I quote, 'Dad won't have to take any crap from McGinley if I'm not in the picture.' ''

Ely grunted. "Well, he won't have to worry about that any-more."

Eliza was driving, so she could not get a good look at Ely's face as he leaned back against the headrest. "How much are you planning to tell him?"

"I'll have to tell him I was fired. But I don't think he'll be too disappointed about that. I'll tell him that you recommend I do some substitute teaching."

"And you'll have to tell him he'll be staying at St. Joe's."

"Yeah," Ely said, sighing.

"We should also tell him that I won't be his lawyer any-more."

Ely's reaction was delayed for a second, then he sat straight up. "What?"

"With the photos the detective took of us, you would stand a better chance with someone else."

"I don't believe that."

"The judge could be prejudiced against us. You would be accused of having the bad judgment to sleep with your attorney. He could find my arguments suspect because we're personally involved."

"We just talked about this last night," Ely said. "Lawyers represent members of their families all the time. Wives repre-sent their husbands and vice versa. That judge doesn't know anything about our relationship."

"He is a *family court judge.* They're not known for their liberal morality."

"No," Ely said. "I am not making a move without you. Look, what we're doing, where we're going, together. You care about us. I cannot believe that that won't be better for Jessie in the long run than some impersonal stranger."

"But—"

Ely didn't let her finish. "No buts. "I've heard all your reasons before.

"Things have changed," Eliza protested.

"Not that much," Ely said.

She subsided. Eliza was more convinced than ever that she was right, but knew that reasoning with Ely in his present frame of mind would be pointless. She would tell him later, after he had settled things with Jessie, that she was going to have to withdraw from his case.

"Turn right, then left at the second light."

The only words exchanged for the short remainder of the drive were Ely's softly voiced instructions.

The front door swung open as they approached the house. Rebecca and Hank were waiting for Ely. "Come in," Hank invited them.

"He's made himself sick," Rebecca Tyson said quickly. "You've got to tell him it will be all right. He's in his bedroom."

Ely strode into the house and disappeared, leaving Eliza to reintroduce herself to the elderly couple. They looked tired, and drawn.

"Would you like some coffee or tea?" Mrs. Tyson led her into their spacious dining room.

"If it's no trouble, I'll have a cup of tea, thank you," Eliza agreed. The teapot and the silver were already on the dining room table.

"No trouble at all. It's already made." Rebecca left her alone with Hank Tyson, who stood awkwardly in the doorway.

"You have a beautiful house," Eliza commented, hoping to put him at ease.

"Thank you." Rebecca bustled back into the room, teacup in hand. She gestured to her husband, and he gallantly offered Eliza a seat.

"Sugar?" she asked as she poured.

"No, thank you." Eliza always tried to be as cordial as possible to those she opposed in court. It was a trying exercise, sometimes impossible when she was dealing with abusive parents or guardians. In the case of Jessie's grandparents, it was virtually effortless.

"We'll be sorry to leave here. It's been our home for over thirty years. We raised Jessie's mother in this house," Rebecca said.

"Mmmm-hmmm," Eliza mumbled. There was nothing she could say.

After a moment, Rebecca went on. "You probably knew that." Eliza shook her head. "I'm sure you know all about us."

"Not quite all," Eliza said, forcing a smile. "But we're all bound together by our concern for Jessie, so I feel I know you a little."

"This was terrible . . . today," Rebecca said.

Hank nodded. "He seemed fine when he got here. We were surprised to see him, of course, but we're always happy to have Jessie stop by, so when he said school let out early we didn't really think much of it. By the time we finished lunch, though, it was clear that something was wrong."

"We tried to get him to tell us what it was, but . . ." Rebecca shook her head. "He kept running to the bathroom."

"When he got a little green around the gills, we finally put him to bed. Then, he told us."

"I'm sorry," said Eliza.

"Well, that's why . . ." Rebecca started.

Hank finished for her. "That's why we've decided to cancel our petition for permanent custody. We're not going to fight anymore."

"Have you spoken to your lawyer about this? I'm not sure we should speak without him here," Eliza said.

"Yes, we called him. And we told him we were going to tell Ely as soon as he came to pick the boy up," Hank said.

"We might have kept on," Rebecca explained. "If he hadn't tried to lie to us, poor duck. When he told us he wanted to live with us and not with his dad, and we should take him to the judge so he could tell him, we said he didn't need to do it. He said he loved us more than his daddy, and he was trying so hard not to cry, I'm surprised he got the words out. It nearly broke my heart." Eliza nodded, letting her talk. "We could see how much it cost him, even to say the words."

Ely came back into the room. "He's asleep," he said.

"Ely, I think you should hear this." Eliza waved him into a chair. "Go on, Mrs. Tyson, Mr. Tyson."

"We still think he should live with us. We could give him so much. He'd be ours. We're not too old. It would be just like when we had him when he was a baby.'' Ely shifted in his seat, but Eliza never took her eyes from Rebecca Tyson's face. ''But we couldn't put him through it. What if the judge made him choose? It could traumatize him.''

Hank Tyson took his wife's hand in his. She looked at him, and he confirmed, ''The lawyer said the judge might ask Jessie where he wanted to live. In his chambers and all. We didn't think it would be so bad if that happened, but after today, we just couldn't do it,'' Hank said.

Eliza sensed that the Tysons couldn't handle much more of this conversation. The guilt they were feeling was evident on both of their faces. ''We never meant to hurt our baby.''

''I know,'' Ely said, soothingly.

''He calmed down when we told him we were going to drop the case.''

Ely jumped up. ''What?''

''The Tysons are going to withdraw their petition,'' Eliza informed him.

''We can't do it,'' Rebecca repeated, at his questioning look.

''I know how you feel,'' he said. ''I felt the same way. As much as I love him, I thought about just letting him go for his own good. In the end, I couldn't do it. Not just for me, but for him, too. I was afraid that I would hurt him even more in the long run if I gave up without a fight. He might feel like I abandoned him. I didn't want him to grow up thinking his father didn't want him enough to fight for him.''

''We were worried about that, too,'' Hank said. ''Ever since we found out we had to move.''

''I hope you won't worry too much,'' Ely said. ''He'll miss you a lot, but no one expects grandparents to be parents. I probably shouldn't have relied so heavily on you all these years.'' Hank was shaking his head, but Ely insisted, ''No, really. This whole situation was of my making. Jessie is my son. I should not have taken advantage of you, or taken all the help you gave me for granted.'' They were all in agreement again.

''It was our fault, too,'' Rebecca said.

''It's over now, thanks to you,'' Eliza told the Tysons. ''I wish more parents were able to put their child's interests before their own.'' The Tysons looked gratified by the statement.

She sensed Ely turning to look at her, but she couldn't look at him. She was embarrassed enough at the thought of this sweet little old couple seeing the photos George Baker had taken of her and him. She didn't want to get caught staring, especially not now, when her heart was so full she was afraid they'd see the love she felt for him written all over her face.

Chapter Twenty-Four

Ely's relief, on hearing the Tysons' decision, was staggering. He drew his first really deep breath in months, and it felt fantastic. Unfortunately, his joy in the moment was marred by the fact that Eliza would not meet his eyes. She made the comment about other parents putting their children first and then didn't glance his way once. It kept coming back to him.

He was afraid that that statement had been meant for him.

She had said before that he should worry more about Jessie and less about himself, primarily when they had first been reunited, but they had talked it out, then and since. He had assumed she approved of his decision to fight for his son in court. Eliza knew he was thinking of Jess first, last, and always. Didn't she?

"Daddy?" Jessie said from the doorway. Ely opened his arms, and Jessie ran into them.

"Jessie, Jessie," he said softly, rubbing his boy's back and holding him close. His son clung to him with all the strength in those scrawny, eight-year-old arms. "It's okay," he comforted.

"Gramps says they're not going to take me away," Jessie said in a muffled voice, his face buried in Ely's shoulder.

"That's right. We worked everything out."

"You're not mad at me?"

Ely pulled his son onto his lap. "Not at all. I think what you tried to do was great. I really appreciated it. But everything is going to be fine now."

Jessie leaned back into his dad's chest and peeked at his grandparents and Eliza. They were all smiling at him. Ely couldn't help but smile himself. He supposed his smile, too, had a hint of sorrow in it.

"Do I have to go to school tomorrow?" Jessie asked.

Ely bounced his boy on his knee, once, in a silent reproof. "Yes," he said firmly.

Jessie climbed from his lap and walked over to Eliza. He held out his hand to her and she took it. "I guess you won't be our lawyer anymore, huh?" he asked.

Eliza shook her head. "You don't need one now, kid."

"But we're still friends, right?"

"You bet," she said. "It's all cool, Jessie."

"Good," he said, satisfied.

"I'd better be going. I have some calls to make." Eliza stood and everyone walked her to the door.

"It was a pleasure to meet you again," she said to the Tysons.

"Good-bye, Eliza," they said along with Jessie.

Ely walked her to her car. "When can I see you again?" he asked.

"After I speak with Mr. Daniels, I'll call you and fill you in. We'll get that temporary custody order rescinded."

"Great, but that's not what I meant." He searched her face, but it was blank. She wasn't giving anything away. He tried again. "We should celebrate. Pick a time."

"Do you need a lift back to your car?" she asked.

"I should go back in. I think they're waiting. I'm sure Hank will drop Jessie and me off," he said. "Eliza, you didn't answer me."

"This isn't the time or place," she said emotionlessly.

"I want to touch you," he whispered.

"Don't even think about it," she warned.

"Why not? I'm not a client anymore."

"Our professional relationship has not been completely severed. Unless you're firing me." Her voice had become chilly.

Ely backed off. "No, no. I'm not doing that." He wasn't absolutely sure she'd take his calls if he did.

His earlier, frightening thought returned. "You didn't mean me, did you? When you said that about parents putting their kid's interests ahead of their own." Eliza didn't answer him. She turned to her car. "Did you?" he demanded.

"I've got to go," she said.

"You think I should have given Jessie up rather than fighting for him?" he asked incredulously. "I thought you understood."

"I did," Eliza said. "But I told you what I thought from the very beginning."

"I thought you agreed with me, in the end."

Eliza shrugged. "What difference does it make now?" she asked. "It all turned out for the best."

"I don't understand." Ely was completely confounded. "What are you saying?"

"You figure it out," Eliza said. She got into her car and left him staring after her, feeling as if he had lost his only friend in the world.

It took Ely all that night and most of the next day to calm down enough to think clearly. He alternated between a helpless anger at her dismissal, and the conviction that somehow he had misunderstood her. He thought back over all the times they'd argued about going to court. The very first night, she told him to work it out, outside of the justice system. But they'd ironed out their differences. Or so he had thought.

He tried to remember what Eliza said when she finally agreed to represent him. He'd taunted her with being a sexist, and she'd agreed that he, like any single mother fighting in the juvenile courts, had a right to fight for the best interests of his child. After that, the only subject he could remember debating was his behavior at school. In the end, he thought she approved of his decision to stand up for his students at St. Joe's. Could he have been mistaken about her agreement to his plan to leave the school? Ely didn't think so. Eliza would not have given in just to end the argument. He was sure of it. It just wasn't her way.

Eliza would never have been silent if she felt he was not acting in Jessie's best interest.

The truth hit him with the force of an anvil. She had not been speaking of him when she praised the Tysons' decision. His feelings of guilt had caused him to take her simple statement as a criticism of his own actions. And Eliza had let him do it.

There was a perfectly rational explanation for her dishonesty: she had wanted him to be angry at her. She must have seen his question as the perfect opportunity to start a fight, to get rid of him easily and cleanly. It fit. She'd fought the attraction between them from the first and then put up obstacles between them at every juncture.

Ely chuckled, as he always did, when he thought of the ridiculous list she'd presented him with the night they first made love. The myriad reasons she had given for avoiding personal involvement had included their ages, their lifestyles, their expectations, and the case. He had thought it adorable. Only the fact that she had been so serious, so determined, had kept him from throwing away her legal pad and devouring her on the spot.

He had listened to her arguments and tried to answer them, because he had known that she had wanted him as much as he wanted her. If the passion that had flared between them hadn't already convinced him that she was as eager as he to take their relationship one step further, the dress she wore that night would have. There was only one possible explanation for the enticing way she dressed, her hair, her heels, the scent she wore.

Eliza felt they were incompatible, and she had said so, over and over again. He should have known that Eliza Taylor wouldn't throw herself into his arms just because the case had been resolved. There was not a doubt in his mind that she was completely sincere in saying that their lawyer/client relationship precluded the possibility of personal involvement between them. But he also knew full well she wouldn't be ecstatic at the prospect of an affair between them regardless of their professional relationship.

It didn't take long for him to figure out why.

Ely was on her doorstep that night, half an hour after Jessie was in bed. He'd have come earlier, but he didn't feel right about leaving his little boy alone after the excitement and uncertainty of the day before. Jess was still a little bit shaky after the ordeal, and Ely waited for him to go to sleep before asking his neighbor to sit for a couple of hours.

Eliza's reaction to finding him at her door was less than flattering. After a moment's pause, she stepped back and said reluctantly, "Come in."

He followed her into the gleaming white kitchen, where she asked, "Can I get you coffee? Or tea? Or something stronger?"

"Coffee would be nice," he said, trying to match her nonchalance. But he couldn't maintain the attitude for long.

Before she'd even finished preparing his coffee, he blurted out, "You're still serving penance, aren't you?"

"What are you talking about?"

"Admit it," Ely persisted. "You're planning to spend the rest of your life paying for that boy's death."

"You don't know what you're talking about," she said in an icy voice. Ely circled her, forcing her to face him.

She was afraid. He didn't just sense it, he could see it. Her body was rigid with fear, her eyes wide. She trembled. Not that enticing quiver that shook her when they made love, but a quaking that made her hands shake and her eyelids flutter. She was terrified.

"You're afraid to trust your judgment because of that child who died. What was his name again?" He kept his tone purposely light, but she recoiled as if he had struck her.

"Why don't you go home and leave me alone!" she said wearily.

He felt like a complete jerk, but he couldn't stop. "Let it go, Eliza."

"What gives you the right—" she spluttered.

"I won't let you punish yourself anymore. You did your best, but you couldn't save him. No one could. It was an accident. There was nothing you could have done to prevent it. Nothing.''

"What do you want from me?" she asked bitterly. Ely wanted to take her in his arms and soothe her, but he had to force her to confront her demons. It was the only way he knew to get through to her.

"Talk to me, Eliza."

"And say what?" The words were torn from her. "What?!" She sounded panicky.

"I need you, but you can't accept that, can you?" He pushed a little further. "What were their names? Tell me," he urged softly.

She opened her mouth, but no sound escaped.

"Tell me about it. What happened to you?" He felt her weakening, saw it in the slump of her shoulders. "Please, Eliza."

"Paron. David Paron. His father's name was Bruce." Tears streamed from the corners of her eyes, but her voice was hard. "And I felt like I was going crazy. I went crazy. Okay?" She had given him what he asked, but she hadn't given in. Not completely. The anger was gone, and the panic, but she had withdrawn behind a familiar crusty shell. The softness he had sensed, and the fear, were hidden once again.

"Believe me, you'll feel better if you just get this out. Just say it, Eliza."

He grasped her shoulders in his hands. "I want you to trust me. I need you to trust me, because I love you."

She threw off his hands and her lips twisted into a brittle smile that hurt him more than her tears had. "That's good." She gave a shaky laugh. "I'm supposed to trust you? You're still in love with your wife."

He was shocked into silence. She stared at him, disdainful, daring him to contradict her.

"Helen?" he croaked, disbelieving. Her smile cracked, but she nodded. Ely couldn't keep the chuckle from escaping his lips. She winced. "Helen?" he said again.

"I'm not going to compete with a ghost, even if I were . . .

interested in you, which I am not. Why can't you accept it, Ely. I'm not right for you.''

She was slipping away from him again and Ely strove desperately for some way to regain his former footing. ''Eliza, you're not in competition with anyone. You are the only woman in my heart. That makes you *perfect* for me.'' He was still reeling from the unexpected accusation. ''Where did you get such a crazy idea?''

''In my bed. When you whispered her name in my ear,'' Eliza said.

''I'm sorry. God, I'm so sorry if I hurt you.'' Ely knew men and women who could not accept the death of a spouse and could not move on. He was not one of them. He searched his soul for the legacy of love that had been the gift of his young wife. It was there, as it had been for so long, a warm, comforting glow. Nothing like the feelings he had for Eliza.

It was clear she had convinced herself that his slip of the tongue meant much more than it had. She was grasping at straws, trying to keep a distance between them. But he had no doubt she honestly believed that what she said was the truth. She didn't believe he loved her.

''I loved Helen. But never the way I love you. I'm in love with you.''

''Don't you get it,'' she said. ''I don't love you. All I felt for you was physical attraction. I tried to be honest about it, at least.''

He reacted intuitively. ''Kiss me, Eliza. Kiss me and tell me I'm in love with somebody else. Tell me you don't love me.''

''Oh, no,'' she said. Ely saw the shutters go down over her eyes. He took a step toward her, and she darted a glance at the door behind him, but he kept coming.

''Don't try to run away from me. I won't let you.''

''Don't,'' she warned.

''All these games we've been playing, stolen kisses, secret touches, have they made you as excited as they made me?''

''It's just sex. It doesn't mean anything,'' she said. He could tell that she was trying to convince herself as much as she was him.

He wouldn't let himself be diverted. "I've wanted you for so long," he said, his voice as rough and ragged as his emotions.

"I want you to leave now," she said, but she didn't resist as he cupped her elbows in his hands and pulled her even closer. He lowered his lips to hers.

"Get out," she whispered, but he ignored the command and settled his mouth gently on hers. He tried, with that kiss, to draw out the woman he knew was hidden somewhere inside, but she wouldn't yield to him. Her eyes were still wide open. He closed his own to shut out the betrayal in those shining, hopeless orbs and concentrated on her soft lips.

When he lifted his head, she stood as unmoving as stone. His disappointment was too intense to hide. "What am I going to do with you?" he said sadly, stepping back.

"I'm fine just the way I am," she said, gathering the mantle of her reserve around her. But he caught a quick glimpse of a quiver in her bottom lip and that tiny involuntary movement told him she was not as untouched as she pretended to be.

There was still more he hadn't told her. He knew she didn't want to hear it, but he began to talk anyway. He had no choice. He had to make her see herself as he saw her. Otherwise . . . otherwise she was right, they had no future together. "Do you know why I love you?"

Eliza blinked. "Aren't you finished yet?" she asked in the same exasperated tone his son used when his father nagged him about cleaning his room.

"No," he said unequivocally. "I'm not finished. Damn it, Eliza, you are so rigid, so stubborn, I don't know how I'm ever going to get through to you."

"Give it up, Ely."

"No," he said again. "I am going to convince you we belong together if it's the last thing I do."

"I'm going to get a drink."

He let her past and followed her into the living room.

"You are one of the bravest people I ever met and the strongest." Ely kept talking while she did her best to ignore him. "And you give so much of yourself. You think you don't want a family, but you've made a family of strangers, helping and protecting children who aren't even yours.'' He didn't take his eyes off her. Her delicate hands moved quick and sure over the bar as she poured three fingers of vodka into a tall glass. ''You call yourself a workaholic and say you don't have time for others. You think you're selfish. But you devote your life to the people whom you love.''

She topped off the glass with tonic water. ''I'm a saint,'' she said, taking a healthy swig of the drink.

''Not by a long shot. But you are an amazing woman.'' She was shaking her head in denial, but he had gotten through to her, a little, he thought.

''Why won't you leave?'' she asked in a small voice he'd never heard before. He felt himself falter, but he kept on.

''You're the most maternal woman I've ever seen. You like children, all children, and they sense that. They're drawn to you.''

''Ha!'' she snorted, but her hands shook as she took another swallow of her vodka and tonic.

''You take in children whose own parents don't want them.''

''Someone has to do it,'' she said flippantly, but her voice nearly broke.

''Why you?'' he asked. Then waited. She opened her mouth to speak but clamped her jaw shut tight again. ''Why, Eliza?''

''Children are precious, and they need to be protected,'' she said, then took another swallow of her drink.

It came to him in a flash. It wasn't his feelings for Helen, or the difference in their ages that frightened her. It was the kids she'd devoted her life to that stood between them. The irony struck him forcefully. He had almost lost everything because he, too, believed the needs of the children in his life came first, before anything else. He had nearly lost Jessie, and she was treating him as if he didn't understand, couldn't possibly understand.

''I know,'' he said soothingly.

But she refused to be comforted. ''I wish I were normal and had a family of my own. Don't you think I'd like that? But where would my kids go? Who would keep them safe?'' The words escaped her lips against her will. ''Do you really want a woman who is so busy taking care of other people's children that she doesn't have the time and energy to take care of a pet, let alone a family of her own?''

And finally, he really did understand. She might love him, might want to be with him, but she couldn't let herself do it. She'd been hurt by all the damage she'd seen inflicted on children in her work. That was why she'd accepted the awful responsibility of that little boy's death. It had been a form of recompense for all the children who were lost, hurt, killed. Eliza couldn't forgive herself for being unable to prevent the crimes she saw committed every day. She believed that she had failed to prevent the damage caused the children by their families and the law and the courts. It was what drove her.

He had fallen in love with her when he was seventeen years old because of that pain. With a boy's romantic instincts, he had wanted to rescue her from the evil that haunted her. He had sensed it then . . . that she'd been wounded by the evil done to children.

He loved her so much more now. Her strength and beauty were incredible. It was amazing that she was unaware of the power of her own generous heart. He didn't want only to rescue her. He wanted to be rescued by this incredible woman who had saved so many others.

She was blind to all she'd done for ''her'' kids—giving them support, care, love, and a safe harbor. She didn't know what she had accomplished. And she couldn't see the truth, couldn't accept that she couldn't keep all the children safe from harm. She tallied up the cases in which she could find tangible evidence of danger averted, and still paid penance for every child whose pain she hadn't been able to ward off. She had set herself an impossible task, and then, she punished herself for being unable to fulfill it.

''Don't you see? You can't do it by yourself. You can't save every child. You're just one person. Even if you go on devoting every possible minute of your life to your work, you can't do it all alone.''

''I'll do more alone than I will if I—'' She bit back the rest of the sentence.

"If you what?" He crossed the room in two strides, took the drink, and held on to her hand. "If you what?"

"If I have to take care of you, and your son, and all of your problems."

He backed away. Her words stung. Whether spoken in desperation, or whether they were just a pure statement of fact, they hit hard.

"Please leave me alone, Ely," she begged. "I don't want to hurt you, but you've got to stop pushing me. I can't give you what you need."

"All right." He held up his hands in surrender. He was not going to get any further with her tonight. Perhaps he would never be able to make her see the truth. "I'm going."

He turned and walked to the entryway.

"Ely, I'm sorry," she said behind him. He stopped.

There was always tomorrow.

He hated to leave. She was sure to think he was admitting defeat if he walked away from her now. But she wasn't ready to hear any more. He couldn't force her to listen. He would be back. Even if she didn't know it.

As long as he was giving up the field, Ely thought, he'd get in one last parting shot. "I'll miss you, Eliza," he said. He turned back to face her. "Will you miss me at all?" He was not above using her own soft heart against her. He'd use anything he could to make her open up to him. She might think she was tough as nails, but he knew better.

She stood, her glass in her hand once again, staring at him. He waited for a few more seconds, but she didn't respond.

"Good-bye, then," he said. And left her there.

Chapter Twenty-Five

The morning dawned clear and bright—a perfect early summer's day—in direct contrast to Eliza's dark mood. She felt terrible about the way she'd attacked Ely the day before. She couldn't get the memory of his sad expression out of her mind, when he'd asked if she would miss him. It had been a test. She had known that. And she had refused to respond, rather than fail it. But the pain he had felt had been real, nonetheless. And of course, she would miss him. She missed him already.

When she arrived at the office, Mary Jane and Rosa hadn't come in yet. She dictated the resolution of the Greene case for MJ to type up and left it on her secretary's desk. That should have been it. The end. But she didn't feel much satisfaction, despite the fact that the case had been successfully resolved. She felt unsettled.

It had been a shock, suddenly seeing herself as Ely saw her, but it had probably been good for her. His litany of her faults had been very revealing. It demonstrated to her he couldn't possibly love her—and if he did, he shouldn't.

It hadn't been Ely she had been angry with when she had lashed out at him, but herself. There had been a lot of truth to what he had said about her and the Parons. She'd realized that on her own quite recently. Because of Ely and Tom and Sandy, she had had to reevaluate her life and herself. She hadn't made the connection between her life and her work, but Ely was probably right about that, too. She'd been deluding herself, filling the hole left in her life by her parents' death with an insane mission. But that was over now. Ely had made her understand that she had been pushing herself too hard, and it had been to fulfill a goal that was unrealistic.

She still had a ways to go, but his insight had given her a very different vision of herself, and what she could achieve. Maybe she would even try to achieve less and live more. As she set aside a legal brief to work on before bed that night, Eliza smiled cynically. Oh, yeah, she'd learned a lot from this experience.

She was hopeless. Even if he didn't understand right away, eventually Ely would come to realize that he'd had a narrow escape.

She had dismissed the possibility that he was still in love with Helen. She'd been running scared when she came up with that one, but she was thinking logically now. She could not keep pretending that there was anything as simple as his late wife between them. Too bad he wasn't a little older, a little more sophisticated, a little more ambitious, maybe just a little bit more like herself. They might have managed to continue their affair, if he weren't such a romantic. But he was the marrying kind. And, unfortunately, she was not. It was a pity that he couldn't distinguish between the love she felt for him and the love that he deserved.

Eliza wanted to call him, speak to him, see him, but she didn't know what she would say, or how she would feel. Every instinct urged her to avoid the man. But she felt compelled to apologize, to try and make him understand. If only she could come up with the right words.

She knew she couldn't allow herself the luxury of seeing him again. If she had thought it would give her a sense of closure, she'd have risked calling him, at a time when he wasn't likely to be home, and apologizing to his answering machine.

It was so much easier to speak to the tape recorder than to the man himself.

She heard Mary Jane and Rosa enter the outer office together. MJ called, "Eliza?"

"In here." She came to stand in the doorway to her office.

"Morning," Rosa said.

"Good morning." Eliza cleared her throat. "I've got good news. The Tysons have decided to drop the custody suit. The Greene case is closed."

"Great!" MJ exclaimed. "Are we going to have a dinner party to celebrate?"

"We never have before," Eliza said, surprised at the suggestion.

"Ely and Jessie are different. This one feels personal," MJ responded.

"Well, it's not."

"I think it would be nice," Rosa added. "That sweet little boy and his father are something special."

For once, Eliza didn't appreciate Rosa's advice. "No dinner party, MJ," she said firmly.

"There's no need to get snappy," MJ commented. "It was just a suggestion."

"Let's just forget about it," Eliza said. "Okay?"

"Sure," Rosa agreed. "Now we can get back to normal around here."

Eliza stepped back and closed the door on the two women. She couldn't help wondering if they suspected something had happened between herself and Ely. Did they know she'd crossed the line with a client? What had Mary Jane said?

Eliza shook her head. She didn't suppose it mattered. As Rosa said, everything would be returning to the way it had been before. Sandy was settled back in with her foster family, and Jessie was all set. Ely had given up on her. Wasn't that what she had wanted.

No, the little voice inside her insisted. But it was definitely better this way, she told herself. She didn't have time or space in her life for Ely Greene. The way he made her feel was too scary. It was beyond her control, and that wasn't something she was used to. Love. It was impossible even to imagine.

What would there be in her to love? Her work with her kids took it all out of her. She wasn't the hero Ely thought her. Far from it. She was bound to disappoint him. Even if she did, for once, listen to her heart instead of her head, and throw caution to the winds, Ely wasn't that different from anyone else. He couldn't love her.

"If at first you don't succeed, try, try again," he said, as he barged into her office that afternoon with Jessie trailing behind him.

"Ely!" Eliza knew her jaw had dropped open, but she was shocked to see him.

"You might be able to resist me. After all, I'm just a man. But I don't think you can hold out long against Jessie. He's irresistible."

"Hello, Eliza," Jessie said, staring at her curiously.

"We're a team," he said cockily. "And whether you'll admit it or not, you love us." The two of them faced her while Eliza tried to stem the laughter riding in her throat.

No matter how adorable they were, she knew it was safer to guard her heart. She'd learned that so long ago, she'd almost forgotten how to use the organ. It had taken Tommy's honesty, Sandy's aggressiveness, Jessie's dependence, and Ely's hero worship to remind her of the possibility of love. Even if she was tempted by the prospect of being loved by, and loving, Ely, Eliza couldn't imagine giving in to that temptation.

"If I have to bring him in here every day, I will," Ely promised.

She tried frantically to figure out how to convince Ely that he was making a huge mistake.

"I didn't expect to see you again," she said, stalling for time.

"You should have." Ely's dark eyes impaled her, making it difficult to look away.

"I didn't think . . . after last night, I thought we had settled this . . ."

"I came to ask you to marry me." Her eyes fell from his to find Jessie grinning up at her.

It was an absolutely ridiculous notion. Marriage? With Ely? Coming home in the evening yelling, "Honey, I'm home," and finding them there waiting for her. Instead of finding the image of herself as wife and mother laughable, it was clear and quite seductive. She could picture Ely taking her coat and Jessie telling her about his day at school, just as they had done the last time she'd been by their apartment.

Eliza shook herself. Just because it was easier to imagine than she would have thought, didn't make it any less impossible. She and Ely had nothing in common. He didn't want her. He couldn't. She was, as he said, stubborn and unbending, selfish and a workaholic. That did not make her very good wife and mother material.

"Have you lost your mind?" she asked Ely, smiling apologetically at his son.

"No, just my heart."

She couldn't believe he could stand there so calmly, while her world broke into a thousand pieces. Jessie was looking expectantly from her to his father and back again, while he waited for her answer.

"But I know that you don't believe in following your heart, so . . ." He paused and with a flourish, he pulled out a small stack of three-by-five index cards from his back pocket. "I've got a whole list of practical reasons for my proposal."

"What?" Eliza asked, dazed.

"First, I love you, and I don't think I can live without you. So, you'd be rescuing me from certain death. Is that practical enough for you?"

He looked at her searchingly. "No?" He nodded. "Okay. How's this. By the way, you can take notes, if you like." He smiled and went on. "Second, you love me, too. That's not a hunch, it's a logical, reasonable deduction. You've admitted you're attracted to me, and that you can't . . . umm . . . resist me, by deed if not by word."